BOOKS BY P. J. HOOVER

The Hidden Code

Game of the Gods Series
A Broken Truce
A Ruined Land
A Buried Spark

The Dying Earth Series
Solstice

Tut: My Immortal Life Series
Tut: The Story of My Immortal Life
Tut: My Epic Battle to Save the World

The Forgotten Worlds Trilogy
The Emerald Tablet
The Navel of the World
The Necropolis

Camp Hercules Series
The Curse of Hera

FURIOUSLY AWESOME

BY

P. J. HOOVER

ROOTS IN MYTH, AUSTIN, TX

FURIOUSLY AWESOME
The Demigod Chronicles Volume 1

A Roots in Myth Book
Austin, TX
For more information, write
pjhoover@pjhoover.com
www.pjhoover.com

ISBN: 978-1-949717-08-2 (trade paperback)

First trade paperback edition: December 2018

For Mari, thanks for the encouragement

CHAPTER 1

ANCIENT TROY, AGE OF HEROES

So there I was, invading the palace of Troy. The battle was almost over. There was a brief second when I thought that maybe my mom was wrong. That I'd live for another fight. Then the bow string snapped, and the pace of the world slipped into slow motion.

From across the royal garden, a victorious grin covered Paris' face. A stupid grin that I wanted to smack away.

"Achilles!" he shouted, and my name echoed off the burning timbers that had been the palace. "Today, you will die!"

Damn, I hated how my mom was always right.

Dying was going to suck. It wasn't that I was afraid. I was a warrior. This was my life. Well, I guess my death, in this case. I was just really pissed that Paris was going to be the one who killed me. Sure, I'd killed his brother, Hector, but that was one warrior to another, an honorable fight. Maybe not such an honorable end. I never claimed to be perfect. But Paris? He wasn't even a warrior. The gods were having a good laugh at my expense.

The arrow got closer with every limited beat of my heart. Paris was getting the revenge he so desperately wanted. His aim was dead on. Which was unbelievable. Paris couldn't have hit the walls of Troy from two feet away on a sunny day. It wasn't sunny, and this aim was not Paris'. Someone else was also getting their revenge. Someone who really wanted me dead. Sadly the list was long.

I dove to get out of the way, like some last bit of me wanted to deny my fate. It was pointless. This was my end. The arrow spun as it got closer. I lifted my shield, holding it out in front of my body, curling into a ball with my spear held above. But the arrow was relentless, and it had one target in mind. Even if somehow I managed to throw the spear and sink it into Paris' cowardly heart, I would still end up dead.

When the arrow found its mark and sank into my ankle, I fell to the ground and pain ripped through me. Then a second arrow hit, burying itself in my chest. Then a third, hitting my side.

Paris lifted his arm in a victory motion, glorious in his evidence that I wasn't invincible. I never claimed to be invincible. I didn't need him to prove it to the world. But he had.

I accepted death like the warrior I'd always been. My vision clouded around the edges, and reality started to slip away. I saw Patroclus, waving and beckoning me to come toward him, to join him in death. Next there was Hector, standing on an island with other heroes from the ages. A glorious spot waited for me. Had always been saved for me from the moment I agreed to join this fight against the Trojans. I nearly took a step toward Hector and Patroclus. I was ready to join them. My time had come. That's when my mom appeared, the immortal nymph Thetis.

I was sure she was ready to go into some long lecture about the mess I'd gotten myself into or how I should have never gone off to this war in the first place. I opened my mouth to tell her I was sorry, but before I could summon up the strength to utter a word, she pressed a hand over my face, closing my eyes with her fingers and covering my mouth with her thumb.

"Sleep, not death," she said.

The world slipped away.

CHAPTER 2

Unlike Paris back in the Trojan War, I had perfect aim, which I was more than happy to demonstrate every chance I got. I stood five feet behind the line and threw all three darts, one after another. Only two hit the bullseye.

"You missed," my roommate Ethan said.

"On purpose." As much as I loved to show off, doing so in a downtown bar wasn't the best idea. I was already pushing it by standing so far back from the line.

"Whatever you say." Ethan retrieved the darts from the board. "That means you buy the next round."

"I bought the last one."

"Your point?" Ethan said.

"I got no money," I said. "It's your turn."

"Fine, Achilles. But you really need to find a way to make

more cash."

Truer words were never spoken. As it was, the gym was two memberships away from putting me in the red. Then I'd have to start running specials and crap like that to get people to join.

We wound our way back to the outdoor second-story patio of Maggie Mae's and found a spot at the bar. The bartender nodded when he saw us, and I waved my darts, letting him know I was ready to trade them back in. Ethan had carefully stored his away in their case. He never borrowed bar darts, claiming they were bent and blunt. I'd made the obvious comparison on more than one occasion.

Since it was a Wednesday night, the place wasn't packed. Just crowded enough to blend in but not where we had to elbow our way through and wait forever to get a drink.

"What can I get you?" the bartender asked once he made his way over to us. He had full sleeve tattoos on both arms and giant holes stretched in his earlobes that I could have easily thrown the darts through.

"Whiskey Sour," Ethan said.

"Same. But make mine a double," I added, handing over the darts.

Ethan scowled, since he was paying, but I was going to make the most of a free drink.

"So fine," Ethan said. "You're still better than me at darts. But let's go target shooting, and I could seriously kick your ass. You haven't been out to the range in months."

"I've been busy," I said, though we both knew that guns weren't really my thing. Also the last girl I dated hated guns. We'd broken up months ago, but I hadn't picked a gun up since.

"What's next then?" Ethan said. "Golf? We haven't played in at least a year. And I've been practicing." He'd been on a mission to prove he was better than me at something besides keeping shit organized around the condo. Ethan bordered on OCD when it came to putting stuff away, which was the complete opposite of my habit of wearing whatever was on top of the clean laundry pile. Our appearances were pretty much the opposite of each other also. Ethan was black with short brown hair he got trimmed every two weeks at the barbershop. My skin was nearly golden in color, year-round, and the last time I'd gotten my blond hair cut was when I lost a bet to him over a football game. It had finally grown back to the point where it just grazed my shoulders.

"Golf takes too long," I said.

"Then disk golf," Ethan said. "They have this new course down at Zilker. And there's that tiki bar on Barton Springs where you could buy me drinks once I win."

"You won't win," I said.

"I declare myself the winner until you can prove otherwise."

"That's not winning," I said. "That's lame."

"Whatever, Achilles. What about video games?"

The bartender slid our drinks across the bar to us and Ethan handed him a twenty.

I was about to launch into my explanation of why video games were not valid when it came to competition, but this girl slipped into my peripheral vision and walked right up beside Ethan. The entire time she approached us, her eyes were fixed on me.

She stopped when she got between us and smiled, like she was part of our group.

"Buy me a drink?" she said in a thick Texas drawl, the whole time keeping her eyes on me. She wore a red cowboy hat, red tank top, super tiny denim shorts, and red cowboy boots with a black scrolling pattern. Both her arms were covered with tattoos of snakes twisted around and intertwined.

Also, she was smoking hot. A quick glance around told me that every guy in the place was staring at her and wishing they could be the one she'd decided to walk up to. But my skin prickled just looking at her. Something was off but I couldn't put my finger on it. Maybe it was the tattoos.

I patted my pocket. "I'm out of money."

"I'm not," Ethan said, grabbing for his wallet.

"You are." I tried to give him a subtle hint that something was not quite right with this girl.

"No, really. I can totally buy you a drink."

But the girl wasn't looking at Ethan. Instead she said, "You're Achilles." Not a question. A statement of fact. She knew who I was. She was specifically here in this bar to see me.

I took a deep breath and went through options of who she might be. Maybe she worked for Ares and he'd sent her to give me some message. Or maybe Mom had sent her. Another girl she was trying to set me up with. Mom was relentless when it came to my love life. She was determined to have me married because as she put it, neither of us was getting any younger and she wanted grandkids. Of course neither of us was getting any older either, but she chose to ignore this logic any time I pointed it out.

"What do you want?" I asked, glancing at her tattooed arms, because for a second, I swore the snakes had moved. But that was crazy.

"Just a drink," she said, drawling it out like she was some flirty little cowgirl straight off the ranch.

"No you don't," I said. "What do you really want?"

The girl angled her head and turned slightly away from me, looking off to the side, where, at the other end of the bar stood two other girls, both watching us. One wore a green cowboy hat and one wore a black one. They each had matching tank tops and boots on like all three of them were part of some costumed trio.

"I'm Tish," the girl in red said. "And my sisters and I want to talk to you."

I crossed my arms, flexing my muscles out of habit. "So talk."

"Oh, let's talk outside, Achilles," Tish said. "Where we can have some privacy. We like privacy."

"You don't want the drink?" Ethan asked. He seemed to be watching the exchange like he was one step behind. I get that he wasn't a demigod, like me, but he knew about the world of the gods. I couldn't believe that his skin didn't itch from this girl's very presence. Every second that went by, the size of my goosebumps doubled.

"She doesn't want the drink," I said. "And we don't have anything to talk about."

"It will only take a minute," Tish said, the twang in her voice simmering through.

I set my now empty glass on the bar. Apparently I'd already managed to drink the entire thing. "Either tell me what you want or this conversation is over."

"Outside," Tish said. "It's not . . . proper . . . to talk in here."

If for a second I'd thought there was a chance that she was any kind of normal girl, this comment would have made it clear otherwise. Not proper meant not normal, and not normal meant that it must have something to do with the world of the gods.

"What's not proper?" I asked.

"Outside," Tish said again. "We can't talk in here."

I grabbed Ethan's arm. "Sorry. We're busy now. Maybe we can talk some other time."

Meaning I could ask around and figure out who these girls were before meeting them outside in some dark alley. Demigod instincts were nothing to ignore. I was alive because of these instincts. I knew how to recognize a fight days before it started. I kept a low profile. I could talk to Tish and her sisters tomorrow. Or next week. It didn't matter much to me.

"So you're refusing to talk to us?" Tish asked.

"Yeah, something like that."

"Are you certain?"

Hadn't I just said that?

I didn't bother with a reply. Instead I pulled Ethan away from Tish and toward the stairway. By the time we got downstairs, he seemed to have snapped out of whatever stupor Tish had cast over him.

"Who was she?" Ethan said. He still had his drink, so I grabbed it and took a huge sip.

"Nobody we want to talk to," I said.

"But that accent. Man, that shit makes me crazy."

My skin still tingled, like I could feel the three of them watching me even now. I glanced upstairs, but if Tish or her sisters were around, they were staying out of sight. I passed the drink back to Ethan. "Finish it. We need to go."

Ethan downed the drink and set it on a nearby ledge. "You're a total buzz-kill, you know that?" His words slurred just enough that it was obvious his buzz had not yet been killed.

"So you've told me." I led him out of the bar and onto Sixth Street.

It was a good mile back to the condo, and it was January, but given the fact that we'd both had more than enough drinks and that I didn't want to spring for a rideshare, we opted to walk. But we hadn't made it ten blocks when from around the corner appeared the three girls. Tish stood in the center with the other two flanking her.

"How'd they get here before us?" Ethan asked. He kept

walking, but I pulled him to a stop. It was hard to see them clearly since the streetlight above us was out, but I'm not gonna lie. They had curves in all the right places with lots of skin showing. But the smile that had been on Tish's face back at Maggie Mae's had been replaced with a fierce look that seemed like it belonged on a crabby old statue in a museum instead.

"Achilles," Tish said. "You stand accused."

I knew it. I knew there was something more with these girls.

"Accused of what?" I flexed my fingers at my sides and steadied my breathing.

"You tell us," the girl on the left in the green cowboy hat said. She had dark skin that nearly disappeared into the blackness of the night. Tattoos also covered her arms, but they were inked in white instead of black, lighting up against her skin.

"I didn't do anything," I said, scanning through my memories even as I said it.

"Tell us what your crime is, and there may be leniency for you," the girl on the left, with the black cowboy hat, said.

"I've committed no crime."

"He hasn't," Ethan said.

Tish shook her head and pointed at him, and he flew backward, landing in a giant hedge. Immediately, the branches of the bush wrapped around his wrists and ankles, tying him in place.

Shit. My mind slowly started telling me exactly who these girls were, no matter how much I wanted to deny it. And if my mind was right, I was screwed.

"You have," Tish said. "Tell us now and your punishment will be less severe."

I tried to ignore my suspicions about them. I didn't want to go where my mind was taking me.

"Tell me what you think I did," I said.

"You killed a dryad," the girl on the left said.

"A dryad," the girl on the right repeated.

"Admit your crime and you may still repent," Tish said.

"I didn't kill a dryad," I said. "I haven't seen a dryad in . . ." Damn it. Telling the truth on that wasn't going to get me out of the accusation. I'd seen a certain dryad up until about six months ago. Seen her and spent a lot of time with her. But it had been completely consensual. If anything she'd been the one driving the relationship, visiting me at all hours of the night. Until we'd had our fight. Since then, I hadn't seen from her or heard from her.

"Liar!" Tish said, and anger slid onto her face like a mask merging with her skin.

"I'm not lying. And which dryad are you talking about?" Gods, they couldn't be talking about Syke. The thought of her dead . . . It was too much.

"Don't pretend you don't know," Tish said. "You stand accused of false oath and murder."

"I didn't lie and I didn't kill anyone," I said.

"You have been judged," the girl on the left said.

"Tell me what happened." If someone had killed a dryad, I'd find out who and seek revenge myself.

"You're punishment has been set," the girl on the right said. "You shall spend your eternity in Tartarus under eternal torment."

As the words spewed from her mouth, I became one hundred percent certain who these three girls were. My worst fears had come true. The Furies. This situation had spun completely out of control faster than Zeus' lightning bolt spinning to Earth. If I didn't find a way out of this mess, real quick, I'd be in a heap of immortal trouble.

They dove at me, all three at once. I jumped to the side, swatting at them. Tish, whose full name I knew was Tisiphone, tore at me with her long fingernails, which had extended into claws, making me hiss under my breath. My skin was tough and almost impossible to tear by mortal standards, but her nails were sharp enough to slice through my defenses. Unlike normal mortal weapons, they burned.

I lunged to the left, narrowly missing the Fury in green, Megaera. But all my moves did was push me closer to the Fury in black, Alecto. It was like they had anticipated my moves and were fighting in formation. Like they'd choreographed their attack ahead of time. Like they knew I would deny their accusation. And yeah, sure, I was a pretty good fighter—okay, the best; just ask anyone who knew me—but three Furies? This would take more than awesome evasion.

The Austin street was dark and empty, which made it the perfect place for them to attack me. This was why Tish had been so insistent about wanting to talk outside. As creatures of the world of gods, the Furies had to be under the same rules I was. Don't let mortals know about the immortal world. Don't interfere with mortal issues. If I could get out in the open, in front of other people, I could stop them from attacking me. Problem was it was midnight and every single street light seemed to be out. I had to get back to the main street.

I jumped behind a brick half wall, just missing Megaera— Meg—as she flew at me. She hissed and circled back faster than I could move. Then she went for my ankle. Like if she couldn't capture me, she would kill me.

"I didn't kill anyone," I yelled, tucking and rolling out of the way.

"You're a liar and a murderer," Tish responded, cool and calm as if they weren't trying to destroy my immortal future.

"I'm neither."

The slices on my arm throbbed. If they caught me in the ankle, that would be the end.

I jumped from the brick wall to a row of trashcans. Meg and Alecto—Alex—picked one plastic trashcan up after the next and threw them so hard they shattered in the middle of the street. Then Tish came right for me, fingers extended, teeth dripping with what I was sure was poison. I jumped again, this time taking cover behind a BMW.

The sound of tearing metal filled the air as Tish connected with the car, slicing giant gashes through the hood and roof. The owner was going to have a very bad day when he woke up to that. Almost in mockery, the car alarm blasted to life, beeping and flashing the few lights that hadn't been shattered. But the alarm didn't even make them flinch.

I dove behind a stone pillar attached to a fence. Fight. I had to fight. Had to get rid of these monsters. I glanced from left to right, looking for something I could use to defend myself. The fence was wrought iron, but even though I was stronger than a mortal, I still couldn't tear an iron fence apart.

Sadly, they could. Megaera slammed into the metal fence, twisting it more easily than Silly Putty on a hot day.

My head swam with my next step, and my arm throbbed anew. Shit. If there was poison in my bloodstream, I'd collapse, and that would be the end. Life as I knew it would be over. I grabbed one of the pieces of iron fencing Tish had torn loose and swung it around my head. It smacked into something soft.

A hiss erupted from Alex. But instead of incapacitating her, like I'd hoped, it just made hatred burn in her eyes.

"Achilles," Tish hissed, still with the Texas twang, but almost like a sick joke version of a cowgirl.

I swung again in answer, wildly. Meg and Alex fell back,

hovering in the air behind their sister.

"Come with us," Tish said. "It will make this so much easier."

I swung the iron fencing again. "I'm not going with you anywhere."

"You will go to Tartarus," she said, and she bit through her bottom lip with her fangs. Blood dark as the River Acheron dripped from the wounds. Then she spit at me.

I jumped back. Scratches from a Fury were bad enough. Blood of the Furies was most definitely worse.

"You can go to hell," I said, which was lame, but with the car alarm and the hissing of the three crazy monsters, I was totally off my game.

"Your punishment will become more severe with every moment you deny us," Tish said.

I had to get out of here. Buy some time. I could figure out why they were after me later.

"Give me a chance to prove I'm innocent," I said.

"You had your chance to tell us the truth," Alex said.

"But you lied," Meg added.

"I didn't lie."

They ignored my words. The three sisters hissed, and Meg and Alex dove in harmony.

I rolled backward and took off again, focusing every bit of effort on planting one foot in front of the other. I had one block to go. One block until I would be out among people. Then I could circle back and free Ethan. I could do this. I was a freaking hero after all. I was Achilles.

I swung the metal bar over my head as I ran, hoping it would hit at least one of them. Could Furies even be killed? But the bar came up empty. I felt their breath on the back of my neck. I heard their hisses of anger. I didn't stop.

Neither did they. Meg and Alex continued to attack, each time getting closer and slicing my already aching arms. I only had a few houses to go. I was going to make it. I sprinted the final distance and passed into the light.

The three Furies held back, staying in the shadows. They drifted to the ground and their claws shrank back into fingernails, their fangs back into teeth.

"One week, Achilles," Tish said.

"Seven days to clear your affairs," Meg added.

"To finalize your life," Alex said.

"To say goodbye," Tish said.

Gods, these girls were complete downers.

I almost opened my mouth again, to declare my innocence. But before I had a chance, the air around them seemed to suck in on itself, flickering them away in an instant.

Seven days.

Three Furies.

And an eternity of torment to look forward to unless I could figure out what the hell was going on.

CHAPTER 3

I texted Ares the second we got back to the condo.

No response. Damn the gods. They were on their own schedules. But without talking to him, I had no clue how to figure out what was going on. It's not like I could Google *dryad murder* and expect anything to come up. Next I had Ethan text Ares, and he still didn't reply.

"You need to carry a weapon," Ethan said, pulling a knife the size of my forearm from a table in the corner of our condo. The metal was shiny enough to cast my reflection back at me and looked sharp enough to slice through dust particles.

He tossed it to me. I caught it easily by the wooden handle.

"I can't walk around Austin with this thing," I said, even though it was a pretty sweet blade. Ethan made weapons for a living. Totally legit. He'd gotten his degree from UT in Materials Engineering and worked for the Army as an independent contractor.

"Sure you can," Ethan said. "This is Texas. You can do whatever the hell you want in Texas. That's what makes it the best state in the entire world."

Texas was pretty badass, but I wasn't quite ready to go all Rambo, so I set the knife down.

"Don't say that I didn't warn you," Ethan said. "When those Furies show up again and try to flirt their way into dragging you off to hell, you'll be wanting the knife. Man, that was some scary shit. I damn nearly pissed myself when she tossed me through the air."

"I thought you wanted to buy her a drink," I said.

"Yeah before she went all psycho-bitch on us," Ethan said. "She can forget the drink. But I sure as hell could use one."

So I grabbed us a couple beers from the fridge and Ethan got out a first aid kit so he could wrap my cuts. As far as I could tell, the Furies hadn't actually gotten any poison inside me. And they'd given me one week to get their accusation sorted out. I should be thankful, but instead I was pissed. Seven fucking days to prove I was innocent of something I didn't do.

* * *

THE NEXT MORNING, I UNLOCKED THE DOOR of Heroes Gym, looking left and right just to make sure the Furies hadn't changed their minds and come back early. There was no sign of them. No sign that anything was out of the ordinary. It was everyday Austin, complete with coffee shops, hungover college kids, and bloated traffic.

Once I was inside, I texted Ares again, asking him to come by the gym if he got a chance. Which he better. He was my connection to the immortal world. Kind of my patron god. He'd been the god who'd woken me from my immortal sleep. He was the reason I was here. And he better have some answers for me.

A dryad. I hated even the thought of it. The dryads were about the most peace-loving group of gals you could imagine, always worrying about Mother Earth and crap like that. No one would have any reason to kill a dryad. But my concern ran deeper. I had to make sure Syke was okay. It had been over six months since I'd seen her, and we hadn't parted on the best of terms, which I'm sure didn't weigh in my favor. Actually the last time I'd seen her, she'd told me she never wanted to speak to me or see me again. But still, I'd never in a million years kill one of the dryads. This whole thing was a complete mess.

After an hour at the gym and a seriously good workout, I felt ready to call back the Furies and tell them that I didn't need a week. That I could take them on now. I was ready. But there was no sign of them.

I took a quick shower and flipped the sign out front to OPEN. Sure enough, my regulars were coming through the door before I'd even gotten back behind the counter to boot up the computer. Which of course wouldn't boot. The thing was on its last leg. But a customer had given it to me for nothing, and given my shortage of funds, I wouldn't be upgrading anytime in the near future.

Jack was the first one in. He was this tall skinny real estate agent that owned twenty office buildings downtown. He gave me a fist bump then looked morbidly at the computer.

"No log in today?" he said.

"It's taking a while to start," I said, hitting more of the buttons on the keyboard to try to get the blank screen to do something other than stare back at me in frozen mockery.

"I don't want to miss my workout credit," Jack said.

Stupid workout credit. I'd thought it would be a good idea to incentivize people to work out more, and I guess it had, but it had also been a serious pain in my ass. Accounting was not my strength, and all it had become was one more thing I needed to take care of on a daily basis.

"You'll get your credit," I said, clicking the mouse to see if that would help. A single green bar blinked slowly in the top left corner of the screen.

"That's every day this month," Jack said, which I was well aware of. Only five customers had made it every day so far this month. The contest was simple. Whoever worked out the most days in a given month got five free personal training sessions with yours truly. Not like most of these people couldn't afford to pay for the training upfront. I catered to a pretty affluent crowd. But it was the competitive side of human nature.

Jack grabbed the last fresh towel and headed to the free weights. Which reminded me that I really needed to run a load of laundry. The stack of dirty towels had not only grown nearly as tall as me—six foot five, not that anyone was measuring—but it smelled like dogs had pissed on it and left it to smolder. I could start a load while the stupid computer decided if it wanted to come on or not.

I checked my phone one more time to see if Ares had texted me back. He hadn't, and even though I had to figure out this mess with the Furies, gods didn't like to be rushed. Ares would get back to me. Either that or I'd be dead within a week.

It was that pleasant thought that filled my head as I made my way to the back of the gym and grabbed a handful of towels, throwing them in the washer. I stuffed as many in as I could while still being able to shut the door, then I reached for the detergent.

Shit. I knew there was something I forgot at the store.

Maybe I could just run them with no detergent. Okay, no, that was stupid. Then it would just smell like wet dog piss instead of smoldering dog piss. I'd go get detergent during lunch once Keith got here to cover the counter. Or maybe by lunch, I'd have figured out a way to clear my name and could take care of that.

I headed up front and greeted a few more regulars. Simon, this super muscular Asian dude who worked out every Tuesday, Thursday, and Friday, stood at the computer, clicking the mouse.

"I'm booting it up," I said.

"It's not making any noise." Simon craned his neck like he was trying to look inside it. "Are you sure it's booting?"

"Of course I'm sure it's booting. What else would it be doing?"

"Okay, man," Simon said. "Just don't forget to log me in."

"I'll log you in." Not that it would matter. Only coming three times a week, Simon had no chance of competing with the ilk of Jack.

"You ever think about creating a sign-in app?" Simon said.

"You're kidding, right?" Was my lack of computer skills not clear? Simon thought I was going to design some app?

"I don't know, man," Simon said. "It's pretty easy to make apps these days. You could hire some high school kid to do it for you. My little brother could do it. I could get a good deal on it."

"I'll think about it," I said, even though, good deal or not, I didn't have spare cash to make an app.

Sophie and Scott were next. They were this married couple that worked out each morning before work and bickered all the time. It used to be that they worked from home, but Sophie told me in confidence that Scott drove her "fucking nuts" so they rented offices at one of those work co-op places up in the Domain. They can't even be on the same floor any more. Before she could ask about the computer, I slapped a notebook and pen next to it on the counter and wrote <u>Sign-In Here</u> at the top. It was like the Dark Ages, but it hadn't been that long ago that the gym didn't even have a computer.

I'd owned Heroes Gym for ten years, since I'd been woken from my immortal sleep by Ares and come to Austin. The gym had been open forever though, with a signature muscle arm hanging out front like a landmark. It went along with the giant daisy next door for the flower shop. Or at least it used to be a flower shop, until dear old Mrs. Barker (pretty sure I never knew her first name) finally kicked the bucket. And sure, it kinda tore me up inside since I'd known her for ten years, but it also opened up the florist space which I immediately bought with what little money I had in my bank account. Problem was that she made pack rats look like minimalists.

With Ethan's help on weekends, I'd made progress in the last month. I'd gotten rid of all the giant shelves where she'd stacked vases for years. I'd painted the walls, hoping to cover up eons of flower pollen. Busted a door through to the gym. Changed out the ancient fluorescent light fixtures. How she managed to sell flowers for decades with those lights shining down from above I had no clue. But she did. People used to rave about Mrs. Barker. Her wedding flowers were known as the best in town. Weddings in Austin would never be the same. Brides-to-be still came by looking for her, asking me when she'd be back.

Hopefully by now Mrs. Barker was enjoying her days in the Elysian Fields, decorating the entirety of the Underworld with bouquets. She and Persephone had probably connected on the best color of orchids.

Today though, I had to clean the floor. The gym mats I'd ordered were going to be delivered within the month. I spotted Jack for a couple of reps then grabbed a broom from the back. But the dustpan was nowhere to be found.

Oh wait, it was probably still up front. Keith had dumped an entire bag of Chia seeds earlier in the week. I had the feeling I'd be finding them forever. I heard the bell for the front door as I squatted down to grab it. Carly. It had to be Carly. She'd only been coming a couple of months, but I could tell that she was a sticker. After ten years in the business, I could always tell. But when I stood up, it wasn't Carly. Instead it was some girl I'd never seen before, which was totally my loss because this girl would have given Aphrodite a run for the money. Her skin was dark and virtually unblemished, which I could tell because she wore a tank top and yoga pants that showed off her muscular figure. Her dark hair was straightened and tucked behind her ears. The only thing off about the whole image was the fact that she had a purse slung over her shoulder that looked like it was big enough to hold ten footballs.

"Can I help you?" I said, even though I already knew why she was here. She kept looking over to the old florist shop. She was probably another bride-to-be trying to get flowers.

"I was wondering about the shop next door," she said.

I put on my best sad face. It wasn't hard. Mrs. Barker really was a sweetie.

"She passed away a couple months ago," I said. "She was pretty old, so it wasn't really unexpected."

Confusion clouded the girl's face. "Who died?"

"Mrs. Barker," I said. "The florist."

"Oh, is that why it shut down?" the girl said. She turned to get a better look at it, and her giant purse slammed into the counter with a metallic clang.

"You're not here for flowers?" I said, cringing at the sound. Even though the counter was solid, it could still break with enough force. I clicked off the computer and turned it back on again since it still hadn't come to life.

"Flowers are kind of stupid," the girl said, her eyes glancing to the computer monitor then back to me. "You cut them. They die. It's kind of pointless."

"Very true," I said, still trying to puzzle out why she was here. I doubted she was here to lift weights. She was already doing enough of that with her giant purse. "So are you here to work out?"

"Maybe," the girl said. "Do you have yoga?"

I blinked, trying to make sure I'd heard her correctly. "Yoga?"

"Yeah, you know, like downward dog and sun salutation and things like that?"

"I know what yoga is," I said. Sometimes, when we were bored, Ethan and I would watch yoga on YouTube on the TV. Perverted possibly, but also pretty satisfying.

"So do you have it?" she asked.

I looked around at the gym, crowded with weights. "Where would we have yoga?"

She gave me this look like I was the stupidest person on the planet. "Duh." And she motioned with her head toward the old florist shop.

"Yoga?" I said.

"Yeah, it would be perfect for yoga classes," she said.

"We don't have yoga," I said, clicking the mouse because the stupid computer had done nothing.

"You should."

"No one would come," I said. "This is a gym. For people to lift weights."

"People would come," she said.

I shook my head. "It doesn't matter. We don't have it."

"Bummer," the girl said. Then she punched three buttons on

the computer keyboard—three, I'm not kidding—and it sprang to life. "You know you should really get a new computer."

That I would agree with her on. The yoga? No way.

"Thanks," I said. "I got this one for free."

She raised an eyebrow in mock surprise, like I'd just told her that Dionysus preferred wine over club soda. "Free. What a bargain. You know you can get one five times better than this at Goodwill."

"I'll keep that in mind," I said.

"If you want a working computer you will," she said. "Anyway, I'll see you." She turned to leave. I would have said something else but I was too shocked at the fact that she'd fixed my computer in two seconds flat to say anything. Then she was gone.

CHAPTER 4

I grabbed my keys the second Keith walked in the door to the gym. "I need to go. You got this?"

Keith was this college kid I'd hired to work in the afternoons at the place. He was a complete hipster, with curly red hair he wore in a man bun, a skinny frame, and a beard that was so well groomed I was sure he combed it when I wasn't watching. He was mostly responsible for checking people in and wiping the equipment when people forgot to. It gave me the flexibility to run errands and take care of other business that I couldn't do at the gym. Like right now.

He set his kombucha and gluten-free pretzels on the counter and cracked his knuckles. "I got this, Achilles," he said. "You know, you really should give me a raise, as much as I've been closing up after you these last few weeks."

"How long have you been here?" I said. "Like three months?"

"Five," Keith said. "I started right after school went into session." Keith, like so many other kids around here, went to UT.

"Ask me again in another few months." Maybe by then, I'd be making more money. With the florist shop expansion, hopefully more people would join.

"Three months," Keith said. "I'm putting that on my calendar."

I only hoped that in three months I'd still be around. If the Furies had their way, I'd be suffering out an eternity in Tartarus within the week.

I walked outside and called Ethan to let him know where I was going, just in case I didn't make it back.

"I'm going to visit the dryads," I said once he finally answered the phone. In the background, loud noises went off like sonic booms.

"What?" he yelled into the phone.

"The dryads," I said again, trying not to yell since visiting dryads was not a normal everyday activity. "I'm going to visit them."

"You think that's a good idea, Achilles?" Ethan said.

"I got no choice," I said. "And can you stop the explosions in the background?"

"Can't," Ethan said. "I started an automated test. There's no way to stop it now."

If anything, the sonic booms only got louder. Maybe whatever weapon he was testing was a noise attack, designed to make any enemy who heard it go crazy.

"Dude, you need to stay the hell away from that shit," Ethan said. "Those chicks were going to kill you."

"They weren't going to kill me," I said. "They were going to haul me off to Tartarus for an eternity of torture. And they weren't chicks. They were Furies."

"They were hot Furies," Ethan said.

Which was true. Had the Furies not been psychotic monsters out to make the rest of my existence torment, I might have wanted to go out with one.

Your average mortal doesn't know anything about the god world. Like I said, it's one of the rules. It was a rule I always stuck to, since the punishment for breaking it could be anything from having your liver eaten by a giant bird every day for a year to getting your eyeballs plucked out. I wanted both my eyeballs and my liver. For the mortals who found out about the world of the gods, their minds were wiped clean, like a giant whiteboard being erased. So I never broke the rules of the gods.

Gods on the other hand . . . they broke their own rules all the time. Gods, like Ares, who'd had Ethan in one of his classes at UT. I think it was Modern Warfare. Anyway, once he discovered Ethan's uncanny ability to design epic weapons, he'd taken him aside and told him everything. I was pretty sure they'd worked out some sort of bargain, but I didn't want to get in the middle of that. Anyway, now Ethan and I were roommates.

"It doesn't matter what they look like," I said. "I have to get them off my trail."

"Wait until I get off work," Ethan said. "I'll go with you."

I shook my head. "I'm going now."

"What if they try to kill you again?"

"I'm visiting the dryads, not the Furies," I said. "You remember Syke. I need to make sure she's okay." Unlike most of the gods I knew, the dryads had a strict no-technology rule. It wasn't like I could text Syke and check what was going on.

"Didn't she try to kill you the last time you saw her?" Ethan said.

"She was a little upset. But that was six months ago."

"She tried to stab you with a tree branch."

"Fine. A lot upset. I'm sure she's over it by now."

"Just wait for me," Ethan said. "And what about Professor Reese? Did he ever—"

Professor Reese was what Ethan always called Ares, a hold-over from college, I guessed, since he knew about Ares' immortal status.

"Not yet." I tried not to crush my cell phone out of frustration. But seriously? If someone gets a 911 text about a Fury attack, I would think that should at least merit a response.

Oh right, these were the gods we were talking about.

"It's fine," I said. "I'll catch you later tonight."

I hung up and nearly tripped over a wagon on the edge of the curb outside of the gym. Two little girls held the handle of the wagon, and a third little girl stood behind, stuffing her face with a box of cookies. Her pudgy waistband looked like she'd been eating a bit too much of the product.

"Hi, Mister, would you like to buy some Flower Scout cookies?" the little girl with a head full of red curls asked. She bobbed up and down like she was trying to look all cute and stuff.

"They just went on sale today," another little girl said, this one Indian with bushy dark hair and huge glasses.

I paused, and all three of their eyes got super big, like I'd given them hope.

"You'd be our first sale," the little blond girl said with a full mouth. Small pieces of chocolate cookie flew from her lips as she spoke.

I reached for my wallet and pulled out a ten. "Yeah, sure. I'll take some cookies. How many can I get for ten dollars?"

"Well, for two more dollars, you can get three boxes," the red-headed girl said.

The last thing I needed were three boxes of Flower Scout

cookies.

"Just give me two," I said. "Peanut butter if you have them."

A tall, dark-haired woman stepped forward, next to the girls. Her sweat suit was the same color green as the girls' vests, making her look like a grown up Flower Scout. "They're trying to sell enough to earn a trip to Hawaii," she said. "Right, girls?"

All three girls nodded. The dark-haired girl grabbed my ten and the red-headed girl dug through the wagon and handed me one orange box of cookies and one red.

"Do you want the change, or can we keep it?" the red-headed girl asked.

Given that I had no money, I wanted the change. But these were Flower Scouts. And they were working toward a goal. Hell, I'd sell cookies if it would get me a trip to Hawaii.

"You can keep it," I said.

"Thanks for supporting Flower Scouts," the little blond girl said. She grabbed for another box of cookies.

"Sarah, stop eating the cookies," the dark-haired girl said, and they wheeled the wagon on down the sidewalk.

I shoved the cookies back inside the gym then grabbed a rideshare down to Treaty Oak Park. I wasn't sure if I'd be able to find Syke there, but it was a place to start. Dryads tended to cluster around their matron tree. Treaty Oak was something like five hundred years old, and the dryad who inhabited the tree didn't have a name that I knew of. All the other dryads simply called her Mother Dryad.

There was a chill in the January air, but the sun shone high above in the sky. That changed the second my driver pulled to a stop at the curb.

"This the right place?" she asked, checking her phone to make sure. Thankfully, she hadn't been one of those chatty rideshare drivers. We'd said all of three words the entire ride.

I glanced at the massive oak tree to my right. The last survivor of an entire council of elder dryads who'd once lived here. The others had died slowly, one by one.

"Yep."

"Isn't this the oldest tree in Austin?" the driver said. "That one they tried to poison?"

"Yeah, crazy, right?" I said. Back in the eighties someone had tried to kill this final tree, Mother Dryad. The official story was that it was some crazy guy trying to cast a spell, and that he'd dumped an entire truckload of herbicide into the roots. Like I said, that was the public story. Syke had told me that the not-so-public story had everything to do with the world of the gods.

The city had managed to save the tree, but not without a lot of damage. The dryads had gone through an entire decade of mourning, refusing to talk to anyone, but as Mother Dryad's health had returned, they'd opened up a bit more. That was when I'd started hanging out with Syke.

"Seriously. What kind of hater would poison a tree?"

"Seriously." I got out before she could ask any more questions. The last thing the dryads wanted was any renewed interest in the tree. As it was now, most people drove by it on a daily basis having no clue about its history.

No sooner had the car pulled away and I'd placed one foot onto the curb, the sky darkened. I tried to pretend that it was all a coincidence, but one more step and thunder rumbled in the sky. I had to clear my name. The dryads had to know that whatever happened, I wasn't to blame.

I took a deep breath and walked forward. I had done nothing wrong. When I got to the base of Treaty Oak, I placed a hand on the rough bark.

Even with no technology, there are a couple different ways to communicate with dryads. In tree form, communication is telepathic, transmitted through the bark. But when the dryads took human form, they talked and walked like everyone else. Just without cell phones.

"You're not welcome here," Mother Dryad said in my mind, and immediately a tree branch snapped out and twisted around my wrist, holding me tightly against the tree, cutting into the skin.

On instinct, I struggled against the branch, pulling my hand back. But she held it too firmly.

"Is Syke okay?" I asked, needing to know that before anything else. I tried to relax, but the branch dug deep.

"She won't speak to you," Mother Dryad said, and bitter hatred filled her telepathic voice.

Relief washed through me. Her not wanting to speak to me at least told me that she wasn't dead. As the waves of relief cascaded through me, the sky lightened up, almost like Mother Dryad could feel my emotions.

"I just wanted to make sure she was okay," I said.

"Why did you do it, Achilles?" Mother Dryad asked, and the branch tightened on my wrist. "We trusted you. We thought you cared."

"Do what?" I struggled again because at this point my hand had turned completely white and lost feeling. "I didn't do anything."

"The proof is there," Mother Dryad said, holding me close, making my struggles useless.

"What proof?"

Moments of silence passed. I was having a hard time focusing on anything because my wrist hurt too badly. I swear if she tightened it any more, it would snap off.

Finally she released the branch. Blood pulsed back into my hand, and a giant welt circled my wrist.

"You are not welcome here anymore," Mother Dryad said. "If you come near the dryads again, we will end your existence. No questions will be asked. We have the power."

"But . . . what proof? I swear I'm innocent," I said, holding my wrist with my other hand.

Mother Dryad didn't say anything else. I pressed one thought after another into her, but all were ignored. Her warning had been clear. She could end my life. She could and the Furies could. I was doubly screwed.

I dared to touch the bark one final time and said, "Please tell Syke that I would never harm her or any of her sisters. Please tell her that I'm sorry."

There was no response. I could only hope that my message was delivered. Sure, I hadn't found out what had happened, but I did know that at least she was safe.

CHAPTER 5

Ares sauntered into the gym next day, dressed in gym shorts and an athletic shirt, obviously planning to work out. His dark hair was pulled back into a short ponytail at the base of his neck. He ducked as he came through the door, something that had become habit given the fact that he was six feet eight inches tall. And though I was stronger than legend, Ares dwarfed me when it came to sheer width and muscle. Yet somehow, for his day job as a professor—he was the top military history professor at UT and also lectured around the country— he managed to pull it all together into a respectable suit and tie each day.

I let out the breath I'd been holding since the Furies attacked. Finally, I'd be able to get some answers. And Ares, being on the council of gods, would definitely have those answers.

"I'm not spotting Jack," Ares said the second he walked

through the door, glancing over to where Jack stood gawking at him. I was pretty sure Jack had a serious man-crush on Ares because he never took his eyes off him and he found every excuse he could to talk to him.

"'Sup, Professor Reese?" Jack called from across the gym, waving. Professor Reese was what everyone here at Heroes Gym also called Ares. But unlike Ethan, none of them had any clue that he was really a Greek god.

Ares flexed his muscles and nodded in Jack's direction. He didn't bother with signing in. Mortal competitions were below the gods.

"I'm going to spot him," I said, trying to act cool, like it didn't bother me that Ares had completely ignored my text messages for the last twenty-four hours.

"You need to spot me." Ares grabbed a towel from the pile of dirty laundry. "Jack can find someone else. And what the hell is wrong with this towel? It smells like ass." He tossed it at me. I threw it back into the pile.

"I forgot to do laundry," I said. "Oh, you know, because I have a couple other things on my mind." Like staying alive.

I might insert here that there is no arguing with the gods. They do what they want when they want without answering to anyone. Anyone except other gods on the council of the gods, that is. And no, I'm not a part of the council of the gods. I'm a demigod. Half-god. In this case, my mom, Thetis, happened to be a goddess. My dad was just this mortal guy, a king, so pretty important in the mortal world, but just a mortal after all was said and done.

But anyway . . . I was immortal, but wasn't a god. So I didn't argue with Ares. Instead I found a clean towel for him in a cabinet and followed him to the free weights to spot him.

"So about my text . . . ," I said when he was benching two fifty. He set the bar down and motioned for me to put on more weight. I had to be careful to not draw too much attention. Guys like Simon would put that shit online, and that's how rumors got started.

"Could you seriously have picked a worse time to get into this mess?" Ares said.

"Get into this mess? Are you kidding?" I held my hands under the bar even though there was zero chance that Ares would drop the weights.

"Yes, get into this mess," Ares said. "You're a pain in my ass, you know that, right?"

Like I said, there was no arguing with Ares. "Yeah, whatever. But the good news is that if you don't get me out of this mess, I'll be in Tartarus for the rest of eternity and won't ever bother you again."

"Tartarus," Ares said, like it was some kind of joke.

"I'm serious. The freaking Furies came after me. Tried to haul my ass off right then and there."

"No shit. Did you kick their hideous asses?"

"Did you not read my text messages?" I said.

Ares shook his head. "I skimmed them but didn't have a chance to read them."

Again, not the time to explain that it would have taken all of ten seconds to read a text message.

"They gave me a week," I said, maybe a little too loudly because Jack looked over at us.

"Those Furies are nothing to mess around with," Ares said. "They'll slice out your intestines and eat them for dinner."

"Wow. Thanks for that utterly wonderful imagery."

"You know, I tried to ask one of them out one time," Ares

said. "Meg. She's the one who wears green and has that amazing dark skin. And those white tattoos. You know she has a tattoo on her . . . never mind. Did you meet her?" He didn't wait for an answer. "Anyway, she actually listed out twenty different crimes that she said I'd committed. Things that as she claimed could have my testicles pulled off and fed to me with a spoon. Man, you have never seen me get the hell away from a girl so fast. You should be smart, Achilles. Stay away from those Furies."

"What? You think I'm trying to ask them out?" Sometimes I was sure that Ares lived on an entirely different planet.

"Women are monsters, Achilles," Ares said, way too loudly.

"Hell, yeah, they are," Jack hollered and gave a thumbs up, as if this comment made him fall in love with Ares that much more.

We both ignored him.

"They came after me," I said. "They said I killed . . ." I lowered my voice, because this was not anything I wanted Jack to hear. "They said I killed a dryad."

"You killed a dryad? Are you fucking kidding me? You know killing dryads is some serious shit, Achilles. That's the kind of shit that will get you put in Tartarus for the rest of your days."

I wanted to pull my hair out in frustration. "That's what I'm trying to say. They said I did it. I didn't do it. But they don't care. They're trying to haul me off anyway."

It was like understanding finally dawned in Ares' eyes. "Oh. Man. That is a problem."

"Yes. Exactly. It's a problem. That's why I texted you. You need to get them off my tail."

Ares seemed to think through my words while he continued to lift. "I haven't heard anything at the council about this. And you would not believe the shit I have had to hear. Just the other day, I had to listen to some dispute between Castor and Pollux.

You would think that after gods know how many thousands of years those two could stop bickering."

"Like how you and Athena don't bicker?" The fights between Ares and his sister Athena were the thing of legend.

"Just like that," Ares said.

"Anyway, why are we talking about Castor and Pollux?" I shoved the weight pin in the highest weight hole. "What is up with this dryad shit?"

"Like I said, I haven't heard," Ares said.

"You're a god."

"And . . . ?"

"Do you think you could find out?" I suggested.

Ares gritted his teeth, like this was asking entirely too much. "I could ask the council, but if this shit were on the level, I'd already know."

"So you think they're going rogue?"

"Maybe," Ares said.

"How about you ask around? Maybe ask Athena?"

Ares cocked his head like I'd finally had a good idea.

"Tell you what," Ares said. "Athena and I are meeting later for drinks at the Driskill. You can meet us and ask her yourself."

Forget if I had any other Friday night plans.

The bell chimed, letting me know someone else had come into the gym.

"Hello, beautiful mortal," Ares said, thankfully under his breath.

I turned to look, and there, standing by the counter, was the same girl from yesterday. The one who'd asked about yoga.

"I'll be right back," I said to Ares.

"Not if you're smart," Ares said. "That is one nice piece—"

I put up my hand to cut him off. Ares wasn't always the most appropriate of gods.

Actually none of the gods were the most appropriate of gods.

"We still don't have yoga today," I said, strolling up to the front of the gym.

The girl, who was again wearing a tank top and yoga pants, but this time her long dark hair was pulled back with a hair tie, stuck her hand out. "I never properly introduced myself," she said. "I'm Nicole Earley."

I shook her hand. "Achilles Stevens. I own the gym."

"Achilles," she said. "And you own a gym called Heroes Gym."

"Funny, right?"

"Super funny," she said, but I think she was just trying to get on my good side, though I had no clue why.

"I'm named after Saint Achilles. My mom's all religious and into stuff like that." That was the cover story I always used when people brought up my name. Achilles was not an unheard of name, but it also hadn't cracked the top one hundred.

"There's really a saint named Achilles?" Nicole said.

"There's a saint named everything," I said. "Saint Achilles used to cast out demons."

If only I were Saint Achilles, maybe I could cast out the Furies and be done with the entire mess.

"Ooh, sounds scary," Nicole said.

"Very scary," I said. "So are you here for a membership?" It had been way too long since I'd signed up anyone new. One membership wasn't going to make a huge difference, but it would be a start.

She shook her head. "I'm here to make you an offer."

Not bragging here, but women made me offers all the time.

"What kind of offer?" I said, sure I sounded like a complete douchebag but not really caring.

If she caught on to what I was thinking, she didn't let it show. Instead she motioned with her head toward the old florist shop. "I'm going to teach yoga for you."

I let out a small laugh. "That's funny."

Nicole grabbed her ponytail and smoothed it. "No, I'm serious. Since you don't have yoga already, I'll teach it for you."

"But I don't want to have yoga here," I said, even though now that she'd planted the idea in my head, all I could imagine was a bunch of nice looking women bending over in yoga pants. Why hadn't I offered yoga years ago?

"Sure you do," Nicole said.

"No one will come to yoga here," I said. "We're a workout gym."

"People will totally come," Nicole said. "I'll advertise on Facebook and Twitter and we can do some giveaways and offer up some free memberships."

"I don't do Facebook," I said, but the idea of more memberships coming in was pretty attractive.

Nicole moved forward and started tapping keys on my computer. "No worries. It's super easy to set up an account. All I have to do is . . ." She stopped talking because the computer did to her what it did to me all the time: acted like a big piece of shit.

"I don't Facebook," I said again, but I guess Nicole wasn't listening to me. She scooted around behind the counter and started doing gods-know-what to my computer. A bunch of windows popped up on the screen and she typed words that weren't even really words and clicked the mouse faster than a bunny rabbit having sex.

"About the yoga . . . ," I said.

Nicole didn't look my way. Instead she bit her lip and creased her forehead. And I couldn't help but notice how amazingly full her lips were.

"You know you have a virus on here," she said.

"I do?"

She nodded. "A Trojan Horse. But don't worry. I can get it cleaned up."

"You can?"

I realized that with my two word sentences, I was sounding more like an idiot every second, but where had this girl come from? First she's offering to teach yoga and now she's going to fix my computer? And what the hell was she talking about, a Trojan Horse?

"Sure." She kept working, typing things, pressing buttons. The computer screen went completely black which is never a good sign. I was about to open my mouth and say something, but then it winked back to life and started counting through some routine in percentage done.

"I'm running a full scan," she said. "It'll take a while. But I can start on Monday."

"Start what?" I said, still staring at the little bar on the computer. It was at two percent.

"Yoga," she said. "I'll start teaching on Monday. Oh, and I can get your computer working better, too."

"It works fine."

"Your computer's a piece of shit," Jack called over. Had he been listening this entire time?

I looked from the computer to Nicole then back to the computer. It was already at seven percent and seemed to be doing exactly what she'd wanted it to do because a smile crept onto her face.

"Why are you so good with computers?"

Nicole shrugged. "I'm a programmer."

"I thought you were a yoga teacher."

"That too."

"Don't you have a job?"

She crossed her arms. "I'm between jobs right now."

"So you want to teach yoga?"

"How does two hundred a class sound?" Nicole said.

Two hundred dollars for an hour of yoga? Was she kidding? She'd be the only person in there.

"No one will come," I said. I did not have yoga clientele.

She looked at me like I was a small child. "People will come. Trust me. Now show me where your cleaning stuff is so I can get the room ready."

Nicole wrinkled her nose when she saw the pile of dirty towels. "You should do some laundry."

Which only served to remind me that I'd once more forgotten laundry detergent. I'd have to get some this weekend or the pile might grow enough bacteria to come to life.

"I will." I pointed out the broom and cleaning stuff and left her to it.

Ares was finishing up his workout when I got back.

"Did you make a date for later?" he said, watching Nicole's every move. She'd made her way to the old florist shop and was officially frowning. Maybe she'd give up and go home.

"She's going to teach yoga," I said.

"Here?"

"Yep. You gonna sign up?"

He threw his towel at me. "Let me know when classes are. Anyway, I'll see you tonight."

That was definitely a date I wasn't going to miss. If anyone knew what was going on, it was Athena. Word had it that she was on the good side of the Furies, if it was possible to be on the good side of torturous soul-sucking she-demons. She'd know why they attacked me. And that was something I had to figure out if I was going to survive the week.

CHAPTER 6

In the very likely event that Ares and Athena got into a fight, I did not want to get in the middle of it all by myself.

"Come with me," I said to Ethan after I got out of the shower. He sat on the sofa with a game controller in his hand.

"Professor Reese didn't invite me," Ethan said.

"Ares wouldn't give a shit," I said. "You know that."

Truth was that I was pretty sure Ares liked Ethan more than he liked me. Ethan made amazing weapons, and Ares, being the god of war, dug that shit. I could fight like a total badass, but Ethan was like Ares' personal version of Hephaestus, only with twenty-first century technology.

"True," Ethan said. "But I have plans for tonight."

"What plans?"

He shrugged. "This girl I met earlier today when I went to get a sandwich. We were both waiting in line at the counter and really hit it off."

"You asked a girl out at the sandwich counter? What was she getting? A salami sandwich?" Ethan had asked girls out at the laundromat, the grocery store. He'd even asked a girl out one time when he was on a date with another girl.

Ethan laughed. "Yeah, something like that. And when you see this girl, you are going to shit yourself."

"What? Is she prettier than the last one?" I said. Ethan claimed every girl he met was the best looking ever. This was nothing new.

"Dude, you have no idea," Ethan said. "Just don't wait up for me."

Seeing as how I had no idea what my own night entailed, I didn't see that happening. Best case I'd be fighting the Furies with Ares and Athena by my side. Worst case . . . I didn't want to even imagine.

"Have fun," I said, and left.

Ares was already waiting when I got to the Driskill. He got us one of those half-booth half-tables, and he sat in the booth side so his back was to the wall. No matter the circumstances, Ares was always ready for an attack. He may now be some stodgy college professor, but underneath his polished exterior, he was still the god of war. Still ready to engage in battle at the slightest sign of trouble. This was why, of all the gods, I related to him the best. Battles were pretty few and far between these days, but I was always ready. I had the spirit of a warrior. I always would.

Ares gave a small nod of acknowledgment.

"I got you Scotch," Ares said, shoving a glass my way when I walked over.

Scotch wasn't my favorite, but I took the glass anyway. I'd way have preferred straight up whiskey. Scotch always had a funny aftertaste, sort of sweet. But he was paying and I didn't complain.

"Where's your sister?" I asked, taking a sip from the crystal tumbler.

Ares downed his Scotch in one shot. "Late, like always."

I resisted the urge to point out that Ares was never on time. Instead I did what any demigod with a self-preservation instinct would do. I laughed along with him and drank my Scotch.

"You didn't bring Ethan," Ares said.

I wiped my mouth with a napkin. "He had plans."

"Hopefully making me the new flame thrower I requested," Ares said. "He claims it can throw ammo up to forty-nine meters with dead-on accuracy."

"Not fifty? That's trash. And what the hell do you need a flame thrower for anyway?"

"Preparation," Ares said. "Because you don't know what's coming."

"What's coming?"

"That's the point," Ares said. "I don't know either."

"You know one of these days, Hephaestus is gonna find out you have someone else making weapons, and he's gonna be pissed."

Ares slammed his tumbler down on the table. "Hephaestus can suck my—"

I put my hand up. That was a visual I didn't need.

"Anyway," Ares said. "You should get Ethan to make you some new weapons."

I won't deny it. The idea of brand new weapons still made my heart speed up. But weapons without a place to use them sucked.

"What for? To hang on the walls?"

"Preparation," Ares said. "Like I said, you don't know what's coming."

Just then silence filled the room, and I knew Athena had

gotten here. Every head in the bar turned to look. Athena was over six feet tall, but she didn't do that slouchy thing that some girls do when they're tall. Instead, Athena pushed her shoulders back and held her head high. Her blond hair was pulled back from her face, and she didn't have on a shred of makeup. Being the goddess of war, you'd almost expect her to come in wearing full battle armor, and I had seen this various times in the past, during the war, but today, she had on faded jeans and a gray undershirt tank top. Every single line of her muscles was defined, from her arms to her upper chest.

She cast her special glamour over the people in the bar and slowly their eyes drifted away. That was another thing that set me apart from the gods. They had special powers, things like casting a glamour over mortals to draw their attention away from unusual occurrences. I had nothing like that. I was resistant to their glamour, but not completely.

"Don't stare at her," Ares said, smacking me on top of the head.

I thought I'd stopped, but I guess I was wrong. The thing is that Athena is possibly the most beautiful goddess in the universe. Sure, there had been lots of debate about it over the ages. There had even been this whole contest between Hera, Aphrodite, and Athena to decide who was the most beautiful. Paris, the asshole who killed me back at the end of the Trojan War, had been chosen to judge. It had ruined his life. And seeing as how he was the one who shot me with the arrow, I didn't feel the least bit sorry for him.

I forced my eyes away. "I'm not staring," I muttered before Athena got to the table. "But your sister is . . ."

Ares put up a hand to stop me. "Don't talk about that shit in front of me. That's my sister, you know."

I didn't get a chance to say anymore because that's when

Athena got to our table.

She grabbed my shoulders and started running her hands all over my muscles. "Damn, Achilles, you are looking good these days."

"These days?" I said, trying to keep my cool so I didn't act like a teenage boy. It took every bit of my self-control.

She gave my shoulders a final squeeze then sat down next to Ares, across from me. "Always," she said, and she winked.

Goddess or not, if Athena ever made any kind of advances on me, sexual being my preference, I would take her up on it in a second. Sadly, those advances had never come. She was just an incredible flirt.

"You don't look so bad either," I said. "You been working out? You know you could come by the gym any time. I'd be happy to spot you." I wasn't all bad at flirting right back.

"Maybe I will," she said. Then she grazed her leg against mine under the table.

Damn, she was fine.

"Enough," Ares said. "What did you find out?"

I wasn't ready to call enough. The Furies could have come at me and started hauling my ass off to Tartarus, and I would have been willing to flirt just a bit longer with Athena. That said, I did also want answers.

Athena grabbed Ares' Scotch and licked the entire rim before taking a sip. He scowled but didn't say anything. Then he waved the waitress over.

"Bring the bottle," he said.

It was the start of what I was guessing would be a long night.

"So what's new, Achilles?" Athena said. She licked the rim again and took another sip, and I swear each time she did it, it drove me a little bit crazier. My palms were sweaty, and my pants were starting to feel really tight.

As soon as the waitress brought over the bottle, I poured some in my glass and drained it. The Scotch worked its way through my blood, helping me focus. Or at least relax.

"Oh, I don't know," I said. "I got new furniture from IKEA. I went to DC last year. I got attacked by the Furies. You know, just the usual."

"Also Achilles is taking up yoga," Ares added.

"Yoga?" Athena said.

"I'm not taking up yoga," I said.

"I love yoga," Athena said, which was perfect because now images of her in impossible yoga poses filled my mind. Almost like she could read it, she rubbed my leg again.

I poured more of the Scotch.

"Can we talk about the Furies?" I said, even though a large part of me—a very large part of me—wasn't thinking about the Furies at all.

"You sure?" she said, and her leg rubbed a little higher.

Ares elbowed her. "Can you just stop?"

"Stop what?" Athena said, and smiled like she most the most innocent goddess in the entire world. Which she was not. Actually there was no such thing as an innocent goddess, no matter what the stories said.

"The Furies . . . ," Ares said.

"Fine, the Furies," Athena said. "Did you let their blood touch you?"

I shook my head. "No. They scratched me. But that was it."

"Did the snakes bite you?"

"Snakes?" I said.

"I'll take that as a no. What happened? How did you get them to go away?"

"I fought them off," I said. "What do you think? And they gave me a week." As the words came out, I realized two days were already gone of that week.

"It's good they didn't do more damage," she said. "If their blood touches you, then you're totally screwed. It can boil your skin off. And the snakes . . ."

"That shit never heals," Ares said. "You know that's what they do to their victims in Tartarus. They boil their skin off and pull out their intestines and fill them with disease and madness. And over the ages, their tactics get more creative. Victims don't have a chance."

"You guys suck at inspirational talks, you know that?" I said.

"Sorry, but my sister's right," Ares said. "You are screwed."

"Why are they after me in the first place?" I said. "I didn't do anything."

"I did some asking around, and lots of gods on the council disagree," Athena said. "They think you killed a dryad. And you know, I always thought you were smarter than that."

"I didn't kill a dryad," I said. "I haven't even seen a dryad in over six months."

"So you're saying that you didn't visit Mother Dryad just yesterday?" Athena said.

What? Was she following me?

"Okay, fine, until yesterday. I went to talk to her," I said. "To try to clear this whole mess up. To make sure this one dryad I know pretty well—"

"Syke," Athena said.

Did Athena know everything about my life?

"Yes, Syke," I said. "I wanted to make sure she was okay."

"And was she?" Athena said.

I nodded. "Yeah, she's okay. It was a different dryad."

"And you're telling me straight up that you didn't kill this dryad?" Athena said.

"Right," I said. "That is exactly what I'm telling you."

Athena drummed her fingers on the table. Her nails were cut short and unpolished which was a complete turn-on, just like everything else about her. Light blond hairs dusted her arms. But that moment of flirtation was gone. I needed answers.

"Are you lying?" Athena said, and her gray eyes bore into me, almost like she was trying to pull the truth out of me.

I stared her down. "No. I'm not lying. Why would I kill a dryad?"

"Maybe you and Syke had an argument?" Athena said.

I shook my head. "We didn't . . . I mean we did have an argument. But it was nothing. I sure as hell wouldn't kill a dryad."

"And yet a dryad is dead," Athena said.

"Not by me."

She narrowed her gray eyes at me, like she didn't believe me.

"Why would I even be a suspect in the first place?" I said. "Just because of some stupid argument? That doesn't make any sense. If someone killed a dryad, why would the gods blame me?"

"Because of the weapon," Athena said.

"What weapon?" I asked.

"The spear of Achilles," Athena said. "That's the weapon that was used."

"Bullshit," I said.

Athena stopped drumming her fingers on the table, and she eyed me like she was trying to determine my guilt right then and there.

"That's impossible," I said. "The spear is locked away. No one can get it out except me."

"Exactly," Athena said. "Which brings us back to why the

Furies were sent after you."

I drained my glass and filled it again, trying to squelch the anger that was burning up inside me. I hadn't killed a dryad.

"Let's back this shit up a second," Ares said. "How do you know it was the spear?" He grabbed the bottle and filled up both of their glasses. I shoved mine forward and he topped it off.

Athena held up her thumb, like she was counting on it. "The spear leaves . . ."

"There's no mistaking a wound delivered by the spear," I said, interrupting her. This was my weapon we were talking about. Mine to use. Mine to lock away.

Athena nodded. "Achilles is right. Since it's capable of killing immortals, it has a distinct infliction pattern. Study of the dryad's body was obvious. It was without a doubt the spear."

"It wasn't me," I said. "Someone else used it."

Athena smirked. "We all know that's impossible."

"What's impossible about it?" I said. "I didn't do it."

"And yet you're the only one who could have," Athena said.

"Why wasn't the spear locked up?" Ares said. "All weapons—including some exceptionally badass ones that I would really love to get my hands on—are kept secure."

"Exactly," Athena said. "And the only person who can take them out of security is the one who put them there. In this case, Achilles."

I squeezed the glass tumbler with so much force, it shattered in my hand. Glass and Scotch sprayed all over the table. That was the least of my concerns. "I never took it out."

"You must have," Ares said, tossing me a napkin. "You're the only one who can."

"And I didn't," I said. "Which means that it's still locked away. Which also means that there has to be some mistake."

"A mistake with what?" Athena said. "The evidence is clear. The body was left where anyone could find it. The wound was evident."

Her logic made perfect sense and yet was completely flawed.

"The body was left out in the open?" I said. "Not hidden away."

"Nope. Other dryads found her and reported it right away."

I grabbed Ares' glass and took a sip, trying to piece through it. Something about this felt off.

"Let's just say that I had done it," I said. "Not that I did. But let's just say that I had. Don't you think I would have tried to cover the evidence? Otherwise everyone would know it was me."

"Generally," Athena said. "The accusing gods thought about that. But then your anger came into play."

"My anger?" My anger had nothing to do with any of this. If anything, this whole mess was only a trigger to make me furious. "That's the biggest bunch of bullshit I've ever heard. And where the hell is the waitress? I need a new glass."

Ares waved her over. She frowned at me when she saw the broken glass but brought me a new tumbler anyway.

"All the gods know how you get," Athena said after the waitress left. "So it came up. And they determined that maybe you killed her out of anger. Like maybe you weren't thinking about your actions."

"Or I was framed," I said. "Did that ever occur to these accusing gods? And which gods are accusing me anyway?"

Athena blew out a breath, like I'd insulted her. "Of course it occurred to the gods. And I can't tell you which ones. You know that. But you're forgetting the part about the spear. You filed it away in the Hall of Artifacts. Only you can get it out. Only you."

"Which I didn't do," I said. "So it must still be there. And the wounds on the dryad were made to look like the spear."

Athena leaned forward and flexed her arm muscles. "Possibly."

Okay, I was making progress. It was at least a start.

"How about this?" I said. "How about I prove to you I'm innocent? Can the council give me a break from the Furies until then?"

I had to get the Furies off my back or this week would be my last on Earth. If the Furies managed to drag me off to Tartarus, I'd never have a chance to clear my name.

Athena sat back and licked her glass again. Then she drained it. And then she rubbed her leg against mine once more, just like we'd never had the entire conversation.

"I'll see what I can do, Achilles," she said.

Thank the gods. Tartarus was about the last place I wanted to be.

We went through another bottle of Scotch. The waitress eyed our glasses like she wasn't sure where the liquor was going. She must not wait on many immortals. But when Ares slipped her a hundred as an extra bonus, she brought us a bowl of popcorn, too, covered with some sort of brown dusty crap she called truffle powder. I skipped the popcorn, drank the Scotch, and let myself sink into the fact that Athena was totally hitting on me. It was only after the three of us were the last ones left in the bar that I accepted the night had to end.

My head swam only for a moment when I stood. My demigod status meant that I could handle more liquor than an average guy.

"You're not an average guy," Athena whispered in my ear, almost like she could read my mind.

"And I think you're totally gorgeous," I said, because that much Scotch would make even Dionysus spit out the first thing that came to his mind.

The streets were pretty empty, since it was well after two in the morning.

"I'm walking Achilles home," Athena said, and she stepped close and lay her hand flat on my stomach.

Ares snickered under his breath. "Yeah, like I said, I don't want to hear about that shit." And without another word, he was off, walking toward campus in the direction of his house.

"You tired, Achilles?" Athena said, and her hand trailed down lower.

"Not at all," I said.

CHAPTER 7

We got back to my place, hardly shutting the door, before Athena was on me. All over me. Making me wish I'd skipped the Scotch so I could remember everything totally unhindered. I had no clue if Ethan was home and wasn't going to waste time checking. He'd be smart enough to stay out of the way.

We started out in the kitchen, moved from the countertop to against the refrigerator then into the family room, to the coffee table in front of the television. I had a vague memory of Athena kicking over the TV but couldn't have given a shit. She moved like liquid fire and crawled on top of me with desperate urgency, like she'd been waiting her entire life for this moment. Or maybe that was just me.

"You don't disappoint, Achilles," Athena said as we lay on the stairs, me collapsed between her legs trying to catch my breath.

I thought we were done. But Athena's trailing hands made me realize how wrong I was. We went at it again, moving from the stairs to my bedroom, where, once we were really done, I fell into a deep sleep.

I woke up hours later with two thoughts. One, what had happened last night was a complete dream because Athena was nowhere to be found. And two, if it was a dream, I was going to spend the rest of my life sleeping in hopes of reliving it. Scratches covered my chest. Not scratches like the Furies had delivered. Scratches that made me incredibly horny all over again just thinking about it. Damn. I always knew Athena was fine. I just had no idea how right I was.

Then I heard sound coming from the kitchen of my condo.

I didn't bother putting clothes on before checking on it. If Ethan had been home last night, he would have already had plenty of entertainment. There, in the kitchen, was Athena, opening every single cabinet.

"Looking for something?" I said, even though I knew instantly what was going on.

"Maybe," Athena said. She, unlike me, was fully dressed in her jeans and tank top. She eyed me up and down and grinned.

"I told you I don't have it," I said, and anger flashed inside me. "And you could have just asked to look around."

"You could have lied."

"But I didn't," I said.

Athena stepped forward and reached down. I kept my eyes looking straight ahead and focused on the anger. Had she seriously slept me with just so she could come in here and search the place?

"I had fun, Achilles," Athena said.

"We could have more fun," I said.

She leaned forward and kissed me, slow and hard, full on the mouth while she kept her hand moving. Then she said, "Not today."

And that was the end of that.

My entire body ached as I watched her walk out the door.

After she left, I looked around for Ethan, but he wasn't home. I jumped in the shower, keeping the water running for an extra-long time, trying to sort out everything. I had to check on the spear. Make sure it was still safely tucked away in the Hall of Artifacts. Once I did that, I could easily prove my innocence. Get rid of the threat of Furies forever. The Hall of Artifacts was in DC, and I wasn't particularly excited about making a trip halfway across the country. Good thing I didn't have to.

Ethan must've gotten home while I was showering, because when I walked out of the bathroom, with just a towel wrapped around my waist, he sat on the sofa staring at the television stand.

"What happened to our TV, Achilles?" he said.

I shrugged. "It got knocked over."

"How?" he said, then looked my way. "And holy shit, what happened to you?"

I glanced down at my exposed torso. It was covered with scratches, as were my arms and back.

"Oh, you know," I said.

"Is that a hickey on your neck?" Ethan asked.

I hadn't looked too closely in the mirror. "Maybe?"

"You and . . ." He motioned with his hand like he was afraid to say her name.

"Yeah. I got no words," I said, because the only place the experience could live on was in my mind. And damn it was a great memory to have.

Ethan let out a low whistle. "Dude . . ."

"Yeah."

"But you're buying us a new TV."

Unless I made some money, that wasn't going to happen.

"Where were you last night?" I said. "Was it . . . ?"

"Elle," Ethan said. "The sandwich girl. And yes. I mean no. I mean, I stayed at her place, but nothing happened."

I was about to call bullshit when the doorbell rang. I motioned at my half nakedness, so Ethan got up and answered it while I went into the kitchen to grab a glass of water.

"You got any cash?" Ethan called.

"No," I said, even though I always kept a spare twenty under the microwave.

"Bring me your spare twenty," he said.

"No."

"But it's Flower Scout cookies," Ethan said.

I grabbed the twenty and passed it to him. "Get me some of those peanut butter ones. Not Skinny Mints though. Keith brought some in the other day and they tasted like crap."

While Ethan finished the Flower Scout transaction, I went upstairs to get dressed.

"Did you get your Furies shit resolved?" Ethan asked after I got back down. We sat on the sofa with five boxes of cookies in front of us on the coffee table. I didn't mention that it was the same table where just hours ago Athena and I had . . . Anyway, I didn't mention it.

"She's gonna try to buy me a few extra days. To prove my innocence."

"And can you?" he asked.

I nodded. "Someone is trying to set me up. But I should easily be able to prove that."

"I hope so," Ethan said. "It's going to suck if you get hauled off to hell. I'd have to live here all alone. No one to beat me at every single game we play. No one leaving dirty dishes in the sink. No one to knock over my fucking TV. You know, actually, maybe it wouldn't be such a bad thing."

I flicked the rest of my cookie at him, hitting him on the forehead. "Thanks for the concern."

"I'm kidding," Ethan said, snatching up the piece of cookie and eating it. "I'm here for you, man. You know that."

He put out his fist, and I fist-bumped him. I did know he was there for me, and I was glad for it. Glad Ares had brought him into this crazy, fucked-up world of gods.

CHAPTER 8

I survived the weekend with no sign of the Furies. I dreamed about Athena. Ethan and I shot darts downtown, worked out, and tried to find a decent television at Goodwill, which wound up being impossible. Sure, they had a bunch of those old ones that were so big I could have used them at the gym instead of barbells, but neither of us was willing to lower ourselves to that level of desperation.

Monday morning when I got to the gym, Nicole was waiting for me outside. Nicole and a yellow cat with hair so long, it could have doubled as a throw rug.

"What is that?" I asked, stepping away from her as I unlocked the door.

"This is Nano," Nicole said, snuggling it up against her face like it was her best friend.

I hurried inside. "I hate cats."

Nicole put on the perfect pout. "You can't hate cats. No one hates cat."

"I hate cats. They claw at you every time you try to get near them. They hiss at you when you look at them. No cats allowed at the gym."

"But Nano helps me with yoga," Nicole said. "And he never claws stuff. Also, I told everyone he would be here. You know having a cat in the room really helps lower anxiety and bring about relaxation. It's something about their purring."

If by purring, she meant the buzzing sound like a broken microwave coming from the general directly of Nano, then it wasn't doing anything to relax me.

"Everyone who? It's not like we have a yoga clientele," I said, because I had no clue how she thought people were just going to magically show up to a yoga class.

"We'll see," Nicole said. Nano squirmed out her hands and immediately jumped to the counter where he grabbed a crocheted ball and started batting it around.

"He's messing with my balls," I said. There were at least seven of them sitting on the counter, all different colors.

"Sounds like a personal problem," Nicole said. "And why do you have so many knitted balls anyway?"

"They're crochet, and someone made them for me," I said, which wasn't entirely a lie. The fact that I happened to be that person was irrelevant.

Any more discussion about Nano was cut short when Jack came in, followed by Simon and Carly.

"Aw, you got a cat," Jack said. He reached down for it.

I waited for it to swipe him with one of its deadly claws. Instead, the stupid cat jumped to the floor and rubbed against his skinny leg.

"Man, I love cats," Jack said, scratching the cat behind the ears. The cat's buzzing sound only got louder.

"You'll be able to sign in in a few minutes," I said to change the subject. I pressed the power button on the computer, ready for my daily frustration of seeing whether it was going to cooperate or not. But unlike nearly every other day since I'd had the thing, it immediately lit up and started booting.

"Virus is totally cleaned off it," Nicole said. "I spent a couple hours on it while you were holding weights for people on Friday."

"Spotting," I said. "And I thought you were cleaning the flower shop on Friday."

"Yoga studio," she said. "I cleaned it and worked on your computer. It was a mess." She looked at me like she was expecting me to say something.

"Thanks."

"You're welcome, Achilles," Nicole said. "Oh, and I got you some laundry detergent. You can thank me by doing some laundry because it smells like dirty socks in here." She slung a bag off her shoulder and set it on the floor with a loud thump. "Now I'm going to get ready for class. First one is at nine."

She was so excited about the whole yoga thing, and I didn't want to be a total dick, especially seeing as how I'd forgotten laundry detergent yet again, so I decided not to say anything else about the yoga. Once she saw that no one was coming, she'd give up and go back to looking for a real job. She was probably just doing this whole yoga thing to make herself feel better.

A few more of the regulars came in and got settled. I carried the detergent to the back and started a load of laundry. Nicole was right about one thing. By now the pile of towels smelled totally rank, and it was permeating through the entire gym. I might have to run each load twice just to get rid of the smell. By the time I got back up front, the computer was ready. I checked in everyone who was already there then dug the piece of paper out of my pocket that I'd brought from home. I'd log into the Hall of Artifacts website and check the inventory on the spear and that would be the end of that.

I'd just pulled up my browser when the bell chimed. When I looked up, two girls stood there decked out in tank tops and yoga pants with mats rolled up and slung over their shoulders.

"Hello," I said, trying to make sense of it. "Oh, you're here for the yoga class."

They were probably friends of Nicole's. That's how she planned to get a couple people to come. She must've told them about it.

"Are we in the right spot?" the one girl said, looking up at the row of shields hanging over the mirrors around the walls.

"For yoga? Sure. It's over there." I motioned with my head toward the old florist shop.

"Is it already filled up? Do we need memberships?" the other girl asked. Both of them looked like they were maybe in their twenties, possibly even college students.

"Um . . . ," I said, because I hadn't thought it through that far. I didn't think anyone was going to come.

"First class is free," Nicole said, strolling up. Then she did some bow thing and said, "Namaste."

The girls must've known what she was doing because they bowed back and said the same thing.

"How did you hear about us?" Nicole asked.

"Facebook," one of them said.

"Yeah, what a great idea, yoga at this place," said the other. "I always thought it was just a smelly old gym."

I bit my tongue and smiled. I also hoped they didn't smell the dirty towels.

Nicole hardly had time to point them in the right direction before a few more girls came in, all dressed about the same, carrying mats. They went through the whole routine again, except this time they'd found out about it on Instagram. But it didn't stop at females. At least seven guys came in, knowing the bow thing, too, like they were all part of some secret club.

I sat kind of speechless, but Nicole had no trouble saying, "I told you so," after over twenty people, guys and girls alike, had arrived. If even a fourth of these people actually signed up for memberships, I'd be able to replace the TV and cover the next round of drinks.

"Class starts in five minutes," she said. "You think you can handle it from here?"

"Sure," I said. I doubted we'd get that many more.

But no sooner had she gone to the florist shop—or I guess it was now the yoga room—the bell chimed again. And in came this amazingly perfect female, with long dark hair that fell in curls around her face and deep blue eyes that seemed like they were full of the ocean and long slim legs that any straight guy would want wrapped around him. A tiny mole sat over her right eyebrow, but instead of detracting from her appearance, it only made her face that much more alluring.

"Hello," she said, and her eyes roved over my entire body, from top to bottom, making me want to smooth my hair and stand a little straighter.

"You're here for yoga?" I said.

"I'm in the right place?" she said.

I nodded and motioned to the yoga room.

"Thanks." She started in that direction. But then she stopped and smiled at me once again. "I'm Elle."

I felt like I should have somehow already known this, which

was ridiculous. I'd never seen this woman before in my life. Elle. Where had I heard that name before recently?

"I'm Achilles," I said.

Her smile softened. "It's really nice to meet you, Achilles. I've heard all about you." Then she was gone, before I could ask how she'd heard about me, slowly walking toward the yoga room.

I watched her every step. Watched the way her lower half shifted just slightly from side to side, the way she tucked her hair behind her ear and smoothed down her pants along the lines of her hips. I kept watching until Jack came up to the counter.

"You got some nice eye candy, Achilles," he said.

"I thought you were going to take yoga." After all, he'd half encouraged Nicole on Friday.

"I'm going to watch yoga," he said. "I thought that would be much more rewarding."

"Just don't stare," I said. The last thing I needed were complaints from these yoga people that lecherous creeps were ogling them. We'd never get memberships that way.

Jack went back to his workout, and that's when it hit me. Elle. She was the girl Ethan had gone out with on Friday night. He'd stayed the night at her house. He must've told her about the yoga class. And I'll give him this. His description of her wasn't even a slight exaggeration.

I turned back to the computer, because it seemed like everyone who was coming, which by now was at least twenty-five people, was already here. I pulled the piece of paper from my pocket and typed in the website address for the Hall of Artifacts. It didn't have a name like most normal websites, just a string of numbers with dots between them. It also wasn't accessible by the normal public because the Hall of Artifacts was no normal place.

After my near death, the spear had been kept with me, on

my island, the White Island. Kept with me during my immortal sleep. And when I'd been woken by Ares and I'd found out how much time had passed since the Trojan War, how the gods were regrouping, living among mortals, I was *asked* by the council of the gods to secure it away.

Truly, I think they were scared of it. Scared of any of the weapons that could kill them. I hadn't wanted to part with it, but a request by the council of gods is hard to deny. So I carried the spear to the Hall of Artifacts and filed it away, where it still had to be.

The website that finally pulled up was a black screen with two green boxes. They didn't even say anything like username or password. It was just assumed that if you had access to the Hall, you knew what to do.

I typed letter for letter the username and password on the scrap of paper I'd brought from home. Once I hit enter, a green circle appeared and spun around and around for what felt like a million minutes but was probably closer to thirty seconds. Then the circle disappeared and the green boxes showed up again. I must've gotten a letter wrong.

I tried again and the same thing happened. But then I realized that what I thought was a zero was really the letter O. Once I got that straightened out, the circle spun and a single green box appeared. Success. I was in.

I typed the series of ten numbers from the piece of paper. This was the number for my inventory item. For the spear. The gods had assigned it to me when I'd secured it ten years ago. I'd never actually logged into the site before now.

I hit enter and the circle appeared again, spinning away. Finally, after at least a minute, the circle vanished, leaving nothing but a blank screen. Since I had never logged in to check on the thing, I wasn't sure what was supposed to happen next. Still, I was willing to bet that a blank screen wasn't it. But the thing was that without a green box to try again, I was stuck. I had to close the browser and try the entire thing again. But the same thing happened. Then it was time to spot Jack, and Sophie and Scott were arguing about something, so I shoved the paper back in my pocket and went over to the free weights.

"How's yoga?" I said.

"They hung a sheet over the door," Jack said. "You know I could send a crew of guys over to help with some of the remodeling this weekend. It would be nice to have windows where we could see in there. You know, just to make sure no one needs help or anything."

"What kind of help would they need?" I said, listening as best I could. But from here, all I could hear was a bunch of deep breathing and some sort of chanting music.

Jack put up his hands. "I'd be happy to help with anything. You name it, I'm your guy."

"I'm sure Nicole will appreciate knowing that."

I spotted Jack through his reps, then had to settle the argument between Sophie and Scott about the proper weight to maintain but not increase muscle mass, and before I knew it, the sheet was lifting from the door and a bunch of sweaty people were coming out with rolled up yoga mats slung over their shoulders. They were all smiling, which I took as a good sign. They waved and thanked me and said they'd be back and asked about yoga memberships. So I wrote down some names and promised I'd add them to the system.

Elle stopped at the counter and leaned over while I was writing, exposing so much of her luscious cleavage that it was hard to look at anything else. I tried to pull my eyes away since she was maybe sort of dating my roommate.

"I love this place," she said, looking around. "How is it I've never known about it before?"

I managed to force my eyes away from her chest and up to her eyes. But that was no better. The blue drew me in almost like it was hypnotizing me. "We don't really advertise."

"I'm so glad you started," she said. "I'm so glad Ethan told me about it. I'll definitely be back." Then she reached out and traced her fingers over the back of my hand, sending little chills through me. Gods, if Ethan walked in right now, he would flip his shit. But man, it felt like there was some sort of instant connection between us.

"Good. That's good."

"What's good?" Nicole asked.

I pulled my hand back. "Elle liked the class."

Nicole beamed. "I'm so glad. I thought it went really well, too."

Maybe I was wrong about this yoga thing. Who would have ever thought there would be such a demand for it?

"You can't be staring and making people feel uncomfortable," Nicole said as I watched Elle leave.

"Uncomfortable? Are you kidding? I was being polite," I said.

"If you say so."

"I do. And if you don't mind, I need to go put the towels in the dryer."

Nicole was crazy. I ran the gym. It was my responsibility to take note of whoever came in and out of this place. Just because Elle was pretty didn't mean I was staring at her. Also Ethan wasn't here right now anyway.

I shoved the towels from the washer into the dryer and started another load, managing to get all the rest of the towels jammed in the washer. Anything would be better than the smelly pile on the floor. By the time I got back up front, Nicole was in her yoga room. Wait, not her yoga room. My yoga room. No, not even that. I still wasn't sure this whole yoga thing was going to stick or even if I wanted it to.

I sat back at the computer and pulled up the browser, going through the login routine for the Hall of Artifacts once again.

"Whatcha looking at?" Nicole said, coming up behind me.

I nearly jumped off the stool. And to make matters worse, her stupid cat, Nano, jumped on the counter and started swatting at the computer mouse.

"Nothing," I said, minimizing the window.

But damn if Nicole wasn't nosy. She grabbed the mouse and clicked the window back open in under two seconds flat.

"What website is this?" she said, shoving onto the stool next to me.

I tried to grab the mouse back, but she pulled it away.

"It's nothing," I said.

"It's just an IP address," she said. "What's it for?"

"Nothing. I told you."

She narrowed her eyes at me. "Is this some porn site? Because that's probably the reason you had a virus on your computer. Those sites always put crap on computers. Once you visit one, your computer will never be the same."

"It's not porn." I tried to think through all the websites I'd ever visited. Had I gone to some porn site online and messed up my computer that way? Or maybe Ethan had.

"Then what is it?"

This girl was impossible. But also, kind of smart. And knew a hell of a lot about computers. And possibly able to help.

"It's this website I'm trying to get information from," I said. "But it's not working."

"What do you mean it's not working?"

So I walked her through my login until we got to the screen where I was supposed to type the number.

"The screen went black," she said.

"Right. That's the problem. I can't get the information I need."

"You must've done something wrong," Nicole said. She went through the same routine I had, and I couldn't help the smugness that slipped onto my face when the same thing happened to her.

"Have you called anyone about it?" she asked.

"Who would I call?"

She shrugged. "I don't know. Whoever runs this website. The webmaster."

Right. Like that was going to happen. I could just call up the gods and ask them why their website was a piece of shit. They'd probably send the Furies after me anew.

"I don't know who runs it," I said.

"What information are you trying to get?"

"Nothing," I said.

"If it's nothing, then why are you trying to get it?"

Okay, this was a bad idea. I grabbed for the mouse again, but she held it out of reach.

"It doesn't matter. It was just something I was looking for."

"Have you checked the source code?" Nicole said. "Or checked the IP location and registry?"

Since I didn't know what any of those things were, I was pretty safe in guessing the answer was no. Nicole started clicking away, pulling down menus, and causing all sorts of things to pop up on the screen. But after a few minutes she took her hand off the mouse and scowled.

"You know your computer is a real piece of crap," she said.

"Yeah, you told me that already." Possibly I'd have to buy a new computer with any new membership money that came in.

"I could get you into this website from my computer," she said.

"Really?"

"Sure. You can come by after you get off work. I'll show you."

There were about a million reasons why this was not a good idea, the first and foremost and really the only one that mattered was that Nicole, being a mortal, should never know anything about the Hall of Artifacts. That was a can of worms I didn't want to open.

"It's not that important." I closed the browser, returning to the customer check-in screen. I could work on this Hall of Artifacts thing later.

"Whatever," Nicole said, standing up. "Anyway, I need to get ready for my next class."

Turned out Nicole had scheduled two classes a day. The second was more packed than the first, and after it was done, I was in agreement with Jack that some windows might be nice. And all these yoga people were super Zen, bowing at each other and taking off their shoes and shit like that. Mom had nagged me for the last five years to take up yoga. She said it would help with my anger issues, not that I had anger issues. This may be the perfect time.

Almost like the thought had triggered it, my phone rang.

"Damn the gods," I said, checking the caller ID. Sure enough, there was a picture of Mom holding her two fingers up in a peace symbol.

I could not answer it. Except she'd know. She always knew. It was a crazy sixth sense she had. Some sort of immortal psyche. I swiped my finger across the screen.

"Hey, Mom."

"You were going to ignore my call, weren't you?"

"Never," I said. "I would always answer your phone calls."

"I know when you're lying, Achilles," she said.

"I'm not lying. I'm talking to you right now, aren't I?"

"That's because you knew I would know," she said.

"I look forward to your phone calls."

"Then why haven't you been by to see me?" Mom asked. "You haven't come by the house all month. And your brother says that he hasn't seen you in three years."

Brother my ass.

"I've been busy," I said, but I left it at that. There was no need to mention the Furies. If Mom didn't already know, I wasn't going to tell her. She'd go crazy worrying about me. And as things were, she was already overprotective.

"There's something you're not telling me," Mom said.

"There are lots of things I'm not telling you. I'm a grown man."

"But I'm your mother. You should tell me everything."

My mind went instantly to the crazy Friday night with Athena. There was no way I'd share that with my Mom.

"What's her name?" Mom said, burrowing into my mind.

"Who's name?"

"If you're not coming to see your own mother, there must be a girl. You should bring her by. Introduce her. I could make you two lunch."

"There's no girl," I said.

This was exactly the reason why I didn't call and visit more often. She had this overwhelming need to know every single detail of my life.

"Next Tuesday," Mom said.

"Next Tuesday what?"

"You and your girlfriend can come for lunch."

"Mom, I own a gym. I can't just go out for lunch any time I

want. I have responsibilities."

"So you admit there is a girl."

This was enough. There was no more reason to trudge down the current path of conversation.

"So what's new with you?" I said. If I could get her on to the next topic, I'd be golden.

"Your counselor called," Mom said.

Inwardly, I groaned. I should have stayed talking about my imaginary girlfriend instead.

"He said you skipped your last two appointments. If you skip appointments, you'll never get better."

"I've been doing fine," I said.

"You're stressed," Mom said. "I can tell."

I grabbed one of the crocheted balls from the counter and squeezed it. "I'm not."

"Have you been meditating? Like I showed you?"

"Maybe," I said. I'd had every intention of meditating, but it always seemed like I had too many other things going on.

"And how about the coloring books? Are they helping?"

"They stress me out. There are all those little spaces to color. And I suck at art. You know that."

"It's not about art," Mom said. "The coloring is supposed to help you relax."

"I'm plenty relaxed," I said. Or at least I would be once this whole Spear of Achilles thing was sorted out.

Nicole walked up but stopped a few steps away when she saw I was on the phone.

I covered the receiver. "It's my mom," I said, though I wasn't sure why I felt like I had to tell her.

"Okay," Nicole whispered, but it was one of those whispers that was louder than if the person had talked in a normal voice.

"Is that her?" Mom said.

"Who?"

"Your girlfriend?"

"I told you I don't have a girlfriend," I said.

Nicole's eyebrows raised. I rolled my eyes and shook my head.

"How about the crocheting?" Mom said. "Did you make the blanket like I showed you?"

I squeezed the ball again, curling my fingers completely around it. "Crocheting is fine."

Truth was that the crocheting was great. Sure, I kind of felt like a girly-man when I started, but it was a great way to get my mind off everything else.

"I'll make you a sweater," Mom said.

"I don't need a sweater."

"You can wear it to your counseling appointment," Mom said.

"I don't have another appointment scheduled."

"You do now," Mom said. "I scheduled it for you. Two weeks from yesterday."

"Mom . . ."

"And if you even think about skipping it, I'll drag you there myself."

There were few things I could imagine which would be worse, so I wrote down the date and time of the appointment and promised Mom I would go. Then she changed her request to dinner for next Tuesday with my alleged girlfriend and we said goodbye.

"You crochet?" Nicole said, sticking her phone in her sports bra.

"Maybe," I said.

She started laughing. So I threw the crocheted ball at her, hitting her perfectly in the forehead. But that made her laugh even more, so I threw two more at her and headed to the back to get the towels out of the dryer. But the stupid cat jumped into the basket and started rolling around.

"Come get your cat," I hollered.

"Aw," Nicole said, standing at the door of the back room. "I think he's starting to like you. Aren't you, Nano?"

"Too bad the feeling's not mutual," I said, tipping the basket over in an attempt to get the cat out.

"You just wait," Nicole said. "Within a week you two will be inseparable."

Two days ago I hadn't thought Nicole would still be here in a week. But now, after seeing the turnout for the yoga class, I wasn't so sure.

"You actually got people to come to your class today," I said.

"Of course I did. What did you think? No one would come?"

"Pretty much," I said.

"Well, I'm glad I could prove you wrong." She turned her palms up, and the cat jumped right into her arms. "Guess I'll see you tomorrow."

"Yep. See you tomorrow," I said.

Nicole left and I folded the towels and put them back on the shelves. My clients were going to be thrilled to have fresh towels once again. I really did have to get better about staying on top of things like laundry. When I got back up to the counter, Keith had texted, telling me he couldn't make it in today. That there was a fermenting seminar that he just had to go to so he could learn to make his own sauerkraut. Seeing as how he should have been here and hour ago, it would have been nice to know. I'd planned to go back to Treaty Oak Park to see if the dryads would talk to me, but now it would have to wait until later tonight.

I managed to do three more loads of laundry and get half

the names of the yoga people entered into the computer before eight o'clock when I finally turned out the lights and locked up. Then I headed out back to dump the trash. That's when the Furies found me.

CHAPTER 9

They came up from the sewers. The manhole cover blew up from the ground like the cap on a volcano, shattering a streetlight above before falling to the asphalt. Immediately, the alley was cast into darkness, lit only by the light coming through the open gym door.

"Your week is up, Achilles," Tish said, landing solidly on the ground. She sauntered toward me with her red cowboy hat still perched on her head. With each step she took, her black and red boots clicked on the pavement, echoing around the empty alley.

"What do you mean, my week is up? I still have two days." Two days that I needed.

Tish looked to Meg who cocked her head like they were somehow considering this. Then she looked back to me and drawled out in her Texas twang, "Well, isn't that something? It seems you're right. We lost track of time. Guess your time is cut short."

"But—" I started, as if negotiating with the Furies was an option.

"How do you plead?" Alex said. Her black hat leaned slightly forward, covering part of her face, but in an almost imperceptible movement, it tipped backward on its own until it was straight.

"Not guilty," I said. "I didn't kill the dryad."

"Still the same lie." Meg touched the brim of her green hat. "The same lie that will sentence you to your eternity of torment. How do you wish for your torment to begin, Achilles? Do you want us to pluck out your eyeballs and devour them? Or shall we slice open your fingers and suck every drop of blood from your body like a straw? Or perhaps you would like us to strip every bit of skin from your flesh and use it to make new boots? If you tell us the truth, we may give you a choice."

Holy gods, none of those choices sounded good. Ares had really tried to hit on her? He was either completely insane, or he had the worst judgment in the entire universe.

"If you want justice to be served, you have to give me more time," I said, holding my ground even as Tish walked closer. I had to stand up to the Furies. I was not some pathetic mortal who'd committed a petty street crime. Also I'd done nothing wrong.

"Your time is over." Alex shifted her black cowboy hat and stepped to the far left side of Tish at the same time Meg stepped far to the right.

My hackles went up. A typical battle posture. They were ready to strike.

I hardly had time to jump out of the way as they dove for me. They flew upward and circled back, coming in for another attack. I jumped and rolled and looked around for something to fight them off with. If I really did have the Spear of Achilles, I would do away with these she-demons and be home in time for dinner.

"I didn't kill a dryad," I yelled as I evaded them.

"Liar and murderer," Alex screamed back. They dove for me again and again, all the while making sure I stayed in the alley behind the gym, away from mortal eyes. They clawed at me as they attacked, covering my already scabbed over skin with fresh scratches. Each time they dove, they got lower and lower. They were trying to reach my ankle—which I was not going to let happen. If they did manage to reach my ankle, I'd be hosed. They'd incapacitate me, drag me off to Tartarus, and I'd never have a chance to prove my innocence.

The attacks came, one after another. Their shrieks and accusations filled the air.

"Tell us the truth," Tish said.

"Admit your crime," Meg whispered.

"Confess and we will be more lenient," Alex hissed.

They were the ones who were lying. They wouldn't be lenient no matter what came out of my mouth.

"I did not do it!"

At my words, all three landed on the ground.

"You choose to continue with your false words," Tish said, and she ripped the red cowboy hat from her head and threw it aside. Underneath the hat, instead of hair, was a mass of writhing red snakes, twisting and coiling and hissing.

Alex and Meg did the same, each tossing their hats aside, each exposing a head full of snakes. The snakes on Meg's head were bright white, matching the tattoos on her arms, and the snakes on Alex's head were black. So black they blended into the darkness of the alley.

All at once, they reached up and pulled a snake from the top of their heads and threw them at me. The red snake was easy to see but was also the fastest. I jumped and stomped on it, stifling its movements before it could reach my skin. The white snake came up immediately after. I tried to stomp it, but it leapt into the air, fangs exposed as it snapped at me.

I caught it and swung it around, slamming it into the brick wall behind me, silencing it. But by then, the black snake was on me, sinking its teeth into the skin of my leg, near my ankle, but just missing it. Immediately the venom began to move into my body, and pain exploded from the wound. With the fresh wave of pain, anger filled me.

How dare they attack me? Me, who had not committed a single crime. Me, who was unjustly accused. The rules of the gods sucked, and this was a perfect example of why.

Blood leaked from my wounds, but I couldn't feel them anymore. All I could feel was my rage. My vision narrowed and focused in on one object at a time in the alley. Trash bags. Dumpster. Piles of junk next to the Dumpster. I grabbed at the pile, pulling out a metal shelf bracket from the old florist shop. Then I let the anger explode. I went after Meg first since she was the closest, swatting at her, determined to destroy her. She pushed back at me, delivering blow after blow. I countered each of her attacks, using all my anger to fight back.

Each hit drove home. I swung again and again, relentless, channeling my anger with every single motion. I was not going to let this happen. I would not be punished for something I hadn't done. Each hit was harder than the one before it until, with one solid hit by the shelf bracket, Meg finally exploded into a cloud of dust.

Silence filled the alley as the dust slowly settled to the ground.

Tish and Alex stared at the spot where their sister had been, then cast their eyes on me.

"This crime has been added to your list, Achilles," Tish said. "This only makes your sentence worse."

"Meg will reform," Alex said.

"She will get her revenge," Tish said.

"And we will hold you captive until she does," Alex said. "We will let her have at you first."

I held the shelf bracket out in front of me, channeling my anger through it.

"You cheated me out of time," I said. "Give me the time I deserve."

"No," Tish said.

"You have to. If you want this to be fair, if you want to be the true judges you claim to be, then you have to give me the time. Otherwise everything you're doing is false."

Tish looked to Alex, and silent communication passed between them. I held my breath, not daring to move as they considered my request. My fingers gripped the metal bracket as the seconds passed. I was ready to strike.

Then Tish said, "One week."

One week. Shit, I was hoping for two days, but I wasn't about to tell them that.

"I want my two extra days also," I said, holding my face even.

Tish smiled at me, almost with camaraderie. "You'll have your two extra days, Achilles. May they cause you torment."

That was nice. But it bought me a solid nine days.

Tish and Alex each extended a hand, and their cowboy hats flew into their fingers. Then in a flash of darkness, they vanished, into the night.

Silence filled the alley. Moment after moment passed as I tried to catch my breath. But the anger was still there, fresh and pumping through me. I threw the shelf bracket against the back wall of the gym, cracking some of the bricks. Then I picked it up and hit the bricks again, releasing every bit of my tension. This was way better than any coloring book. I hit it over and over until the bracket was nothing but a twisted, flattened shred of metal and my arms ached like I was Atlas, holding up the world. I threw the mangled bracket to the side. Only then did I finally sink to the ground.

CHAPTER 10

The pain from the snake bite returned, hot and throbbing with each beat of my heart. I dared to look down. My pant leg was torn and covered in blood. I lifted it out of the way, checking the damage. The two puncture wounds went deep, well into my skin, and were already turning black from the venom. If I didn't take care of this, I would be too weak to face them when they came back. And they would come back. I was certain of it. I had to heal.

After I'd been born, Mom had dipped me in the River Styx, and its waters along with her blessing had made my skin like armor. Made me able to withstand way more than any mortal. There were two problems with this. One, she'd held me by the right ankle, so that part of me had never been covered with the water. It was my true weakness. And two, when I was injured, like I was now, the protection wore off, and I had to heal to renew it.

To heal it, I had to visit the Underworld: The River Styx where my original protection had come from.

But getting to the Underworld was going to be impossible with venom clouding my mind and blood dripping from every appendage. I couldn't exactly flag down a rideshare or hop on the city bus.

Think. I had to think. The first thing I had to do was get some clothes that weren't torn and covered in blood. I yanked on the back door of the gym which had slammed shut during the fight, but it was locked. I fumbled in the pocket of my sweats and grabbed my keys, finding the one for the back door. It took me a few tries, but I managed to get it into the lock and turn it.

I stumbled inside and closed the door behind me. There was Nicole, folding the towels.

She dropped the one she was folding. "Oh shit, Achilles, what happened to you?"

As if my day wasn't already bad enough. I focused on each and every movement I made. I couldn't let her know anything was off.

"I fell and scratched myself," I said, pulling the shirt off over my head.

Nicole grabbed a towel and pressed it against my chest then my arms. "Scratched yourself!" she said, wiping at the blood. "You look like you fell into a lawnmower. You must have fifty cuts."

Each swipe felt like it was going to rip the cuts wide open even more and I would bleed out, so I took the towel from her and pressed it flat against one cut after the next, hoping to staunch the blood.

"It's nothing." But the blood wasn't slowing down. The Furies had cut deeper than I'd thought.

I pulled off my sweats next, not caring that I was down to my sliders.

"Oh, god, your leg," Nicole said. "Is that a . . . ?"

"Snake bite," I managed since there were two dripping puncture wounds.

"Snake bite! Do you know what kind? Was it poisonous?"

I shook my head but that made my vision swim even more from the venom. "Sort of."

"Sort of? You need to go to the hospital. I'll call 911."

That was the last thing I needed. I grabbed another towel and ran it under the sink. "No hospital." Hospitals were not places guys like me went.

"I'll take you. Come on." She pulled at my arm, trying to get me to move forward.

I shook my head. "It's okay. I have a friend who can help."

"A friend? What? Is he a doctor?"

"Kind of." I pressed the wet towel over some of the scratches, which I thought would bring relief, but hot pain seared through each one, like the snake venom had already gotten to them. I had to get this healed pronto or my future wasn't going to look so bright.

"Kind of isn't going to cut it, Achilles," Nicole said. "You could die if you don't get this fixed."

At least we were in agreement about that. But the problem was that where I needed to go was at least three miles away, and no way was I going to be able to walk. Still, I didn't have much choice. I grabbed a clean pair of sweats from a shelf and managed to get them on, then tugged a fresh t-shirt over my head. I took a step toward the door, but my head swam and I stumbled, falling against the washing machine. This was not good and only getting worse.

Nicole reached out to stabilize me. "I'll take you."

Seeing as how I was about to fall over on the spot, I couldn't think of a single reason to say no.

We went out the front door, and I know I was losing it because I told her at least five times to lock to the door. My brain was really fuzzy and it was hard to keep one moment distinct from the next. Nicole sat me on a bench and said she was going to get her car, and I was pretty sure she'd left me to die, but then some tiny car pulled up and she helped me into the passenger seat.

I was feeling really bad about bleeding on her seat, and I guess I said this aloud because she said, "That's okay. Where are we going?"

"Zilker Park," I said, and closed my eyes. When those Furies came back and I got ahold of them, I was going to find the spear and kill them for good.

"What spear?" Nicole said.

My eyes snapped open. I must've spoken aloud.

I mumbled something that not even I could understand, and she didn't press it. And the entire time she drove, she bit her lip and gripped the steering wheel so hard, I thought her knuckles might pop.

It felt like it took ten years, though it was probably more like ten minutes, but we finally pulled up to the entrance to Zilker Park.

"This is it," I said, motioning at the entrance to the gardens in front of me.

"The Botanical Gardens?" Nicole said.

"My friend lives here," I managed to say, and I fumbled with the door handle until it finally opened. I could do this. I was so close.

"At the Botanical Gardens?"

I nodded.

"Achilles, this is ridiculous. I'm taking you to the hospital," Nicole said.

But I shook my head and got one foot out of the car, thinking that way she couldn't drive off.

She got out on her side and hurried around to the passenger side like she was going to shove me back in, but by then, both my feet were on the ground and I gripped the doorframe.

"Get back in," she said.

"It's okay, I swear." I hoisted myself out, feeling bad that I'd now gotten blood on the silver paint, too.

"I can't let you leave," Nicole said. "If you die . . ."

"I'm not going to die." Though every second that went by that I didn't get healed, the chances that I was wrong got higher. "I'll see you tomorrow."

"Tomorrow? Are you kidding?"

"Tomorrow." Everything would be better tomorrow. I started forward, toward the gated entrance. I was so close. I didn't check to see if Nicole was watching as I stumbled around the gate and slipped into the trees. I almost felt Nicole's eyes on me, but I couldn't waste the time or energy looking. I had to heal.

Zilker Park's Botanical Gardens were only a cover for the real purpose. This was, in fact, a garden of Persephone herself, goddess of the Underworld, wife of Hades. I trailed down the pathways, managing to put one foot in front of the next. I was so close. If I collapsed and died now, there would be nobody around to save me. When I'd nearly reached the pagoda, I took a side path, traveling down a bit, falling only once, until I came to the place I needed to be. In front of me stretched a pond, still as ice and black as a raven.

I stepped one foot into the pond, then the other, disturbing the quiet. Ripples extended from my legs. I moved forward, sinking lower and lower, until I came to a stop in the center of the pond. And because the Underworld recognized me, it accepted me, and the earth opened up.

The quiet pond became a writhing mass of silver, like liquid mercury, and it swallowed me whole, covering me and sealing me away from the world above. My heart sped up from the sudden immersion, a fight sensation I'd never been able to shake. I tried to hold my breath—I always did—but the pressure from the silver liquid forced my mouth open. It was the River Styx. I had to breathe in. It was the only way I would heal.

As soon as the quicksilver covered my mouth and nose, I sucked in, drawing as much of the liquid into my lungs as I could. The water cushioned me and worked its way into my skin, and within seconds the pain coursing through my body started to fade. I felt the flesh stitch itself back together. I flexed my fingers, and the river worked its way through my blood and washed the snake venom away. I sank into it and let it heal me and rebuild the protective shield around me.

All except for my ankle. Since it hadn't been included in the original ritual, it could never be protected.

I sank to the bottom of the River Styx, drifting slowly enough to relax fully, and once my feet touched hard ground, the silver liquid ebbed away. It seeped into the ground like a waterfall cascading around me, and my surroundings transformed. Instead of the pond in the middle of Zilker Park, dirt and rocks covered the ground. Instead of the sky, a ceiling of stone loomed over my head. Instead of the sun, lanterns hung from the hewn walls, spaced evenly, casting eerie shadows around the underground cavern like campfires.

I ran my hands over the skin of my calf, looking for any evidence of the snake bite, but the puncture wounds were gone. It was perfect, like always. So was every other scratch on my entire body, both those from the attack by the Furies and those from my crazy night with Athena.

Even though I knew it wasn't protected, I ran a hand over the back of my right ankle. Though it had been so long ago, the pain from the arrow that pierced the area still throbbed, almost like the touch of a ghost arrow. A dull ache that would never go away. A permanent reminder of my failure.

In front of me stretched an endless river of black water. Not the River Styx. That was the silver liquid I'd just come through. The River Styx was the barrier between the outer world and the Underworld. It was one of five rivers in the Underworld. Another, the black river in front of me, was the River Acheron, the river every dead person had to cross to get to the Underworld. And one person brought all those people across.

On cue, a black wooden boat pulled up to the shore. I cracked my neck and let out the last bit of tension from the attack and went to face the inevitable.

"Charon, you came to see me. What a surprise." Not sure it was a nice surprise, given his job. I walked over to shake the old ferryman's hand.

"Just checking to see if you were dead," he said. Charon was a giant of a man, with brown wrinkled skin like old leather and small tufts of white hair over either of his ears. Most of the world thought Charon was some guy that wore a black cloak that covered him completely, like the Grim Reaper or some shit like that. I'd only seen him dressed that way once, one time when he actually had to visit the world above. I think he did it more as a Halloween prank rather than for any required reason.

"Not yet, though you already had your chance once," I said.

Charon laughed. "Hardly. That mother of yours was hovering

around you like flies hover around . . ."

I put up my hand and laughed.

"Yeah, you get the idea. I never had a chance," Charon said.

"Hopefully you'll be waiting a long time for another chance."

Charon's old face creased into a frown. "Not if you don't watch out for those Furies."

I ran a hand over my calf again, like I had to make sure the snake bite was really gone. That had been close. Too close.

"Guess you heard about that," I said.

Charon hesitated before speaking. "It's a popular topic. Everyone knows. In fact Hades and Persephone want to talk to you."

"Talk about what?" Entering the Underworld should never be taken lightly, not even for a demigod. Just because I knew about the world of gods didn't make me unaffected by their rules. And the rule was that those who entered the Underworld could never leave. It was like a real Hotel California.

Almost like he could read my thoughts, Charon said, "Don't worry. You're not dead."

"So you promise you'll bring me back?" The last thing I wanted was to get stuck in the Underworld. Not only did I enjoy my life above ground, the Underworld was also where the Furies actually resided. I did not want to run into them by accident, especially not after what had just happened with Meg. They were going to be full-on pissed.

"I'll bring you back if you pay me." Charon held out a big, meaty hand.

Pay him. Shit. I dug my hands into the pockets of my sweatpants, but I'd changed so fast that I hadn't even thought about money or ID or anything. All that was back at the gym.

"Um . . ."

"You don't have any money?" Charon said.

I shook my head.

"Not even a single penny?"

"Nope."

Charon put his hand to his chin and stroked it, like he was deep in thought. "You realize this is a problem, right Achilles?"

"Can I owe you?"

Charon scowled. "You don't want to owe me. That won't ever end well."

I put my hands up and took a step back. "Okay, you know, I don't really need to cross anyway. I should get back and clean up."

"Nope," Charon said. "You have to cross. Hades and Persephone told me to bring you to them."

"Then they should pay," I said.

"And you're going to ask them for money?"

"Sure." Hades was a reasonable guy a lot of the time . . . except when he wasn't. I just had to hope that he was in one of his reasonable moods. The fact that Persephone was around increased the odds. When she went off to the outer world, his mood turned to shit.

"Okay, it's your eternity you're messing around with," Charon said, and he motioned for me to climb into the black boat. Once I was aboard, he stepped on behind me, causing the boat to rock in the bubbling water.

Charon ferried me across the water, which even though I'd crossed three other times, never got any easier. It was black and choppy and filled with monsters that swam just below the surface, every once in a while nipping at the air. But the monsters weren't what unsettled me. Worst of all were the bubbles that constantly rose to the surface. Each one contained a single thought: the last hope of a dead person. The sorrow. The thing they wanted to leave behind on their way to death. Depressing shit to say the least.

I listened to the confessions of murderers, rapists, tax evaders. I tried not to hear as mothers cried for their unborn babies and women pleaded for their lives. And even though I was a freaking fierce and awesome warrior, I nearly broke down as children begged for their mothers to protect them, to hold them one last time.

"I hate crossing this river," I said to Charon once the boat bumped into the dock at the opposite shore. "How do you stand this shit?"

Charon gave a small smile that I swear had the hints of sadness. "It never gets easier, not even for me." Then with a push of the long pole he'd used to move us across the river, the boat floated back out, ready to pick up the next deceased soul.

Unlike the barren shore I'd started on, this side of the river steamed like a rain forest. Water droplets hung in the air, dripping off weeping willows and falling onto the thick grassy ground. I glanced around, looking for Hades, trying to shake the sorrow of the river from my shoulders. It eased a bit when I saw him step out of a tunnel and head my way. Next to him stood a giant three-headed dog: Cerberus.

Cerberus took one look and me and charged, bounding across the grassy swamp.

I braced myself, but when Cerberus hit me, it was no easier than the last time. I flew backward, landing hard on my back. Then he placed both his giant paws on my chest and bared all three sets of his teeth right in my face. At least for a couple of seconds he did. But then, the giant monster dog couldn't take it any longer. Drool dripped from his mouths as he opened them wider, and he started licking me with all three of his disgustingly long and slimy tongues.

"Good dog," I managed to say, and tried to push him off me.

But Cerberus wasn't having any part of it. He licked even harder.

"Down, boy!" Hades called, at least five times.

Finally Cerberus gave me one final full-facial lick and leapt off, running back to Hades' side.

I jumped to my feet and wiped my face with the bottom of my t-shirt.

"Achilles, man, it is good to see you!" Hades said, slapping me on the shoulder, way harder than necessary. But then again, Hades was a god, had god powers, and acted like he was twenty even though he was thousands of years old. He also looked about twenty, with dark hair, and dimples on either side of his face. He kept a hand on one of Cerberus' heads, as if to hold him in place.

"Hades!" I said, slapping him back, extra hard also, I guess because of some stupid macho thing. He hardly flinched.

"Could you just go ahead and die?" he said. "Man, they're waiting for you over on the island of heroes. Hercules bitches about it every time I see him. Claims he is totally going to kick your ass."

"I would love to see him try," I said. "What is that guy? Like seventy? Does he roll around with a walker and drink Metamucil?"

Hades laughed. "I'll be sure to tell him that you asked."

I followed Hades and Cerberus back to the actual place where they lived. It was this posh pad decked out in red and black and designed by Persephone, his wife, who lived there with him for half the year. The other half she spent with her super-protective mother above ground. Hades kind of won the lottery when it came to wives because Persephone was this sexy as hell goddess (not that I'd ever say so when Hades was listening) who not only looked great on the outside, she did good things. She made plants and flowers and food grow and shit like that. Like the botanical gardens where I'd entered the Underworld from. She had that kind of crap all over the world, not just in Austin.

Just before we went inside, Hades leaned over. "Can you please not go on and on about how great things are out there?" he said. "She's really missing her mom."

Everyone knew Persephone's mom was crazy. Well, everyone except Persephone herself.

"I got attacked by Furies," I said. "I'm not so happy with the world right now."

"Yeah, good point. But just don't mention all the awesome things she's missing out on, okay?"

Which gave me a great opportunity. "I promise. If . . ."

"If what?"

"If you give me a couple coins." I motioned back at the river. "Charon. I didn't really think ahead."

"Oh, yeah, sure." Hades dug a handful of coins out of his pocket and shoved them my way. I didn't count out two, just took the whole bunch. I was not above taking money from the gods.

He slapped me on the back in thanks, way harder again that he needed to, and we went inside.

"Oh, Achilles! It is so good to see you!" Persephone said, hurrying over to hug me. Her bare feet padded across the red and black mosaic floor. Every time I saw her, she had some new crazy hair style. Today she had her long curly blond hair twisted up into some complicated braid that circled around her head so many times that it didn't seem possible.

"Hi, Persephone," I said, giving her a chaste hug under Hades' watchful eye.

"That is so silly, Achilles. Can't you give me a real hug?" She yanked me into the hug so hard that I tried not to blush. I could not think about how nice looking she was. At least not if I didn't want to end up here in the Underworld forever. And I had the feeling that if Hades did kill me because he was jealous about his wife, he'd gift wrap me himself and hand me over to the Furies.

Persephone grabbed my hand and dragged me over to a red sofa, forcing me to sit down. "Do you want something to eat? Something to drink? We could sneak you some Ambrosia if you promise not to tell my mom."

I shook my head. Persephone tried to force Ambrosia on me every time I came here. And sure, I'd tried it once or twice, but eating the food of the gods was not generally allowed for demigods. The last thing I needed was the council of the gods coming after me for one more thing.

"I'm already in enough trouble," I said, but Hades pressed a glass of wine in my hand anyway.

"Did you really do it, Achilles? Did you seriously kill a dryad?" At this Persephone's eyes got super huge and her whole face shifted. Tears filled the corners of her eyes.

I shook my head frantically because the realization that Persephone was like the biggest fan of dryads was not lost on me.

"Gods no!" I said. "I would never do it."

"But Mother Dryad said that you and Syke had an argument," Persephone said.

Was my love life the knowledge of every immortal on the planet?

"An argument," I said. "That doesn't mean I would kill a dryad."

"She said it was a really bad argument," Persephone said.

"Maybe. But that doesn't matter. Don't you guys argue?"

Persephone shook her head, even as the tears still brimmed in her eyes. "Never."

I rolled my eyes. "Oh, come on. You've been married forever. And Hades even told me about some of the things you've fought over. Like he said this one time—"

I stopped mid-sentence because Hades cast me a look like he would incinerate me on the spot, something he was more than capable of doing.

"You tell people about our arguments?" Persephone said, turning her eyes to her husband.

He put up his hands, still giving me the death glare. "Only one time. We went out drinking."

"Who is we?" Persephone said.

If I could have sunk into the red leather sofa, I would have, but otherwise there was no way to extricate myself from this situation.

Hades shrugged. "Just me, Achilles. Maybe Ares."

"Ares!" Persephone said. "You know I can't stand him. I told you not to hang out with him."

"We can talk about it later," Hades said. "Remember right now we're trying to figure out if Achilles needs to spend the rest of eternity in Tartarus."

His eyes continued the thought. My future was looking pretty horrifying right now.

"But Ares . . . ," Persephone said. "You remember what he did."

I didn't know what he did. I also didn't see myself asking.

"It was a business meeting," Hades said.

"I don't care," Persephone said, crossing her arms. "I don't trust him."

Anyway," I said. "Back to what we were talking about. I didn't kill a dryad." I just wanting to get this entire visit over with. A marital dispute between the king and queen of the Underworld was the last thing I needed to get in the middle of.

Persephone bit her lip. "But the spear . . ."

"Someone's trying to frame me."

"Who?" Persephone said.

"I was hoping you guys might know."

"Do you have any enemies?" Hades asked, and the way he still looked at me, like he wanted to rip my throat out, hinted that if things didn't smooth over with his wife, I might be adding his name to the list.

"Enemies." I laughed. "Not that are alive." I'd had plenty of enemies back during the Trojan War, but that was thousands of years ago. All of them were dead now. Hector. Paris. Agamemnon.

"I wouldn't be so sure," Hades said. "If you are telling the truth—"

"I am telling the truth."

He put a hand up. "If you are telling the truth, you're still being blamed."

"Are you telling the truth, Achilles?" Persephone said, wiping at her eyes.

"Yes, I promise. I adore dryads. You know that." Besides Syke, there may have been a couple of other dryads I'm managed to get friendly with. None were ever as serious as Syke.

"May I judge you?" Persephone said, reaching a hand toward me.

Even though I had no idea what went on when Persephone or Hades judged a soul, instantly, I wanted to yank my hand back, like some sort of base reaction ingrained in humans out of survival.

"Um . . ."

Her eyes held mine, waiting.

I finally held my hand out. "Yeah, sure."

Big fucking mistake.

Persephone's eyes darkened, and her hand touched mine, resting lightly on top. And in that moment, a mask of darkness covered her face and transformed her from the bright and vibrant goddess of spring into the terrifying dread queen of the Underworld.

My mind froze, as if I'd been placed in the immortal sleep once again, except this time, I was wide awake, but paralyzed. Then every single thought began to be pulled from my mind. Every desire. Every hope. Every action. My night with Athena. My days at the gym. Drinking at the bar with Ethan. One by one, Persephone pieced through my mind, tearing into my memories.

When I thought that I couldn't take it any longer, when I was sure I would do anything to pull back my hand, Persephone withdrew. The darkness lifted, the light around her returned.

"Okay, I believe you," she said, her bubbly voice returning as if she hadn't just transformed into some brain-sucking demon queen in front of my very eyes. But the memory of what she'd been stayed in my mind, and helped me remember what Hades and Persephone did all day. They judged people. Every single soul that Charon carted across the river. They looked at each dead soul and decided what kind of life they lived, where they belonged in the Underworld. The really nice, good people . . . they went to the Elysian Fields, which was as close to paradise as possible. The bad people—the ones who had committed unforgivable sins—they were the ones who ended up in Tartarus. When people talk about hell, like the real place, that's what they're talking about. The place of eternal torture. I shuddered just thinking about it.

"So you guys can get the Furies off my back?" I said, reaching for my glass which I realized was empty. Not sure when I'd finished that.

I guess Hades had gotten past being mad at me because he refilled my glass with wine.

"Athena already tried," he said, "She pleaded your innocence to the entire council."

"And . . . ?"

"Oh, and she told everyone about how she even sacrificed and had sex with you so she could search your place," Hades said.

"Sacrificed? Are you kidding?" My face heated up so fast, I was sure it was the color of the wine. But come on. Athena had loved every second of it. Or at least she'd acted like she had. She couldn't be that good of an actress. Could she?

Persephone lightly punched Hades' arm. "Don't be mean. She also said it was fun."

"Fun?" I said, which though that was better than sacrificing, it still didn't match the epic feeling I'd woken up with the next morning.

"Fun is good," Persephone said.

"Anyway . . . ," I said, because it was humiliating to know the entire council of gods knew about my night with Athena.

"Anyway, she called for the Furies to be retracted," Hades said.

"But they just attacked me," I said.

"Because they don't answer to the council of the gods," Hades said.

"How can they not answer to the council of the gods?" I said. "I thought you guys were the most important people in the entire world."

"We are," Hades said.

I stared at him, unwilling to open my mouth and point out the flaw in his logic.

"The council does its best to control the Furies, Achilles," Persephone said. "It gives them orders. It helps mediate. But the Furies are older than the Olympians. The only one they truly answer to is Nemesis."

"Nemesis," I said. "Like the goddess of retribution and

vengeance?" Nemesis was the daughter of Nyx, the night, granddaughter of Chaos, the void where original creation began. If rumors could be believed, Nemesis was in charge of the justice of the entire world, both the world of humans and of immortals. She was also void of emotion, ruling solely by facts. And with facts like a dead dryad and the spear of Achilles being the alleged murder weapon, there wasn't much hope.

"That's the one," Hades said.

"But . . ."

"Right," Hades said. "Not exactly the goddess you want deciding your future."

I drained my glass of wine while I went over what they'd said. I wasn't guilty. Hades and Persephone knew I wasn't guilty. Athena knew I wasn't guilty. Yet even with that, the Furies were still after me. They would drag me to Tartarus because that was what they wanted to do.

"You would think they would want to find the real person responsible," I said. "If the entire council thinks I'm innocent."

"Not the entire council," Persephone said.

"Who doesn't?"

She shook her head. "You know we can't tell you. It goes against the rules of the gods."

"Seriously? But my life is on the line here."

"Rules are rules," Hades said.

"Can you at least put in a good word for me with the council?" I said. With enough of the Olympians backing me, maybe that would be enough power to call off the Furies.

"Of course," Persephone said. "If . . ."

"If what?"

"If you tell me how things are. What's going on with the world?"

Hades immediately shot me a look of death, so I proceeded to mention every horrible thing on Earth and what a joy it was to actually be able to visit with them in the Underworld. And by the time I was done, her eyes were once again enormous and tear-filled.

"I worry about the world," Persephone said. "It needs me."

Hades' face darkened.

Shit. I guess I'd laid it on too thick so I back-pedaled and threw in some of the fun things like the yoga class and how it was Flower Scout cookie season and that Ethan had some girlfriend he met at a sandwich shop. The glow returned to Persephone's face and once again, she wiped away the tears. I could see why Persephone was tied so intricately with the seasons and the climate. In addition to being able to cry on demand, she was also moodier than the weather in Texas.

The scowl disappeared from Hades' face which I took as a good sign. I may not be dead yet, but at some point I would finally be—of this I had no doubt—and when that time came, I wanted to make it to paradise. To the Island of the Heroes so I could finally have that battle with Hercules.

"Time for you to go, right?" Hades said, which I guess was his polite way of telling me I'd done all the damage that could be done.

"Back to the world of the Furies," I said.

"Oh, please be careful, Achilles," Persephone said, and she planted a kiss on my forehead. Hades watched the entire thing, so I tried hard to stay as far back from her as was humanly possible.

Once she'd finally said her goodbyes, Hades and Cerberus walked me back to the riverbank. Charon was just pulling up.

"She misses her mom," Hades said.

They only got to see each other half of the year. It was already a messed up situation.

"She misses you when she's above ground," I said.

"Yeah," Hades said. "But not as much as I miss her. It gets lonely down here. That's when you need to come visit. During the summer."

"If I'm still alive when summer comes, you can count on it," I said.

"You know, this thing, with the spear, with the dryad, it feels like something more is going on."

The air turned icy around us. "Something like what?"

"Not sure," Hades said. "Just something. Like a battle brewing among the gods, simmering below the surface."

"And you think this dryad thing is part of it?"

"Maybe," Hades said. "Keep your eyes open. And let me know if you hear of anything, will you?"

"Yeah, I will."

We said our goodbyes, which included a wet sloppy kiss from each of Cerberus' heads, then Hades and his monster dog walked away. I pulled two coins from my pocket and handed them to Charon.

"Look at you, good for your word," he said, flipping them around his long, weathered fingers until they vanished.

"I got them from Hades."

Charon rubbed his fingers together as if he could still feel the coins. "It's not good to owe the gods favors."

"That's the least of my problems right now," I said. This thing with the Furies was far from resolved. It was great that some of the gods were putting in a good word for me with the council, but I couldn't count on that. What I needed to do was find Nemesis and see if she would call the Furies off my back.

"Can you tell me where Nemesis is?" I asked, offering him

another coin.

Charon took the coin and made it disappear like the others. "Don't know where she is."

I let out a long sigh. "Do you have any idea how I can find out?"

"Ask Athena?" Charon said. "Seems like the kind of thing she might know."

Yeah. Might know and might not tell me. Though she had pleaded my case to the council. Still, the fact that she termed our night together as a sacrifice . . .

"But you might want to be able to prove your innocence," Charon said. "Nemesis is . . ."

His words trailed off. Nemesis was vengeance. And retribution. And as likely to torment me herself as to hand me over to the Furies.

"Thanks for the advice," I said. Then I climbed on board and he ferried me across the River Acheron. I slipped back through the silver of the River Styx and found myself in the middle of the pond in Zilker Park. The world seemed a little darker, not because it was nighttime but because it felt like so much more was going on. Things I didn't understand. But somehow I'd found myself right in the middle of it.

CHAPTER 11

I hadn't thought about what would happen the next day. When I walked into the gym, Nicole was already there. Nano hissed at me the second I got through the door and swiped a paw at me, so I threw a crocheted ball toward the back of the gym. He dashed after it, easily distracted. But not Nicole. She gaped at me.

"You're okay!" She hurried over and pulled up the leg on my sweatpants before I had a chance to stop her. She looked from my completely smooth leg to my face then back to my leg. "You're all better," she said.

I tried to look all casual, like me healing was no more miraculous than finding steak for sale at the grocery store. "I told you my friend could help."

She took a step back, still holding my pant leg up. "But you don't even have a single scar."

"I just had some scratches," I said, pulling my pant leg out of her hand.

"But you don't even have a mark," she said, running her hand over my unblemished forearms.

"I heal fast." I walked around the counter so I could start up the computer, ignoring the fact that it felt kind of nice with her rubbing her hands on me. Or I guess not quite ignoring.

"Nobody heals that fast," Nicole said, following me. "I mean except Wolverine, but he's a comic-book character. Unless you're a super-hero. Are you a super-hero? Like in disguise?"

"I'm not a super-hero."

"You're sure?"

"Sure."

"Then how?"

"It's my diet," I said. "I eat lots of protein."

Nicole narrowed her eyes. I knew she didn't believe me. I would have doubted her intelligence if she had. But she'd forget about it soon enough, once her yoga class started. What I had to do was find out who was framing me and clear my name with Nemesis before the nine days were up. Because if I didn't and if Meg reformed by then, she would be ready to tear my kidneys out and eat them.

"Did they have the snake anti-venom?" Nicole asked.

"Luckily yes."

She put her hands on her hips. "Okay, be honest, was it some special plants they grow at the botanical gardens? My friend Jordan is always going on and on about natural healing. He says that there's a plant to cure everything. He says the pharmaceutical companies keep them secret so they'll make more money and that it's all a huge conspiracy."

I snapped my fingers. "Yes, exactly. But it's not the pharmaceutical companies. And you can't tell anyone. It's part of this group of people I know who want to be all holistic and shit. My mom hooked me up with them."

This was actually pretty close to the truth and the perfect alibi.

"I can't even tell Jordan?" Nicole said.

"Definitely not Jordan," I said. Whoever this Jordan was, he certainly didn't need to know. "Anyway thanks. You know, for the ride."

"You got blood all over my car," Nicole said, looking like she wanted to ask more about the special healing herb garden but picking up on the fact that I was trying to change the subject.

"Is it bad?"

"It looks like someone got murdered in there."

"You're exaggerating." I hoped.

"Are you kidding?" She pulled out her phone and loading up some pictures. "Look at the passenger seat. And the carpet."

I cringed. Both were covered in blood.

"I'll pay for you to get it cleaned," I said.

"Perfect," Nicole said. "You can take it at lunch."

I was about to argue with her, because I had to figure out who was framing me, but the blood was totally my fault. Also she had kind of saved my life. So instead, I said, "I'd be happy to." And I smiled. And she smiled. And that was the end of that.

Yoga had even more people the second day than the first. I admit that I got a happy grin when all the people started pouring in, and I wondered why I hadn't started this years ago. Jack gave me a huge thumbs up, and I made a mental note to talk to him again about making sure he wasn't gawking. The last thing I needed was someone feeling uncomfortable because some mid-life crisis testosterone-boosting real-estate agent was leering at them.

"Am I late?" someone said.

I looked up to see Elle, Ethan's kind-of girlfriend, hurrying into the gym.

"They're just about to start," I said, trying not to think about how attractive she was.

"Oh, good," Elle said. "I did not want to miss. I haven't felt this invigorated in ages. I forgot how great it feels to exercise."

"You should stay and lift weights sometime," I said, though it wouldn't have surprised me to find out she already did. With a figure like hers, she had to do something.

Elle giggled and batted her eyelashes in a way that totally made my lower half tingle. "Oh, I don't know anything about lifting weights."

"I'm sure Ethan would be happy to help you."

Elle squished up her mouth into a pout. "Hmmm . . . doesn't he work way on the other side of town?"

"Well, yeah."

"What if I want to lift weights during the day when he's at work?" she asked, and she batted her eyelashes again.

"Oh, uh, I guess I could help you," I said. Which was a horrible idea. Elle was going out with Ethan. Kind of. I had no right to get within ten feet of her.

Her eyes got wide. "You'd help me?"

"Well, yeah. I guess. It is part of my job. We could set up an appointment if you want."

Elle placed her hand on mine, just like she'd done yesterday. And I felt the same connection. Like somehow were we linked together. Except that was totally not good.

"I would love that," she said.

I wanted to pull my hand back because if Ethan was to see this, it would totally look like I was hitting on Elle. Which I wasn't. But I didn't see a way to do it without offending her. So instead, I waited until she pulled her hand away. Then she gave me a small smile and walked off to the yoga room. I watched her the entire time, trying to force my eyes away, but the connection held them in place.

After that, the day slipped into routine. I spotted Jack who insisted he wanted to go up in weight, to bulk up just a little bit more. He stared at the curtained yoga room door with every rep. Sophie and Scott came in, bickering about what kind of cabinets they should have installed for their kitchen remodel. I finally got them settled by sticking Scott on an elliptical machine and setting Sophie up at a punching bag. She went at it with a vengeance, like it was Scott's face and she was letting out every bit of pent-up aggression that ran around in her OCD brain. After that I ran a load of towels. By noon, Keith still hadn't gotten in. I texted him, just to be sure he'd woken up.

"Were you planning on coming in today?" I texted, even though the answer should obviously be yes.

"Dude, can't make it til five today. New farmer's market opened up eastside. Got to get there early to get the good kimchi," he texted back.

If Keith ate any more fermented food, his entire stomach was going to be pickled for the winter.

"You do remember I pay you to come in?" I texted.

"LOL dude. Thought I told you about it. You want some kimchi?" he said.

I didn't bother texting back. The last thing I wanted was kimchi.

I let Nicole watch the place at lunch while I took her car to get it detailed. The guy at the car wash asked what had happened, and I made up some story about buying steaks at the grocery and having them leak all over. Fifty dollars and an hour later, the car looked brand new. Sadly my bank account hurt.

"Did you get your computer thing figured out?" Nicole said when I got back.

I tossed her the keys. "Haven't tried again. And you're welcome for cleaning your car."

"I didn't realize I was supposed to thank you," Nicole said. "Oh, and someone came by to see you when you were gone. She said she'd be right back."

"She?"

"Oh, there she is now," Nicole said.

I felt Athena's presence before I saw her. A small breeze picked up inside the gym, and tingles covered my bare arms. Then the door opened, and she was there.

I smiled and attempted to say something, but she beat me to it. Except she didn't wear a smile.

"We have a problem," Athena said, storming up to the counter. She wore dark jeans and a gray t-shirt, and looked delicious enough to devour.

"A sacrifice?" I said, referring to how she'd described our night together to the gods. "You said it was a sacrifice?"

"Whatever, Achilles. We need to talk." She cast Nicole a glance. "Alone."

Nicole put up her hands. "Don't mind me. I was just going to clean up the yoga studio." She walked away, Athena drilling holes with her gray eyes into Nicole's back the entire time.

Once Nicole was out of earshot, Athena leaned close. Close enough that my thoughts drifted to what we could do right there on the counter. But those thoughts evaporated when she spoke.

"Another dryad was killed, Achilles," she said. "Last night.

With your spear."

A sick feeling moved into my stomach, and I clenched my hand into a fist, like somehow I could fight off the truth. "Another dryad?" I hated even saying the words.

"Yeah," Athena said. "And guess who the prime suspect is?"

The world wavered around me as the truth sunk in. It was like every past misdeed I'd ever done was coming back to haunt me.

"I didn't do it," I said. Sure, I'd killed plenty of people in my life, with the wars and battles I'd fought in, but I would never kill someone who didn't deserve it. Especially someone like a dryad.

"Where were you last night?"

"I was in the Underworld," I said. "Just ask Hades and Persephone."

But Athena shook her head. "After that. I already talked to them."

"After that? I was back at my condo."

"Was anyone there with you?" She motioned with her head toward Nicole. "Maybe her?"

"Nicole? Are you kidding? We aren't . . ."

Athena waved her hand. "I don't need to know the details of your sex life."

"Good," I said. "I don't really want to tell you."

"So she wasn't there?"

"No. But Ethan was. Ares knows him. You remember he's my roommate."

"I know Ethan, but I didn't see anyone at your place the other night," Athena said. "And I'm pretty sure we checked every room."

My face flushed, but in a good way.

There was no humor in her face. "So Ethan will vouch for you. Will say that you were at your home."

"Well, he wasn't there when I got home. He got there a couple hours later."

"A couple hours?" Athena said. "And nobody else saw you in that time?"

I shook my head.

"You realize that doesn't look good for you, Achilles. The murder took place between the botanical gardens and your home."

At the word murder, the world seemed to compress around me. It hadn't seemed real until right then. Hadn't sunk in. "Who was it?" I said in barely a whisper. Gods, let it not be Syke. I could not live with that. Just the thought of it sent my stomach into terrible knots that threatened to burst from my insides.

"I told you. It was a dryad," Athena said.

"Which dryad?"

Athena's face softened. "Oh, right. I forgot. It wasn't her. It was a young dryad named Balanus. An acorn dryad. She was barely past her thirtieth year. From the new generation."

The knots in my stomach twisted even as the relief mixed in. "That's so young."

"Achilles, you have to tell me the truth," Athena said. "Did you do this? Do you have it?"

Anger flashed through me, pushing aside the relief at knowing Syke was okay. "This is ridiculous. I didn't kill a dryad. And I don't have the spear, which you know, seeing as how you sacrificed and had sex with me so you could search my place."

Athena didn't look the least bit ashamed. "Maybe you have it somewhere else."

I threw up my hands. "Where? Here? Search the place. I'll take you on the grand tour."

She motioned with her head toward the yoga room. "Maybe you have it at your girlfriend's place."

"I told you. She's not my girlfriend."

"It doesn't matter," Athena said. "I can only protect you so far. If anyone on the council thinks you're guilty, they will never do anything to call the Furies off. You will go to Tartarus."

"I'm not guilty," I said through gritted teeth.

"Then prove it," Athena said.

Prove it. That's what I had to do.

"How?"

"Figure it out," Athena said. Then she leaned forward, so close her mouth was right by my ear. "Oh, and it wasn't a sacrifice. Not one bit. It was actually enjoyable. Very very enjoyable."

My body responded immediately. "Maybe we can . . ."

"Prove your innocence," she said. Then she licked my ear, causing all sorts of tingles to run through me. Without another word, she left the gym.

It took me a good five minutes to collect my thoughts. It was only when Nicole finally came back up front that I blew out the breath I'd been holding.

"Friend of yours?" she said.

"Kind of," I said, though I didn't think there were words to describe Athena.

"Did you tell her about yoga?" Nicole said.

At this, I actually let out a laugh. "No, I forgot to mention that. But I do have a favor to ask."

"Another favor?" Nicole said. "What? Do you need me to drive you to your woo-woo doctor again?"

I shook my head. "Can we do that computer thing?"

At the word computer, Nicole grinned like she'd just gotten tickets to the Super Bowl. "Computer thing? Sure."

"Keith's supposed to get here at five," I said. "Does that work?" I didn't want to waste any more time. I had to not only clear my name. I also had to keep more dryads from getting killed, because that was not good. That's the kind of shit that brought bad karma forever.

"Works for me," Nicole said.

* * *

AT FIVE-THIRTY, WHEN KEITH FINALLY AR-rived, we walked to Nicole's tiny little car. She set Nano on the top of the car and ran a finger along the clean silver paint, like she was inspecting how good of a job I'd done.

"I took it to one of those professional places," I said. "I'll have you know that it was fifty dollars."

She nodded and unlocked it. Nano immediately launched himself into the back window area.

"Try not to get anything on it this time," she said.

I hoped the Furies would never appear again. I also hoped that my refreshed healing would protect me a little better if my nine days managed to go by without me proving my innocence.

No, that wasn't an option. I had to prove that I hadn't done this. And I had to find out who had.

Turned out that Nicole only lived a couple miles from the gym, east of the highway. She pulled up in front of a one story house that had probably been built back in the fifties but was in a part of town that was completely being revamped. People were buying these little houses, remodeling them beyond the point of recognition, then selling them for millions. Not a bad way to make money.

"How long have you lived here?" I asked as I got out of the car. A fence ran around the perimeter of the yard, which didn't have any grass. Only rocks with cactus and benches all over the place. Nano ran out of the car and through the rocks up to the front door, evading the cactus like a ninja.

"Just over a year," Nicole said. "It was closer to work. Of course now that I don't work there anymore, that's kind of irrelevant." Her voice took on a hint of bitterness.

"Did you get fired?" I said.

She turned to me like I'd insulted her very being. "No way. Are you kidding? I didn't get fired."

I put my hands up in defense. "I was just asking."

"I got laid off," she said.

My eyes narrowed. "Same thing as being fired."

"It's not," she said. "It's completely different."

"How is it different?"

She twisted up her mouth. "People get fired for not coming to work or sleeping in their cubicles or stuff like that. People get laid off when there's not enough work to keep everyone employed."

"So there wasn't enough work," I said.

"Right. The company lost a few contracts, so they let about fifty people go."

"And now you're all looking for jobs?"

"Not me," Nicole said. "I have a job."

"Teaching yoga? Instead of computer programming?"

"It's much more relaxing."

"And the pay?" We still hadn't been able to settle on a price for the yoga.

Nicole shrugged. "Yeah, there is that. But I got a couple months' severance."

"So in two months, you're out of money?"

She finally let out a deep breath. "Maybe. But I'll figure something out."

Nicole walked up the steps leading to the house and unlocked the door, Nano at her heals. And if I thought one cat coming to the gym was bad, what I saw inside was a train wreck.

Four cats dashed right for her. That's four on top of Nano who darted off into the dark recesses of the house. Hanging on the walls were all sorts of photographs of cats. There were cat cushions on the sofa. A cat quilt hanging over the back of it. There was even a cat apron hanging on a hook by the entrance to the kitchen.

"You like cats?" I said, daring to take a step inside. Two of the cats immediately started rubbing up against me, getting their hair all over my sweatpants.

"Love them," she said. "And all these guys came from the shelter. I couldn't very well let them be homeless."

"I guess," I said. "But how many do you have?" Also at the entrance to the kitchen were four food bowls, lined up in a row.

"Eight," Nicole said. "Though you know I volunteer at the animal shelter on weekends and sometimes those little kitties are so hard to resist."

"I could resist them," I said.

"That's because you're a cat hater."

"I'm not a cat hater," I said, trying to disentangle myself from the purring felines. "Cats just aren't my favorite animal."

"So what is?" She threw her keys on a table near the front door and dropped her gigantic purse to the ground beside it, making a huge thudding sound. One of the cats vaulted up to the table and started pawing at the keys.

I shrugged. "Dogs, I guess." A dog like Cerberus would be perfect, though there would be no way to hide that from mortal eyes.

"I'm guessing you don't have one?"

I shook my head. "No dogs over twenty pounds are allowed in my condo." Cerberus was definitely over twenty pounds.

"You could get one under twenty pounds."

"Get a little dog?" I'd never much seen the point.

"They're cute. And lovable. And really great companions."

"And small," I said. Mom had nagged me before about getting a dog, saying they were good for stress relief. But to me, it just seemed like one more thing to step on.

"You want something to drink?" Nicole said "Or eat?"

My stomach growled, and I realized that with taking her car to get cleaned, I'd never actually taken the time to eat lunch. Immortal or not, I needed food.

"That would actually be great."

Nicole walked into the kitchen to get the promised grub, and I took the time to look around. In addition to the cat photos, on all the shelves and flat surfaces were cat figurines. Brown cats. White cats. Cats with no hair. I stepped away because I didn't want any chance of the cat fever that she was apparently inflicted with rubbing off on me. She came out a few minutes later carrying a bottle of wine, a couple plastic red cups, and a box of saltine crackers.

"It's the best I can do," she said, setting it down on the coffee table. "I hate to cook."

"It's perfect," I said, grabbing a few of the crackers. Ethan and I had made a meal out of Flower Scout cookies at least twice in the last week, so crackers were almost a luxury.

She poured us each some wine, and while it wasn't the caliber of what Hades served in the Underworld, it still tasted pretty damn good. Also, knowing my immortal soul wasn't about to be sent to Tartarus made it taste even better.

A laptop sat closed on the coffee table. "Is this your computer?" I asked. I wasn't sure what was so powerful about it compared to mine at the gym. It was thinner than one of the saltine crackers.

Nicole shook her head. "It's one of them. But not the one we're going to use."

I followed her down a short hallway into what might have been a bedroom in a normal person's house, but on top of the cats, I had now determined that Nicole was not a normal person. The entire room was packed with computer crap, like printers and monitors and keyboards.

"What do you do with all this stuff?" I asked as I looked around, trying to mentally count just the monitors alone.

"I buy it at Goodwill," she said. "And try to restore it. Do you have any idea how old some of these computers are?" She picked up something that looked like a relic from the seventies. "This is a Commodore 64, the most awesome, revolutionary home computer ever invented. This thing changed the world when it came out."

"You weren't even alive when it came out," I said.

"That's how amazing it is," Nicole said. "Its awesomeness stretches across the ages."

Kind of like mine, I thought, but I kept that to myself.

She dragged a second chair up to the main desk surface and motioned for me to sit down. "Did you bring the IP address?"

"The what?"

"The piece of paper you were using to log in?" she said, like somehow I should know that equated to something called an IP address.

I dug it out of my pocket. "Oh, yeah." I smoothed it out on the desk.

"The numbers," Nicole said. "That's the IP address."

"Okay," I said, because I really wasn't in a position to question any of this computer shit.

She started pushing buttons and clicking things and the computer did all sorts of stuff, like flash from blue to green to a background that said, "Illuminati Lives." Her fingers moved like she'd been typing computer code since birth. She bit her lip and kept nodding her head and saying things to herself and smiling, and her confidence was actually way sexy. Once that thought was in my head, I started thinking about her in her yoga poses and her sports bra, and my brain started traveling down a path I didn't have time to waste on.

"Did you hear me?" she said.

I shook my head, snapping myself out of my thoughts. Thank the gods she couldn't read my mind.

"Your user id," she said. "Is this supposed to be a capital C or a little c?"

"Little c," I said. "And the zero is actually an O."

She typed the user id and password into the little green boxes on the website and the computer did the same thing where the circle appeared and then the green box.

"Now the number?"

I read it off to her and she typed it in. And it did the same thing it had done back at the gym. Nothing.

"Perfect," I said. "It's broken."

But Nicole put her finger up and went through the whole routine again. "Don't give up yet, Achilles," she said. And this time, no sooner had she typed the inventory number for the Spear of Achilles, she hit some other button on the keyboard and the circle froze in the middle of the screen.

Nicole turned to me and smiled.

"Is that good?" I said.

Nicole nodded. "Totally good." Then she clicked a bunch of other stuff and made some other windows pop up on the screen and kept saying things like "okay" and "strange" and "hmmm." I tried not to interrupt her because whatever she was doing, she wasn't running out of ideas. Then after clicking some more, she went back to the screen with the box for the inventory number and typed it in again.

The circle spun. The screen went to black. But then, words appeared in small green type: ITEM CURRENTLY NOT IN INVENTORY.

Nicole slapped her hands on the desk. "There's your answer. Whatever you're trying to get isn't there."

"That's impossible."

"Why? This is obviously some kind of database tracking system. Someone must've checked it out. Like a library."

It was kind of spooky how on the mark she actually was.

"Nobody can check it out except me," I said.

She shrugged. "But somebody did."

"Who?"

Her face fell just the smallest amount. "Oh. Is it supposed to say?"

You would think the Hall of Artifacts which was run by the council of the gods would keep track of that kind of information. And the gods, unlike me, were way excited by all this computer crap. That was the whole reason they'd used a computer tracking system for the Hall of Artifacts. Ares, who'd told me about it in the first place, said it was to make everything trackable.

"I think so. Is there a way to check?"

Nicole cocked her head in the cutest way and smiled. "If there is, I can find it."

She turned back to the computer and started hitting some more buttons. The same ITEM CURRENTLY NOT IN INVENTORY message appeared a few more times, but nothing else. Five minutes went by. Then fifteen. The cats incessantly rubbed against my legs and pawed at my right ankle, almost like the little beasts knew it was my weak spot. I crossed by legs at the ankle as best I could and shooed them away.

I tried not to bother Nicole, but sweat beaded up on my forehead. It was bad enough that I was being framed for something I didn't do. It was even worse that someone had dared to take my spear.

"I don't know, Achilles," Nicole finally said, pushing the keyboard away.

"But I thought you knew everything about computers."

"Yeah, me, too," she said. "I won't lie. This one's kind of tough. But I can keep checking. I can run some scraping routines overnight. Maybe that'll turn up something."

I shoved my chair out, trying to control my anger. I was not going to end up in Tartarus. I had to find a way to prove I was innocent and I had to stop any more dryads from getting killed. Unless I did the first, I'd never be able to do the second.

I went over the options in my head. I could seek out the Furies and try to vanquish the other two just like I had done to Meg. But the last fight with them had left me nearly dead. I wasn't sure picking a fight with them was a viable option if I wanted to stay alive. I could find Nemesis and plead my case, ask her to call them off. I didn't know where Nemesis was, but I'd figure out a way to find out. Of course none of those things would tell me who the real killer was. None would make the dryads stop dying.

"What's so important anyway?" Nicole said.

I ran a hand through my hair, thinking about how to find out where Nemesis was. I could ask Ares and hope he returned my text. Or I could ask Athena if she came back by. I was pretty sure I couldn't find Nemesis via Google maps.

"It's just . . . nothing," I said. There was no way to explain to Nicole, a mortal, the divine hell I was somehow right in the middle of.

"Then why are you so upset?"

"I'm not upset," I said.

"You look like you're about to explode," she said. "Does this have something to do with your *scratches* from yesterday? Like did you get in a fight with someone over whatever's going on?"

It had everything to do with that. And nothing to do with Nicole. Dryads were already dying because of me. I wasn't going to get Nicole in the middle of the situation, too.

"It's nothing," I said. "Anyway, I need to go."

Nicole glanced back to her computer, like she was somehow going to will it to suddenly work.

"But . . ."

"It's not that important," I said. "We can just forget it."

Or at least she could forget it. I'd find another way to get the information I needed.

"Fine, Achilles," she said. "I guess I'll see you tomorrow."

I nodded and left, avoiding the cats as best I could on my way out. Maybe that's what my torture would be in Tartarus. Cats clawing at me and hissing and . . . okay, cats weren't that bad. I doubted my fate would be as simple as that. I'd probably end up more like Prometheus, having my liver devoured every single day by an eagle pecking at me.

Gods, this sucked.

CHAPTER 12

When Nicole walked into Hero's Gym the next day, she had bags under her eyes that stood out even against her dark skin, but she still grinned like she'd just benched two hundred.

"Got your info," she said, dropping her enormous purse to the counter and Nano to the floor in one synchronized motion.

"What?" I said, because her words didn't really register. My night had started with me texting Ares and having him not text back. Like always. I was going to have to crash one of his history classes at UT. So instead, Ethan had convinced me to go out to a bar and get my frustrations out over a game of darts. And a drink. Maybe a bunch of drinks. It got a little fuzzy after the fifth one. He'd used the logic that if we were out in public, the Furies wouldn't attack.

"The website," she said. "I got in."

"You got in?"

"And I found some interesting things out," she went on.

"Interesting?"

I sounded like a parrot, but my brain wasn't kicking on all gears, thanks to the late night.

She nodded. "Yep. And I have some questions."

Questions were not good, but if she really did have information for me, I couldn't ignore it.

I grabbed one of the crocheted balls and started squeezing it, trying to channel my anxiety through it. "What did you find out?"

Nicole leaned close. So close her arm brushed against mine. But for once in my life, my brain wasn't thinking about sex.

Okay, maybe just a little bit.

"First off," she said. "It looks like whoever took the item you're after tried to cover up their tracks."

"What do you mean?" I said.

"Like I think it was stolen," Nicole said. "And whoever stole it entered some fake info in the storage records. Like first they tried to say that it was still there. Then, when it looked like that was discovered, they went back and added another entry, saying that it had been checked out."

"By who?"

She shook her head. "There wasn't a full name. Just the letter A. Almost like it was entered really fast."

"I didn't take it," I said, because obviously whoever had was trying to make it look like I'd been the one to put in the information.

Nicole put up her hand. "Wait. There's more. The logs showed that the letter A entry got booted, like the admins kicked it back, so a full name was put in."

"What name?"

"Alexander," she said.

Relief drained through me. Whoever Alexander was, he sure as hell wasn't me. I could take this information to the council of the gods and prove to them that I wasn't the one who had it. They would have no choice but to petition Nemesis themselves to get the Furies off me. It would be the only way to keep justice and order.

"This is good," I said. "Really good. I can use this." The stress seemed to seep out of me and into the ground. I was not going to have to worry about Tartarus. And there was a solid clue as to who had the spear.

But the smile slipped from Nicole's face. "Okay, there might be a problem with that."

"What kind of problem?" As far as I could tell, everything was moving back on the perfect track.

She grabbed her dark ponytail and pulled it over her shoulder fiddling with the ends. "I stayed up really late checking on this."

That would explain the bags under her eyes, though I didn't dare say anything, especially since I'd been out drinking.

I motioned for her to go on.

"And I kept digging deeper," she said. "And when I got to the point with the name, the website rebooted."

"Okay. Why is that bad?"

"Because I went back and tried to get the information again. I retraced my steps. But this time, none of the same information was there. I typed in the item number, and a file started downloading on my computer. Like it was installing a virus or something. So I tried again, and this time I couldn't even pull up the item number."

"Maybe you did something wrong," I said.

She rolled her eyes. "I didn't do anything wrong. And I tried like five more times, all with the same result. The record got deleted."

"Are you kidding me?"

Her face was the only answer I needed.

"Fuck."

I stormed to the back room, pulling my sweatshirt off over my head. The council would never believe me just on my word. Why should they? And without the record available, I had no way to prove my innocence.

I heard someone clear their throat behind me. When I turned, Nicole stood there in the doorframe.

"There's something else," she said.

"What?" I couldn't imagine anything worse than what she'd already told me.

She scratched the back of her hand, like she was trying to distract herself into saying what she wanted to say. "When I was digging around, I got more information. A few things actually."

I waited. Maybe some good news would come out of this after all.

"You told me it was a library," she said.

I nodded slowly. "It is."

"Hall of Artifacts?" she said.

"It's like a library where things are kept," I said. "And books." The Hall of Artifacts had a little bit of everything.

"Things like the Spear of Achilles?" she said.

One second went by. Then two. Then ten. I wasn't sure how to respond.

"It's a . . . ," I started.

"A what?" she said, tapping her fingers on the doorframe.

"A . . ."

"I did some research on it," she said. "It's a weapon from the

Trojan War. And the Hall of Artifacts? I dug around and looked at some of the other things filed away there."

Inwardly I cringed. The council of the gods would send me to Tartarus for letting a mortal get this kind of information. Then, they'd wipe her memories to make sure she never said a word about it.

"Shield of Perseus? Artemis's arrows? Helm of Darkness?"

My mind spun. I could lie my way out of this. I could lie my way out of anything.

"Okay," I said, piecing together my words as I went. "I don't tell people this because it sounds really dorky, but I'm part of this gaming group."

"Gaming?" She looked amused at my answer.

I nodded. "Gaming. Like live action role playing."

Nicole busted out laughing. "LARPing? You're telling me you're a LARPer?"

I crossed my arms and tried to own it even though the last thing I'd ever do was LARP. I had no desire to pretend to fight. What I craved—what was in my blood—were real battles.

"All the time."

She stepped forward. Got right in my face. "You know what, Achilles?"

"What?"

"I don't believe you."

"It's true."

"Bullshit."

Damn. I was screwed.

"Look, do me a favor," I said.

She waited.

"Don't say anything else about it, okay?"

"Why not?" Nicole said.

I shrugged. "It kind of destroys my cool image, you know?"

"What cool image?" she said.

Oh, this girl. She was maddening.

"Just—" I started.

"I won't say anything, Achilles. Not yet. But you owe me some answers."

As far as I was concerned, I'd given her the best answer I could. But I nodded and pushed past her and out of the back room. People were just starting to come in so I was saved from having to say anything else about it. And once students started showing up for her yoga class, Nicole went on about her day like nothing was the least bit out of the ordinary. Except everything was. I walked a thin tightrope over Tartarus, and if I slipped, I would fall in for eternity.

CHAPTER 13

I didn't spot Jack while he lifted, and I didn't play mediator for Sophie and Scott. I didn't even hardly talk to Elle when she came through the door for yoga. She went on and on about lifting weights, trying to set up an appointment—I swear she was flirting with me—but my mind was spinning. And for me to not even have time for mild flirting, regardless of the fact that I shouldn't flirt with my roommate's girlfriend, that was really saying something about how upset this whole thing had me.

I'll give Elle this. She tossed her dark curly hair and stroked her shoulder and bent over to pick up a pen that she'd dropped and it almost worked. Almost got my mind off the mess and back where it didn't belong. But no. I was too deep. So Elle flipped her long hair over her shoulder and went off to the yoga room. Me? I headed for the punching bag.

I wrapped tape around my knuckles and fell into the rhythm,

one hit after another, until my mind started working again. Nicole was good with computers. Way too good. And the more I thought about this, the more I realized that it was probably a blessing from the gods that the record had been erased, because if I'd gone to the council of the gods with the information Nicole had dug up, they would have wanted to know how I got it. And they would have pressed and pried and somehow found out that I'd involved her. In addition to my life being over, I'd also be responsible for destroying Nicole's life. She'd be subject to the gods' whims. At best she'd have her memories erased. At worst, she would be sentenced to time in Tartarus. And even if the gods never found out, the fact that Nicole now knew something else was going on—that she knew the Hall of Artifacts even existed—blew wads the size of elephant balls.

"Who pissed in your Cheerios?" Ares said, grabbing the punching bag to stop its swaying. He must've finally decided to grace me with his presence.

"The world," I said, and I kept punching, reveling in the extra resistance Ares holding the bag gave. I guess he must've sensed this because he stayed there, pushing back and shifting around with each of my movements. Sweat poured off me, dripping onto the floor. My muscles started to weaken, so I punched harder. And harder. Then I counted, pounding out one thousand more punches without stopping. It was only then that I finally stepped back.

"Damn," someone in the gym said. Maybe it was Simon.

When I looked up, every single person stared at me, Ares included. He released the bag and handed me a towel.

"You want to talk about it?" he said.

Gods how I wanted to talk about it. And of course he would be the first person I would talk about it to. But I couldn't mention anything about Nicole and the Hall of Artifacts. He was my patron god, but he was also subject to the council of the gods and their rules.

I shook my head. "I feel better."

"You texted me," Ares said.

"Oh, you noticed? I figured when you didn't respond, like you always never do, that maybe you didn't get it. I don't know why you even have a cell phone."

Ares pulled the phone from his pocket and looked at it like maybe he'd wondered the same thing. "The university makes me carry the stupid thing, you know, in case some student procrastinates for the entire fucking semester and then needs to get in touch for an extension. Like I'm going to give them an extension. They can stick that extension up their ass. Man, I hate that shit."

"So do you answer their texts?"

"Hell, no," Ares said, shoving his phone back in his pocket. "But I came by here, didn't I?"

"Yeah, you did," I said, and unwrapped the tape—or at least what was left of it—from my knuckles. It fell to the floor in pieces.

"You said you had something to tell me," Ares said.

Shit. I couldn't tell him, even though he might be able to find out more. Or maybe I could. No, I couldn't. Ares was a god, but he wasn't going to get himself in bad with the council either. Not if there really was something brewing between the gods like Hades had said.

"I had another thought," Nicole said, walking up just then. But she stopped when she saw Ares. "Oh, sorry. I thought you were done working out."

"Hello, gorgeous," Ares said.

Nicole, to her credit, rolled her eyes, which actually made Ares laugh.

"Nicole, this is Reese," I said, going with Ares' common name.

"He's a professor at UT. Reese, meet Nicole."

"Any time she wants," Ares said.

Inwardly I groaned.

"Anyway . . . ," Nicole said.

"Don't let me interrupt," Ares said. "What do you have a thought about?"

I shot her a look with my eyes, praying to the gods that she wouldn't say another word. Forget that one of the gods stood right there between us.

My prayers were answered.

"Oh, um . . . I was just thinking more about yoga," she said. "But it can wait."

"I want to hear about yoga," Ares said, taking a step closer to Nicole.

This situation was going down the toilet faster than I could flush it.

Nicole sighed deeply. She then wiped her brow with the towel she was holding. "Oh, it was about class size," she said. "I don't know if you saw or if you were too busy, you know, punching your little bag to death, but we had fifty people in there."

"That's great," I said, playing along even though the reference to my 'little bag' was a bit demeaning.

"It's not great, Achilles," Nicole said. "It's way too many for anyone to get a good workout."

"So what? You want to start limiting class size?" Limiting class size would limit new memberships which wouldn't help keep the gym afloat. It also wouldn't help me get a new TV or computer.

"No," Nicole said. "I want to add two more classes. In the afternoon."

"I'd come," Ares said. "If you make one of them after three."

"You do yoga?" Nicole said, stepping back since Ares had

stepped toward her again.

"I do now," Ares said. "I hear that it can really help get to some of those hard to reach muscles."

"Exactly," Nicole said, ignoring or oblivious to Ares' intended innuendo. "That's what I've been trying to tell Achilles, but I think he's scared to try."

"I'm not scared." I also was not going to have Ares doing yoga in my gym, but that wasn't the point right now.

"So what about the extra classes?" Nicole asked.

"That sounds great?" I said, though it came out more like a question.

"Perfect. We can start them in a couple weeks," Nicole said. "So I'm just going to go clean up before the next class starts." And off she went, casting one final glance, telling me with her eyes that I owed her, yet again.

"That is one fine looking lady," Ares said. "Man, they are getting better looking every day. Somebody better thank the gods for that shit."

"She's not your type," I said, suddenly feeling overly protective of Nicole, though I hardly knew her. Still, I'd known Ares a long time. His idea of a relationship was not something I could imagine a girl like Nicole putting up with.

"Everyone is my type," Ares said.

"Anyway," I said, lowering my voice. "I need you to tell me where one of the gods is."

"Right here," Ares said, pointing both thumbs back at himself.

Oh, the gods. They drove me crazy.

"Not you. Nemesis."

"Oh, Nemesis," Ares said. "That's a little different. She's not right here."

"Yeah, I see that. Can you tell me where she is?"

Ares stroked the short dark hairs on his chin, like he had to contemplate this deeply. I waited and did my best to not let any anger build up inside me again. Finally he looked back to me.

"Well?"

"I'll have to get permission first," Ares said. "I mean, I know exactly where she is. Also, technically, she's not really a god. She's more of an immortal entity. But that's kind of semantics."

"You think?" I was ready to stuff semantics where the sun didn't shine.

"So can you get permission?"

"I can ask," Ares said. "Meet me tonight for drinks." Not a question. Not a request. Just like the gods.

"Perfect," I said. Drinks would help, and Ares would be able to get permission. By tonight I'd know where Nemesis was. I'd be able to petition to her, have her call off the Furies. Then I'd find out who the hell this Alexander person was who'd stolen the spear.

By the time Ares left, the next yoga class had started, so I couldn't ask Nicole what she'd been so excited about. But as soon as everyone from her class left, she hurried over to me at the counter.

"It wasn't a virus," Nicole said, shoving herself right next to me on the stool.

"What wasn't? My computer? But you said that's why it was so slow and crappy."

"Not that," Nicole said. "You did have a virus. I'm not talking about that. I'm talking about the file."

"The file?" I was trying really hard to follow along, but with as excited as she was, she wasn't make it easy.

She slapped something down on the counter. "The file that downloaded onto my computer last night. Remember when I told you how I thought your Hall of Artifacts LARPing place was trying to install a virus on my computer. I deleted it from my computer, but I put it on this thumb drive. I always do that with virus files in case I need to look at them later."

"Which is a common occurrence?" I said. "Looking at viruses?"

Nicole shrugged. "It can help when I'm trying to clean off old computers. Anyway . . ." She set a thumb drive on the counter. "What if it's not a virus?"

"And . . . ?"

"And what if it's actually a file. With information about your spear."

"Not my spear," I said.

She eyed me.

"I mean kind of my spear. Anyway. What information?"

She flipped the thumb drive over, looking at the inside connector part. "I can't look at it on my phone. But with your computer . . ."

"I thought my computer was a piece of crap," I said.

"Yeah, but it's not a giant piece of crap," Nicole said. "Just a sort-of giant piece of crap. At least it has USB connections."

"And this is a USB connection?" I said.

Pity filled Nicole's eyes. "Oh, Achilles. You're embarrassing yourself. Maybe you should take a computer course or something. Computers are actually really simple if you get to know them."

Nothing about computers was simple as far as I was concerned. But with all this technology the gods had started using, maybe it was time to take a class at the local community college.

Nicole shoved the thumb drive into my computer and grabbed the mouse and started clicking away, biting her lip like she always did when she worked on a computer. It was only a few seconds and she said, "This is it. And look, here, at the beginning of the file if we look at it like a text file. I think it's actually a video file."

The only part of what she said that made sense was the video file part. A video would be good. And bad. I mean I wanted to see whatever was in it, but I also wasn't sure that Nicole should see it. I also was pretty sure that at this point I didn't have much choice.

She closed whatever she was looking at and double clicked the file. A window opened and started playing a video. It wasn't some old dark black and white grainy video. Instead it was full color with perfect lighting. And right in front of the camera was the Spear of Achilles, smooth wooden shaft with a dark spearhead that stole the light. It sat on a shelf with a tag in front of it clearly marking what it was. Except instead of being marked in English, like might be normal given that it was here in America, it was written in Ancient Greek.

"We take our LARPing pretty seriously," I said.

"So you use Greek letters?" she said.

"You know Greek?"

Nicole shrugged. "I'm an engineer."

"Engineers learn Greek?" I said.

"The letters. For math." She pursed her lips together as we watched the video, waiting for something to happen. A small clock ticked seconds by at the bottom right but they kept skipping forward in time as shadows moved in the background. "I think it must be motion activated. There must be other stuff going on. Maybe there's a big LARPing thing coming up and Artemis needs her arrows."

She elbowed me in the side and I laughed, like she'd made a joke. She had no idea how right she was.

The lighting on the camera shifted as a shadow was cast over it. Then a shape moved in front of the camera.

"Oh look, something's happening," Nicole said.

Whoever the shape was, their back was turned to us, blocking the spear from view. But then the person in the video feed turned around and looked directly into the camera.

I sucked in a breath before I could stop myself. "You have got to be shitting me."

"You know him?" Nicole said.

Did I know him? Only too well. I'd known him thousands of years ago. Had wanted to believe he was dead, just like he should have been. Just like I should have been, too. But if the gods had woken me from immortal sleep, then the same could have happened to him. This was none other than Alexander of Troy. Also known as Paris, prince of Troy. The same Paris who had shot the deadly arrow at my ankle, trying to end my life so long ago.

"I know him." My heart pounded. I wanted to believe my eyes were making this up, that my anger and need for vengeance were twisting what I was seeing. I blinked, looking again, but he turned away. Then he grabbed the spear, wrapping his disgusting, unworthy fingers around my weapon, and walked from view of the camera.

"Who is it?" Nicole asked. "Is this Alexander?"

How in the names of the gods would I ever explain this? What answer could I possibly give?

"This is Alexander," I said. "And we're not on the best of terms."

"He's taking your spear," she said.

It completely made sense. He was trying to frame me for murder. He'd taken the spear and killed the dryads and made it all look like it was me who did it. When I found him, I was going to stab the spear up his ass.

"Sure looks that way," I said, taking deep breaths to keep from punching my hand through the monitor.

"So that's good, right?" Nicole said. "You know who took it now."

"It's very good," I said.

"Do you know where he lives? We could drive over and get it."

"We?"

"Sure," Nicole said. "I'd love to see you LARP."

I didn't even bother with the facade. "I haven't seen him in years. I have no idea where he lives. I don't even know what name he's using these days."

"I thought you guys were in this group together?" Nicole said, but a suspicious edge had crept back into her voice.

"He's part of the group," I said. "But I guess you could say we're on different teams. If I knew where he lived, I would have . . ." My voice trailed off. It's not like I could sit here and tell Nicole all the various ways I'd dreamed of killing Paris.

Nicole grabbed the mouse again and clicked back on the video. "No problem. We can run his face through some recognition software."

"We can? Recognition software?" Was that even a thing?

"Sure. We just need a good shot of his face. Then I have a friend who can totally do it." With a couple more clicks, there was a still shot of Paris' face. It made me seethe just to look at. And I swear he taunted me with his eyes, like somehow he knew I'd be seeing this.

"Wow, he's gorgeous," Nicole said.

"Are you kidding me? Gorgeous?"

"Totally." She pointed to his face. "Look at those eyes. And his cheekbones. They look so regal. Like he's some kind of hero, looking off into the camera, ready to go fight down monsters."

I almost threw up in my mouth. Paris was no hero. He would run from monsters, not fight them. I never understood what girls saw in him. Like Helen for instance. Total bad judgment on her part. Not that Helen was known for making good decisions. Ever. Every decision she'd ever made resulted in death and destruction, the top of that list being the fact that she left her husband to run off with Paris. Granted, her husband, Menelaus, was a crotchety old man so overweight and out of shape that he could hardly lift a sword. Her marriage to him had been purely for alliances. But still, to run off with Paris. Even his brother, Hector, would have been a far better choice. Hector at least had been brave. A true hero. Paris wasn't worth the dirt he stood on.

"He looks like a douchebag to me," I said.

"But look at those eyes."

The last thing I wanted to do was look at Paris' eyes. They were the final thing I'd seen before he lamely fired the arrow at me.

"He's an asshole," I said. "And also, let's not forget that he's the one who took the . . . the thing I'm after."

"The spear," she said, in a whisper.

"Can we just not say that aloud anymore?"

Nicole looked around the gym. A couple of girls were in the back, using the leg machine, and Jack had come in a second time to help push himself over the edge in the competition, but other than that, the place was empty.

"Who's going to hear?" she said.

I put up my hand. "Just don't mention it."

"Okay, fine, so he took your little toy."

I nodded. Paris had the perfect reason to frame me. He'd always been jealous of me. Also, I'd killed his brother, Hector, back during the war. He would hold that against me forever, even though I'd done it to take my revenge. I'd had every right to do it. This dryad killing thing though . . . Nothing could justify that.

"So you really think we can figure out where he lives?" I said.

"My friend can."

"What friend?" I said.

"This guy I used to work with."

"Did he get fired, too?" I asked.

"I didn't get fired. I told you that. I got laid off."

"Did he get laid off?"

"No, he got fired for hacking into the corporate computers. He'd been doing it for years, but he finally got caught. Best hacker I know. I'm sure he can hack his way into the right places and track this guy down."

This was the first piece of good news I'd gotten.

"I'll text him," Nicole said, pulling out her phone.

I placed a hand over it. "Can we not tell him any of the details?"

"Like what?"

"Like, you know, about the Hall of Artifacts, or the spear?" I whispered this last part.

"You and your secret LARPing life, Achilles," she said. "Fine. I'll send him the picture. Make it a challenge. He won't be able to resist."

"And you really think it will work?"

"Totally," Nicole said. "The government tracks everything these days. Hell, they probably know exactly who you are and where you go on a daily basis."

That was not a comforting thought, and was definitely something I'd have to look into . . . a different day. For today, I had to figure out where Paris was, clear my name, and destroy the Furies. No big deal.

CHAPTER 14

Nicole scanned through the contacts on her phone until she found the one she was looking for and then texted the image.

I swear, not twenty seconds later, her phone rang.

She swiped the screen and put the phone to her ear.

"Hey, Jordan," she said, in a super singsongy voice, like she was crazy excited to be talking to this Jordan person.

I couldn't hear the other end of the conversation, but her face darkened within seconds. Then she pulled the phone away and looked at it, like she was trying to figure out what had happened.

"What?"

She shook her head and clicked off the phone. "I forgot how paranoid Jordan is. He says he doesn't want to talk on the phone or by text. That I have to meet him if I want to talk to him."

"So go meet him," I said. "Your classes are done for the day, right?"

"Yeah, that's true. I'll go by his place."

I couldn't get her out the door fast enough. This was the best lead ever. And I didn't have to wait long. Within an hour, she was back.

"What'd you find out?" I said.

"Jordan wants to meet you," she said. "I gave him the picture, but he says that he won't do anything with it unless he meets you."

"Why does he want to meet me?" Computer people were so strange.

"He thinks you're some kind of spy."

I laughed out loud. "Oh come on. A spy? For what?"

"The government. Or Russia. He doesn't know. That's why he insists he has to meet you himself. I told you he was paranoid. Anyway I told him we'd meet him at six."

I wasn't meeting Ares until later, so even though it was the last thing I wanted to do, six worked.

"Not at your house, right?" I didn't want to live through the cats again.

Nicole scowled. "There's nothing wrong with my cats. But don't worry. He wants to meet at Zilker Park."

Zilker Park. Great. If the guy only had a single clue how much of an immortal subculture hung around Zilker Park. The entrance to the Underworld was only the start of it. There were dryads and water nymphs and . . . well, strictly speaking, according to the rules of the gods, I wasn't supposed to say anymore.

"Great," I said. "I'll meet him." If he really could tell me where Paris was, then I didn't have much choice.

* * *

NICOLE PICKED ME UP IN HER ITTY-BITTY CAR a few hours later. "We should get dinner afterward," she said. "Shady Grove."

I let my appetite through just enough to imagine the thick grass-fed beef burgers that Shady Grove was known for. But I was also meeting Ares later.

"Maybe?" I said. "We can see what time it is."

"Why? You have a hot date?" Nicole asked.

I wouldn't call meeting Ares for drinks a hot date. Not unless he brought Athena along.

"Nope."

Nicole cocked her head. "Not even with Elle?"

"Elle?"

"Yeah. From yoga," Nicole said. "Don't try to act like you haven't noticed her flirting her ass off with you every chance she gets."

I paused, imagining Elle's blue eyes, dark hair, and generous assets.

"She's dating my roommate," I finally said.

"Then what's she doing flirting with you? I don't think that would make your roommate happy."

"You think she's flirting?"

Nicole took one hand off the steering wheel and smacked my arm. "You're a bad liar, Achilles. Either that or a complete idiot."

I was neither, but now was not the time to defend myself.

She drove us downtown, toward Zilker Park, cutting in and out of rush hour traffic in a way that reminded me why I didn't bother with a car. Most everything I did was contained within a one mile radius of Heroes Gym, and what that couldn't resolve, rideshare took care of.

"I was down here for the Trail of Lights last month," Nicole said. "Did you come?"

"Never been," I said.

"Never?" Nicole asked.

I shook my head.

"How long have you lived in Austin?"

"Ten years," I said.

"And you're how old?"

"Nosy much?" I said. Defining my exact age wasn't really possible since I hadn't gotten any older once Ares woke me from the immortal sleep.

"Oh, please," Nicole said. "Don't you dare tell me that you're one of those people who's all vain about their age."

"Of course not," I said.

"So how old are you then?"

"How old do you think I am?"

We were stopped at a red light, so she looked over at me. And for some reason, having her eyes on me, knowing she was studying me, gave me goosebumps. Not in a bad way, like the Furies had. More in the way that reminded me she was really good looking.

"Thirty," she said finally.

"That old?" I'd been twenty-seven when Paris had fired the deadly arrow that had ended my current existence and catapulted me into immortal sleep.

She shrugged. "Okay, fine, twenty-nine."

"Twenty-eight," I said, since it was at least in the ballpark and kept me under thirty.

"I was close," she said. "But don't worry. You look really good for your age."

I eyed her sideways. "Are you hitting on me?"

At this, she rolled her eyes. "Please. Don't flatter yourself, Achilles."

"What? I'm not worthy of being hit on?" I was seriously worthy. Good looking. Strong. Tall. An entrepreneur. Sure, I had no cash, but that was a minor problem.

She shook her head. "You're just not my type."

"What type are you looking for?"

"I don't know," Nicole said. "Just not . . ."

"Not what?" I said, because at this point, it was a matter of pride.

She motioned with her hands, like words would magically appear there. "Oh my god, can we please stop this conversation?"

"You brought it up," I said.

"Then I'll stop it. Now."

The light changed and she shot out into the intersection. Then it was only another half block until we got to Zilker. There was a parking attendant waiting at the entrance, and Nicole eyed me.

I pulled out my wallet and handed over a ten. He gave us a couple dollars back which Nicole shoved in her pocket before driving forward and finding a spot.

"Where are we meeting this guy?" I said, getting out of the cramped little car. They didn't make cars these days for anyone over five-six.

Nicole beeped the car, locking it. "He didn't say."

"Are you kidding? Zilker Park is huge."

Nicole looked one way then the other, searching for Jordan. Maybe, if he really was paranoid, he'd have just left us another note as to where to look. But if this whole thing turned into some giant nerdy scavenger hunt, I was out of here. I didn't have time for that.

"Oh, I think I see him." She pointed in the direction of the playground. But seeing as how there were about two hundred people that way, I wasn't sure who she was talking about. Still, I followed her over in the general direction. But instead of walking to the playsets, she went to the train ticket office.

"Jordan!" she said, and she gave some guy a hug.

He totally hugged her back, wrapping his arms tight around her until his fingers laced together. The kind of hug that made it completely clear that he wanted to be way more than friends with her. It was only when the hug was done that I could get a look at the guy.

He was maybe five foot ten, wore a blue sweatshirt with a funny white emblem on the front that hung on him, maybe meant to make him look bigger, though I was willing to bet he was a skinny little dweeb. The hood was pulled up, but not so far that I couldn't see his spiky dark hair. His facial features looked like he was at least part Asian, and his eyes were glued on Nicole.

"I'm Achilles Stevens," I said, shoving my hand forward.

Jordan did his best to drag his eyes away from her, but with her standing there in a tight tank top, I couldn't really blame him.

"Oh, yeah," Nicole said. "Jordan Carbery, Achilles. Achilles, Jordan."

He eyed my hand before actually shaking it, and his eyes roved my entire body.

"What?" I said, taking a step back.

"You're not wearing a bug are you?" Jordan said.

"A bug?"

He nodded.

I glanced sideways at Nicole who motioned for me to answer him.

I patted the front of my shirt and my pockets. "No bug."

Jordan stepped forward. "Let me see your ears."

"My ears?"

"Just show him," Nicole said.

So I tilted my head and leaned forward until first my right ear canal and then my left had been properly inspected and deemed bug-free. Only then did Jordan kind of half-way smile in my direction. For Nicole though, he had plenty of smiles.

"You guys want to go for a train ride?" he asked.

The last thing in the entire world I wanted to do right now was go for a train ride, but somehow there I was, pulling my wallet out again and buying three tickets for the kiddie train. The whole time we waited for the train to pull around, Nicole stood there asking Jordan about a bunch of people I guess they used to work with. They spoke some crazy language with a bunch of acronyms, and I had no clue what was going on. TLAs and DMAs and RAMs and ASCII. Finally the train came around, and Jordan picked the seats right up front, behind the engine.

I soon found out why.

The train was one of those little kid ones, the kind that puttered around the entire park. It was made to look all old-school and authentic, and as such, it had the loudest steam engine I'd ever heard in my entire life.

Jordan smiled at the sound. "Now we can finally talk."

I had to sit way forward to hear him, but I was just happy that we were finally going to make some progress.

"Nicole said you were a hacker," I said.

He put up a finger. "We don't use that word."

I think the word we wanted to use was crackpot, but I kept my mouth shut.

"Nicole said you could help us," I said, hoping she'd already explained our entire situation so I could get this episode of my life over with.

"Yep," Jordan said. "I can help."

I tucked my hair behind my ears because the air from the hot engine was blowing it everywhere. "How long do you think it will take to identify him?"

Jordan looked at me like I'd put all my clothes on inside out. "It's done. What? Do you think I'm some kind of amateur?"

"You know where he is?" I'm sure the surprise showed on my face, but I could not believe that I was finally making forward progress.

"Of course I know where he is."

"Where?"

Jordan sat back and smiled. "It's gonna cost you."

"Are you kidding?" I'd already paid for this guy's train ticket. If he thought I was going to fork over hundreds of dollars for his information, he was crazy.

Okay, maybe he wasn't. I needed to know where Paris was. I had no clue where I'd get the money, but I'd find a way.

"Of course I'm kidding," Jordan said. "Information should be free. That's the whole reason I exist. I take from others the information they try to keep to themselves, and I distribute that information as I see fit."

"So where is he? Nicole said.

Jordan turned to Nicole, and his eyes lit up. "Turns out it was almost too easy. The guy's famous."

"Famous?" I said, hearing the disgust drip off my words.

"Yep," Jordan said. "He's a famous poet."

"Poets can be famous?" I mean, I knew dead poets could be. Like Homer. Or Virgil. But I didn't think any poets who were still alive were anything close to being considered famous.

"Guess so, because this guy is," Jordan said. "Alexander is his middle name. His full name is Paris Alexander Parsons. You heard of him?"

I shook my head and tried not to let my face react at the use of his name.

"Yeah, well he lives in a giant house on Lake Travis. Has more money that any of us could ever dream of having."

Rich and famous or not, I could still kick Paris' ass any day of the week.

"Paris Parsons?" Nicole said, and she started googling on her phone. "He must have a website."

I leaned over her shoulder so I could see her screen and was greeted by a picture of none other than Paris himself, gazing off in the distance like he was contemplating the deeper meaning of life. There were a bunch of tabs that said things like THE POET HIMSELF and PLACES THE POET SHALL BE.

"He has a new book of poetry coming out," she said, clicking on the NEWS FROM THE POET tab.

"No one will buy it," I said.

"Are you kidding?" Nicole said. "He's a best-seller. Do you know how hard it is to be a best-selling poet?"

"Well, he could have gamed the system," Jordan says. "Happens all the time. In fact, I've had at least one request to do just that."

"Did you make him a best-selling poet?" I asked Jordan.

"No way, man," Jordan said. "I'm not much about the poetry."

"Check this out," Nicole said. "He's having a private reading. At his house this Friday night. Invitation only. Since you know him, Achilles, you could call him up and get us on the guest list."

"Us?" I said. What? Did she think we were all in this together?

"Definitely us," she said. "When I get a picture with this guy, my friends will never believe it."

I blinked a few times as her words made sense. Or at least

made sense as best they could. "You want to get a selfie with Paris?"

She nodded and smiled.

I guess she could do that right before I ripped his arms off.

"Look, I know him," I said. "But like I said, we're not on the best of terms. I can't just call him up and get us on the guest list."

"Oh, really?" Disappointment filled her voice.

"He actually tried to kill me," I said.

She smacked my shoulder. "Get out of here."

"No, really," I said. "Did you not hear the part where I told you he was a douchebag?"

This time is was her turn to pause. "He seriously tried to kill you?"

I nodded.

"Is that what happened the other night?" she said. "When you were bleeding all over my car?"

"You bled in Nicole's car?" Jordan said. "That's not cool at all."

"I got it cleaned," I said. "Anyway, this was when we were younger."

"When you were kids?" she said.

"Something like that."

"So maybe he's over it," Nicole said.

Paris was like me, from another age. An age of heroes and epic wars. He would never get over it, just like I would never get over it. It was an immortal feud to go along with our immortal lives.

"He's not over it," I said. "So the reading is out."

Nicole did that thing where she twisted her lips up and I could tell she was thinking.

"What? You don't think I can get you on the invite list to some lame poetry party?" Jordan said.

"You can?"

Jordan crossed his arms and sighed. "Of course. Do we really have to go over this again?"

Nicole smacked me again. "See. I told you he was good. You can do formal attire, right? These kinds of parties are fancy."

Oh, I could do formal attire. I looked damn fine in a tux.

"I'll see what I can scrimp up," I said. "But you can't use my real name."

"Why do you want to go anyway?" Jordan said. "You're obviously not a fan. And I don't think you're going to walk in there and kill the guy, unless I've totally pegged you wrong."

"You don't peg me for a killer?" I said.

"No, not really," Jordan said.

If I had to, I would kill Paris. It would be much neater though to deliver him to the council of the gods and have them dole out his punishment. But that wasn't an answer I could give Jordan.

So I kept it simple. "This guy stole something from me. And I want to get it back. So I'm thinking that during the party, when he's occupied, I can search the house."

"Oh, I see," Jordan said. "You want me to get his house schematics, too?"

He wanted me to say yes. He was dying for it. Right then, the train whistle blew. Jordan jumped in his seat.

I bit my lip to keep from laughing.

"Only if you think you can," I said.

"Of course I can," Jordan said. "I mean, you know, I'll probably have to dig through a few layers of encryption at the security company that manages his property. But it won't be a problem."

"Great." I thought everything was settled.

But then Jordan said, "What can you do for me, Achilles? I'm an Information Specialist. I trade in information."

I looked to Nicole, but her face gave nothing away. She and I were going to have a serious conversation about this whole meeting once it was over.

"Information?" I said. "I own a gym."

"Heroes Gym," Jordan said. "I did some research on you."

Any research this guy did on me online was golden. I had nothing to hide.

I nodded. "It's great gym. Just over on Guadalupe. We could set you up with some personal training sessions, maybe for a month. See how you like it."

"I found some interesting things out about you," Jordan said, and for some reason, my palms got all sweaty.

"You've owned the gym for ten years," Jordan said.

I nodded. "I bought it right out of high school. College wasn't really my thing."

"Where'd you get the money to buy it?" Jordan asked.

"Inheritance," I said.

Jordan nodded as if this answer checked out. I knew it would. According to records, I'd inherited a chunk of change when I turned seventeen from an uncle who died, and I'd used it all to buy the gym.

"It's a nice gym," Nicole said. "We offer yoga."

"We?" Jordan said.

"Nicole teaches there now," I said.

This seemed like the first real piece of new information so far in the conversation. "You're teaching yoga, Nicole?" Jordan said. "What about looking for a job? I thought we were going to look for something together."

She shrugged. "I'll look for a job eventually. But for now, this is fun."

"She's really good at it," I added, thinking it might help.

Jordan's face darkened. Guess not.

"I want information, not personal training sessions," he said.

"What kind of information?" Sure, I had information, but it wasn't the kind I could share with anyone.

"You be thinking about that, Achilles," Jordan said. "I'll get you on the list and get you details from the security company about the party. And after that's all done, we'll talk."

I could hardly wait.

Nicole leaned over and hugged him, and once again, he hugged her back, way more intensely than he needed to.

"You are the best, Jordan," she said.

I plastered a smile on my face because I didn't want to lose his promise of help. Then they continued to talk to entire rest of the ride, which was a good ten more minutes. The second the rickety little train made its way back to the station, I jumped out. I was more than happy to check the entire episode off my to-do list.

"We should get together sometime," Jordan said to Nicole once they got out.

"That would be so much fun," Nicole said, and it seemed like she genuinely meant it, even though spending any more time with this guy would have made me want to disembowel myself. But I kept the fake smile on my face, suffered through watching them hug once more. Then Nicole and I walked off, leaving Jordan alone at the train station.

"Oh my gods," I said once we were out of hearing distance.

"What?" Nicole said.

"That guy."

Nicole smacked me. "Jordan's sweet."

"Sweet on you," I said.

"Oh, come on," Nicole said. "He is not."

"Are you stupid?" I said. "Because up until this point, I didn't think you were, but seriously?"

"Shady Grove?" Nicole said, trying to change the subject. She pointed in the direction of the restaurant. "We can walk."

I checked my watch. It was only seven. I wouldn't meet Ares until nine.

"Sure," I said. "But it's your treat unless you can admit he likes you."

"I won't admit anything of the kind," she said. "Jordan and I are just friends."

I kept my mouth shut about it until we'd gotten our beers.

"So Jordan . . . ," I said.

"You can't be serious," Nicole said. "We've known each other for like seven years. We're totally just friends."

"Does he know that?" I said.

"Of course he knows that," Nicole said.

"How do you know? Did you ask him?"

Nicole looked like she was going to pull my hair out. "I don't have to ask him. I just know it. I worked with tons of guys."

"They probably all want to go out with you," I said, having way more fun with this conversation than I ever could have imagined.

"None of them want to go out with me," she said. "We're all professionals."

I rolled my eyes.

"It's true," she said. "Guys and girls can work together and not like each other, you know."

"If you say so."

I enjoyed dinner a lot more than I ever would have thought. So much so, that I was almost willing to stand up Ares just to stick around for a little bit longer. But I guess Nicole wasn't having the same level of fun, because come eight thirty, she told me she had to go.

"You never admitted that Jordan likes you," I said. "So dinner's on you."

Nicole pretended to look aghast. "I never agreed to that deal. And anyway, you owe me. My connections are getting us into the party on Friday."

She did have a point. I pulled out my last bit of cash and left it on the table.

Once we got outside, I walked Nicole back to her car and motioned with my head toward downtown. "I'm going that way. I'm meeting that guy Reese. The one you met earlier today." I don't know why I felt the need to make it clear that I was meeting a dude.

"Oh, that guy," Nicole said. "Seems kind of like a pig."

"I'll be sure and tell him you said that," I said, though I had no intention of doing so.

"Great. See you tomorrow then."

"Right. Tomorrow." I watched her pull away then headed off toward downtown. Ares should be waiting by now, I hoped with answers.

CHAPTER 15

"You're late," Ares said the second I sat down at the table.

"I'm right on time." Ares had never actually specified a time. Nine o'clock was more our assumed time for meeting.

"Right on time for what?" Ares said. "The thunderstorm?"

"Thunderstorm," I said. "Right?"

"You think I'm kidding about this shit? Zeus is pissed."

On cue, thunder rumbled outside, shaking the glassware and chandeliers in the Driskill bar.

I sat there, unblinking, looking at Ares until it finally stopped a good twenty seconds later. I had no clue how this would be explained on the local weather channel. Not five minutes ago, there hadn't been a cloud in the dark sky.

The waitress stopped by our table, dropping off a couple

drinks. If this was Ares' first drink, I couldn't be that late.

"Why is Zeus mad?" I asked once she walked away.

Ares placed his fist on the table after taking a drink. "'Cause the council are a bunch of idiots. They seem to be having a disagreement."

"Hades mentioned something brewing," I said. "Is that what they're fighting about?"

"They fight about every fucking thing they can," Ares said. "And trust me, I'm always up for a good fight. I will jump into a fight whether I'm invited or not. You know that. But I get sucked into the council meetings every time there's even the slightest issue. It's like taking care of a roomful of two-year-olds."

I decided against mentioning that Ares acted like a two-year-old on many occasions.

"Did they get it figured out?"

"Hell, no," Ares said.

"So what's gonna happen?"

"War," Ares said, and shrugged, as if that was the most normal response ever.

"The gods are going to war?"

"Not yet," Ares said. "But it's coming. Trust me. Thousands of years of dealing with this shit, and I know these things."

A war between the gods was not going to end well. The Trojan War had been a mask for deeper issues among them, and an entire civilization had died. I didn't think America would take it very well if a war of the gods erupted again. And as much as I loved a good fight, unlike Ares, war was not my passion. It generally ended up hurting innocent people because of power-hungry rulers trying to take control. The only upside I could see was that if I couldn't get the Furies to stand down, I may not have to be involved in the war. I'd be in Tartarus.

I almost told Ares then, about Paris, about finding out that he was still alive and where he lived. Sure, Ares probably already knew this information, but he didn't know that I knew. And he didn't know that Paris had been the one to take the spear. But I had to find a way to tell him without letting him know I'd gotten Nicole and Jordan involved.

"Someone else took the spear," I said. "I'm sure of it."

"That's what you said," Ares said. "But without proof . . ."

"Can you check the records?" I asked. "Log into the Hall of Artifacts and check for me."

"HOA is locked down," Ares said, taking another long drink from his glass.

"Locked down? Since when?"

"A week or so. Something about needing to upgrade security."

"It's a little late for that," I said. "They should have upgraded security before Paris stole my spear."

Ares raised an eyebrow and fixed his gaze on me. "Paris?"

Deep breath. I could get through this. I just had to pick my words.

"It has to be him," I said. "He hates me. He has every reason to want to frame me."

"He's dead," Ares said.

"Is he? The same way I am?"

"What are you saying, Achilles?"

"I'm saying that if you woke me from my immortal sleep, then a different god could have done the same for Paris. For any of the other demigods."

"It's a theory," Ares said.

"Bullshit it's a theory," I said. "You know it's true, so don't act like you don't."

Ares waved at the waitress. "I know that I need to keep my

mouth shut about things that you aren't supposed to know."

"So I'm right?"

"I'm not saying you're right," Ares said. "And even if you were right, it's not like I'd tell you. Do you know the shit I'd get from the council if I did that?"

"Oh, I'm sorry," I said. "Would you get in trouble? Maybe we could spend the rest of eternity together in Tartarus. That sounds like a great time."

"Don't be ungrateful," Ares said. "I got something for you."

"What? The Furies off my back?"

"No. Not that. It's about Nemesis. I talked to Athena who told me no way in hell could I tell you where Nemesis was."

"Perfect," I said.

"Man, I hate when she tells me what I can and can't do," Ares said. "She acts like she's my boss or something. It gets really fucking tiresome."

Even I was tired of Ares and Athena bickering.

"Anyway," Ares said. "Nemesis oversees the council."

"Of the gods?"

"No, of the unicorns," Ares said. "Of course of the gods."

I bit my tongue because we were getting somewhere.

"And because Athena told me not to, you can sure as hell bet I'm going to tell you where you can find Nemesis."

This was definitely progress. Finally their fights were working to my advantage. "Where?"

"Downtown."

"In Austin?"

"No, in Istanbul," Ares said. "Of course in Austin. At the main courthouse. Nemesis is a judge. Fiftieth precinct. Council of the gods meets there, too, during off hours."

"There's a courtroom downtown used for the council of the gods?"

"Sure," Ares said. "But her courtroom oversees other cases, too. Mostly murder. It's tight security though, so there's no way you can possibly get in. So when you find a way to get in, don't mention I told you."

"You're serious about all this?" I said.

"Don't say I never do anything for you," Ares said.

"You want to talk to her for me?"

"Hell no," Ares said. "I hate talking to Nemesis. Gives me the runs for a week every time I do. She'd got some juju power that messes with your insides."

Perfect. That was just what I needed to add to my list of problems.

"Oh, and one more thing," Ares said. "Meg, the Fury you decided to obliterate . . . she's rematerializing. Slowly. It'll still take her a while. But when she finally does, she is going to be pissed."

"Are you trying to make me feel better?" I asked. "Because if so, you're kind of crappy at it."

"Yeah, yeah, I know," Ares said. "Anyway, find a way to get your ass into the courtroom. Maybe ask Athena."

"I think your sister likes me."

Ares busted out laughing. "Yeah, I think so, too."

"Do me one more favor," I said. "Look into the Paris thing, will you?"

He fixed his eyes on me. "Fine. I'll check him out."

"So you admit that he is around?"

"I didn't say that. Only that I'll check."

I decided not to push my luck with Ares. I'd get my spear back from Paris and I'd find a way to talk to Nemesis. Clear my name. I could drag Paris into the courthouse and drop him on the floor in front of her. And if her unwavering justice was in any way truth, she would see through his lies and know that he was guilty and I was innocent.

CHAPTER 16

I got home from the gym on Friday and showered since eight hours of sweat and body odor covered me. Nicole was set to pick me up at seven thirty. Ethan was just getting home as I came down to grab my jacket.

"You should bring a weapon with you." He pulled something out of his backpack and tossed it at me. It was a knife, which I easily caught by the handle. "Take this one. I made it for you."

I gripped the knife in my hand, feeling the leather handle which fit into my palm so perfectly, it almost became one with my fingers. The blade had to be six inches long, made of some sort of dark metal that didn't reflect the lights around our condo. It reminded me of the same metal my spear was made from. I could almost imagine sliding this knife into Paris' side before he could make a sound. But as sweet as it was, a weapon like this would be impossible to hide.

"Dude, I like it," I said. "A lot."

"It's yours," Ethan said. "There's not another one like it in the world. You can't believe the shit I had to pull together to get the metal right. That metal is crazy proprietary."

My heart rate quickened just looking at the black metal. There was nothing more epic than brand new weapons. "Thanks, man."

"Keep it with you," he said. "I don't like all this shit that's going on."

I didn't like it either. And damn, keeping the knife with me was tempting. But a weapon this nice was something I didn't want to risk losing. I threw it across the room, embedding it into the wall with a solid thud. Ethan cringed as bits of drywall flaked off.

"Security's supposed to be tight," I said. "I'll find something on site." I was more than capable of finding a makeshift weapon. Or I could just wrap my fingers around Paris' neck.

"I could come with you," he said, yanking the knife from the wall and running his finger along the blade like he wanted to make sure I hadn't hurt it.

"Don't you have plans with Elle?" I asked. He'd been talking about her non-stop, and he'd seen her nearly every night.

"She has plans."

"Without you?"

"Yeah, I'm sure it's nothing," Ethan said. "She said she was busy."

Busy flirting with someone else, no doubt. The more I saw her, the less I wanted Ethan to hang out with her. Girls like Elle were more trouble than nine-headed hydras.

"Anyway, you should bring me along," Ethan said. "I could stay in the car and cover your back."

It was tempting. Ethan, for only being a mortal, was a better fighter than most of the foot soldiers back during the Trojan War.

And the weapons that he created were totally badass. But, he was a mortal. And even though Paris was a pansy douchebag, he was still a demigod. I didn't want Ethan to get caught in the crossfire.

"Nah, I got it," I said. "Paris is an idiot."

"An idiot who killed you before," Ethan said.

"Thanks for the reminder," I said. "It's nice to have salt rubbed in the wounds."

"I'm just saying, Achilles, Paris has immortal help, just like you do. Probably Apollo. And unlike you, I'm guessing he's told his patron god exactly what's going on. It wouldn't surprise me if Apollo was actually—"

I put up my hand to stop him. I had the exact same thoughts. If Apollo was helping Paris, then he could be involved in the killing of the Dryads. But accusing the gods, whether they were guilty or not, was not something any mortal should do. The gods had ears everywhere.

"Don't say it," I said. "I got this under control. But keep your cell phone close, just in case."

"If you change your mind, text me," Ethan said. "I can be there in ten minutes."

It warmed me to know Ethan had my back.

"Thanks, man." We clasped hands in the old style, like warriors back in ancient times used to do. It was sign of solidarity. I knew Ethan would fight with me. Fight for me. But I also wasn't willing to risk his life. Not today or any day.

I finished putting on my bow tie and went downstairs to greet Nicole, already expecting the reaction I knew I would get.

She wasn't even looking my way.

I rapped on the window, stirring her from whatever dream world she'd been trapped in.

She unlocked the door. "Oh, that was fast," she said, once I opened the door.

I stood back motioning at my amazing tux. I'd picked it up from the cleaners earlier since I didn't want it to smell like mildew. I hadn't worn it in two years.

"Well?" I said.

"What?"

"Aren't you going to say anything about how I look?" I said.

"You look fine," Nicole said.

"Fine?"

"Sure. Fine." She shifted the car into gear before I'd even had the chance to buckle up.

"Gee, don't knock yourself out with the compliments," I said.

"I just don't want to be late," Nicole said. She smoothed her hair, which come to think of it, looked silkier than I'd ever seen it. And her bare shoulders, though I'd seen plenty of those, too, given her constant yoga attire, seemed even more exposed in her navy blue spaghetti strap dress. Her dark skin looked so smooth that I almost reached my hand out to touch it. Except no way would I do that. I was not going to give her the satisfaction of knowing how sweet she actually looked.

"Not to worry," I said. "You'll have plenty of time to ogle Paris."

"I'm not going to ogle Paris," Nicole said. "And was that your roommate I saw a few minutes ago?"

"Ethan," I said, nodding. "He's a little preoccupied recently."

"Because of Elle?" Nicole said.

"Yeah," I said. "They've been spending a lot of time together."

"She seems really sweet," Nicole said. "And pretty. Like really pretty."

I wanted to disagree, to say that Nicole was way nicer looking, except it wasn't true. Elle was pretty enough to compete with a likes of a goddess, not that I'd ever tell Athena or any other goddesses that. Pissing off the goddesses was good for a one-way ticket to Tartarus.

I kept up the conversation the best I could while Nicole drove, but all I could think about was getting back the spear. That and hauling Paris off to the Underworld to be judged by Hades and Persephone. It wasn't just about clearing my name. I had to keep any more dryads from getting killed. Syke could be next, and that was one thing I could not let happen. After this was all over, I would resolve things with Syke. If she died . . .

No, I wasn't going to even let my thoughts go there. Syke was not going to die. No more dryads were.

We pulled off the road and into a private driveway near the lake. Nicole stopped at the guard desk and gave them our names. Well her name and whatever name Jordan had put me under. Achilles may be gaining popularity on the naming charts in the world, but I didn't want to draw any unwanted attention.

"Nicole Earley and Myron Poppins," she said.

I shot her a look. "Myron Poppins?" I said under my breath.

"Jordan picked it." She tried to look like it was all normal and stuff, but she couldn't keep the little smirk off her face.

"Jordan and I will have words after this." I imagined the words would involve me grabbing the front of his sweatshirt and holding him against a wall . . . oh, wait, I still had a favor I needed to ask him. The retribution for the dorky name would have to wait.

The guard wore a green uniform that looked like it had been sprayed with enough starch to stand on its own. He stood straight, like he had a stick up his ass, and not once flickered anything close to a friendly greeting. He lifted a tablet from the desk and barely glanced down at it, like he didn't want to risk taking his eyes off us for a second. Paris must be pretty paranoid, like always. It's not like poets were prime assassination targets. Unless people hated his poetry so much that they would do anything to make it end.

Even after the guy looked up from the list, he didn't smile.

"Do you two have ID?" he asked.

Nicole handed over two licenses. I guess Jordan had even made me a fake ID. I could become Myron Poppins full-time. The guard studied them with suspicion. Jordan better be as good as he pretended to be. After a solid thirty seconds the guard passed back the IDs.

He pointed down the long driveway ahead. "Follow the path down the hill and around the trees until you get to the estate. There will be a valet out front to meet you."

Damn, this was seriously fancy. Estate? Valet? Here I couldn't afford a new television, and Paris had a valet? I was going to have to talk to Ares about new funding options.

After we pulled away and Nicole had rolled up the window, I said, "That guy needs to loosen up a little. What the hell did he think we were gonna do?"

"Oh, don't be upset, Mr. Poppins. At least we got through."

"Let's stop with the Mr. Poppins stuff before we even start, okay?"

"But it's such a cool name," Nicole said.

"Then maybe you should use it. Jordan better have a good explanation."

"He probably thought it was funny," Nicole said.

"Yeah, that's probably it." More likely Jordan was trying to make me look like an ass. I'm sure it had something to do with his obvious crush on Nicole.

"I can't believe I'm really going to meet this guy," Nicole said.

Oh gods, she still was all dreamy-eyed about Paris. Once she saw how pathetic he really was, that would evaporate.

"Just try to keep it in check, okay?"

Nicole patted me arm. "Don't be jealous, Myron."

I gritted my teeth so I wouldn't say anything I would regret.

A valet took the car, but before we could get into the house, we had to go through the entire security routine again, except this time it also included a pat down.

I stepped back. "No pat down."

"Then no entry," the guard said, and he whistled back to the valet like he was supposed to go get the car pronto.

Nicole smacked me. "Get the pat down, because we are going inside."

And even though we had completely different motivations, we both wanted inside. I spread my legs and let the guard run a wand up and down my pant legs and under my arms. I checked out fine since I'd left the knife Ethan had made me at home.

"You're clear to pass," the guard said.

I flipped him the bird.

His face didn't move.

Nicole grabbed my hand and pulled me inside.

If I thought the outside of Paris' house was fancy, the inside was like a portal into another world that I couldn't even imagine. The entire place seemed carved of marble. There were little alcoves with hidden lights, sculptures of Greek and Roman figures, and chandeliers so large that if one fell, it would take out at least twenty people. Silk curtains draped the floors, and carved furniture festooned every corner.

"He did not make this much money from poetry," I whispered in Nicole's ear. But when I got that close, I couldn't help but notice how amazing she smelled, like a fresh ocean breeze.

"His poetry is really good. I read some of it earlier," she said, turning just enough that her hair brushed my cheek, and suddenly

I couldn't think about anything else except how nice she looked.

"Not that good." I pulled away because I didn't want to distract myself.

We walked through the entryway which was already crowded with other guests and into a living room. A guy walked by with a tray of drinks, and I grabbed two, handing one to Nicole.

"Cheers," she said, holding the glass up.

"Cheers," I said back, clinking glasses with her. Maybe once this whole mess was over, I could let myself think more about her, because as women went, Nicole was definitely worth giving more thought. Not that it would be a good idea to get involved with someone who worked at the gym. But I could figure that out later.

I took a sip of wine and studied the room. The walls were made out of limestone blocks, and dark globes and abstract sculptures offset the white. A massive fireplace stood against the wall, off to the left. And hanging over it was a bow. A massive bow with a single arrow.

Every muscle in my body tensed. This was it. This was the bow Paris had used to shoot me. The very arrow, too. My ankle ached with pain, just from its near presence. I felt it sink into my flesh, tearing through the connecting tendon, ripping apart my life.

"Are you okay?" I heard Nicole say. Her voice sounded far away, like she was down a long tunnel. I never should have brought her here. This entire thing, this immortal battle between Paris and me, had nothing to do with her.

How dare Paris not only still have the bow and arrow, but how dare he display them so brazenly, like he was still gloating over his alleged victory? I fought against the pain in my ankle. I should go over there and tear the bow from the wall. Snap the arrow in half. Let him gloat over that. What right did he even have to display them? Without the guidance and strength of Apollo, Paris never would have been able to pull the string let alone have it drive home.

"Myron," Nicole said.

It didn't even register.

"Achilles," she finally said, grabbing hold of my arm and whispering it in my ear.

"What?"

"Are you okay?"

I gripped the glass hard, wanting to shatter it on the spot but knowing that would only draw attention.

"I'm fine," I said.

"Your face is red," she said. "You look like you want to kill someone."

Oh, how right she was. Not only did I want to kill Paris, maybe I should. Maybe that would be the best end result of this entire thing.

"It's nothing," I said, even though it was everything.

Nicole's eyes followed the path of mine to the bow and arrow mounted on the wall like a trophy. Then they traveled down, toward my feet. Toward my ankle.

I had to get out of this room. Get on with searching the house, looking for the spear.

There was no such luck, because right then, someone walked into the room, toward the fireplace, and used a spoon to ding their wine glass. Other people joined in, making the whole place like a wedding reception. Then the room quieted down. Everyone looked toward the fireplace, toward the bow, so there was no chance I could look anywhere else without drawing attention. I'd missed my chance to excuse myself to the bathroom.

I clenched and released my free hand, trying every technique

Mom and my counselor had ever given me to stay calm. But nothing worked. Nothing until somebody rested their hand over mine.

I glanced down to see Nicole's dark hand resting lightly on top of mine. She brushed my skin with her thumb, and the world seemed to refocus.

The guy introduced himself as the luckiest guy in the world, partner to the world famous poet, Paris. I almost threw up on the spot because the guy seemed so over the top in love with Paris, I wondered how much of it was actual love and how much of it was some demigod power Paris had cast over him. Power like that would explain how Paris had drawn Helen's eye, back before the war. That whole thing had never made sense.

After the guy had said enough nice things about Paris to make even a person with no gag reflex throw up, he said, "And now, it is my highest honor to introduce to you all, the inimitable Paris Alexander Parsons."

The entire room exploded into applause, Nicole included, who got caught up in the awesomeness of it all. Sadly this meant she took her hand off mine, and the anger inside me instantly returned. Then it doubled because Paris glided into the room.

He hadn't changed a bit since the last time I'd seen him. His curly dark hair hung in ringlets, just grazing his ears. His skin was like mine, unmarked by the passage of the years, unblemished by divine means. I took a small amount of pleasure in the fact that he hadn't grown a single new muscle. He was still the scrawny little weasel he'd always been. I had no clue what anyone saw in the guy, but I was apparently the only one because the entire room cheered, and I think everyone in there, guys and girls alike, would have slept with him on the spot given half a chance.

Including Nicole.

I leaned close. "You can't seriously tell me you think he's good looking."

"Are you kidding?" Nicole said.

I guess that was my answer.

The applause went on for over a minute. Paris did that thing where he tried to motion the crowd into quieting down even though he didn't really want them to stop. False humility never looked good on him. Not thousands of years ago. Not now.

Finally they did get quiet, and Paris launched immediately into a poem.

Every single person in the room was transfixed on his voice. It made no logical sense. But then I realized that it didn't need to make logical sense. It was part of him being a demigod, just like my resistance to harm was part of mine.

After the first poem, the applause returned, and I knew I had to get out of there before I had to suffer through yet another bullshit poem. So I gave Nicole a look to let her know I was going, and I kind of ducked backward, through the crowd. I'd find the spear first, and then I'd confront Paris with it.

Most of security seemed to be there to protect Paris, not to guard the house. I grabbed a drink off a tray and acted like I was looking for a bathroom. Since according to Jordan there were twelve bathrooms in the house, it shouldn't be too hard to find one. A security guard stood in the back of the room, but he wasn't looking my way, so I headed away from the party, into the rest of the house.

With each step I took I decided that this place where Paris lived couldn't be considered a house. Money dripped from every crystal light fixture. It wrapped around the motion control light switches. It paved the marble below my feet. How had I not known that he was right here, in Austin? Right under my nose. I couldn't believe that Ares had never told me. The gods drove me crazy at times. Okay, all the time. But it made sense. I was here because this is where Ares was, where the council of the gods apparently was. And other demigods would be here, too.

The house/palace looped around until I wound up off to the left of where we had come in. I hurried across the foyer and over to the stairway, trying to remember what Jordan's schematics had shown about the place. I went over his words in my mind.

"Four levels if you included the wine cellar carved out of the limestone ground. Family and living rooms on the main level. Bedrooms, game room, and media room on the second level. Observatory and sunroom on the upper level. And a small attic for ventilation off to the side of that. Twelve thousand square feet," Jordan had said. "Over seventy security cameras." I could hear his voice now. "Do you realize how many cameras that is? Do we need to try to keep you off those cameras?" he'd asked.

I actually had softened to the guy after that. That was forward thinking, and I realized that even though a guy like Jordan and I would never have been friends organically, maybe having someone like him in my corner wouldn't be such a bad thing. Except for the Myron Poppins thing. That was unforgivable.

I'd shaken my head. "I don't care about the cameras." I was going to confront Paris before the night was through. If Paris didn't want that on his security cameras, he could deal with it.

I closed my eyes and thought through the house plans. Since I was already on the second floor, that's where I would start. I went through each bedroom, looking in closets that were big enough to house entire families. I checked under the beds. I shot the bird at every camera I came to, hoping Paris' guards would have a chance to look through the video footage.

The second floor came up empty, so I continued on to the third. Every place I looked, the sheer ridiculousness of this opulence overwhelmed me. Paris was still the spoiled brat he had always been. His selfishness had started the Trojan War. How was it that someone like him was still alive? If the gods were just, his life would have ended like any mortal, with death. What god would deem his existence worthwhile enough to bring back?

Of course the answer to that was Apollo, a god who I'd managed to piss off on more than one occasion. Apollo had definitely been the one to wake Paris. May have been the one to place him in immortal sleep in the first place. And if Paris had been preserved and woken, then others could have been also. It was an entirely new can of worms I couldn't spend the time to consider right now. Right now, I focused on Paris.

By the time I'd finished looking around on the third floor, rage almost consumed me. Between Paris' very existence and not yet finding the spear, I had just about come to my end. I grabbed a bronze sculpture off a small table, and before thinking about what I was doing, I threw it as hard as I could. Maybe if I wasn't so angry, I would have thought this out more, but . . . well, there was no going back.

The sculpture slammed into the glass of the upstairs sunroom, shattering it, sending a shower of glass everywhere. Instantly, an alarm started blaring, and I knew I had to get out of there pronto or I'd never have the chance to search the rest of the house. Not that I expected to find anything at this point. Paris had probably stashed the spear somewhere else, which made me all the angrier. I was going to have to capture him first and force him to tell me where it was.

I looked out the broken window just enough to see an intermediary roof covered in shattered glass. It was my only chance. I jumped, landing hard on the roof then lowering myself to the ground. I hurried around the corner of the house, out of view of the guards should they decide to look down. I straightened my tux and smoothed my hair and took a deep breath. Then I sauntered to the front door, like maybe I'd somehow just gotten turned around. The guards from the front door were no longer there, maybe called up to the third floor for the investigation, so I went inside, and my breathing slowed. So far, so good. And seeing as how they were all occupied, I could finish my search down here.

"There you are, Achilles," Nicole said, hurrying over to me. "You won't believe this, but—"

She didn't get the chance to finish because right then, none other than Paris himself walked up, with that smug look on his face that I had hated thousands of years ago and hated even more now.

"Yes, there you are, Achilles," Paris said. "I had no idea you were such a poetry connoisseur."

"And I had no idea you were such an asshole," I said. "Oh, wait. Yes I did."

Nicole's mouth dropped open like she could not believe I'd just called her literary hero an asshole. Paris put on a look of mock offense.

"Really, Achilles? After all this time? I thought you would have missed me."

"Hardly," I said, trying to tamp down the anger that was boiling inside me. I needed something else to throw.

"How's the ankle?" Paris said.

"It's fine," I said, trying to play off the comment like it was nothing.

Nicole glanced down at my foot, and I wanted to clamp my hand over Paris' mouth to keep him from saying anything else. I guess he didn't follow the rules of the gods like I did.

"I'm sorry to hear that," Paris said. "After our last meeting, during that little battle, I figured that was the end of you."

"And I figured that you crawled away into a hole to die," I said. "But I guess both of us were wrong."

"I'd be happy to change that," Paris said. "Finally make good what you started."

"What I started?" I said, unable to stop the words. "You were the one who started the entire thing."

"And you were the one who killed my brother," Paris said. "I'll never forgive you for that."

"Your own brother forgave me," I said. "He knew he brought it on himself. And he knew that you were responsible for everything."

Paris shook his head. "No, I'm not." In that moment he sounded so much like a little bratty teenager.

"Have you grown up at all? Even kind of?"

"The gods are the ones to blame for everything," Paris said. "You and I both know that."

There was truth behind his words. When it came down to most of humanity's suffering, it was due to the petty squabbles and jealousies of the gods. I hated to think that was coming again, another battle raging between them. The entire world would suffer. But even still, Paris could have gone beyond that. Tried harder not to play into their games.

"The gods?" Nicole said.

Both Paris and I looked over at her, and the conversation replayed in my mind. Gods. War. Killing.

"Oh, Achilles, you brought a friend along," Paris said. He looked her over from top to bottom, and even with the rage boiling inside me, I could tell he liked what he saw. "A very nice looking friend, too. Maybe you two would like to stay for a drink. It seems all my other guests are leaving. Something about a security breach? I'm sure you don't know anything about that, though, do you, Achilles?"

I grabbed Nicole's hand, dragging her toward me and away from him. She didn't need to be enmeshed in this at all. Bringing her here had been a bad idea from the start.

"She was just leaving," I said. "But I'd be happy to stay for a while." I could get Paris alone and force him to tell me where the spear was and what game he was playing.

"I wasn't leaving," Nicole said.

"Yes, you were," I said. "We can catch up tomorrow." I tried to give her non-verbal signs so she would take a hint and get away from Paris, because now that we were here, talking to him, I realized that I may have brought her into a trap. Paris had stolen my spear, and he had gods on his side. His lifestyle alone made me sure of it.

Nicole planted her hands on her hips. "No, I wasn't."

So much for sticking around for a while. And so much for keeping everything a secret.

"Just tell me where it is," I said. "And tell me why you're doing it."

"Where what is?" Paris said, glancing back into the room with the fireplace.

I stepped forward and grabbed him by the collar of his stupid velvety shirt, pulling him close. Four guards stepped toward us, but Paris waved them back.

"Don't play stupid," I said. "You know what I'm talking about. Don't act like you don't."

"Let him go," Nicole said, pulling on my arm.

"Not until he tells me."

"I can't tell you if I don't know what you're talking about."

"You know," I said, getting right in his face.

"The bow?" he said, motioning with his head back toward the party room. "You must've seen it back there. Over the fireplace."

I shook my head. "Not the bow, and you know it."

"I don't," Paris said, and real fear shone in his eyes. It was right then that I was reminded of what a coward Paris truly was. A coward without even the strength to fire the arrow all by himself. Paris was the kind of coward who, as much as I wanted him to be, did not have the cunning to kill a dryad with my spear.

"The spear of Achilles," Nicole said before I could stop her.

Paris' eyes went wide. "The spear?" He shook his head. "I don't know anything about it."

"You do," I said, though with every second that went by, doubt began to creep in.

"Isn't it locked away?" Paris said. "In the Hall of Artifacts? That's where everything is supposed to be."

"Everything like your bow?" If the gods really insisted all immortal relics be kept safe and secure, then why was Paris allowed his bow and arrow? The very arrow that had nearly killed me.

Paris looked like I'd insulted him. "I got permission for that. From the gods."

I was never going to talk my way out of this one with Nicole.

"How did you possibly get permission?" I'd had no choice about turning over the spear.

His face seemed to relax, as if he thought there was a ray of hope that I wouldn't beat the pulp out of him. "I put together a case for it," Paris said. "Went before the council. Had a bunch of gods petition for me, stating that it was the only way I could protect myself. Agreed to their security requirements."

"Liar," I said.

"No, it's true. It's for protection."

My ass. That was absurd.

"I can prove it," Paris said.

"Oh really?"

He pulled back from my grasp, and I finally let him loose. "Yes, as a matter of fact, I can."

"How?" A huge part of me figured Paris was bullshitting to distract me. But then there was also the part that reminded me he was a coward.

"Try to take it off the wall," he said. "You won't be able to."

"Of course I will," I said.

"No, you won't," Paris said. "That's part of the security. Nobody can remove it. Not even me."

"Not even you," I said. "I call bullshit."

"Okay, fine," Paris said. "I can. But only in the extreme case of an emergency. It's my protection, just like your invincibility is yours."

"So why don't you grab it now?" I said. "Because I will kill you if you're lying."

"I'm not lying," Paris said. A flash of anger passed over his face. "That's the thing. Just try to take it down if you don't believe me. You'll see."

I shot him a look to let him know what I thought of his bullshit story then stormed into the room with the fireplace. It had cleared out completely because the guests were all by now either on their way home or waiting outside for the valet. Even though the room was huge, my strides quickly brought me to the fireplace.

The bow was in reach, perched on a single nail. The arrow rested on two hooks beside it. I reached up, prepared to grab the arrow from the wall and shove it up Paris' ass. But just before my fingers wrapped around it, I stopped. Not because I wanted to.

Not because I believed him. But because I couldn't do it. Couldn't bring myself to actually touch this weapon that had very nearly ended my life. Would have ended my life if not for my immortal mother.

I rested my hand on the mantel and took a deep breath. I could do this. I had nothing to fear from this arrow. Better yet, what I could do would be to yank the thing from the wall and snap it in half right there in front of Paris. Let him mourn that for a couple hundred years. Maybe write some pathetic poetry about the loss.

I reached up . . . and stopped again.

I still couldn't do it. Here I was one of the most invincible people in the entire world, a demigod, and I couldn't even do this simple task.

I was about to turn around and let my rage show, but before I could, a hand wrapped around the arrow and yanked on it.

"That's weird," Nicole said. "He's right. It won't budge."

Without waiting for a reply, she lifted her hand from the arrow and tried the bow, but it didn't move either, no matter how hard she yanked and pulled.

I grabbed her hand and pulled it back. "You shouldn't touch that," I said. She shouldn't even be here, but that was beside the point.

"You weren't doing it," she said. "And we needed to see if he was lying."

We? This was definitely going to merit a discussion later. Much later.

As much as I hated for it to be the case, it seemed like Paris was in fact telling the truth. I turned, and he was standing there gloating. It made me want to smack the smug look right off his face, but security guards still flanked him. Who were these security guards anyway? Just regular guys or some sort of immortal guards of the gods?

"I told you, Achilles," Paris said. "And I also told you that I don't have your little spear."

"But there's video footage of you taking it," I said.

"Taking the spear? That's impossible."

"Except it's not," I said. "We downloaded the video from the archives and saw it for ourselves."

Paris took a step back and looked like he'd been insulted beyond reason. "Well then, it's obviously fake."

"It's a pretty good fake then," Nicole said. "Because it looks exactly like you."

"What can I say?" Paris said.

"You can say that someone's trying to frame you," I said. "The same way they're trying to frame me. And because of that, I have a trio of Furies after me, trying to haul me off to hell."

"Sounds like you have a problem," Paris said, brushing his hands together as if he were done with the entire mess.

I stepped forward. So did the guards.

"You're going to have a problem if you don't . . ." I stopped. I wasn't sure what I wanted from Paris at this point. If he didn't have the spear, I couldn't bring him in front of the gods.

"Achilles, you've already ruined my party," Paris said. "So if you'd be kind enough to get the hell out of my house, I'd appreciate it."

I flexed my fingers but held them at my sides to keep from punching him.

"This is not over, Paris," I said. "I don't trust you. And you know what? I never will. So you can live here and pretend that you're peaceful and all that bullshit, but I'm not buying it. You know more than you're telling me."

"Oh, Achilles," Paris said, and he plastered on the most patronizing look in the universe. "You need to move past your anger.

It's only hurting you."

So I punched him, because if my anger was hurting me, it might as well hurt him, too.

Damn, it felt great when my knuckles connected with his nose. Bone cracked under the blow. My anger wasn't hurting me at all. In fact, it made me feel fantastic.

Blood gushed from Paris' nose, and the guards were on me in a second. Paris dropped to the ground and covered his nose with his hands. The guards tried to manhandle me, but they were no match for my strength. I shoved them away.

"What should we do with him?" one of the guards said, making another pathetic attempt to grab my arm.

I pushed him off and gave the universal 'Get the Fuck Away from me' sign. I was not in the mood. They looked from me to Paris.

"Get. Him. Out," Paris managed to say from under his hand.

"Don't worry. We're leaving." I shot him one more heavy dose of hatred. I wasn't sure how it was possible, but I despised him more now than I had back in Troy.

"I cannot believe you did that," Nicole said as I grabbed her hand and pulled her outside. Her car was already out front, doors open, running.

"Damn, that felt good," I said. It was great to be me. I stuffed myself in the passenger seat and slammed the door, leaning my head back to relive the moment.

That's when my high finally settled down because Nicole turned to me.

"So, we got some things to talk about, don't we, Achilles?" she said, drawing out my name.

Reality exploded back into my world. The web of lies I'd been perched on was breaking. I was falling. And if the web caught me, I'd be stuck forever.

CHAPTER 17

I gripped the door as she drove off, wishing I had some knitting needles, except instead of knitting, maybe I'd just pin Paris to the wall with them. That would definitely make me feel better. Nicole didn't say a word as we trailed back up the long driveway and onto the main road.

"So now what?" she said.

Nicole was an entirely different problem. She wasn't supposed to know anything about immortals. It completely went against the rules of the gods. The gods hated when you broke their rules. It put me at risk. But worse. It put her completely at risk. If they found out, they'd dip her in the River Lethe in the Underworld, and her memories would be obliterated. But not just memories of me. Memories of everything. Her family. Her job. Even her cats.

"Can you drop me at my condo?" I said, holding out just the smallest hope that she wasn't nosy and wouldn't want to know anything more.

"Huh," she said, with a small laugh. "I don't think so."

"Umm . . ."

"How about a drink?" she said.

After the fiasco of a poetry party, a drink would be the perfect solution. Sure, I'd had a couple already, but with all that adrenaline pumping through my body, they'd completely worn off. But still . . . drinks with Nicole meant conversation with Nicole.

"I'm not really up for it," I said.

"Too bad, Achilles," Nicole said. "Because you have serious explaining to do. And if you think that I don't already know, then you're not giving me a hell of a lot of credit."

Shit. The clues were all there. Nicole would have to be an utter moron to not have figured it out. Maybe there was some way I could convince her otherwise.

"Fine," I said. "A drink would be great."

"I thought so," Nicole said.

She drove to her house and parked the car, and we walked to a nearby bar called Spiderhouse Café. It was an Austin original decorated with antique furniture and headless statues peeing water into basins and plenty of beers on tap. We ordered a couple of local brews, then Nicole grabbed my hand and dragged me through the place to the back where she found an unoccupied table near a fountain.

"Dish," she said, taking a giant sip of her beer.

"We should've gotten the pitcher," I said, downing half my beer in one sip. I wasn't sure an entire pitcher would be enough.

"Yeah, you aren't lying," Nicole said, and she flagged down a waitress.

I tried to sink into my chair and replay the night, to see what I could have done differently. To see how I could convince her that she didn't know anything.

"Achilles," she said, snapping her fingers in front of my face. "Time to talk."

Time to talk. Also time to figure out what the hell to do next.

"Do you think he was lying?" I asked. It wasn't that I was trying to change the subject or avoid the inevitable. I just needed to know. Wanted her opinion. Her honest opinion.

She let out a huge sigh, like she'd been holding it in for the last hour, and she shook her head. "It's not like I'm some psychology expert. Hell, I'm a computer engineer. I work in ones and zeros. But that guy, Paris . . . I don't think he was lying. He seemed too . . ."

"Pathetic?" I suggested.

Nicole actually laughed. "Yeah, something like that."

I drained the rest of my glass. "So he didn't meet your expectations of rock star poet?"

This made Nicole laugh even harder. "Well, he is cute, but he's also just kind of . . ."

"Pathetic," I said again.

"Yeah. Pathetic. And I'm guessing if he really did have that bow and arrow at the same Hall of Artifacts place, and he was able to get them, then there would be video footage of him doing it. Someone could have taken that video and used it to overlay the real video footage of the spear."

I put my head in my hands. "People can do that?"

"People can do anything with videos and computers," she said. "But we're not really talking about the main thing here, are we?"

"The main thing," I said, letting the alcohol fill my brain. "My LARPing?"

She set her glass on the table and trailed her finger around the top. Once. Twice. Then she looked me directly in the eyes.

"Who are you? Really?"

The moment of truth. Or not. I had to come up with some plausible scenario which would totally explain everything because the LARPing wasn't cutting it.

"Who do you think I am?" I said, praying that maybe she was stupid.

She grasped her glass but didn't pick it up. "I think . . ." She shook her head. "It just doesn't make any sense."

She knew. There was no doubt about it. She knew as sure as I knew that I was royally screwed.

"What doesn't make sense?" I asked.

"You can't be Achilles," she said. "I mean, not that Achilles."

"Which Achilles?" Maybe she didn't know jack about ancient history.

She rolled her eyes. "The one from the Trojan War. What? Do you think I'm an idiot?"

Fine. She knew about ancient history.

"There was an Achilles in the Trojan War?" I said, falling down the path of lying.

"Yeah. There was," Nicole said. "And every single thing I've seen or heard in the last week and especially tonight makes me sure that you and the Achilles from then are one in the same."

"But that would make me thousands of years old," I said. "And we agreed that I was only twenty-eight years old."

She stared me right in the eyes. She didn't let my gaze go. Then she said, "I think you're older."

The seconds ticked by. The waitress brought the pitcher, but neither of us even looked up. I tapped my teeth together, thinking of the right words to say.

"So you realize that what you're saying is impossible," I said. "Nobody lives that long."

"I know it's impossible," she said. "But I also know enough about logic to realize that there isn't any other solution to the problem. You have to be the same Achilles. Just like Paris is the same Paris. It's the only thing that makes sense, even though it doesn't make sense. So please, just tell me now, truthfully, if I'm totally crazy. Actually, don't, because, really, at this point, nothing you say is going to convince me any differently. So just tell me how you did it. How it's possible? Is this like some crazy time travel thing you have going on? Is that what happened?"

I shook my head. "Time travel's not real."

She laughed. "You're telling me what's real or not?"

Good point.

"I'm not a time traveler," I said.

Before I knew what was happening, Nicole grabbed the fork from the table and stabbed my hand where it lay flat on the table. Really hard, too, like she was trying to amputate it.

"What the hell are you doing? Trying to kill me?"

"No. Just proving something."

"What? That they shouldn't give forks to crazy people?" I said.

"Tell me this. If you really aren't that Achilles, then why aren't you bleeding right now?" She motioned at my hand which was unblemished. The fork wasn't nearly strong enough to make it through my skin.

"Because that was a lame attempt to stab someone with a fork," I said. "Really lame."

"It wasn't lame, and you know it." Then she struck again, even harder this time. "See, no blood. It didn't even break your skin."

"I have thick skin," I said, but even I didn't believe myself.

She didn't say a word. Just put the fork down and took a long sip of her beer. And I had to admit that the way she licked her upper lip when she was done was totally hot.

What was I thinking? Here I was about to be completely outed, and I was thinking of how good she looked? But she did look good.

"What are you thinking?" she said.

If only she knew.

"I'm thinking that you have an issue with silverware," I said.

She tilted her head and waited.

"I'm thinking you're some kind of history buff?"

Nothing.

"I'm thinking—"

She put up a hand. "Lie all you want. I know the truth. And you know what? Maybe if you don't tell me what's going on, I'll just call up Jordan and have him hook me up with his connection from the *Austin Chronicle*. I bet they'd be all over this story." She motioned her hands like a news banner. "<u>Ancient Immortals Roam the Streets of Austin, Texas</u>. That has a nice ring to it. I bet I could go viral with this story. *Washington Post. New York Times.* You're going to be famous."

That was the last thing I wanted. She might not know it, but it was the last thing she wanted, too, if she wanted to remember who she was in the morning.

"You're not really going to tell the newspapers are you?" I said, trying to act all cool, like it didn't bother me.

"Do you want to test me to find out?" She took another sip of her beer.

I had never been in this situation before. Never felt so trapped.

"You're blackmailing me?" I said.

"Call it what you want," she said, and smiled like she'd just won at poker night. Which I guess she had, because no matter if the news believed her or not, this was not the kind of story I wanted to get out. The gods would kill me, her. Their damage control would be epic.

I took a deep breath. "If I tell you the truth, do you swear not to go to the news? Not to tell anyone, actually. Because if you tell anyone, your life is over. Like seriously over."

She laughed.

I didn't.

And she said, "No shit?"

"No shit."

"What do you mean by over?" she asked.

So I told her about the whole memory thing and the river in the Underworld that would make her forget.

"Oh," she said, and her face got really serious.

"That's why you can't tell anyone," I said. "Like not a single soul. You can't even tell your cats."

Nicole blew out a long breath. "Okay, Achilles, I promise. I won't tell a soul. Not even Jordan."

"Not even Jordan?" I said. "Of course not Jordan. I told you not to even tell your cats. Why would you tell Jordan?"

"I wouldn't tell Jordan," she said. "That's what I'm saying."

"But are you guys that close?"

Nicole blinked at me like I was crazy. "Are we talking about that now? Seriously?"

Oh gods, she was right. How had I gone down the Jordan trail?

"Of course not. That's great if you and Jordan are good friends. I don't care. Just don't tell him."

"I won't," she said. "So go on. Tell me."

So I did. I told her about who I was and where I'd come from and how I'd been in immortal sleep for thousands of years, thanks to Mom. She hung on every word, asking a couple questions here and there, like she wanted to make sure she got all the details right.

I talked for like five minutes straight, and when I was finally done, she said, "So is it true?"

"Is what true?" I asked.

"The ankle thing. Will it really—?"

"Kill me?" I said. "Yeah. Tested and true, thanks to Paris."

"He really shot you?" she said. At least she kept her voice low so no one else nearby overheard.

I tightened my fists. "Yep. The very same arrow you saw. I couldn't bring myself to touch it." Which still bothered me. I should have been able to snap that arrow in half.

"Well, if it helps, I'm glad you punched him," she said.

I laughed at that. "Yeah. Me, too. But I should mention that even though he fired the arrow, he didn't aim. Apollo aimed for him."

"Apollo," she said slowly. "That's just crazy. I can't believe the Greek gods are really alive."

I thought of all their pain-in-the-ass rules and tricks and ir-ritations. "Alive and annoying."

Nicole sat back and drained her beer. I filled it again from the pitcher while she thought through everything I'd said. Greek gods. Immortals. The Trojan War.

"What are you thinking?" I asked her this time. Maybe, if I was lucky, she was thinking about how hot I was.

"I think you're crazy," she said. "Completely flat-out crazy."

"Yeah, maybe."

"And I don't want to forget how crazy you are," she said. "So I'm not gonna say anything to anyone."

That at least, out of this whole evening, was a bright spot.

"But you owe me, Achilles," Nicole said.

"Owe you what?"

"I don't know," she said. "I just know you owe me."

CHAPTER 18

We ordered another pitcher and finished that. Nicole grilled me with one question after another, and I did my best to answer them without divulging every messy detail of the immortal world. Then I walked her home. I really hoped for some kind of invitation in, since we were all up close and personal now, but that didn't happen. She waved me off from the sidewalk and went up the front path to her house alone, leaving me standing there looking like an idiot. But what did I expect? Her to be ready to jump my bones since she now knew I was immortal?

Okay, fine. The thought had crossed my mind. Whatever.

About a block away from her house, I was finally able to drag my mind away from Nicole enough to think about my next steps. If Paris didn't have the spear, then somebody had faked the records, like Nicole had said. But who would have done that? Who else would hate me that much that they'd want to sentence me to Tartarus forever?

I was going over the list of everyone who'd ever taken issue with me—most of whom were long dead—when the tree about ten feet away from me shuddered and groaned as if something had slammed into it. I was near the medical center, in one of the wooded areas, and I immediately jumped back and looked around for something to use as a weapon. This was way too soon for Meg to have reformed. Except it wasn't Meg. It wasn't any of the Furies. Instead Syke slipped from the tree, taking human form. She took a tentative step toward me and away from the giant Ficus tree behind her.

"Syke!" I said, and relief flooded through me. It was one thing to hear she was alive. It was totally another to see her here, tonight, alive and well. "Thank the gods you're okay."

I took a couple steps in her direction, but she immediately backed up and pressed herself against the tree, blending into it right before my eyes until there was nothing but bark and foliage.

I jumped back. "I won't hurt you, I promise."

Nothing happened.

"I swear it on my life, Syke. Please."

The wind blew through the leaves of the tree, making them quake. I remembered this sound so well, every time I used to visit Syke. We'd always meet near Zilker Park, out past the Nature Center where people rarely came. I closed my eyes and imagined that time had turned backward and that none of this had happened with the dryads. The leaves rustled, and I tipped my head back and breathed in the heady scent of her tree.

A full minute went by before the tree began to creak. I opened my eyes in time to see her morph once more into her human form. Syke was tall, probably five-nine, with a willowy frame and tan skin the color of the figs her tree bore. Her long hair was brown with a green tint, reflecting the leaves of the tree. At any given moment, there might actually be leaves stuck in the tangles of her hair, like there were right now. I wanted to reach forward and pull them free, like I'd done so many times in the past, but I held back. I couldn't scare her again.

Syke reached out, like she wanted to touch my arm, but then she touched her fingers to her mouth.

"I swear that I won't hurt you," I said again, because I wanted her to know this more than anything.

She gave a small nod. "You look really nice, Achilles, but you have an awful lot of clothes on." She stepped forward, running her hands over her skin from top to bottom. As she did, clothes materialized. Not substantial clothes. A brown halter top and a brown skirt, just enough to cover her.

I glanced down, realizing that I was still wearing the tux. Most of the times I'd been with Syke in the past had been the spring and summer, when her tree was bursting with new life. Winter was when dryads were supposed to be hibernating. Saving their energy for the next growth. Not running from a murderer.

"I can take some of them off it you want," I said, trying to lighten the mood. I gave a small smile, hoping for a reaction like I used to get, back before we'd ever had our disagreement.

Syke shook her head. A few of the leaves fell to the ground. "Why are you doing it, Achilles?"

"Doing what?"

She crossed her arms over her chest and took a step back. "Killing the dryads."

Oh gods. She really thought I'd done it.

"Why would you do it?" she said. "We trusted you. Mother Dryad trusted you."

"It's not me, I swear," I said, even though my heart cracked knowing that she thought I was guilty. "I would never harm a dryad. You know that."

"How would I know that?" Syke said. Tears welled up in the corners of her eyes.

"Because you know me," I pleaded. "You know who I am. I would never do that."

A single tear slipped down her brown face. "I thought I knew you. I thought . . . never mind."

"You thought what?" I said.

"I thought we were going to be together," Syke said. "Forever. I know it's silly. My sisters told me I was wasting my time with you. But I defended you. Even back then. And when you got so angry. The things you said . . ."

The night of our fight replayed in my mind. My stupid anger had ruined everything. I'd said so many things that weren't true. And I'd hated myself even as I said them, and yet I couldn't stop. And then, once Syke was gone, I wanted to take back every stupid word. Except I couldn't.

"I am so sorry about the fight," I said. "I thought about it for days. Weeks. I tried to get in touch with you so many times. I looked for you. I went to all the places we used to meet. You never showed up."

"I thought I could trust you," Syke said. "But you lied to me. You betrayed me."

I had. There was no way around it. I'd lied to Syke, and when she'd confronted me, I'd twisted it around to try to make it seem like she was to blame.

"I'm so sorry. It was completely my fault. My anger . . ."

"Your anger is the problem," Syke said. "It's always been your problem. And even now, you say that you're sorry, but how would

I ever know that you wouldn't act the same way again?"

"I've been working with my mom," I said. "She sent me to a counselor." I left out the fact that I'd skipped more counseling appointments than I'd gone to. "And I would never harm a dryad. Never, even if my life depended on it."

Syke looked backward toward the tree and ran a hand over the bark. "You lied before. How can I believe you now?"

"Because it wasn't me," I said, willing her to believe me. "Someone is setting me up. I would never harm you or any of your sisters. I swear it."

She continued running her hand along the bark, closing her eyes as if she were deep in thought. I hoped it would be thoughts of my innocence.

"I was the one who found her," Syke finally said. "Carya. She was the first one killed. I found her in the clearing, on the ground, near her tree. Her arms were stretched out, like she had been trying to reach it, maybe to find safety within. But it was too late. Nectar leaked from the wound in her chest. Her tree had already started to wither."

"I'm so sorry, Syke." I wanted nothing more than to move forward and hold her in my arms to comfort her.

"And the wound . . . ," she said, and looked directly at me. "Mother Dryad said there was no mistaking it."

The accusation in her eyes floored me. She believed I'd done it. She actually thought I was guilty. My stomach twisted as the reality sunk in.

"I don't want to believe it, Achilles," Syke said. "But there is no other explanation."

"There is," I said. "Someone is setting me up."

"Who would do it?"

"I thought it was Paris, but it's not."

"Then who?" Syke said. "Give me something to work with. Something to convince Mother Dryad that you're innocent. I want you to be innocent so much. To not have done this horrible thing."

Damn it. Why couldn't Paris have actually been the one who'd taken the spear? It would have made sense and it would have proved my innocence. I had to figure out who was doing this. I had to find the spear. And I had to stop any more dryads from getting killed. Because if any more did—if Syke did—I wasn't sure how I could keep my rage under control. It would destroy me and anything that got in my way.

"You have to promise me that you'll stay safe, Syke," I said. "You can't come out anymore."

"I know," she said. "I'm not supposed to be talking to you even now."

"Then why are you?" If she truly thought I was guilty, then why would she risk it, especially after our fight? Unless she still cared about me.

Syke's face softened. "If you are innocent, find a way to prove it. Please."

"I will."

"I miss you, Achilles," Syke said, and her face betrayed her. Her hand reached out, almost like she was going to touch me. I wanted to feel her hands on my skin. To be back with her once more. For our fight to never have happened. But she pulled her hand away, quickly letting it fall to her side.

"I miss you, too, Syke," I said, and I held my ground, not moving toward her. I didn't want to scare her. I would keep her and her sisters safe. I had to.

She gave a small nod and stepped backwards, into the tree, blending in with the bark and leaves until there was no visible sign of her anymore.

Maybe I shouldn't have, but I stepped forward then, once she was gone, and I placed a gentle kiss on the bark of the tree before walking away.

* * *

ETHAN HAD FALLEN ASLEEP ON THE SOFA WITH the game controller on his stomach, but I slammed the door loudly enough to wake him up. I figured telling him it was the same sofa Athena and I had sex on wasn't required information. I didn't want to have to buy all new furniture.

"How was the party?" he said, squinting through his sleep haze. "Did you kick Paris' ass?"

"Kind of," I said, and I filled him in on what had happened.

"Rat bastard doesn't have it?" Ethan said.

"Nope. And he has no clue where it is." I'd been sure Paris had the spear. Absolutely certain. And now I had nothing. Nothing except a cloud of guilt hanging over my head and a bullseye painted on my ass. I only had five days before my time was up and the Furies would be back. And if their timekeeping skills didn't improve, they might show up at any time. The whole thing with Paris had been my best chance.

"That sucks."

I grabbed us each a beer from the fridge and sank down into a chair across from him. "Why did Ares tell you about the immortal world? Was he not worried about . . . you know . . ."

"Getting my memories wiped?" Ethan said. "Hell, no. I don't think Professor Reese even gave that a thought."

How very considerate of him.

"He was all about the weapons, you remember?"

"Yeah, but what made him tell you? He could have just hired you to make shit for him." I wanted all the details, even the ones that might not have seemed all that important at the time. Maybe it would help with this mess I'd gotten into with Nicole.

Ethan took a long sip from his beer. "He never told me why. He just told me."

Again, so Ares-like.

"Okay, fine," I said. "But you must have a theory. Why do you think he decided to actually tell you? And what did he tell the other gods?"

"I have a theory," Ethan said. "A theory that he didn't want any of the other gods to find out how good I was. You know, you may not believe it, but I'm pretty exceptional when it comes to weapons."

"I believe it," I said, eyeing the knife he'd made me. It sat on the coffee table, and I picked it up and held it in my fist, letting the leather once again connect with my skin.

"Right. So back when I was in college, remember how Professor Reese was my professor for Modern Warfare senior year?"

I nodded. That was the first time Ares had introduced me to Ethan. And after Ethan had left, Ares had said, 'Pretty smart guy, right?' I hadn't thought much about it at the time until the semester ended and Ares told me I had a new roommate.

Ethan set his beer down and rubbed his eyes. "He told me to come by after class one time. Said he wanted to ask me about some of the newer metals we were using in my Materials Engineering class. I didn't think anything of it, so I went by his office, even though it was way past office hours. I climbed the stairs. No one was around. When I got to his office, his was the only light on in the entire place. I walked over and was about to knock on the door, except then I looked through the little window."

"And . . . ," I said, because he paused to take a long sip from his beer.

"And," he said, wiping his upper lip. "Professor Reese was in there talking to a centaur. A freaking centaur. This guy had the head, shoulders, and chest of a man, but had a horse's body. Like on first glance, I was sure it was fake, because that shit's just not normal. But then the more I looked, I was like, that is a damn fine fake. And then this centaur says something else, nods to Professor Reese, and starts toward the door. Of course he kind of stops when he sees me, looks to Professor Reese, then shrugs and continues on, opening the door and walking out right past me, all four feet clattering on the linoleum floor in rhythm. I guess my jaw was probably down near my chest because Professor Reese said something like, 'You don't see that shit every day, do you?' And I tried to act all cool, like seeing a freaking centaur didn't blow away every image of reality I had. Except I'm a horrible actor. And it was a centaur. Dude. A mother-fucking centaur. So I went in and shut the door and crossed my arms and waited. And that's when he told me."

"He didn't try to lie his way out of it?" I asked. I'd heard the centaur story before. Never knew which centaur it was. But what I never got was why Ares had just fessed up. He was a god after all. He should have been able to use some kind of god woo-woo to make Ethan forget. But instead, he violated the rules of the gods and told him. Just like that.

"Nope. He laid it out. The gods. The world of immortals. And he asked me to start making weapons for him. Only for him. Said he needed somebody like me on his side. Even put in a good word for me to get the job at Camp Mabry."

"And none of the other gods know, do they?" I said.

"Only Athena," Ethan said. "But she is his sister. Pretty sure she was pissed when he told her, but she still vowed to keep it quiet, although, man, she never smiles and always gives me the stink eye when she visits the armory."

"Athena visits the armory?" I said.

"Professor Reese gave me permission to make her a couple things from time to time, too," Ethan said, like it was no big deal. "But she's always studying everything I'm working on really hard, like she's trying to find flaws in it. Not that she's going to. I make some pretty sweet shit."

Funny the things I had no idea went on in the world of the gods.

"You do know your entire memory will be wiped if the other gods find out, right?" I said.

"I try not to think about it," Ethan said. "And it's not like Professor Reese gave me a choice. Who am I gonna complain to anyway, if I wanted to complain?"

It was a good point.

"Why all the questions? You don't like having me as a room-mate?" Ethan said.

"You bitch too much about me leaving my dirty clothes all over the condo."

"That's 'cause you're a slob," Ethan said.

"Yeah, well you're an anal-retentive Einstein, but you don't see me complaining."

"So what's up, then?" Ethan said. "What's going on?"

I let out a deep breath. There was no getting around it. "Nicole knows."

"About . . . ?"

"Everything," I said. "She knows who I am. Who Paris is. That the gods are real."

"Oh," Ethan said. "That shit's not good. You can't let them

find out."

"You don't think I could even tell Ares?" I said. If I could tell Ares, it would make everything so much easier. I wouldn't have to dance around explanations and half-truths.

"Are you kidding?" Ethan said. "Have you seen him get mad?"

I laughed at that. I had seen Ares so mad, I thought the entire world would die as a result. I'd seen him grab countries by their hilltops and threaten to turn them inside out. I'd seen him grow into the size of a titan and stroll through battlefields, wiping out entire armies. If Ares was angry and someone got in his path, they risked extinction. This new Ares—the one that had woken me up from my immortal sleep—was only a small shadow of the one I used to know. It was almost like right now he lay in a dormant state, building up an army, waiting to strike.

"You have no idea," I said. "But Ares told you. He already broke the rules of the gods."

Ethan shook his head. "Do you really want to risk some girl's entire existence? Just find a way to work around it. Do what you need to do."

"I need to find out who's framing me," I said. And I had to do that within two days.

"Weren't you going to talk to Nemesis? What about that?"

"Yep, that's next on my list," I said. "I just need to make a couple arrangements first."

* * *

I TEXTED NICOLE THE NEXT MORNING, WAIT-ing until eight o'clock because Ethan told me that I should never text anyone before eight o'clock.

"It's just rude, man," he'd said. "People like to sleep in on the weekends."

"People who have Furies breathing up their asses don't like to sleep in," I'd said, but I waited until eight just the same.

"What's Jordan's number?" I texted to her.

She replied right away. "Can't tell you."

"haha," I texted.

"no really," she said. "You remember how paranoid he is. He'd kill me if I gave you his number."

I gripped the phone in my hand, taking a couple deep breaths so I didn't break it. What the hell kind of conspiracies did Jordan think the world had brewing? He had to get over being such a drama queen about it.

"can you have him text me?" I finally texted back.

"you can give me your message and I'll pass it on," Nicole said.

Even though I'd told Nicole everything last night, I didn't want her to get any more involved. It had already gone too far. If there was a way to take back everything I'd told her, I would have done it faster than Hermes could deliver a message to his next door neighbor.

"please just have him text me," I said.

"fine," was her only response. I could almost see the chilly look on her face when she typed it. But whatever. This was my issue, not Nicole's.

Ten minutes later my phone buzzed with an incoming text. It had a bunch of extra digits and came through with only the city as an identifier: Moscow.

"don't try to trace this number," the text said.

I was willing to bet my favorite shield that this was Jordan. I had no clue how he'd gotten it to come through under a Russian number, but I didn't care so long as I was able to talk to him.

"like I would know how, " I texted, opting against calling him some sort of insulting name although *paranoid nerd* came to mind.

"what do you need?" he texted.

"I need you to get me on jury duty," I texted.

"it's your obligation to do jury duty. I'm not getting you removed," he texted back.

"not off jury duty. On jury duty."

There was a longer pause this time, like he was trying to figure out why anyone in their right mind would go out of their way to get on jury duty.

"which court and when?" he finally texted, so I gave him the details.

"you think you can do it?" I said.

"there's no reason to insult me," Jordan texted, which I guess meant that he thought he could. So I hung tight and waited a couple hours like he told me to. Sure enough, right around noon I got another text, this time from a different number in Russia.

"you're in. Show up on Monday at eight and bring your id I gave you."

The Myron Poppins ID? I was going to kill him.

"thanks, " I texted.

"what is the hall of artifacts?" was the next text that came through.

Nicole had not told Jordan, had she? Seriously? I was going to kill her, too.

"no clue what you're talking about, " I texted back.

`"challenge accepted,"` was the only response.

I didn't text back because I didn't want to push it. But I also cringed when I thought about Jordan poking around in the stockroom of the gods. Maybe he'd forget about it.

Okay, who was I kidding? The guy had gotten his text messages to come through Russia. I was digging myself deeper with every second that went by. But I'd worry about that after I got rid of the Furies. One problem at a time.

CHAPTER 19

"You can't wear that to jury duty," Ethan said Monday morning, right before I walked out the door.

I glanced down at my jeans and gray hoodie. "What's wrong with this?" I couldn't have looked more normal. I'd even put the jeans with tears back in the pile.

"It's the hoodie, man," Ethan said. "A gray hoodie is a sure way to not get selected."

"What's wrong with a gray hoodie?"

He shook his head. "It's what dopers wear. All winter. Gray hoodie and jeans."

"Dopers?"

"Yeah, you know . . ."

I put my hand up. "I know what you mean, but dopers? What kind of word is that?"

"Ah, it's what this old retired general at Camp Mabry is always calling the high school kids who stumble through the museum. He tells me to watch out for the dopers. That they always mess with shit."

"And do they?"

"Always." He grabbed our last box of Flower Scout cookies from the counter. "Also, if you see any of those Flower Scouts selling cookies, get me some. Those caramel things. Oh, and those peanut butter sandwiches."

"Give me some money," I said, since I had none except for a handful of coins I shoved in my pocket.

Ethan pulled a twenty from his wallet. "That should get you five boxes. And don't eat any."

"I get one box." I took the twenty.

"Don't say I didn't tell you about the hoodie," Ethan said, just before I shut the door on my way out.

I used some of the change and caught the bus downtown since I didn't want to risk being late. Even at that, it was painstakingly slow. I swear it stopped at every corner to pick up at least five new people, all the way from Fifty-First down to Twelfth. By the time it finally pulled up next to the courthouse, I'd been jammed in the far back of the bus, so I had to say 'Excuse me' about twenty times just to get to the door. This was the last time I was going to take the bus anywhere, ever.

Getting into the courthouse was more of an adventure than Odysseus trying to get back to Ithaca. The line to get through security moved at the pace of continental drift. Some guy covered in piercings set off the metal detector ten times. The girl behind me smelled like vomit. I closed my eyes and took deep breaths so my annoyance wouldn't turn into full-on rage. Finally, it was my turn to pass through. I dumped my keys and phone into a bucket and went through.

Of course it beeped.

"You sure you emptied your pockets?" the guard said.

I patted them again to be sure and nodded.

"How about the hoodie pocket?" she said.

Damn hoodie pocket. I found the handful of coins in there and dumped them in the same bucket.

"Hoodies are never a good idea," she said, eyeing the coins extra hard like she thought they were made of gold.

Wait a second. They were made of gold. Somehow I'd shoved the remaining coins Hades had given me in my hoodie pocket. Before I could stop her, the guard grabbed one.

"Don't see these every day," she said, and bit it, like she was some Miner Forty-niner checking to see if it was twenty-four carat.

"No, you don't." I grabbed the other coins from the bucket and held out my hand, waiting for her to give the final coin back to me.

"I think I'll keep this one. You got a problem with that?" She fixed her eyes on me and her mouth thinned into a line.

Fuck. I did not have time to argue over a coin.

"Just go ahead and keep it," I said. She could use it when it was her turn to head to the Underworld. I didn't care. I was in.

"Thanks." She flipped the coin around on her hand, until it disappeared like a magic trick. Just like Charon had done.

I scanned the area, looking for the nearest stairwell, but was met by a sea of people sitting on benches against walls, cruising down the hallways, waiting for the elevator. I had two minutes to get to the courtroom or else I'd be late for the jury duty I'd gone out of my way to get assigned to.

I ran for the stairs, which were off in the corner, and hurried up the five flights. Nemesis' courtroom was on the top floor. There had to be some alternate way in here. I couldn't imagine the gods mixing with mortals in such vast numbers. Thankfully, most of the people had not come up to the fifth floor. There were only maybe fifty people who were just now filing into the courtroom. I got in line behind the last person, some girl with dreadlocks, a halter top, and so many tattoos I wasn't sure what the original color of her skin actually was.

When I got up to the door, I stopped dead in my tracks. There was Athena, dressed in a gray business suit and looking all kinds of sexy, holding the door open.

"Well, isn't this a surprise?" she said, glancing at the tablet like she was trying to find my name.

Surprise wasn't even the start of it. Athena worked here? In the courtroom of Nemesis? She could have told me. She could have gotten me in to talk to Nemesis without having to bother with this jury duty crap.

"Yeah, surprises all the way around," I said, holding out my phone with a screenshot of my summons. "Myron Poppins reporting for jury duty."

"Myron Poppins," Athena said. "Oh, let's see, here you are on the list. Did you bring your umbrella with you?"

I ignored the Mary Poppins reference. I'd already heard it at least fifteen times from Nicole on Friday. "Do you think you could just—?"

"No getting out of jury duty, Myron," Athena said. Then she closed the door behind me and walked to the front of the courtroom.

I took my assigned seat, which was sandwiched between the dreadlock girl and a guy in a full-on Starfleet uniform, complete with shiny black boots and an emblem sewn on the front. The second I sat down, he turned to me.

"I always wear my uniform for formal occasions," he said, like I wanted to know that.

"What the hell are you talking about?"

He motioned at himself. "My Starfleet uniform. It's very important to look my very best in public. Since I do hold the rank of captain, my actions reflect on the entire Federation of Planets."

"You don't want to get picked, right?" I said.

"I have no idea what you're talking about." He turned back to the front.

"Dude, do you have a pipe?" the dreadlock girl on the other side of me said. "I could really use a hit."

"Uh, no, I left mine at home," I said.

Did everyone in this entire courtroom except me want to get out of jury duty?

"Too bad," she said. "I'll have to wait until they give us a bathroom break."

She hadn't seriously smuggled pot in, had she? Here I'd been stopped for pennies in my hoodie pocket and she was the one who had weed?

"I'll share if you want to join me for a hit," she said.

"Oh, tempting," I said. "But I . . . never mind." I didn't want to bother explaining that I wanted to get selected. This was the only chance to get face time with Nemesis. Or at least I thought it had been before I saw Athena here. Speaking of which, she watched me from the front of the courtroom. If she made sure I wasn't selected, I was going to challenge her to a sparring match, which actually would be a ton of fun come to think of it.

"All rise," Athena said.

It took at least twenty seconds because some of the jurors tried to explain why they couldn't rise because of religious reasons or crap like that, but a couple well-chosen words along with an invisible wave of immortal awesomeness from Athena and they were on their feet, ready to bow before Nemesis. Once everyone was standing, Nemesis walked in.

I'd never seen Nemesis before. I had envisioned Nemesis to be giant, almost titan-like, with her head nearly touching the ceiling and her stern hair pulled back into a bun so tight it cut off any circulation to her head. Instead, a short black woman walked in.

When I say short and black here, let me try to explain. Nemesis only reached about half the height of the doorway. That's what I meant by short. Her jet black hair was spiraled around in some stiff beehive do, lending another full foot to her height. Her skin was black like ebony without a single wrinkle, and her dark eyes looked like black stones that had been placed in her eye sockets. It was as if midnight itself was encompassed in this tiny woman who couldn't have been over four-foot-eight. That's what I meant by black.

She walked to her bench with her black robe trailing behind her, sitting without looking at the courtroom or the potential jurors. She studied the stack of papers in front of her and scanned the room. Her eyes settled on me. Blackness flashed in my mind, and immediately images of death and destruction filled my vision. I stood in a battlefield, surrounded by the dead. And when I raised my hands, blood covered them, dripping to the ground. At my feet was the body of Hector, Paris' brother, dead at my hands. Guilty, yes, but so was I. Guilty of so many things.

The vision vanished and the courtroom reappeared. I took a deep breath, forcing away what I'd seen. Nemesis still had her eyes fixed on me. Athena leaned over and whispered something into her ear. I assumed it was about me, but maybe it was about the case, because Nemesis picked up her gavel and tapped it on her bench.

Athena next told us about the case, which as luck would have it turned out to be a murder trial. Then the most boring three hours of my life ensued, with the lawyers on both sides asking every single one of the fifty jurors the same questions. What do you do in your spare time? What are your views on capital punishment? Have you ever filed a lawsuit against a doctor? What television shows do you watch? Do you fold your toilet paper or wad it?

Okay, they didn't ask that last one, but it wouldn't have surprised me if they had.

"Myron Poppins," Athena called when it was my turn to stand. I could almost hear the snicker under her breath.

I smiled at her and stood and answered as best I could, giving the answers that I thought would get me selected. When Nemesis held court over the council of the gods, did they get asked the same boring questions? Like, if the Furies ever did manage to drag me in, and I had a chance to stand before the court, would they be dealing with monotonous logistics like this?

"You can sit now, Myron," Athena said, and she continued on.

Finally they finished with juror number fifty. It was then that Athena called out the numbers of those selected.

My number, thirty-one, was not called. Nemesis left the room. The lawyers left the room. Then Athena instructed us all to leave.

Are you kidding me? After all that and I didn't even get picked.

I immediately looked to Athena who winked at me as she held the door for the jurors to file out. But I was not going to leave. I crossed my arms and waited until everyone left.

"I need to talk to Nemesis," I said once the last person was through the door. "Now."

"Myron," Athena said.

"It's Achilles," I said. "And seriously, Athena. Do you not understand that there are dryads being killed? Killed, Athena. Not injured. Not immortal sleep. Killed. And even though I'm not the one doing it, if I'm hauled off to Tartarus for something I'm not doing, then I can't be here to stop it from happening again. More dryads will die. And I cannot let that happen? Do you not get that?"

She watched as I spoke, not moving until I finished.

"That's what I needed, Achilles," she said, crossing her arms.

"What?"

"That. What you just said."

"What part of it?"

Athena finally smiled, despite what Ethan said about her never smiling. "That you're more concerned about the dryads than yourself. That's the part I'm talking about."

It took a few seconds for her words to register. "Wait. You think I'm some kind of asshole who doesn't give a crap about anyone else?"

"Well are you?" Athena said.

"No. I'm not. And I'll thank you for not thinking so."

Athena stepped forward and got right in my face. "You know, Achilles, I like you more each time I see you." She reached down and placed her hand on my lower abdomen.

Wrong place, wrong time, no matter how much I wanted it to be different.

"Can you get me in to talk to Nemesis?" I asked, forcing myself to step back even though no part of me, especially my lower half, wanted that.

"She's already waiting for you," Athena said. And she led me to an office and opened the door.

CHAPTER 20

Inside the office, Nemesis hovered five feet off the ground.

Yes, hovered. Two giant wings extended behind her, so white they almost reflected the sun coming in through the high windows. They contrasted sharply against her otherwise black appearance, as if the two opposite ends of the color spectrum had joined. And in that moment, both the presence and the absence of color glowed, casting light around the entire room. Athena closed the door behind me, staying out in the hallway.

Though I was a demigod, immortal myself, I dropped to my knee and bowed my head, and the awesomeness of her presence overwhelmed me. I almost started spewing honorifics but managed to stop myself. Still, I'd never been in the presence of a primordial entity. Compared to her, the Olympian gods like Ares and Athena were no better than mortals.

"You can stand, Achilles," Nemesis said, and finally I was able to lift my head and look at her. She drifted to the ground and settled in her chair. "Do you want some coffee? I grind the beans myself."

I opened my mouth, but before I could even respond, a pure white mug appeared in front of me, almost as white as her wings. Nemesis raised a pot and poured coffee so black that it looked like ink into the white mug. Next to the mug was a coin. The same gold coin the guard had taken at security. They'd known I was here from the second I walked in the door.

"Thanks," I managed. "Coffee is good."

"It's all organic," Nemesis said. "Smells great when I roast it."

Maybe she roasted the beans in the fires of the Underworld. Maybe she had the Furies do it for her. I sat in the chair across from her and took a sip even though it was scalding hot because Nemesis held her black eyes on me, watching me the entire time. I smiled and nodded and set the steaming mug back down. Then the world shifted into blackness, like it had done back in the courtroom. But instead of a battlefield, I stood in a forest, in the darkness of night. I paced around a clearing, keeping my eyes away from the center of the clearing, afraid of what I knew I would see.

"You have to look," a voice that sounded like Nemesis seemed to say.

But I didn't want to look. I didn't want it to be reality.

"Do it now," the voice said.

I stopped pacing and turned to the center of the clearing. There lay the body of a dryad. Death leaked from the wound in the center of her chest like sap, pooling to the grassy ground beneath her. I stepped closer, needing to look at her face. Her brown hair splayed out around her head, tangled with leaves. But before I could take another step, the weight of an object in my right hand stopped me.

I lifted my hand. Gripped in my fingers was the shaft of a spear. And the wound in her chest could not be mistaken for anything else.

The blackness vanished. I clutched the armrests of my chair, and my breathing was heavy. I'd been there, in the vision, standing over the body of the dead dryad. But that had never happened.

"I—"

"I know you didn't do it," Nemesis said.

She knew I didn't do it? Then what the hell was up with the vision?

"She was dead," I said, still trying to get my breathing under control.

"Someone's killing dryads," Nemesis said, as casually as if she'd told me her coffee beans came from Brazil.

"And it has to stop," I said. "Which is why you have to call the Furies off me."

In a quick motion, Nemesis flicked her wings and folded them in. They disappeared under her black robe as if they'd never been there. "Which is why I can't call the Furies off you, Achilles."

"That doesn't make any sense." I hated to question her judgment, but the logic left me no other choice.

Nemesis tightened the muscles in her jaw. "Well, someone has to pay for what's happening."

"But not me," I said, my voice filled with determination.

"Why not you?" Nemesis said, matching my tone. Then the world flickered around me again.

I was back on a battlefield, slaying anyone who came my way. I cut down one enemy after another, until no one was left before me.

"Were they all guilty?" the voice of Nemesis boomed. "Did

they all deserve to die?"

"This is war!" I screamed in the vision. My hands gripped my sword, and I scanned the area looking for more enemies to vanquish. Battle lust raged inside me. This is what I was born for. The fight is what I craved, even if it meant my own death. I had to have it.

"This is death," Nemesis said. Across the battlefield I saw her, standing in a chariot drawn by griffins with a whip in her hands. The chariot raced for me.

I widened my stance and prepared for her.

The vision vanished, leaving my heart pounding as Nemesis watched me.

"Why shouldn't you be the one to pay the price, Achilles?" Nemesis said. "You've done more than your share of killing in the past. You've taken lives that didn't deserve to be taken. You've been the cause of suffering."

"I hate war more than anyone," I said. "But in war, people die. It's the way of things."

"And my justice is the way of things, too," Nemesis said.

"But my death won't be justice. This isn't about past deeds. This is about now. About dryads dying."

I wrapped my fingers around the handle of the mug, forcing myself not to grab it too hard. If this was how Nemesis acted when she thought I was innocent, then if she believed I actually had done something wrong, I would burn for eternity. I took another sip of the coffee and set the mug down. It was almost hot enough to burn my lips off, but I didn't complain.

"You don't agree with my justice?" Nemesis said, and the edges of the room started to blacken again, as if another vision was coming.

I fought it, unblinking and fixing my eyes on her, even though my insides twisted.

"No. I don't agree with your justice," I said, gritting my teeth to keep the vision from taking over. "You know I'm innocent, and yet you sent the Furies after me. How is that justice?" This was maybe not my best choice, but it the only one I had.

"Here's the thing, Achilles," Nemesis said. "I know you didn't do this, but I don't know who did."

I nearly knocked the mug of coffee over. "How can you not know who did?"

She pressed a finger to her black lips. "That is an entirely different problem, one that we're not going to be talking about right now."

"Okay. Fine. So you don't know who took my spear or whose killing the dryads. So what? I just suffer the fate because someone has to?"

"That's one option," Nemesis said.

"What's another option?"

"You tell me, Achilles. Why would I send the Furies after you?"

"I don't have any clue," I said.

"Then think it out," she said. "Tell me what happened?"

I blew out a deep breath and thought through everything I knew.

"The Furies attacked me," I said. "I fought them. They almost killed me, but I managed to defeat one of them and buy some more time, just barely."

Nemesis raised an eyebrow. "Just barely?"

"Yeah, just barely. They were trying to kill me. I hardly got out of there without them ripping my ankle off."

"Right," Nemesis said. "Anyway . . ."

"Anyway, I fought them off, and then I asked Ares what the

hell was going on. That's when I found out about the spear."

Nemesis nodded but didn't say a word, so I went on.

"But I didn't have the spear. Someone else did. And I figured that I had to find out who."

"Yes," Nemesis said. "That's it. That's exactly it."

It was like I was part of a different conversation because I had no idea what she was talking about.

"What's it?"

"You had to figure out who," Nemesis said.

That's when it finally dawned on me. "You're using me to do your dirty work."

"It's not that dirty," Nemesis said.

"Furies are trying to kill me. I got bit by a deadly snake."

"And survived, once again," Nemesis said. "Do you see a pattern?"

If she was trying to say that the Furies were going light on me, she was cracked.

"You want me to figure out who's killing the dryads," I said.

"Exactly. Athena said you were smart."

My face flushed at the thought of what other things Athena had said about me.

"Why me?" I said. "Seriously? You have hundreds of gods at your command. Why do you need me to figure this out?"

"Because, Achilles, the actions of demigods attract far less attention. If I put Athena on this, every other god out there would take notice. You? Hardly anyone is watching."

I let that go. Better to be humbled than to be center stage to every folly of the gods. I took another sip of the black coffee while I figured out what to say next. It wasn't like I could argue with Nemesis. If what I'd seen really was the Furies taking it easy, then I'd be doomed if they upped their game. But this entire situation also sucked. I was some pawn? Did Ares have any idea? Did Athena? She'd been scouring my condo, looking for the spear, and she worked here, for Nemesis. Unless that had been part of the plan all along so I would be further convinced that my life was almost over unless I could prove my innocence. Or maybe she just wanted to have sex with me.

In your dreams, I could almost hear her say.

"Fine. You got what you want," I said. "I am definitely trying to figure out who's doing this. So in the meantime, can you call the Furies off?"

Nemesis drummed her short dark fingers on the desk. One. Two. Three. Four. One. Two. Three. Four. "No. I can't do that."

I wanted to stand up and get right in her face and demand that she do it. But I was not an idiot with a death wish.

"Why?"

"Because you'll stop trying," Nemesis said.

"I won't. I swear. I have to stop any more dryads from getting killed."

"It's not enough, Achilles. You need the Furies."

I swallowed the words I wanted to say, that I needed the Furies like I needed a hemorrhoid. And instead, I said, "Can you make their attacks less . . . violent?"

"No again," she said. "In fact, each attack will get worse. To give you added motivation."

"I don't need added motivation," I said.

"We all do, Achilles," she said. "So if I were you, I'd find that spear before whoever is doing this strikes again. Oh, and another thing. Don't tell any of the gods about this."

"Not even Ares?"

"Not any of the gods," Nemesis said. "That's the thing. I don't know who's behind this. Which is why the Furies are after you.

It's a perfect little circle. But if you tell a single god that I think you're innocent, it ruins the perfect little circle. Which is why, like I said, don't tell any of the gods."

"What about Athena?" I said. "Does she know?"

"None of the gods," Nemesis said. "Oh, and next time, don't wear a hoodie. It shows so little respect."

Nemesis smiled, exposing brilliantly white teeth that sat against her black lips. Her wings extended in one quick motion, and she floated back into the air.

Almost like she'd been listening outside, the door opened, and Athena's head appeared.

"Time to go, Achilles," Athena said.

I'd had enough of this entire situation. I was no plaything for the gods, and yet somehow, here I was. I was going to find the spear and figure out who was setting me up, and then, once that was resolved, I was never going to get in the path of the gods again.

I turned, not bothering to say goodbye to Nemesis. I had to find the spear.

CHAPTER 21

I got to the gym by noon. Keith gave me a high five when I walked in the door.

"Seven new sign-ups this morning, all from the yoga babes," he said, slapping his hand on the clipboard on the counter. "Well, two of them were yoga dudes, but they were pretty swole."

Yoga babes. I was sure Nicole would love that.

"Oh, and that one babe who you said was dating your roommate? She wants you to call her. She left her number."

"Thanks," I said, taking the slip of paper he handed me. Like I was going to call Elle. Talking to her here at the gym was one thing. Calling her, on the actual phone, was another and was not going to happen.

"So that's it, right?" Keith said. "I can go?"

I actually had a million things to take care of, but he was already halfway to the door, kombucha in hand. I'd do what I could from here, and once I closed up, I could do the rest.

"Fine," I said. "Thanks for coming in early."

Keith took a long sip from his drink. "Yeah, let's try not to do that again. Seven o'clock is way too early to wake up."

Oh, to be twenty and carefree and not have Furies and gods using you like a pawn in a chess match. After my conversation with Nemesis, I knew my life would never—no matter how much I wanted it to—be that way.

Almost like the gods were testing me to see how much I could take, my phone rang. It was Mom.

I stared at the screen, hearing her voice in my head, telling me to answer it. So I did.

"You were going to not answer my call again, weren't you?" she said.

"No, of course not," I said. "I just have a lot going on."

"I'm calling to remind you about tomorrow night."

Tomorrow night? I tried to remember what she was talking about but came up short.

"You forgot already," Mom said. "Which is why I'm calling. Dinner. At my place. You and your girlfriend."

Oh, shit. I had forgotten.

"She's not my girlfriend," I said.

Mom ignored this. "Seven o'clock. Don't be late." Then she hung up.

The only positive of the impending Fury attack was that if they happened to attack early again, I wouldn't have to worry about dinner plans.

"Your mom?" Nicole said, walking up beside me. She wore yellow yoga pants and a black top and toweled off her chest and face. She also looked really good. Not that I was looking at her that way. She wasn't my girlfriend.

"Look," I said. "I know this sounds totally weird, but can you go to my mom's with me tomorrow night for dinner?"

"You want me to go to your mom's house with you?"

I nodded. "Just this once. It'll make her really happy. And she'll be totally cool with . . . you know, with everything." Mom would never do anything to put me in danger.

"With everything?" Nicole said.

"Well, not the part about the Furies trying to kill me. That'll kind of piss her off."

"She doesn't know?"

"Hell no. You know how moms are."

"Not really," Nicole said. "My mom left when I was a baby."

"Seriously?"

She shrugged. "Yeah. No big deal. Anyway . . ."

I could tell that she didn't want to talk about it from the way she started scratching Nano behind the ears, so I went on.

"Yeah, well my mom is crazy protective. When she finds out about the Furies . . . You know, maybe we could just not mention it."

"We? You assume I'm going."

"Oh, right. Can you make it?"

"Maybe," Nicole said. "Speaking of which, how was jury duty? Was it everything you ever dreamed of?"

"Not even close," I said. "I need to find the spear, and I'm out of ideas."

Nicole pursed up her lips. "The last place you knew it to be was that hall museum place?"

"Yeah. And did you really tell Jordan about that?"

"Jordan? No. Why would I tell him?"

"Why does he know about it?"

"Maybe because he's smart? You did get him to do the facial recognition."

"You got him to do the facial recognition," I said.

"We did. Anyway, he could have pulled the information off the picture."

"You can do that?" I said.

"You can do anything with computers and technology, Achilles," Nicole said. "If it can be done, Jordan can do it."

"Well that's just great," I said. "Anyway, yes, that's the last place where I knew it to be. I put it there myself."

"Okay," Nicole said. "Where was it before that?"

I shrugged, trying to play it off without sounding completely crazy even though Nicole now knew about the immortal world. "It was with me during my immortal sleep, on the island. And before that, I used it during the war."

"What war?" Jack said, walking over with a dumbbell in either hand, pumping one arm after another as he strode by. He'd upped to twenty-five pounders though it looked like he could drop them at any given second.

"I fought in the Middle East," I said quickly. "And get the weights back on the mat." Jack was tolerable most of the time, but right now I wasn't up for him joining the conversation. The last thing I needed—the very last thing—was one more person getting involved. Jordan even hinting at knowing something already sucked.

"You fought in the Middle East?" Jack said.

"Yeah. With Reese." I hoped just the image of Reese's hulking form would shut Jack up.

But instead his eyes got really big like they did every time Ares came into the gym. "Man, I knew that guy was in the war. With those muscles and the way he takes command. He had to be a general or something like that, didn't he?"

I glared at him, and he finally got the hint and hurried back to the mat.

I opened the front door for Nicole. "Let's talk outside."

Nicole grabbed a water and followed me out.

"Okay, so you had it during the war," Nicole said. "And before that?"

"It was my dad's," I said. "Made special for him by one of the gods."

"Which god?" Nicole said.

Which god indeed. My mind started spinning. Hephaestus crafted items for gods and demigods all the time. It was what he was known for. Famous for. And he had a reputation to uphold. A reputation I was willing to bet he took precautions to protect.

"Never mind," I said. "I have an idea."

"What?"

"Nothing." I needed to visit Hephaestus and see if he could help. And for that, Nicole didn't need to be involved. Hephaestus was a god, and unlike Mom, he might tell the other gods about Nicole.

"Are you kidding me?" Nicole said.

I looked her right in the eye. "Look, it's not personal. It's just that whole thing where you aren't supposed to know. Just don't worry about it. If I need your help, I'll holler."

"You'll holler?" she said. "Are you kidding me? What? Like I'm a dog? You can just holler and I'll come running?"

"I didn't mean it that way."

"Then what way did you mean it? Tell me, Achilles? Because as far as I can tell, there's not a good way to mean that."

"It's just . . ." Gods, this was frustrating. Could she not see that I was doing this to protect her? "I got this, okay."

"Fine, whatever," Nicole said. She stomped back inside and grabbed her stuff, including Nano who scowled at me, too. Then she buzzed past me and left, letting the door slam behind her. Which was perfect. One more problem to add to my growing list.

I pulled out my phone. I could call Mom back and ask her about Hephaestus, but then she'd ask a million questions that I didn't want to answer.

"Can you hook me up with H?" I texted to Ares instead. I didn't need to be any clearer than that. He knew which H I was referring to. He knew because he'd told me on more than one occasion if I ever mentioned his name again, he'd chop my toes off one by one and make me eat them. I'd seen Hephaestus from time to time since I'd woken from immortal sleep, but he was always moving around. I never knew where to find him. Aside from being a hermit who lived under a volcano, he was also crazy paranoid about shit like that.

Ares' reply came almost immediately. It had to be a record for him.

"No, " he texted.

"Yes, " I texted back, not willing to let him get off that easy.

"Why?" came his reply seconds later.

I had no intention of telling Ares, because he'd say that we didn't need to get Hephaestus involved. Ares would rather I got sent to Tartarus than have to depend on Hephaestus for anything.

"I need him to make something for me," I texted.

"What?" Even though they were all one word responses, at least he was replying.

"A shield," I texted.

It was the perfect answer. In addition to having made me a shield in the past, Ares had seen my shield collection in person at the gym.

"Why do you want another shield?" Ares texted.

"For protection. You don't know what's coming," I texted.

Nothing like using his own words against him.

"Have Ethan make it."

"I want H to make it. I want it to match my other one," I texted.

"I hate that guy," Ares texted.

"I know."

"He's an asshole."

"I know."

"A huge asshole."

"I know."

Then he texted me a phone number. Nothing else.

"Thanks," I texted back, but I got no reply. Given the history between Ares and Hephaestus, I should be really thankful for what I got.

I called the number Ares had sent, and someone picked up on the first ring.

A female's voice said, "Who is this, and why are you calling?"

Right, that would be Aphrodite, Hephaestus' wife. Also the reason Ares and Hephaestus didn't get along. Ares definitely had her number.

"It's Achilles," I said, sounding all casual, like I called all the time.

"You're not dead?" Aphrodite said.

For being the goddess of love, she certainly let her worst side shine through when she was around her husband.

"No. I'm not dead," I said. "Why do you think I'd be dead?" She must have heard about the Furies.

"Just wondering," Aphrodite said. "Didn't you die once?"

"Once," I said. "But that was a long time ago."

"But if it happened once, it could happen again," she said, like it was just a fact of life. Which I guess, sadly, it was.

"I'm not planning on letting it happen again," I said. "Anyway, I was hoping to talk to your husband."

"Really? You don't want to talk to me?" Her voice got all pouty, and I could almost imagine her there, hands on hips, acting all hurt and stuff.

"Of course I want to talk to you," I said. "But I also—"

"Why don't you just come visit, Achilles?" she said. "Gods, it gets lonely around here. All Heph does is work, all day and all night. And he wonders why I run around on him. Seriously. What's a girl supposed to do? He's always working. And I get so lonely."

I had no clue how to respond to that, so I just said, "I'd love to come visit."

"Great! See you soon."

"Wait!" I said, before she hung up the phone. "Where can I find you guys?"

"Find us?" she asked like the question confused her. "Oh, wait, you're not a god."

"Right," I said. "Not a god."

"Hmmm . . . ," she said. "Where do you live now?"

"Still Austin. Since Ares woke me."

"Shhh . . . ," Aphrodite said, lowering her voice. "Don't say that name."

"Oh, right," I said. "Since I got woken up from immortal sleep, I've been here in Austin."

"Good," she said. "You can access us through that extinct volcano down south. Pilot Knob. It's near some park. I don't know the name of it. Anyway, that'll get you to us. There's a smooth rock wall right near the volcano sign. You can't miss it. That's the door. I'll leave it unlocked for you."

Pilot Knob. Park down south. I was sure I could find it. "Thanks, Aphrodite," I said. "I'll be there soon."

Then she whispered, "Is he there?"

I knew she was talking about Ares.

"He's not here," I said. And I wondered how long it was since the last time they'd talked or seen each other.

"Hmph," she said. "Well, anyway, see you soon." She hung up.

Since Keith was gone, I couldn't leave, especially since Nicole had already stormed out. So I wiped down all the equipment and ran another couple loads of laundry. Finally, at seven o'clock, I kicked the stragglers out and locked the door. I still had the jeans and hoodie on, but grabbed a hat too since it was freezing. Demeter must've been pissed off about something. I'm sure it was Hades related. I stopped by the condo and grabbed the black knife Ethan had made for me just in case I ran into trouble, hiding it under my hoodie.

I had to check the maps for Pilot Knob since I doubted any rideshare drivers would know where the nearest extinct volcano was. It was down south, near McKinney Falls State Park. So I put that in as the address and figured I'd walk from there. My driver, some girl with dark hair who explained how she was trying to make money to buy a drum set and join a band, tried the entire time to make conversation, but my mind wasn't in it. I nodded and gave a handful of one-word response, but when she finally pulled up to the empty parking area, I almost jumped out of the car.

"Enjoy watching the stars," she called. "And stay warm. It's gonna get crazy cold tonight."

She wasn't kidding about the weather. The temperature had already dropped another five degrees just during the car ride down here. Maybe there used to be a volcano here, but the ground was now as flat as a penny on a train track. The wind whipped by, making the tips of my hair blow everywhere.

Hephaestus was a blacksmith and mined metal and crap, so he always set up shop near a volcano. Pilot Knob must've been extinct for eons, but some geology dorks had taken it upon themselves to put up a wooden carved sign, marking a trail to the old peak. I took the trail, twisting through the scruffy brush, until I came to a small indentation in the ground. There was another wooden sign here. There was also a smooth rock wall on the side of a very short hill. This had to be the door Aphrodite had mentioned.

I pushed on the door. Nothing happened. So I pushed on it again. But instead of swinging open, like it should since Aphrodite said she was going to leave it unlocked, it flickered and shifted until a giant padlock appeared. Instead of numbers and a dial, in the center of the padlock was some complicated gold and silver metal puzzle that made my head spin just to look at it.

I shoved on it again, just to be sure, but it didn't budge.

I stepped back and pulled out my phone. I'd call Aphrodite and get her to unlock it. But before I could tap the number, someone said, "Oh, I love puzzles."

I turned and there was Nicole.

It took me a second to register what had happened, why she was here. The only explanation I could come up with was that she had followed my rideshare driver, halfway across town.

"What are you doing here?" I said.

"I followed you," she said, confirming what I already knew.

"Right, I see that. Didn't I tell you that I could handle this?"

"Didn't I tell you that you were being an asshole?" she asked.

I crossed my arms. "I was not being an asshole. Don't you see that? You're already in deep shit knowing about any of this stuff.

You coming here is only going to make things worse."

"Or help," Nicole said. She brushed past me, walking up to the metal lock. She started running her hands over the seams of metal, twisting and pressing and moving squares around that I hadn't even realized were there.

"What are you doing?" I asked.

"Opening the lock." She shifted a piece and jumped back when a crackle of electricity bit through the night air. "Shit!"

"Are you okay?"

She pressed her fingers to her mouth. "It shocked me."

"You should leave."

She ignored me, once again messing with the metal. It shocked her again, this time sending a visible spark through the air.

"Damn. That wasn't it."

"Just step away," I said. "Before you get killed."

"I'm not gonna get killed."

"You need to go, really," I said. With each second that went by, I was sure the door would swing open and Hephaestus would be on the other side.

"Are you kidding? You'd send me out into the dark of night all alone?"

Shit. She was right. If Nicole got mugged and killed on the way home, it would totally be my fault.

"I'll walk you to your car," I said.

"Maybe later." She turned back to the door and went at it again, tweaking the metal pieces around, fitting them into each other in some sort of pattern. I couldn't follow along. This kind of thing had never been my talent. But from the way her hands moved and the intent look on her face, I was pretty sure it was hers.

"Please, Nicole, just stop," I said, and I tried to tamp down the sense that we were both screwed if Hephaestus found her out here—with me. I had no clue what allegiance he held on the council of the gods or how much of a rule follower he was. Mom always stood up for him, but I had no evidence to back up her claims that he was actually a nice guy, deep down.

"Just give me a minute," she said.

"It might be the last minute of—"

I didn't get the chance to finish because right then she moved a final bar of metal. Something clicked. There was a grinding sound like metal that hadn't been oiled in decades, and the door started sliding to the side.

"I told you I'd get it," she said, a triumphant look covering her face.

I knew I had a look of terror on mine, because behind the door, glaring at us, was Hephaestus. He looked like he was ready to tear off my arms with his bare hands and eat them as an after-dinner snack.

CHAPTER 22

"A mortal?" Hephaestus said, looking directly at me. "Why is there a mortal here?"

Shit. Why hadn't I been able to convince Nicole to get out of here? If people thought I had anger issues, Hephaestus was another story entirely. The guy could make entire mountains explode if the wrong thing set him off.

Hephaestus was barely five and a half feet tall but was equally as wide, all solid muscle. Since the beginning of time, I'd always seen him wear the exact same thing, brown leather pants that came to his knees and a brown leather tunic, both that showed off the massive amounts of hair that covered his arms, his legs, his back, his neck. His left foot which had been injured since birth, turned inward, and was at least two inches shorter than the other, giving him the permanent image of standing on a slant. The only thing about his appearance that ever changed was his hair. It was black and so thick that mice could have lived inside it, but it was always styled differently. Today he wore it in a series of braids that hung to his shoulders, each with a metal bead capped on the end.

"Um . . . ," I said, trying to piece together any words that would get me out of this mess.

Before I could say any more, Hephaestus whipped around and screamed, "Aphrodite!"

Nicole glanced my way and raised an eyebrow. I gave an almost imperceptible shake of my head. Hopefully she'd interpret it to mean "keep your mouth shut."

I couldn't see past the hulking form of Hephaestus, but I heard rustling from behind him.

"Oh, I forgot to unlock the door!" Aphrodite said. "Are they here?"

It took a moment for her words to sink in. They? Like somehow she'd known I wouldn't be alone? But how could she possibly have? I hadn't even known that Nicole was following me. Which she shouldn't have been doing. If I'd known how much trouble she was going to be, I never would have hired her to teach yoga. Except I hadn't really hired her. She'd created the job herself and just shown up.

"Why the hell do we have visitors?" Hephaestus grumbled.

"Because I want visitors," Aphrodite said.

Hephaestus shifted enough that I could finally see a petite shadow coming from behind him. Aphrodite appeared and started pulling on his thick hairy arm.

"Invite them in, Darling," she said. "Don't you remember when we talked about manners?" The way she said *Darling* sounded like it could have been exchanged for Bane of my Existence.

Hephaestus grumbled something that I couldn't understand but sounded kind of like where she could stick her manners. I just hoped we hadn't walked into the middle of a marital dispute.

Despite whatever Hephaestus said, he moved to the side, and Aphrodite's beautiful face appeared, beaming and inviting. Her long blond hair was also done up in braids, except she had hundreds of them, decorated with golden thread and beads that spilled out over her shoulders. She wore a brown leather dress also, like she was trying to match her husband, but it clung to her every single curve and was skimpy enough that it pretty much left nothing to the imagination. Nothing. I had to rip my eyes away from her so Hephaestus wouldn't kick my ass. With his thick muscles, he could snap my fingers off one by one.

"Oh, you two! It is so great to see you. Come in!" She stood back leaving plenty of room for us to walk inside.

Nicole was keeping her shit together like a pro. She linked her arm through mine and pulled me forward, into the side of the rock wall, even though a lot of me wanted to find a way to turn back time and never have come here in the first place. But no sooner were we through the threshold, Hephaestus slammed the metal door behind us like it was a flimsy piece of cardboard. I heard the clicking of all the metal pieces lock back into place, sealing us inside what could only be described as a metal box. Metal walls. Metal ceiling. Metal floor.

"How'd you solve the puzzle?" he asked me, narrowing his eyes sideways at his wife as if somehow she were responsible for that, too.

"Oh, I did that," Nicole said.

Hephaestus took one look at her and started laughing, a giant barreling laugh that almost seemed to shake the metal walls around us.

I held my face steady, but Nicole stared at him like he'd lost his mind.

"You! Please!" Hephaestus said.

"What's wrong with that?" Nicole said. "What? Do you think I can't solve your stupid little puzzle because I'm a girl?"

"Because you're a mortal," he said, wiping his eyes where the corners were wet from laughing. He said *mortal* the same way he would have said toadstool.

Nicole's mouth dropped open, but I elbowed her in the side hoping she'd let it go.

"Mortals can't solve the puzzle," Hephaestus said.

She put her hands on her hips. "Well, I did. You want to see me do it again? Maybe you can make it a little harder this time. Like actually give me a challenge or something. I could have solved that with my eyes closed."

"That's because girls can do anything," Aphrodite said, and she gave Nicole a high five. Then she grabbed Nicole's hand and dragged her forward, away from the door and into the metal construct that led to their house.

Hephaestus grumbled something else that sounded like where Nicole could stick her challenge. I was beginning to get the horrid feeling we'd come at a very bad time.

"Females," I said, hoping to lighten the situation before anything bad happened.

"Don't even get me started," Hephaestus said. "They're the reason for every bit of trouble on Earth."

That wasn't my sentiment, but Hephaestus wasn't really the debating kind.

But then he stopped grumbling and sniffed the air, getting closer to me with each sniff, like he was some kind of hound dog and I was his prey.

"What the hell are you doing?" I said, stepping back so he wouldn't be all up in my personal space.

"What did you bring in here?" he growled, and he sniffed again.

I thought he was talking about Nicole, but then he grabbed the bottom of my hoodie and yanked it upward, revealing the black knife hidden below.

Oh, yeah. That would be a problem.

Hephaestus grabbed the knife. "What the hell is this?"

"A knife," I said, even though he was looking for a better answer.

He flipped it around in his hand, running his fingers over the leather handle and black metal blade. His face actually shifted, just for a moment, into something that resembled admiration, like his eyes got all wide and his lips pressed together, and I got the feeling that he wanted to take the knife apart and study how it was made.

"Where did you get this knife, Achilles?" Hephaestus said.

He could not find out about Ethan and his weapon-making skills or Ares would blow a gasket. Not to mention Ethan's existence would be at risk.

I held my hand out, and he surprisingly passed the knife over. I tucked it back under my hoodie. "I got it from a friend," I said. Not like I owed Hephaestus more of an explanation than that.

His lip curled up into a snarl. "Friend. I bet. I'd like to meet this friend."

That was a meeting that could not happen.

I was saved from having to say anything else because Aphrodite hollered, "Honey, we're not getting any younger here."

"We're coming," I called, hoping the knife subject was dropped. And I started down the hall after them.

I'll give Aphrodite this. She'd done the best she could with the materials at hand. Every single corner, every wall hanging, even the ceiling, was made of metal. There were sculptures and lamps and tables and chairs of metal, different colors and some covered with bright pink and purple cloth like she was trying to dress up the place, but underneath it all was that metal core. Cold. Hard. Unforgiving.

Hephaestus grumbled under his breath and followed after me, and I didn't say another word. Besides the knife, I didn't want to bring up the mortal thing again, since I held out hope that he might forget that minor fact about Nicole.

I wasn't entirely sure how it worked, but lots of tunnels led to their home. No matter what city. No matter where in the world. I figured it was kind of like the Underworld: many entrances, one secret location. We wound through the metal tunnel and ended up in a metal room that was obviously where they entertained company, which I doubted happened more than once a century.

Hephaestus grumbled and motioned to a couple of brown leather chairs, so I sat in one. Nicole was over with Aphrodite near the bar, grabbing a silver tray of copper mugs and a couple bottles of what I hoped was alcohol of some type. I could really use a drink.

Nicole set the tray on the table in front of Hephaestus and me and sat in the chair next to mine. She crossed her legs and, maybe she was acting, but she was totally cool with the whole situation. Like this was just another fun, exciting experience. That was the opposite of what I felt. I sat on the edge of my chair waiting for both our lives to end. That's when I saw her hands shake. So she was nervous. Damn if she wasn't good at acting.

"Achilles, what have you been doing? I hear stories about you all the time." Aphrodite said. She filled all four copper mugs from the bottle. The liquid that came out was solid gold. A metal drink? That was taking the whole mining and blacksmith thing just a bit too far. But if I didn't drink it, she might think I was rude. And being rude to the goddess of love could seriously destroy my mojo forever.

"Well, I've been—" I started.

"Why the hell is there a mortal in my home?" Hephaestus said, cutting me off.

I opened my mouth to answer, but Aphrodite said, "I invited her. And we can talk about it later, Sugar." She dragged out the last part and gave him this overly sweet smile that nearly dripped with honey. Then she challenged him with her eyes, daring him to say anything.

I didn't move a muscle. Why in the world did Aphrodite say that? Why would she take the hit for me? Unless she'd talked to Nicole before, maybe actually invited her. Unless she knew Nicole. But no. Nicole had followed me here. She'd admitted it. Aphrodite couldn't possibly know her. Still, I was not going to say a word. I took a sip of the golden liquid, hoping it didn't solidify the second it hit my stomach.

I felt every drop of it go down my throat, and my body began to tingle. My nerves sizzled at the edges of my skin.

Nicole looked skeptically at the drink. "What is this? Some kind of crazy Goldschläger?"

"Gold what?" Hephaestus said. "Are you trying to insult me, mortal?"

They definitely had not hit it off on the right foot.

"Goldschläger," she said, eyeing him like there was no way in hell she was backing down from someone as rude as him, even if he was a god. "You know that drink that supposed to have real gold flecks in it, but it's kind of a bunch of bunk if you ask me. I mean, I checked on Snopes, and it says that it is real gold, but still, do you know how many people drink the stuff? And it's not that expensive."

Hephaestus stared at her like he could not believe she was still talking. I couldn't either. She was completely rambling.

"Are you telling me that there is another drink with gold in it, mortal?" Hephaestus said. Disbelief filled his voice.

"First off, my name is Nicole, not Mortal," Nicole said. "And second, well, like I said, I don't think it's true. We drank it back in college sometimes, because we thought it was cool. But that was mostly on special occasions. You know, like after really hard exams or all-nighters in the lab or stuff like that."

I wanted to clamp my hand over her mouth to keep her from going on. And who did she use to drink with back in college? Was it Jordan? Maybe they'd known each other longer than I thought.

Aphrodite reached over and patted Hephaestus' hand. "There is another drink with gold in it, Honey. I told you that you need to get out more. But you never want to listen to me."

He turned to face her. "You knew about this, woman? And you still let me think mine was the only one?"

"Oh, please," Aphrodite said. "Don't get your panties all in bunch over every little thing. It's a drink. No big deal. So you don't have the only drink in the universe with gold in it. Who cares?"

"It's really good," I said, because my head felt a lot lighter and everything seemed less stressful. Also, I wanted to diffuse the situation. "Way better than Goldschläger." I drained the rest of the glass and pushed it toward Aphrodite for more.

Hephaestus grumbled something.

"What my husband is trying to say is 'Thank you,' Achilles," she said, filling my mug. "Except once again, manners . . ."

"Go ahead and try it," I said to Nicole. "It won't hurt you."

Nicole still looked at it like it would kill her. "Is this going to digest okay? I used to have problems with Goldschläger the next day."

I silently willed her to just drink it, but damn, she was hard headed, even here in the presence of two gods.

"You are a mortal," Hephaestus said. "So I can't make any promises."

Nicole looked to Aphrodite who said, "It's fine. Truly. And if it's not, we'll find some way to summon your spirit back to life."

"Well that's reassuring," Nicole said. Then she let out a deep sigh and took a tentative sip. We all watched. I wondered if she would drop over dead. I also doubted she would. Hephaestus wasn't that careless.

Finally Nicole smiled. "It's pretty good."

"Better than your mortal drink?" Hephaestus said. "Your fake gold drink?"

"Yeah, way better," Nicole said.

Hephaestus grumbled once again. Maybe it was some kind of thank you. Or maybe it was something like 'I told you so.' I figured either way, I didn't need clarification.

"I came here because I need help," I said, thinking a subject change was in order. No need to talk about proprietary gold drinks or mortals.

"Of course we'll help, Achilles," Aphrodite said.

"No, we won't," Hephaestus said.

"Yes, we will."

Oh my gods, here we went again.

"No, we won't."

"Darling," Aphrodite said. "Can I talk to you in the bedroom for a couple minutes?"

Hephaestus glared at me and Nicole, and pulled himself to his feet and followed his wife, limping on his bum leg as he went.

"Do you think we came at a bad time?" Nicole said.

Her upper lip had the smallest hint of the gold liquid coating it. I had a crazy urge to lean forward and kiss her, to lick it off. I think I even did lean forward. I think she leaned forward, too. My mouth opened, the smallest amount. Her lips were less than an inch from mine, and damn if the scent coming off her wasn't driving me completely freaking crazy. I reached a hand out and put it on her cheek, barely touching her dark skin. Her breath mixed with mine.

"What?" I said, because I couldn't remember what she'd asked.

"Um . . ." She blinked a couple times and cocked her head, like she'd suddenly remembered where she was. "Do you think we came at a bad time?"

The connection was broken, but I wanted to lean forward again. To continue through on the kiss and whatever else came next. Seriously. There was nothing else I could think about. Not when . . .

I shook my head and lowered my hand. What was happening? Because whatever was going on, Nicole was looking seriously amazing. Like I knew she was hot. I wasn't saying she wasn't. But normally I could keep it under check. But here, now . . .

"Aphrodite!" I said in a whisper.

"What about her?" Nicole whispered back.

I motioned with my arms between the two of us because I wasn't sure how to explain it without looking like an idiot. "This," I said. "She's the goddess of love."

Nicole nodded slowly. "Yeah?"

"So she's making me feel all . . ."

"All what?"

"You know," I said, because it seemed like she'd been feeling it, too. "All tingly?"

Oh, gods, I was digging myself in deeper with every word that came out of my mouth.

Nicole sat back and smiled, holding her drink in her hand. "Were you trying to kiss me, Achilles?"

"It's Aphrodite," I said. "That's what I'm saying."

"So you were trying to kiss me."

Part of me—a very small part of me—wanted to look the other way and start whistling, pretending it hadn't happened. But come on. I was Achilles, fiercest warrior in the Trojan War. I was not crawling away from anything.

"Fine, yeah," I said. "I was trying to kiss you."

"And what about now?" Nicole said. "Do you want to kiss me now?"

"Yeah," I said. "I do."

That's when Hephaestus and Aphrodite walked back into the room to join us.

"Oh, you two lovebirds," Aphrodite said, clasping her hands together. "That's so cute."

"That's you," I said, pointing at her. "You and your . . . special powers."

Aphrodite giggled. "All I do is highlight what's already there." Then she sat down.

I did not look back to Nicole. Aphrodite and her little goddess love games were maddening.

"So are you guys going to help me?" I asked.

Aphrodite glared at Hephaestus and waited.

He crossed his giant arms over his chest and cleared his throat. "What do you need help with?"

Relief flooded through me. Thank the gods that he was married to Aphrodite. Otherwise he would have been an impossible miser twenty-four/seven.

I took another sip of the gold drink, trying to pick my words carefully. I had no intention of taking his sort of agreement as a sure thing. "You made something for my father, back before the war."

"The Trojan War," Nicole piped in, like she was proud of herself for having that knowledge.

Hephaestus cast her a glance then looked back at me. "Who the hell was your father? Wasn't he some blasted mortal?"

"Yeah. Peleus. King of the Myrmidons. You made him a spear."

"So what?" Hephaestus said. "I've made lots of people lots of things. Why do I give a shit about this spear?"

Aphrodite placed her hand on his arm. "Language, Sugar."

He gritted his teeth. "Why do I give a crap about this spear?"

"Because I need to find it," I said. "When he died, he passed it on to me."

"And you lost it?" Hephaestus said. "What kind of idiot are you?"

I pasted on the best smile I could. "No. Someone stole it from me."

"Why the hell didn't you put it in the Hall of Artifacts like everyone else did with their shit? If you'd put it there, nobody could have stolen it."

I realized at that point that Hephaestus had no clue what had been going on. He really did live under a rock.

"I told you that you should go to the council meetings, Darling," Aphrodite said, and I cringed. I did not have time for them to get in yet another argument.

"Who has time for council meetings?" Hephaestus said. "Do you have any idea how many things the gods ask of me? Athena wants a new helm. Dionysus needs a drinking cup. Artemis' arrows need new tips. It's one thing after another. Council meetings. They're nothing but a ridiculous waste of time."

"Well, if you had gone, like I asked you to do, then you would have known what was going on with this spear," Aphrodite said, and she proceeded to tell him about the missing spear and how it was being used to kill dryads and how I was the main suspect.

"I didn't kill them," I said to all of them, because if Hephaestus didn't believe me, he could haul me off to the council right here, right now. Of course that would mean he'd have to leave his hovel, so odds were against it. But I did want to be clear.

"Everyone thinks you did," Aphrodite said.

"Not everyone," I said. "Not at all. But the Furies are still after me."

"Oh, the Furies! They're horrible," Aphrodite said. "Their fashion sense is the worst. Those tank tops and hats and who wears boots with shorts these days anyway?"

The Furies' fashion faux pas were the least of my worries.

"Look," I said. "I need to find this spear. I need to prove that it's not me and figure out who it really is."

"Sounds like you got a problem," Hephaestus said. Then he drained his mug and waited for Aphrodite to refill it.

She glared at him. I was surprised she didn't dump the entire bottle over his head. But instead she slid her glass toward him. "Why yes, I would love some more, Angel," she said. Then she smiled.

Hephaestus grabbed the bottle so hard I worried that his meaty hands would bend the metal neck and make it impossible to pour. He filled all our glasses and slammed the bottle back on the table.

"How do I find it?" I asked Hephaestus. "How do I find the spear?"

Hephaestus looked from me to Nicole then back again. He grabbed his mug and drained the entire thing in one huge swallow. Then he set his mug on the table.

"I remember this spear you're talking about, Achilles," he said.

I waited, taking a sip, not wanting to interrupt.

"You know why I made your father—a mortal—that spear in the first place?" he said.

"Because . . ." I thought through the possible reasons. He was a king. He had an affair with an immortal nymph, my mom. He led armies fearlessly into battles. But though all these things were awesome, none of them set him that far apart from other heroes of the time.

"I don't know," I finally said.

"Because he proved himself worthy," Hephaestus said.

I nodded. That made sense.

"Are you worthy, Achilles?" Hephaestus asked.

I looked him directly in the eye, not daring to blink. "Yes. I'm worthy."

Hephaestus' grouchy look finally turned into a smile. "Good. You're going to have to prove it."

CHAPTER 23

Prove my worth. This I could do. I could handle whatever Hephaestus threw my way.

"What do you mean by prove it?" Nicole asked.

"I mean what I say," Hephaestus said. "Is Achilles the man he claims to be? His dad was, but it's not hereditary. He needs to prove his own worth."

Aphrodite snatched the mugs off the table and put them back onto the tray. "Is that really necessary, Darling? He fought in the Trojan War."

Unlike every other time she'd challenged him, this time he didn't bend to her will. "You bet your sweet ass it's necessary. And Achilles isn't scared, are you?"

She opened her mouth, like she might complain about his language again. But before she could, I stood and said, "I'm not scared. Tell me what I need to do."

The gods were known for making mortals and demigods prove their worth. Hercules and his trials. Perseus and Medusa. Theseus and the Minotaur. But I didn't think whatever Hephaestus had in mind would be quite as extreme as any of those situations. I didn't have time for twelve trials or to slay the head from a gorgon.

"Follow me," Hephaestus said, grabbing one of the mugs from Aphrodite's tray and chugging it.

I flexed my fingers and tried to imagine what Hephaestus had in mind. The problem was I really didn't know him very well at all. He was such a curmudgeonly hermit. What did he even know about the world outside of this hole?

He led me down a hallway and to a metal door. "Only Achilles and I go past here, understand?" he said to Aphrodite.

She put her hands on her hips and this time, she was the one to grumble. "Your stupid 'boys only' rule is so out of date. You realize it's the twenty-first century?"

"It's still my rule," Hephaestus said.

"Come on, Nicole. We can watch from up above."

Nicole almost looked like she was about to argue with the two gods.

"I'll catch you in a bit," I said. At least I knew she'd be safe with Aphrodite. At least as safe as one can be with a conniving goddess of love.

Hephaestus placed his giant hand on the door and yanked it open, nearly tearing it from the hinges. "My forge is this way."

His forge? Maybe he was going to see how good of a blacksmith I was. Shit. Blacksmithing was not in my immediate skill set. But I followed him through the door anyway. A set of metal stairs with a railing stretched before us. We started down, descending into blackness. Fifty steps down, light once again began to appear. Flickering light like fire. The temperature also increased, making sweat bead up on my arms. I pulled my hoodie off as we continued down, hanging it over the railing, leaving me in only a tank top. By the time we got to the bottom, the temperature was up a good forty degrees.

Hephaestus picked up a giant hammer and pounded it against a gong that hung near the bottom of the stairwell.

The forge was an underground cavern with lava flowing from the walls as far as the eye could see. The heart of the volcano. The ground was rough stone unlike the smooth metal above. There was a huge island in the middle of a pool of lava, and around it, on the main part of the forge, workers wielded hammers and shovels and buckets and every other imaginable tool that might be needed for mining and smelting metal. At the sound of the gong, every eye in the place turned our way. And I do mean eye. The workers were cyclopses. Giant cyclopses. Each one stood at least eight feet tall and had a single eye in the middle of their soot-covered forehead.

The gong vibrated for at least twenty seconds, and as it did, the cyclopses placed their tools on the ground and got to one knee. They bowed their heads and waited.

"I bring a challenge," Hephaestus called, and his heavy voice boomed around the entire forge, echoing against the rock walls. He put his hand out and I stepped forward. "This is the great warrior, Achilles, hero of the Trojan War, slaying of thousands, leader of the Myrmidons."

This was good. At least Hephaestus was letting them know who they were dealing with.

He went on. "He has drawn blood on countless occasions, some warranted, some not. His ego is the thing of legends."

I didn't mind that part. I'll be the first to admit that I'm not exactly modest.

"He boasts that he can defeat every worker in the forge of Hephaestus, single-handedly."

This I did mind. Grumbling broke out in the forge, and some of the cyclopses fixed their single eye on me with hatred. But I kept my mouth shut.

"He believes none of you are worthy of his battle skills."

More grumbling. What the hell was Hephaestus doing? Try to get me killed?

"And I ask you, my workers, who among you would like to challenge this hero for his boldness? Who among you would relish the victory of defeating one of the world's greatest warriors? Who among you wants to fight for your honor? Tell me who!"

At this every cyclops jumped to his feet and roared.

Inside, my blood thundered, and the warrior that I had to keep hidden in my normal life erupted. I would accept whatever challenge Hephaestus threw my way. I relished this fight.

A bridge extended from the center island. Ten of the cyclopses ran down it, carrying their tools, and formed a circle around the edge of the rock island, like a fighting arena. I cracked my neck and my knuckles.

"Don't kill any of them," Hephaestus growled at me. "Unless you want to take over their work for the rest of your life. Oh, and one more thing . . ."

Blood rushed in my ears, drowning out whatever he had to say. The battle called to me. I didn't ask him to repeat himself. I grabbed the hammer he'd used to ring the gong, and I ran for the bridge.

Battle mania took over as the first cyclops charged me. His skin was dark and covered in hair and he wore nothing except a thick leather tunic and leather bracelets along his arms.

I swung the hammer at him, not killing him but leveling him

in one blow. Before the hammer even came full circle, the next cyclops was on me. Then the next. I spun around and swung at them, catapulting them off the island, back to the walls of the forge. Those that I defeated were replaced, one after another. Around the chamber, chanting filled the air. *Kill Achilles. Kill Achilles.* I might not be able to kill them, but they had no restrictions. Every cyclops in here hated me because of the things Hephaestus had said. But I craved this battle. I wanted more and more and more.

I was knocked over twice. A shovel nearly chopped my head off. I dodged axes and hammers. I swung my hammer and fought with everything I had. I fell into the utter joy of a true fight, worthy of my skills. The cyclopses were relentless, and there seemed to be an infinite number of them. But I kept fighting until there were no more cyclopses on the island. They all lay on the other side, unconscious or barely moving. Defeated.

I threw the hammer to the ground. Blood pounded through my muscles. "Is that the best you can do, Hephaestus?" I screamed. "Is that all you have?"

Hephaestus only looked at me and smiled. Then the ground began to shake, one boom after another, like footsteps approaching. I turned, and from the depths of the forge came one final opponent. Only his silhouette was visible in the flickering light of the cavern, but it stretched to the ceiling. He bent to make his way into the chamber, and when he turned the corner, I finally saw him.

He was covered in leather armor and stood well over twenty feet tall. He carried a club and a mace and had oiled his skin until the reflections of the firelight bounced off it. He stopped and my two eyes met his single one. Then he opened his mouth and roared, shaking every wall around us.

I grabbed my hammer in one hand and a shovel from a

defeated cyclops in the other and I roared back at him. Sweat slicked off my skin, and blood trickled down my arms from cuts and scrapes.

The cyclops giant bent his knees and jumped, landing so hard on the island that half of it cracked off, leaving him on one part of the rock and me on the other, with a river of lava flowing between us.

He swung the mace, but it wasn't long enough to reach over the lava. So he jumped again, landing hard on my piece of the island. The entire thing shook, and I prepared myself in case it broke again. But the rock held, so I charged.

I swung the hammer, aiming for his knee. I wasn't going to be able to knock him out the same way I had the others, but if I could drop him to the ground, that would lead to my victory.

He didn't budge. It was like the hammer hadn't even hit him. Then he spun around and swung the mace again, this time connecting with my left arm.

The shovel flew from my hand and landed in the lava, burning up in seconds. Pain exploded from every spot where the mace hit. But the pain only fueled my battle rage. This cyclops was nothing I couldn't handle. Winning a battle had nothing to do with size. I'd proven that time and time again back in Troy.

I jumped when he swung again. Ducked the next time. I darted behind him, using my speed to my advantage. He tried to keep up with me, to keep swinging, but his sheer bulk slowed him down. From behind him, I swung the hammer and leapt to the side. His mace flew from his hands and landed in the burning lava, suffering the same fate as the shovel. Now we were even, with one weapon a piece.

He came at me, swinging his club around, but I jumped to the other island, just barely making it. Except it was still moving, and I tripped. My hammer fell from my hands and tumbled for the edge. I scrambled after it, but it was too late. It rolled off the tilting island and into the lava. And before I could react, the cyclops giant jumped onto the island. It tilted even more. I tried to balance.

He roared again, and he ran toward me. I took the only chance I had. I grabbed the black knife from my waist, and once he was close enough, I jumped to the side and swiped at his ankle, tearing into the tendons that he'd so carelessly neglected to cover. He dropped to the ground, then catapulted forward, carried by his own momentum. And with a final tumble, he rolled off the side of the rock island, into the burning lava.

Shouts and cheers burst from the sides of the forge, from the fallen cyclopses who had regained consciousness. But instead of shouts filled with hatred and rage, they cheered my name. *Achilles. Achilles.* One bent a knee to me then another and another until all of them bowed before me.

I breathed hard, trying to catch my breath, and looked to Hephaestus, still gripped the leather hilt of the knife. The black blade dripped with blood. I'd killed one of his cyclopses, possibly worsening my fate.

"You defeated their overlord," he said, striding across the bridge which had been destroyed in the battle but rebuilt with each step he took. The metal pulled together on its own, twisting and snapping back into place.

"They're cheering for me," I managed to say between gulps of air. Blood still pounded through me, swooshing in my ears like a hurricane.

"He was a very bad overlord," Hephaestus said. "You freed them."

"Why didn't you ever do anything about it?" I said.

"It wasn't my place to interfere with Cyclops hierarchy," Hephaestus said. "And it won't be in the future, either, when they pick a new leader. But for now, thanks to you, that's not a problem."

"Great," I said. Then I looked up. There, at a high balcony, stood Aphrodite and Nicole. Nicole's fingers were clasped so tightly around the railing, I thought her knuckles might pop. I managed to give her a small nod because anything beyond that would have taken far too much effort.

"You proved yourself worthy," Hephaestus said.

"Damn straight," I managed to say. Then I collapsed.

CHAPTER 24

I woke to someone slapping the side of my face.

"Stop!" I tried to say, but it sounded all muffled in my head.

"He's awake," someone said.

My eyelids felt like thick slugs plastered on top of my eyeballs, but I forced myself to open them. The first thing I saw was Nicole staring down at me.

"Achilles?" she said, and she peered down even closer.

I grabbed her head with both hands and pulled her close. "Did you slap me?"

She shook her head loose. "You weren't waking up."

"I just fought fifty cyclopses," I said. "And that last one . . ."

"Was like the king of the cyclopses!" Nicole said. "And you totally took him. I've never seen anything like it."

Never seen anything like me totally getting my ass kicked

for most of the battle. That was something I never wanted to see again.

"I was resting." I sat up and looked over my body. Aside from my red sliders, my clothes were nowhere to be found. My black knife lay at my side. But not a single scratch graced my skin. I knew I'd gotten some, from the mace, the club, the swords and shovels.

Like she knew what I was thinking, Aphrodite said, "I gave you some Ambrosia. I couldn't have you dying here in my house."

"Thanks." I stood up and flexed my muscles, trying to figure out what, if anything, hurt.

"You know you have a really nice body, Achilles," Nicole said. "Not that I'm looking or anything."

She totally was looking. And even though I'd heard this compliment more times than I could count, I still felt my face heat up. It must've been the Ambrosia, pumping through me.

"Yeah, so do you," I said. "Not that I'm looking either."

I left it at that. Another word and I was sure Aphrodite's powers would kick in again until I wouldn't be able to resist Nicole.

"You got any extra clothes around here?" I asked.

"I can ask Heph," Aphrodite said. "If he ever gets back. 'Gone a minute,' he said, but that was like twenty minutes ago. As if no one else's time matters."

"How long was I out?" I asked, lifting my leg and running my hand over my ankle, just to make sure it was okay. I'd sliced through the cyclops king's ankle, using my vulnerability against him. It hurt just thinking about it.

"About a half hour," Nicole said. "But don't worry. We talked the entire time."

That only gave me more reason to worry.

We sat around for another twenty minutes which consisted of

Aphrodite doing her best to ask about Ares without mentioning his name. I was smarter than to bring it up myself. Hephaestus would have probably collapsed half of Austin into the river if he thought Aphrodite was sleeping around on him . . . again. So I answered with vague half-truths and evasions until finally Hephaestus sauntered back into the room.

"What were you talking about?" he grumbled, as if he already knew.

Nicole's eyes flicked my way, and I tried my best to tell her not to answer. I guess she understood because she kept her mouth shut.

"Achilles says we should get out more, Honey," Aphrodite said.

"I hate going out," Hephaestus said. "Bunch of worthless incompetent ninnies that can't build or make anything worth being built or made."

Aphrodite pouted. "Oh, but you know I love going out. Maybe I could go visit Achilles and Nicole sometime. You know. Just go see them. Maybe have dinner. Then come right back here of course."

"That's a horrible idea," Hephaestus said. "Isn't it, Achilles?"

I opened my mouth, trying to think of some response that would make both Hephaestus and Aphrodite happy, which was impossible. Then Nicole said, "You could stay with me. Do you like cats?"

Aphrodite clasped her hands together. "I adore cats! But Heph won't let me have one."

"The cyclopses eat cats," Hephaestus said.

"Oh, what do you say, Heph? Maybe in a couple weeks? I'll just visit with Nicole and Achilles and that's it. You won't even miss me."

What? Did she think we lived together or something?

Hephaestus fixed his eyes on me. "Achilles would have to vouch for you. And if you lie to me and talk to anyone else, he'll suffer the punishment. How does that sound, Achilles?"

It sounded like the most horrible, awful idea I'd ever heard in my entire life. And it also sounded like there was no way I could get out of it. If I said no, Aphrodite's wrath would descend upon me. The wrath of the goddess of love could have deadly aftereffects. If I said yes, then Hephaestus would kill me when he discovered Aphrodite running around on him with Ares, which of course she would do. No matter what, I was screwed.

"It sounds great?" I said. Gods, I just wanted to get the hell out of here.

"I have a network," Hephaestus said. "I'll know what goes on."

"Oh, I'm so excited!" Aphrodite said, as if she didn't realize that she'd just wagered away my life.

"About the spear . . . ," I said. Why hadn't I brought it up five minutes ago before Aphrodite decided she wanted me to burn in hell?

"I got you covered." Hephaestus held forth his right hand. He turned it over and opened his meaty fingers, exposing a black spearhead sitting in the middle of his palm. "You know what this is, pretty boy?"

I let the pretty boy comment slide.

"A spearhead," I said.

"A spearhead cast in the same mold that I used for your father's spear," Hephaestus said.

"And that's a good thing, right?" I said.

"It's a way to track your spear," Hephaestus said. "Items cast in the same mold, with the same type of metal, pull together."

"Like magnets?" Nicole said, and she stepped closer.

I wanted to yank her back, just in case Hephaestus decided

he didn't want a mortal here after all, but Hephaestus actually smiled at her.

"Exactly like magnets," he said, and handed it over.

I took it and balanced it in the palm of my hand. The black metal, like the knife, hardly weighed a thing.

"What do I do with it?" I said.

"I bet you use it like a compass," Nicole said, taking the spearhead from me before I could stop her. "Like this one, since it's attracted to the other one, will lead us to it. Am I right?"

I looked to Hephaestus.

"The mortal's right," he said, and he grumbled something else that sounded a lot like, "Maybe they're not all as worthless as I thought." Then he drained his gold drink and slammed his mug into the pitcher, spilling the rest of the drink everywhere.

"Really, Heph?" Aphrodite said. "I'm not cleaning that up. You're cleaning that up."

I took the spearhead from Nicole. "It will lead *me* to the spear. Not you."

Nicole nodded her head in an exaggerated way. "Oh right. You. Silly me."

"So that's it then?" I said.

"You can leave now," Hephaestus said.

Aphrodite slapped him on the arm. "Don't be rude."

"It's okay," I said. "We need to go anyway."

"Someone's manners seem to have run out," Aphrodite said. "But I'll come visit in a few weeks."

Hephaestus grumbled something else that I didn't even try to hear. I wanted to pretend Aphrodite's visit would never happen.

"Whatever, Darling," Aphrodite said.

She walked Nicole and me back through the metal tunnels and to the door, smiling until she was out of sight of Hephaestus.

Then she spun to face me.

"If you rat on me, Achilles, there will be a price."

I took a deep breath. "Can we just not worry about that now? I have bigger issues."

Aphrodite bit her lip and nodded. "Okay. But tell him I said hi."

"Yeah, sure," I said.

"Sorry to bring up the obvious, but don't you need some clothes before we go outside?" Nicole said. "Not that I'm not enjoying the view."

"Oh, you little lovebirds are so cute," Aphrodite said.

"We're not lovebirds," I muttered.

"Oh, Achilles," Nicole said, and she linked arms with me, pulling me close. And the problem was that I liked it. I really really liked it which was probably completely obvious in my torn sliders. Aphrodite and her stupid pheromones.

"Not lovebirds," I said again. She was totally messing with me. They both were.

"But you will be," Aphrodite said. "Just wait."

"Clothes, please?" I said.

Aphrodite smiled and snapped her fingers, magically dressing me in skintight brown leather pants.

I glanced down to see that nothing was left to the imagination.

"More clothes, please?"

Aphrodite snapped her fingers again, and I got a matching brown leather tank top. "That's what you get. Take it or leave it."

So I took it.

The second Aphrodite unlocked the door I was through it, dragging Nicole with me. It closed behind us, vanishing into the side of the rocky hill.

"That was fun," Nicole said.

I spun to face her. "Fun? Are you kidding?"

She shrugged. "Sure. It's not like I get to hang out with the gods every day."

A million responses went through my mind. She shouldn't be hanging out with the gods. The whole thing with Aphrodite coming to visit would be a disaster.

"Oh, and your leather outfit is really sexy, lovebird," Nicole said.

I didn't reply.

CHAPTER 25

Nicole dropped me off at my condo. I crashed, not even bothering to change out of the leather clothes Aphrodite had gotten so much pleasure dressing me in. If only she wasn't a goddess. She was way more trouble than I wanted to deal with.

I woke early, before my alarm. My heart pounded and pent up energy raged within me, either from the fight with the cyclopses or the Ambrosia. Or both. I threw on some real clothes and shoes and took off for a jog. It was early enough that the streets were still pretty dead, and the cold air of morning helped calm me.

I was going to be able to track the spear and find whoever had it. This would all come to an end. I'd be able to clear my name, stop more dryads from getting hurt, and stay out of Tartarus.

I held the spearhead out, feeling for a magnetic pull, but there was nothing. So I jogged for an hour, trying every few hundred feet. I wanted to try longer, but I had to open the gym at seven. Once Keith got in, I'd try again. I got to the gym and unlocked the door. Immediately my cell phone rang.

Shit. It was Mom. And today was Tuesday.

I did not have time for this now. Not today. Not until this Furies stuff was resolved.

I swiped it to end the call.

It rang again. And again. And finally on the fourth time she called, I picked up.

"What time will you guys be here?" she said before I even had a chance to say hello.

"About that," I said. "We can't make it."

"Achilles . . . ," Mom said.

I ran a hand through my hair. "It's just that I have a crap ton going on right now. I need a few days to get it under control."

"Seven o'clock," Mom said, almost like I hadn't spoken a word.

"Mom . . ."

Her voice got sickeningly sweet. "Achilles, dear, do you know what will happen if you don't show up this evening?"

I might get sent to Tartarus. Another dryad might die. And the Furies would return and decide to tear me limb from limb. Time was nearly up. They could attack any time.

"Bad things?" I said.

"Very bad things," Mom said, though she was not talking about the same things I was.

"Can we please wait a few days?" I asked, knowing it was futile even as I said it.

"I'll see you at seven." And with that, she hung up.

"Who was that?" Nicole said, walking in. I hadn't even heard the door open. I was losing it, one disaster at a time.

I stared at my phone, wondering how Mom managed to cull

me every single time we ever interacted. I was one of the fiercest warriors in the entire world. Hell, I'd just defeated the king of the cyclopses last night. Yet I still bent to Mom's every whim.

"My mom," I said. "Remember that thing about dinner?"

"You're still going?"

At least I wasn't the only one who thought this was not the time for a friendly family get-together.

"Looks that way," I said.

"Oh yeah, there's something I need to tell you," Nicole said, but right then, my phone buzzed again with an incoming text.

It was from a Russian number.

I glared at her.

She tried to look almost apologetic. "He said he wanted to talk to you. I don't know what about."

"Like hell you don't know what about," I said, and checked the text.

"Meet me at noon at Pease Park," the text read.

Of course it was from Jordan.

What? He thought I was just going to cater to his every whim also? He wasn't my mom.

I pocketed the phone without responding, but it immediately buzzed again.

"I know," is all it said.

He knew what? Jordan was full of shit . . . I hoped.

"I'm busy today," I texted back.

"Make time or else," he texted

"What does he know?" I asked Nicole, slamming my phone on the counter. The sickening sound of breaking glass reward-ed me. Which maybe was a blessing. If my phone was broken, nobody would be able to call or text me. I could deal with the important matter at hand.

Nicole kind of shrugged. "Not really sure."

"Not really sure, or you don't want to tell me?"

"Both?" she said.

I was about to grill her more, but the door opened and Jack sauntered in, trying to puff out his chest. Or maybe he was looking bigger these days. Working out every day had to make a difference, even for someone as skinny as Jack.

"Getting an early workout in," he said, and turned the computer toward himself so he could check in.

"And I'm going to get ready for yoga," Nicole said.

"We're not done here," I said.

Nicole blew me a kiss and walked away. Ugh. I was going to kill her and Jordan. What had I been thinking, hiring her to teach yoga? This entire thing was a mess.

The door opened, and it only got messier when Elle glided in.

"Hi, Achilles," she said. "I've been trying to catch you. You are so hard to get a hold of."

She reached out, like she was going to rub my arm or something, and my mind went all foggy like it did every time she got near. Except at the back of my mind, the overflowing bucket of problems pushed forward. Despite how fine she was, I was not in the mood.

"I've been busy," I said.

"Oooh, I hope not too busy to train me."

"Yeah, about that," I said. "I don't think that's such a good idea. You know, with you and Ethan . . . you know . . ." I wasn't really sure how to describe what she and Ethan were to each other.

She shook her head, and her long dark curls flowed back and forth. "Oh, no, it's fine. I already told him that you'd be helping me out. He's totally cool with it."

"He is?"

"Oh sure," she said. "He's really happy about it."

That did not seem right. As cool as Ethan was with everything, and despite the fact that he was my best friend, he was not going to want me having serious one-on-one time with his girlfriend.

"You know what, let me talk to Ethan," I said. "If he says it's cool, then we can set something up."

Elle blinked her huge eyes. "You promise?"

"Sure," I said. "But not this week. I have too much going on." That was putting it mildly.

"Like what?" Elle said.

I was not bringing one more person into the growing circle of secrets. "Like stuff," I said, and I headed over to spot Jack while he lifted.

* * *

I KEPT TRYING TO TALK MYSELF OUT OF GOING, telling myself that Jordan didn't know shit, but sure enough, eleven forty came and I headed out to meet him at Pease Park. Maybe he just had more half-guesses and conspiracy theories, but I couldn't take the chance. If he started spouting off to the news or on social media, it would get traced back to me and the gods would find out. Actually, I could just go ahead and hand him over to the gods. They'd wipe his memory, and everything would be great. Except for the fact that I'd get in trouble, too. Damn the gods and their stupid, archaic rules.

Fine, maybe the rules made sense a little. If the entire mortal world suddenly found out about the existence of gods and immortals, shit would hit the fan. Society as we knew it, across the world, would turn to chaos. Everything would change.

I was going to have to deal with Jordan.

I started in the direction of the park, jogging since the morning thus far had done nothing to quell the energy inside me. My energy level boiled higher and higher with every second that went by. I held the spearhead inside my jacket pocket as I jogged, hoping it would do what Hephaestus had said it would do. But it didn't give the slightest pull in any direction. And I couldn't spend any more time on it right now. I hauled ass to Pease Park, and it took me under fifteen minutes to get there.

Even though it was freaking cold out, a good number of people still milled around. Maybe Jordan planned it that way, so it wouldn't look weird, like we were meeting for some drug deal or something. I glanced around but didn't see him anywhere.

I guess he saw me. My phone buzzed. The screen still worked even though the glass was officially cracked. Not that I'd be able to afford getting it fixed anytime soon.

`"Over by the creek,"` the text read. Again, a Russian number, but a different one than before.

I started over there when three little girls with a wagon pulled to a stop in front of me.

"Excuse me, mister, but do you want to buy some cookies?"

I'd seen these same girls before, downtown and in front of my condo. I glanced up, and there was their Flower Scout sponsor with her dark, poofy hair and weird half-smile.

"They're really trying to sell enough cookies to earn a trip to Hawaii," she said.

That would explain why I'd seen them everywhere.

"Aren't they supposed to be in school?" I may not have kids of my own, but I understood the basics. During the day, kids went to school.

"Homeschool," the woman said, like that explained everything.

I patted my pockets. "Sorry. No cash today."

"Are you sure?" the little girl with the bright red curls said, eyeing me like she wanted me to turn my pockets inside out to prove it. The only thing inside of my pocket was the spearhead, and I wasn't letting anyone near that.

"Cassie!" the Flower Scout lady said. "Manners."

Cassie crossed her arms and frowned.

"Cassie?" the woman said.

Another of the little girls, the Indian one with the dark hair and glasses, pulled on her arm. "It's okay," she said. "We don't need him to buy our cookies."

All three girls turned away.

The Flower Scout lady sighed deeply. "Even if people refuse to buy cookies, we still say thank you. Don't we girls? What do we say to this man who didn't buy the cookies?"

Did she seriously not remember the other times I had bought cookies from them?

The girls turned back. "Thank you," they said, but nothing about their body language said that they meant it. Then they wheeled their wagon away from me and on to their next sugar-addicted victim.

I made my way past the sand volleyball courts and on to the creek, dodging Frisbees and dogs as I went. And there, sitting on a bench all by himself, was Jordan. I knew it was him because he had the same blue sweatshirt on with the hood pulled all the way over his head like he was trying to not be recognized. I took a deep breath and walked over to stand by the bench.

"You should have bought me some Skinny Mints," he said.

Had he been watching me the entire time?

"Dude, what the hell? Are you stalking me?"

He scooted over, trying to give me the hint to sit next to him.

I stayed standing.

"Should I be stalking you, Achilles?" he asked. "Are you hiding something?"

I crossed my arms and glared at him. "I am not hiding anything. Now why am I here? What do you want to talk about?"

"The Hall of Artifacts," he said, and patted the bench.

Fuck the Hall of Artifacts. It had been nothing but a complete pain in my ass.

I gritted my teeth and sat, keeping as much space between Jordan and me as possible. I could not believe Nicole was really friends with this guy. I hoped she wouldn't be too upset when his memory got wiped.

"What about it?" I said.

"What is it?" Jordan said. "And don't give me that lame LARPing excuse you gave Nicole. She might believe that, but it's not going to work on me."

"What's lame about LARPing?" I said, wondering what the hell else Nicole had told him. The last thing I needed was to slip up and dig myself into deeper shit than I already was.

"You don't LARP, Achilles," Jordan said.

"How would you know?"

"Because you're not the type. I know people who do LARP, and you're nothing like them."

"And there's only one type of person who LARPs?"

"Cut the bullshit," Jordan said. "And let's just get this out in the open. What is the Hall of Artifacts? For real?"

I went through possible responses in my mind that didn't mention gods or immortality, and I came up with the best that I could.

"It's a storehouse," I said. "Like a big storage unit."

Jordan nodded. "Yeah. Go on."

"And I store a couple things there," I said. "I rent out space."

"Rent out space," he said, like he wasn't sure if he should believe me or not.

"Right. Have you been by the gym ever? Do you know where it is?"

"Of course I know where it is," Jordan said.

"Great. Have you seen any of those shields that I keep around for decoration?"

Jordan pulled up a picture on his phone. It was of the inside of Heroes Gym. My gym. It confirmed even more that he was stalking me.

"These shields?" he said.

I seriously wanted to throttle this guy.

I nodded. "Those are the ones. Well this storehouse . . . those are the kinds of things I store there. I don't have a very big condo, and this way, I know my shit will stay safe and nice."

"Right," Jordan said. "Until someone steals it." And with his words and the tone of his voice, he called bullshit.

I'd had enough. This was the last thing I had space for in my life right now.

"Look," I said. "What are you trying to say here? What are you really trying to get at?"

Jordan smoothed his finger over the glass of his phone. "I think there's more going on with you, Achilles."

"Okay, fine. Maybe there is. And maybe there's not," I said. "What concern is it of yours?"

He turned his phone on again and pulled up another picture, then held it out for me to see.

It was a picture of Nicole. More specifically, it was a picture of him and Nicole, looking really cozy at Shady Grove, the same place she and I had gone after our visit to Zilker Park.

"This is my concern," Jordan said.

"Nicole?"

"Yep."

"You like her," I said, stating the obvious. "You really like her."

He shook his head, and his face flushed completely red. "No. I just don't want to see her get hurt. Or see her get mixed up in any trouble. The last thing Nicole needs is trouble. She's had too much already."

"What do you mean?" I asked, and in that moment, I realized how little I knew about Nicole's background.

"It's not my place to say," Jordan said. "But let this be a warning to you. I don't care how big you are or how tough you think you are. If you mess with Nicole or if you hurt her in any way, I will kick your ass. You will be sorry you ever met her. And you will be sorry you ever met me. I can make your life miserable, Achilles."

I almost grabbed him by the collar and lifted him off the bench right there, because if one of us was going to make the other's life miserable, it was going to be me. But I held back. Not because he wasn't a total punk. He was. But no. It was the look in his eyes that held me back. The true meaning behind his words. He was here because of Nicole. Because of how much he cared about her.

I got right in his face because I didn't want him to mishear a single word. "Let me tell you something, Jordan, and I want you to listen really carefully. If anyone ever threatens to hurt Nicole, I will be the first one there to stop them. I don't care what you think of me, believe me in this."

He held my gaze, not even blinking as the seconds ticked by. His face shifted, narrowing as he tried to look inside me to see a lie. But he wasn't going to find anything. I would destroy anyone who came near those I cared for.

Finally he pulled back from the gaze and gave a quick nod.

"You better be," Jordan said, and he stood. "But remember what I said. Don't hurt her. She doesn't need it."

I didn't bother responding. I had no intention of hurting her.

"Oh, and one more thing," Jordan said.

"What?"

"I'm going to keep digging, Achilles. Until I find out your secrets. I'm going to keep digging, and then we'll talk again. Trust me."

I didn't want to trust Jordan, and yet somehow, with this whole Nicole mess, it felt like we were on the same side. It was an odd and tenuous alliance, one that could break at any second. I had to watch my back and not let him find out anything more.

CHAPTER 26

By the time I got back to the gym, Nicole was gone. Keith sat behind the counter, chewing on the end of a pencil, staring at his phone like it was his lifeline.

"Achilles, man, do you know what they're saying about global warming these days?" Keith said.

"That it's bad?" I said. Global warming was the least of my concerns right now.

"That it's a Chinese Hoax," Keith said. "Like why China? Why can't it be a Scandinavian Hoax? Or an Egyptian Hoax? Or a Russian Hoax. Russia is always causing problems."

"Because . . . I don't know." I couldn't even bullshit a reason. "Just because."

"Because they're racist," Keith said. "That's why. Which is to-tally not cool man. Not cool at all."

"I feel ya," I said.

"Oh, and your yoga girl said she'd be back by six-thirty."

Nicole would have punched him if she'd heard him call her my yoga girl, but that wasn't my problem.

Six-thirty gave me a few hours, so I headed to the laundry room and shut the door. I swapped out the stuff from the washer to the dryer, then pulled out the spearhead. It rested there on my palm, but still didn't seem in the least bit magnetic. No matter which way I turned it or where I stood in the tiny room, it made no difference. Hephaestus must have been wrong, not that I was going to venture back under the volcano to tell him so. Still, how was I supposed to track the real spear with this?

I wrapped it in some white cloth and shoved it in the pocket of my jacket. I could find a way to bring it up with Mom. She might have an answer. And if she didn't have the right answer, she'd at least have some theory. Mom always had an opinion on everything.

For the next couple hours, I sat at the computer. I'd been putting off all the bills for the gym for the last two weeks. If I didn't take care of them, they'd cut my power. I started at the top of the stack. The first was a bill from the landlord for unscheduled building maintenance. I scanned down the paper to where it was itemized. Masonry work. Painting. Power-washing. This was from the battle with the Furies.

I crumpled the bill and tossed it under the counter and reached for the next piece of mail. But then I walked over and got it. The last thing I needed was the landlord asking questions. I'd pay the stupid seven hundred and fifty dollar bill and leave it at that. Hopefully they just thought someone drove a truck into the back of the building. Not that I had seven hundred and fifty dollars to spend. I could charge it. Then, if I died, no one would be out any money.

I scheduled the payments for the electric, the water, and the trash pickup. I paid for the quarterly exterminator. Then I finally got to inputting and creating accounts for the rest of the new people who'd signed up as part of the yoga special. And there, tenth down on the list, was Elle Teague.

I entered her name and address and set up her with a user id. She had to have the neatest handwriting I'd ever seen in my life, all curves, just like her. Then, because I'd never heard of the street she'd written down, I searched on it. But the search came back with nothing. There was no street named Apple Crescent Street in Austin or any surrounding area. She must've written it down wrong. I thought about trying some different variations, but that felt totally stalkerish, so I continued down the list. But I didn't even make it halfway through when Nicole walked back in.

"Do you know what they're saying about global warming?" Keith said to Nicole.

"That it's a Chinese Hoax," she said.

"Yes, exactly!" Keith said. "Which is so not cool."

"Not cool at all," Nicole said.

Keith, I knew, lived on a different plane of existence. Nicole obviously visited that plane from time to time.

"You ready?" I said. "Or do you want to keep talking about Chinese hoaxes?"

"No, I'm ready, lovebird," she said.

My face got really hot. What was it about this girl? She totally made me crazy.

"Oh, wait, are you two like an item?" Keith said.

"Nope," Nicole said. "Just friends."

I grabbed a few crocheted balls from the counter and stuffed them into my pockets.

"Making sure you don't forget your balls?" Nicole said as we walked out.

"They're for my mom. She's the one who wants me to crochet. It's to show her."

"Your mom wants you to crochet?"

I nodded. "She thinks it will help control my anger."

"And does it?"

I grabbed a ball and squeezed it. "Maybe?"

"If you want me to hold them for you, just let me know," Nicole said. Then she winked.

I stuffed the ball back into my pocket.

Mom lived about ten miles away, on the other side of Austin, near Tarrytown. We pulled up in front of a periwinkle purple renovated two story house with a bright yellow door. White Spanish tiles covered the roof, and the yard was full of some of the tallest trees in Austin. Back when I'd been with Syke, she'd schooled me on how old all the trees in this part of town were. Mom had adored Syke. She'd nagged me weekly since our falling out, telling me I didn't know something good if it hit me in the middle of the forehead. But my love life was not really Mom's business. Of course she disagreed on this, too. The last thing I needed was her dreaming up something between me and Nicole, though it might have already been too late for that.

"About my mom," I said.

Nicole put up a hand. "I'm totally cool with your mom."

"Yeah, but she's just a little—"

"Don't worry, Achilles. I can handle this."

My stomach did not agree with her words. Instead it twisted into something resembling a Gordian knot and stayed that way. This was going to be a disaster. I crawled out of her tiny car and slammed the door, a bit too hard.

"Take it easy on the car," Nicole said, patting it like it was some kind of baby.

I took a deep breath. Why did visiting Mom always do this to me?

Nicole placed her hand on my arm. "Hey, it's okay. You're fine here."

Fine was not the word I would have used. About to get grilled about every detail of my life, from the mundane, like if I was making my bed in the morning (which I wasn't) to the more serious, like when was I going to give her grandkids (which was not going to happen in the near future if ever). Mom nagged the hell out of me, every single time I saw her. Today wasn't going to be any different. And if she found out about this Furies shit, she'd go into crazy-Mom mode and start trying to micromanage my life.

The yellow door flew open before we'd even reached the top step.

"Achilles!" Mom shouted, loud enough for everyone in the neighborhood to hear. She grabbed me in a giant hug hard enough to make breathing an effort. Remember, though Mom barely stood five feet tall, she was immortal, and being so, had immortal strength. I struggled against her for the first couple seconds, because seriously, how embarrassing was it to have your mom hug you when you were twenty-eight years old, but then that thing happened that does every single time. Like my body relaxed, and I sank into the hug, and I wanted nothing more than for her to protect me.

Pretty wussy, I know. But she was my mom.

After a solid minute, I eased out of the hug, stepping back until my heels hung over the edge of the stairs.

"Your hair is purple," I said, though it was stating the obvious. Mom had straight long hair that came to the middle of her back, and every time I saw her, it was a different color.

"It matches the house," she said, running a hand over it. "Do you like it?"

"It's great," I said. "But it always looks great, no matter what color it is."

"Aw, you're such a sweet little boy, Achilles." She reached up like she was going to pinch my cheek.

"So, anyway," I said. "This is—"

"Nicole, Nicole, Nicole, I've so been looking forward to meeting you," Mom said, grabbing her and wrapping her in an immortal hug. I hoped Mom remembered that Nicole wasn't immortal so she'd ease up a bit. I didn't want Nicole to start turning blue just because Mom got too excited.

Finally Mom let her go.

"It's nice to meet you . . ." Nicole's words trailed off, and she looked to me for guidance.

"Thetis," I said. "Wait, what last name are you going by these days?"

"No last name," Mom said. "Just Thetis. It's a new thing I'm trying. Like Madonna. Or Prince. It's artsy. Everyone thinks you're way cooler if you only have a first name."

"But you're already cool," I said.

"You think I am," Mom said. "But what about everyone else? There are so many people out there, it's hard to stand out."

I motioned at her purple house. Her purple hair. "You've never had an issue standing out."

"Oh, you're just saying that to make me feel good," Mom said.

I wasn't, but Mom wanted the flattery. I could tell.

"By the way—" I said, thinking I might as well mention the biggest thing first.

"I know," Mom said. "You told Nicole about the gods."

"She kind of figured it out on her own," I said. "But we

can't let—"

"Like I'd go tell any of the gods," Mom said. "They'd wipe her mind. And of course, they'd probably skewer you."

As if that wasn't already a concern, this statement solidified it.

Mom stepped to the side and waved us forward, into her purple house. I swatted aside the strands of purple beads that draped across the doorway, and held them for Nicole. She smiled at me and walked inside.

Gods, this was so awkward. It felt like a date or something. Curse Aphrodite and her stupid lovebird thing.

"Never curse Aphrodite," Mom said as she stepped inside behind us, not bothering to shut the front door.

"Please don't do that," I said.

Mom didn't respond to me. Instead, she looked to Nicole. "You see, I can read Achilles' thoughts, and he doesn't like it."

"You can read everyone's thoughts, and of course I don't like it. Nobody wants their mind read." Especially not when they were on a weird pseudo-not-date with an amazing-looking girl.

"She is pretty," Mom said, angling her head at Nicole.

I could not look at Nicole. This whole thing was a horrible idea. I had to be redder than one of Persephone's pomegranates.

"Just stop, please," I said.

Mom pursed her lips, like she somehow had to consider this. "But how will I know how you're doing?"

"You could ask me?" I suggested. "You know, that's what normal people do."

"I really like your house, Thetis," Nicole said, and I never liked her so much as I did in that moment. Way to change the subject. "Have you lived here long?"

A giant smile erupted on Mom's face. "Ten years. Ever since Achilles was woken up. Ares brought him here to Austin, so I moved here too. I wasn't about to let my little boy be without his mother. I had the house completely remodeled."

Nicole managed to keep the smile on her face, even though the awakening thing had to be a weird reminder about our immortality.

"Little boy," Nicole said, letting out a small laugh. "It's hard to imagine Achilles as a little boy."

"Oh, he was the cutest thing in the entire world," Mom said, stepping closer to her. "All chubby cheeks and smiles. Do you want to see what he was like?"

"No, Mom!" I said before Nicole could reply.

Nicole glanced over at me, even though at this point she was kind of trapped between Mom and the wall. "What's the big deal?"

I shook my head and pulled on Mom's arm, trying to gently suggest she give Nicole some space. "Mom has this thing she can do."

"It's called shared experiences," Mom said.

Nicole's face didn't change. "Shared experiences?"

"It's like a Vulcan Mind Meld," I said, trying to relate it to the nerdiest thing I knew.

Nicole's eyes got wide. "Really?"

Mom stepped back and glared at me. "You know I don't like when you call it that."

"But that's what it is," I said.

"It's not science fiction," Mom said.

"Like a real Vulcan Mind Meld?" Nicole said, finally stepping away from the wall.

"Exactly," I said. On cue, my stomach growled. "Didn't you promise us dinner?"

Mom's face finally relaxed and her eyes lit up. "Oh, right. Let's go figure out what we want."

Mom pulled on Nicole's hand and led her toward the back of the house, leaving me trailing behind. Not that I was looking forward to vegan dinner. What I really could have gone for was a juicy burger and salty fries. A foamy beer in a pint glass. Some ketchup. But none of those things would be found at Mom's house.

"Because none of those things are good for you, Achilles," Mom said.

I didn't bother responding.

Mom had more crap stashed around her house than they sold at all of Goodwill combined. But the thing about her crap was that everything had a place. It was all in order, though how she determined that order, I had zero clue. From rocks to books to those weird little painted dolls that stacked inside themselves, every shelf and counter and table was covered. I had no idea what the point of having so much stuff might be, but Mom insisted she needed all of it. And it didn't stop at the flat surfaces. Every space of the walls was equally covered with everything from fine art paintings of ladies in dresses playing chess to needlepoint tapestries of gods and goddesses fornicating in forests.

Unlike the front door, no crystal beads hung over the back door, but that was because of the view. There were no other houses behind Mom's. Only her backyard and the greenbelt.

"So I'm guessing you like gardening?" Nicole said, and she stepped out into the cool January air.

Right, so Mom not only was vegan, she grew the majority of her own food. Rows and rows of vegetables stretched before us, and fruit trees edged the sides.

"Do you like gardening?" Mom asked Nicole.

Nicole looked to me like I'd save her. I remembered what

she'd said about hating cooking. But she was a big girl. She could handle Mom. I crossed my arms and gave her a smile.

"Um . . . ," Nicole said, but Mom didn't pick up on the hint and started yapping away in some other language about soil and planting seasons and a bunch of other crap that had nothing to do with the cheeseburger I really wanted.

I headed to a tree whose leaves had already fallen off for the winter. I'd helped Mom plant this tree. This entire garden, in fact. Like magic, a peach began to grow from a branch on the tree, increasing in size until it hung low enough for me to grab it. That was the other nice thing about being a goddess. Mom garden was magical, with anything growing at her smallest command. I plucked the peach and bit into it, letting the juice trail down my face. For a second, with the sun shining above and the birds singing in the trees, even though it was winter, I could almost imagine that none of this stuff with the Furies and the spear was really an issue.

Except it was. Mom was going to freak if she found out.

On cue, her head whipped around in my direction and she fixed her eyes on me.

I took a deep breath. She knew.

"We'll talk after we eat," she said, but not aloud. In my mind.

So I sat through what had to be one of the most tortuous dinners in the history of mankind, answering every question Mom asked me with as few words as possible. She made at least thirty-two implications that Nicole and I were some kind of item, and my smile turned into more of a grimace with each one. I would have thought Nicole would eat a little bit faster, to make dinner end sooner, but she kept putting her fork down between bites and sipping on the sangria Mom had made.

Right, at least there was sangria to dull the pain.

When Mom had eaten the last green bean from her bowl, she once again fixed her eyes on me. And in that second, my brain exploded with her overwhelming presence as she poured her mind into mine. Shared experiences . . . they worked both ways. And they could be unpleasant.

I pressed my hands to the sides of my head, like I was somehow going to be able to push her out of my brain. I squeezed my eyes shut. I looked down, counting the seconds until she was done. And when she finally left my mind, it took a good ten seconds before I could even open my eyes.

When I did, I found her staring at me, concern masked on her face.

"I will hunt those Furies down and kill them myself," Mom said, and rage seeped into the edges of her eyes. The bowls and glasses whipped off the table, smashing into the walls and shattering on impact.

How nice it would be to make my problems go away that simply. But even if I did have Mom step in and save me and get rid of the Furies, I would still be considered guilty until I could prove myself innocent. And dryads would still die.

"I can handle the Furies," I said, even though I wasn't sure how exactly that was going to happen.

"How could they possibly think you're guilty? Nemesis should never had set them on you."

"Yeah, but she did because . . . well . . . ," I said. I wasn't supposed to tell any of the gods, which included Mom.

"Oh, I see," Mom said, doing her mind-reading thing.

"Right."

"But Syke is okay?" Mom said.

"Who's Syke?" Nicole asked.

Welcome, awkwardness. Mom actually looked at a loss for

words, which had to be a first.

"She's a dryad I know," I said. "She and I . . ."

"Oh, I get it," Nicole said. "You used to date her."

My relationship with Syke went way beyond that, but I was fine with Nicole simplifying it.

"Yeah, pretty much," I said. "And since dryads are being targeted . . ."

"You're worried about her," Nicole said.

"But I talked to her this weekend," I said. "She's okay." I specifically didn't look at Nicole when I said that last part. Not that I was trying to hide anything. The whole situation was just awkward. Nicole was not my girlfriend. Not even close. But still it felt weird.

"I'll talk to Mother Dryad myself," Mom said. "I can't have them thinking you're doing this."

I dug into my pocket, pulling out the crocheted balls first, then the spearhead. "Do you know how to use this to track its mate?"

Mom placed her hand on the spearhead and closed her eyes, like she was communing with it.

"Hephaestus made this," she said.

I nodded. "It's a twin to my spear. He said they should be like magnets, but I'm not getting any kind of magnetic pull. Or at least not that I can tell."

"You've already tried?" Nicole said. "Without me?"

"Look," I said. "The last thing I need to do is endanger you more. Don't you get that? It's not personal. It's just that . . . someone is out to get me. And they're killing dryads. I don't need you getting in the middle of that."

Nicole opened her mouth like she was about to say something else, but then she shut it and crossed her arms.

"Do you know how this works?" I asked Mom.

Mom picked it up and held it close to her forehead. Nothing on her face registered, and as far as I could tell, the spearhead didn't change either.

"I don't know, Achilles," Mom said. "But Hephaestus must know what he's talking about."

"Hephaestus is a cranky hermit who ate too many sour lemons," I said.

"Be nice," Mom said. "That's your brother you're talking about."

"Brother?" Nicole said.

"Step-brother, at best," I said.

"Seriously?" Nicole said.

"I raised Hephaestus," Mom said. "When his own mother threw him off a mountain, I took him in. That's blood as far as I'm concerned."

I don't think Hephaestus viewed it as proof of a blood relationship. As far as I could tell, he'd be fine if I was wiped from the face of the earth by the next cyclops king.

"Is that why he helped us?" Nicole said. "Because you're brothers?"

"I'm sure it is," Mom said. "Hephaestus was always looking out for Achilles when he was younger."

"What planet are you from, woman?" I asked. That was not the step-brother I remember at all.

"It's true," Mom said. "Don't you remember that time Aphrodite wanted you to judge that contest between the goddesses. And Hephaestus talked her out of it?"

"If I remember right, he said I wasn't fit to be the judge because all I cared about was fighting."

She patted me on the cheek. "That was his way of keeping

you out of trouble. Then there was the time you hid in the harem. Who do you think made arrangements with the overseer of the place? It was your brother, that's who."

"You hid in a harem?" Nicole said. Not that it should surprise her. We'd just been inside an extinct volcano visiting with the god of blacksmithing and his love goddess wife.

"Just for a year," I said. "It was no big deal."

"No big deal," Nicole said. "Sounds like a good story to tell over beers."

At that, Mom grinned.

I pretended I hadn't seen her.

"Anyway, what I'm saying is that your brother is watching out for you," Mom said. "Which means that he's not wrong about the spearhead."

"Maybe I should just go back and ask him for an instruction manual," I said.

"Maybe you should trust him," Mom said. "It will work."

"And in the meantime, I sit around and wait for the Furies to drag me off to Tartarus?"

"I'll take care of the Furies," Mom said.

At this, blood pounded through my head. "That is not going to happen."

"But I'm your—"

"No!" I said, way louder than I intended, but there were already enough people at risk because of me. Mom was not going to join the list. "Do you not understand, Mom? Don't you get it? The spear could kill you. Kill you. And I don't care what you say, I am not going to let that ever have a chance of happening."

"But—"

"No buts," I said. "You promise me right here and now that you are not going to get involved."

"I can't make that promise," Mom said.

Anger flashed through me, so fierce, my head swam from the tunnel of red that formed in my mind. "Swear it, Mom. Do it now. You. Will. Not. Get. Involved."

I faced her off, waiting, not backing down. Never backing down. She glared right back, but immortal goddess or not, she was not a match for this request. The request ran too deep. A long minute went by with none of us saying a word, until her mouth formed a thin line.

"Fine. I swear it. I will not get involved."

I finally breathed. A promise made like this, made by a goddess, could not be broken. It was a vow that would hold true no matter what. Even if I died. Mom could not get involved to save me.

"Thank you," I said. Then I grabbed her in a hug hard enough to crush her. This was my mother. I was not going to let anything happen to her.

CHAPTER 27

"Where to?" Nicole asked.

It was nine o'clock. Keith should have locked up two hours ago. And aside from wanting to release my frustrations on a punching bag, there was no reason to go back to the gym. What I needed to do was talk to Ares. Athena had to have told him about my visit to Nemesis. And all things considered, it was time to get him involved. He was supposed to be watching out for me, in some weird fashion. So I'd told Nicole about the world of the gods. He'd just have to deal with that fact and keep her safe and me out of trouble.

"Can you take me to UT?" I asked.

"Your wish is my command," she said.

I pulled out my cracked phone and texted him. "Coming to visit. We need to talk."

There was no reply. Like always.

So I texted again. `"It's really important. For real this time. I need your help."`

Nothing.

Could he not at least try to act like he cared?

Nicole drove to campus and I had her circle around until we got as close to the history building as possible. I glanced up but didn't see a light on in Ares' office.

"Just pull over and park here," I said. "I'm going to see if he's in there."

"Ares?" she said. "What are you going to tell him?"

"Everything?" I said. My options were dwindling. I got out.

"I should come with you," Nicole said, getting out of the car also.

"Why?" I wasn't trying to be rude, but there wasn't much Nicole could do at this point.

"Because . . ." For once, she seemed at a loss for words.

But before she could come up with some bullshit reason, the water flew from the fountain in front of us, exploding upward like a mammoth geyser.

"Oh, shit!" Nicole said, backing up and bumping into me.

I stepped in front of her immediately, because out of the fountain of water came two of the Furies: Tish dressed in a red halter top, a denim mini-skirt, red cowboy boots and a red cowboy hat, and Alex, dressed the exactly same except in black.

"Don't get near them," I hissed to Nicole, pushing her farther back.

"Oh my god!" was all she said.

The two Furies landed on the grassy ground and cracked their knuckles.

"Hi, Achilles," Alex said. "Did you miss us?"

Missed my chance to obliterate them like I'd done to Meg.

"Where's Meg?" I called, knowing I shouldn't taunt the Furies but unable to stop myself.

Tish smiled in reply, a sweet smile with a hint of hatred. "She's healing," she said in her Texas twang. "And you better pray that you're all tucked away in Tartarus by the time she mends or she'll be the one to deliver your sentence."

"You won't want that," Alex said, tipping her hat forward.

"You're early again," I said, knowing it wouldn't matter. The Furies had their own agenda. Their own schedule.

"We're right on time," Alex said. "That's why we're here."

Right on time, my ass. I had one more day, but that was irrelevant now.

"Who do you have with you tonight, Achilles?" Tish asked, acting like she was peering around behind me to get a better look at Nicole.

I prayed Nicole would somehow be smart enough to continue backward and get the hell out of here.

"No one," I said.

"No one," Tish said, licking her lips. "You spend an awful lot of time with her for her to be no one."

What the hell? Had they been watching me?

"She works with me," I said. "And she has no part in this."

Almost in the blink of an eye, Alex blurred forward, vanishing then reappearing directly in front of Nicole. I whipped around, and every muscle in my body flexed.

"Works with you," Alex said, walking a slow circle around Nicole. "And she knows about stuff. Knows about us. I can smell it on her." She sniffed the air for effect.

Nicole's eyes went wide, and she stood tall, not taking her gaze off the Fury. But for as scared as she must have been, she stood her ground.

"She was just leaving," I said, cursing Nicole for not leaving when I'd asked her to.

"Oh, but she can't leave yet," Alex said. "We were just starting to have fun." She reached her hand out and traced it along Nicole's cheek. Nicole let out a small whimper but didn't move.

Nothing about this was fun. Nicole needed to get the hell out of here.

"I talked to Nemesis," I said, hoping to draw their attention away from Nicole and back to me.

"Nemesis," Tish hissed, placing herself between me and Nicole.

"She knows I'm innocent," I said, ignoring the instructions from Nemesis. I looked for some way around Tish, but she blocked me.

"Nemesis hasn't called us off," Tish said. "She told us to bring you to Tartarus. She told us you had to pay. And even if she did call us off, you would still have to pay for what you did to Meg."

"Meg was trying to kill me," I said. "You all are. What am I supposed to do? Let you haul me off to Tartarus? Because that is not going to happen."

"Meg is angry," Tish said. "Really angry."

"Oh, I have an idea," Alex said, stopping her circle around Nicole. "Do you think your friend wants to see what's under my hat?" She reached a hand up and placed it on the brim of her cowboy hat, preparing to take it off.

That's when Nicole finally lost her shit.

"What's under her hat, Achilles?" she said. Her voice wavered, and she crossed her arms in front of her, like somehow she could keep Alex away.

"Nothing," I said.

"Nothing." Alex laughed, and she lifted her hat and tossed it aside.

The snakes erupted into a fury of twisting bodies, snapped out in Nicole's direction. Nicole backed up, but the fountain was right behind her, and there was nowhere for her to go.

"Achilles!" she said.

Alex reached up and grabbed one of the snakes. It twisted around her hand and reached its head out at Nicole, stopping only inches away. I lunged forward, but Tish latching onto me, sinking her claws into my arm, hard, but not deep enough to draw blood.

"Not so fast, Achilles," Tish whispered in my ear. Her breath smelled rotten, like flesh that had been sitting out for all of eternity. "Let's watch and see what happens."

"I have a fun idea," Alex said, taking a step closer to Nicole. The snake was so close. Its tongue flicked out, like it wanted to taste Nicole. If it bit her, she wouldn't have the same armor I had. She could die. Would die.

"Let her go," I said. "That sounds like a good idea to me." I pulled forward, but Tish held fast.

"Let's make a deal," Alex said, taking another step. The snake licked again at Nicole then slithered up against her shoulder, tracing itself across her chest and up to her neck. Her eyes flickered from the snake to me.

"No deal," I said, shoving Tish off me. But she only laughed and grabbed both my arms, pinning them behind my back.

"You haven't even heard my deal," Alex said.

I didn't want to hear anything the Furies had to say. Nemesis should have called them off me immediately. She never should have put me in this position. She not only had the wrong person being hunted down, she was putting other people at risk. First Ethan. Now Nicole.

I kept my mouth shut and glared at her.

"If you admit to your guilt and come with us willingly, then we'll let your girlfriend go," Alex said.

"I am not guilty," I said between gritted teeth.

"Then your girlfriend dies," Alex said.

"I'll come with you," I said, pulling one arm free from Tish. "Just let her go, and I'll come with you. We can talk about this."

"Not good enough, Achilles," Tish said, still holding firm on one arm. I pulled against her but her deadly claws held me tight. "You had your chance for that. Now we need your admission of guilt."

"We want your admission of guilt," Alex said, licking her lips.

But an admission of guilt was something I could not give them. If I admitted to the crimes that I hadn't done, then the killings would never stop. More dryads would die. And whoever had taken the spear would get away with it.

"You can't have it," I snapped, and I yanked my left arm from Tish's grasp. Her claws dug into me, tearing down through the skin and muscle, but I hardly felt the pain. With my right hand, I dug into my jacket pocket and grabbed the new spearhead. I leapt forward and swung it around. Then I thrust it into Alex's bare back.

She howled in pain, one scream after another, reaching her arms behind her like she was trying to get the spearhead out. But I dug it deeper. How dare she threaten Nicole? How dare they try to make me confess to something I didn't do? That was not any kind of justice. I twisted it, delivering my own justice. Alex dropped to the ground hard, and both she and her snakes evaporated. A cloud of black mist swirled above where she'd been only seconds before. It seemed to stop and look at me, just for a moment, before sinking into the grassy ground.

Nicole finally dared to breath. But it may have been too early for that.

"You can't deny it now," Tish howled. "That's the same weapon. You have as good as admitted your guilt. And Achilles, for this you are going to pay. You and everyone you care about will pay. Your mother. Your friends. No one will be safe."

She lifted her head back then and screamed into the night. Then she rose up in the air and dove back into the fountain. The cascade of water descended upon her, and she was gone.

Nicole fell to the ground, finally collapsing into an emotional wreck. I scanned the area. I needed to be sure that the danger was gone. There was no sign of Tish or Alex. No sign that they'd even been here, not even the cowboy hat Alex had tossed aside.

"Is she dead?" Nicole asked, looking up at me with panicked eyes.

I sank to the ground next to her and wrapped my arms around her, pulling her close.

"I don't know," I said. "Maybe? Or more likely she can heal. And when she comes back . . ."

"What are you going to do, Achilles?" Nicole said. "How can you fight them?"

"I'll find a way."

I had to find a way. Coming after me was one thing. Threatening my mother and my friends was entirely another. The Furies were out of control. I was not guilty, and I wasn't going to say I was. There had to be a way out of this. I just had to find it.

I scoured the area around the fountain, but there was no sign of the spearhead. It was gone, turned to dust along with Alex's body, dissolving back into the earth. It could be used as a sign of my guilt if and when my case went before the council of the gods. The good news was that Nicole was safe and the Furies were gone—for the time being.

"I'll take you home," I said, helping Nicole to her feet, trying not to think about the missing spearhead.

She nodded and held onto my hand long after she was standing. "Thanks, Achilles."

Not like she should be thanking me. I'd almost gotten her killed. If not for me, she never would be in the trouble she was in right now. And wasn't it just earlier today that I'd promised Jordan I would keep her safe? A hell of a job I was doing so far.

Nicole hardly said a word while I drove to her house. I parked out front and hurried around to her side so I could open her door. She gave me a weak smile which I hated. What I wanted was to see her back to normal. I should have never let her get in the path of the Furies to start off with. I walked her to the door and passed her the car keys.

"Don't open the door for anyone," I said. Not that the Furies would be ringing her doorbell. If they came back—scratch that; when they came back—they would unleash their ultimate fury. No one would be safe. I had to get back and make sure Ethan knew what was going on also. And Mom. Nobody was safe.

"I'll see you tomorrow," Nicole said.

"Maybe you should take the day off?"

She shook her head. "I'll be fine. If I get some sleep." She let out a little laugh.

I only wished that I had some special power to get her out of this entire situation.

I waited until she locked the door, and I started walking back to my condo. My arm had scabbed over where Tish had nearly ripped off the flesh, but I didn't have time to visit the Underworld to get it healed right now. It would have to heal on its own.

I swiped my finger across the phone to call Mom.

"What happened?" she asked, answering before it rang once.

Me calling her was out of the ordinary.

"You need to make sure you're safe," I said, and I gave her the brief and not-quite-as-scary account of what had happened.

"Oooh," Mom said. "Does Nicole want to come stay with me?"

I hadn't thought about that. It was an option. Nicole could stay with Mom, or could even go back to stay with Hephaestus and Aphrodite, since they knew about her. Not that I wanted Nicole to spend any more time around Aphrodite than was necessary. But her safety was the top concern.

"Maybe," I said. "I'll ask her tomorrow, once she'd had a chance to rest. She was pretty shaken up."

Mom gave out a tiny laugh. "Don't let her fool you. She's tougher than you think."

"She was really scared, Mom," I said.

"She's a survivor. Remember that, Achilles. I know these things."

I didn't doubt Mom. She did tend to have a feeling about certain people and places, and most of the time—

"All the time, Achilles," she said, reading my mind.

Fine. All the time.

"I'll let you know what she says."

I texted Ares again, but this time, I needed him to respond. Really needed him to respond.

`"I have a message for you from A,"` I texted.

He'd know who A was. Everyone knew about their affair. It wasn't like he'd ever tried to be subtle. Neither had she, for that matter.

`"I'll come by tomorrow,"` he texted back immediately.

`"What about tonight?"` I texted.

`"Can't tonight. Council business,"` he said.

`"This is more important,"` I texted.

But there was no reply.

Council business my ass. The gods had so little concern for anyone besides themselves that it made me want to scream.

I was nearly to the condo when someone hollered at me from outside the drugstore on the corner.

"Excuse me, mister, would you like to buy some Flower Scout cookies?"

They had to be kidding. But no. There behind a table stood

the same three little girls I'd seen pulling the wagon earlier at the park. And it was nine-thirty at night. These girls were bound and determined to earn the trip to Hawaii. Standing off to the side was the dark-haired lady, decked out in a bright green sweat suit that matched the girl's green vests. Her jacket, like their vests, was covered in patches.

She smiled at me like she'd never seen me before, even though this had to be the fifth time our paths had crossed.

"They're really trying to—" she started.

I put up my hand to stop her. "I know. They're trying to earn a trip to Hawaii."

She put her hands on her hips, like she was annoyed that I'd interrupted her. "Well, it is a mission trip. We'll be picking up trash in the forest preserves for the wildlife."

The little blond girl walked right up to me. "Do you know how much habitat is vanishing every single day for forest animals?"

I didn't really give a fuck.

"Um . . . a lot?"

Her already giant eyes got super wide. "A whole lot, Mister. And if you can spare just four dollars to buy one box of cookies, you'll be helping to send us there to maintain the game preserve."

"Game preserve?" What? Were these little Flower Scouts going to run off and hunt elk in Hawaii for fun?

The woman laughed. "Sarah means the forest habitat." She pulled gently on the little blond girl's arm to get her back behind the table. "They get a little confused sometimes."

"So do you have four dollars?" the dark-haired girl with the big glasses asked.

I patted my pockets, and pulled them out this time to prove the fact that I was penniless. "Sorry. I don't have any money."

The little girl looked at me skeptically. "Are you sure? Where's your wallet?"

This was beyond ridiculous. I did not have time to argue with a group of eleven-year-olds.

"Maybe next time," I said, walking away. With as persistent as these Flower Scouts were, I was sure there would be a next time. And a next time after that.

"Neela, make sure to say thank you," the woman said.

"Thank you for nothing," the little girl named Neela called after me.

"Did you get me any cookies?" Ethan said when I walked in the door. He lounged on the sofa with his feet kicked up on the arm rest. He held a clipboard, but set it down on the coffee table once I shut the door.

"Those Flower Scouts are more persistent than ringworm," I said. "I can't walk two blocks without them trying to sell me Skinny Mints."

"Yeah, they came by earlier. I dug out your special twenty and bought five boxes," Ethan said.

"Great," I said. So much for having an extra twenty stashed away. I'd just replaced it the other day.

I walked into the kitchen and tore off my jacket. I shoved my arm under the cold water and let it clean the cut. Maybe if I pretended it was water from the River Styx that would work?

"What the hell happened to you?" Ethan said, kicking at my bloody jacket with his toe. "You look like shit."

So I told him everything, from the visit with Mom to the chat with Jordan in the park to the Furies attacking and threatening basically everyone in my life.

"Let's see them come at me," Ethan said, patting a set of five knives that sat on our kitchen counter.

I shook my head. "No. You need to stay away from them. You

and everyone else."

"I'm not backing down from the Furies," Ethan said.

I got right in his face. "Yeah. You are. You cannot go after them or try to find them. And if they find you, you need to . . ."

"What? Run away? You know I can't do that, Achilles."

"But—"

"But nothing," Ethan said. "You know me well enough to know that I am not going to back down from a fight. I will kick their asses or I will die trying. And if they come at you, I'll be there with you, by your side. You know that."

As much as I didn't want Ethan to be anywhere near them or involved, his words still warmed me inside. I grabbed him in a hug. "Thanks, man. You're seriously like a brother to me."

Like the brother I'd never had. Mom may try to insist that Hephaestus was my brother, but he'd never stood by me like Ethan had. Ethan may be mortal, but in the five years I'd known him, he'd never let me down.

"Yeah, don't get all mushy on me, Achilles," Ethan said. "And can you stop bleeding all over the sink?"

We'd run out of bandages last week, so Ethan tore one of my t-shirts into strips and used it to cover my arm. I'd heal. Sleep would help. And in the morning, I'd tell Ares everything, about Nicole, and Paris, and even Nemesis. He'd help me find the spear. He could get other gods involved. I didn't care. I just needed it resolved.

CHAPTER 29

"Do you know how magnets work?" Nicole said, busting through the door of Heroes Gym first thing the next morning. Her face was bright and full of life, nothing like when I'd last seen her.

I set down the crochet hook and ball of yarn I'd been holding for the last ten minutes. I'd been trying to convince myself that I should crochet to help reduce my anger, but the thing was that I didn't want my anger to go away. I was furious. I wanted to tear things apart. I wanted that anger to fuel me for what I knew was ahead.

"Yeah, of course," I said. "I'm not quite as stupid as I look, you know."

She flicked her eyes upward as if she didn't have time for my humor, dark as it might be.

"Magnets attract metal and attract to each other because their poles are charged," Nicole said. "Here, watch this." She grabbed a small purple circle magnet off the white board where I wrote gym information. The piece of paper it held fluttered to the floor. Nicole then grabbed the crochet hook. She brought them close together, and the hook jumped from her hand, latching itself onto the magnet.

"Brilliant," I said. "You've discovered magnetism. Is this where we celebrate or something?" I grabbed the crochet hook from the magnet and tossed it across the room. It hit against a mirror on the far wall. A small crack started and traced a line outward in four directions.

"Maybe this is where you act like you don't know everything," Nicole said.

"Fine. So what? Who cares anyway? I lost the spearhead, don't you remember?"

"Anyway," Nicole said, grabbing a second circular magnet from the whiteboard, this one yellow. "Do you know what happens when you put these two magnets together?"

I took them both from her and shoved them together. They bounced apart. "Yeah, they don't like each other. They don't hook on."

"Right," Nicole said. "And do you know why?"

"Because they're the same polarity."

She took the yellow magnet from me and started prying the magnet part out of the back. They'd come in a set of ten for two dollars so I didn't really care. It took her about half a minute, and the use of a paperclip, but she finally got it free.

"What about when I flip this magnet over?" Nicole said, and she did, holding it near the other magnet. "What do you think will happen?"

"Opposites attract," I said.

"Exactly." Nicole smiled and brought the magnets together. They flew together, making a satisfying snap. Then she pulled them back apart.

"This science lesson is all cool and everything," I said. "But I'm not really sure why it matters."

"Because what if the polarity is wrong on the spearhead," Nicole said. "If they were made from the same mold with the same metal, then it stands to reason that they'd have the exact same polarity. And if that's the case, then all we'd have to do is demagnetize the spearhead and repolarize it with the polarity we want."

I admit it. At this point, I wasn't perfectly following along with the science anymore, but that wasn't the main problem. "We don't have the spearhead anymore," I said.

Nicole dug into her purse then set something on the counter, uncovering it with her hand. "Yes, we do."

There on the counter was the spearhead, pitch black and clean of blood as if it had never been used to vanquish the Fury.

"You took it?" I grabbed it off the counter and inspected it, looking for proof that it was actually the same spearhead.

"Maybe," Nicole said.

"And you didn't tell me?" My vision narrowed and my heart rate jumped to the speed of a jackhammer. She had to be kidding.

"You were pretty upset last night," Nicole said. "Also, I wanted some time to study it, and I knew if I asked you, you'd say no."

"So you just took it?" Red started to cloud the edges of my vision.

"Pretty much. Why? Do you have a problem with that? Because as far as I can tell, I've solved the mystery of why it's not working."

She crossed her arms, and with her eyes, she dared me to challenge her.

I counted to ten because if I was going to get angry, I wanted to make sure it was the right thing to do. But everything she said was right. If her science explanation had any merit to it, then there might be hope.

"You know how to do this magnet stuff?" I finally asked.

"In theory," Nicole said. "But I'm sure Jordan could—"

"No!" I said. "We're not getting Jordan involved in this. Seriously."

"But he could—"

"No. You can do this."

"I've never done it before," Nicole said.

"But you know how. And you're smart. You don't need Jordan's help."

Nicole bit her lip. "This is made of iron, right?"

"Something like that. Whatever it is, it's crazy strong. Hephaestus uses only the best materials."

"That sucks," Nicole said.

"Because . . . ?"

"Because that means we need somewhere where we can get this hot. Really really hot."

"Like an oven?"

"Like a really hot oven." Nicole said. "Not like the kind in your kitchen. Or even like a kiln. We need to type of oven they use to reshape metal."

An idea began to form in my head. "Metal reshaping like they do for making bullet casings and guns and stuff?"

"Yeah, that kind of oven," Nicole said. "Consumers don't generally have access to them."

"True," I said. "But I'm willing to bet that I know someone who does."

It took me three times calling to get Ethan to wake up.

"Get out of bed," I said.

"I don't have to go in until noon," he said. His voice was thick and hoarse like I'd literally just pulled him from a dream.

"I need your help," I said.

He didn't respond.

"Wake up, Ethan. This is important," I yelled through the phone.

"So is sleep," he grumbled. "Man, I was up almost all night texting with Elle."

On cue she came bounding through the door, decked out in a lavender yoga top and pants and carrying a matching lavender mat.

"Hi, Achilles," she called.

I waved then turned my back so she wouldn't be able to read my lips, just in case that happened to be in her skill set. "Speak of the devil," I said to Ethan. "Your girlfriend just got here."

"No, that's the problem," Ethan said. "She told me she didn't want to be serious."

For as much interest as Elle had shown in me, Ethan was way better off getting out of a messy relationship with her before it even started.

"Bummer, man," I said. "Anyway, get up and get to work. We'll be by at noon."

"Make it one," Ethan said. "And who is we?"

"Fine, one," I said. "And we is Nicole." Since she was the one who understand the whole magnet process, I didn't see any way to leave her behind.

I disconnected and turned around. Elle was right there.

"Achilles, I was really hoping we could get together and talk sometime," she said, batting her giant eyelashes at me. "You know like a cup of coffee or something?"

That was the last thing I had time for. And yet, this weird part of me really wanted to kick back and have a cup of coffee with Elle. Like I could almost picture us in my mind at an outdoor café, with the sun overhead, her licking the froth off the top of her drink, me watching her do it. The image flashed in my mind, and for a second, I wanted nothing more than for it to come true.

I blinked until it went away. "You know, it's nothing personal, but I'm really busy for the next week," I said. And the week after that. And the week after that. I couldn't go have coffee with her. Ethan like Elle. Had been up all night pouring his heart out to her. I was not the kind of asshole who stepped in the middle of that.

"Maybe," she said, blinking a few more times. "Or maybe your schedule will free up. I really hope so."

Then she smiled and walked away.

"Do you think her eyelids get heavy from those eyelashes?" Nicole asked, coming up behind me. I hadn't even known she was there.

"Um . . ."

"Never mind, Achilles," Nicole said, patting me on the arm. "Did you call Ethan?"

"Yeah," I managed to say. "One o'clock."

"Great," she said. "And you're sure I can't tell Jordan? He could do this way—"

"One hundred percent positive," I said. This already complicated situation did not need any fuel added to it. I had enough problems to deal with as it was.

* * *

NICOLE PULLED HER CAR INTO THE TINIEST spot in the universe in front of the warehouse where Ethan worked. This part of Camp Mabry was always packed with military trucks and Jeeps and Humvees. It was a good thing she had a Fiat.

"Don't we need to get clearance or something?" she asked.

"Ethan called ahead," I said, unclipping my belt.

"Then why are two guys that look like they're constipated hurrying over here?"

I unfolded myself from the car and looked to where she pointed. Sure enough, two military police walked our way. They were decked out in bulletproof vests and had guns on either side of their hips.

"He was supposed to call ahead," I said. But maybe his sleep-addled brain had forgotten that small detail.

"This is a secure area," one of the MPs called once they were within ten feet of us. They stopped there, as if they were expecting us to make some sudden move and attack the place. "We're going to have to ask you to leave."

I held my hands up where they were both visible. "We have special permission from Ethan Webster. He was supposed to get us cleared."

"He didn't get you cleared," the second MP said.

"Okay. I'll just call him and remind him." I reached for my phone which was a huge mistake. Both MPs pulled guns and pointed them directly at me. And though I might be able to heal from a gunshot wound in the River Styx, I didn't particularly want to find out.

"Hands where we can see them!" the first MP shouted.

I dropped my phone, hearing the inevitable sound of more

breaking glass.

"Sorry!" I said. "Can you check with him? We're legit, I swear."

One of them gave a small nod and kept his gun fixed on me, but the other one pulled out his phone and tapped a few numbers. He held to his ear, but if he spoke, I was too far away to hear. Then he called out, "What did you say your names were?"

"Achilles Stevens and Nicole Earley. I'm his roommate."

There was a bit more of the conversation that I couldn't hear, then he put his phone down.

"Mr. Webster says they're legit."

Like I said, I wanted to say, but you didn't fuck around with MPs.

They both holstered their guns and waved us past, but I felt their eyes on us the entire time we walked up to the warehouse. Only when the giant metal door opened and Ethan stood there, did I relax.

"Well that was fun," Nicole said once we were inside. "I'm Nicole, by the way. I'm sure Achilles has mentioned me."

Ethan looked to me, like he was unsure of what the right answer should be. I mentally told him to say yes.

"Oh, yeah, sure," Ethan said, thankfully understanding. "Achilles talks about you all the time. I can't get him to shut up about you."

"We don't need to lay it on quite that thick," I said. "Anyway . . ."

"You make weapons?" Nicole said. If she was embarrassed by Ethan's comment, I couldn't tell. She finally looked around the warehouse and let out a low whistle. It was on the outskirts of Camp Mabry, where not that may civilians came. There was too much bad press about weapons and shit like that. The warehouse was about the size of a football field and was covered in metal equipment and work benches and tools. There was everything from tanks to racks of hand guns and shooting ranges to test them in.

"It's my specialty," Ethan said. "Putting my Materials Engineering degree to good use."

"And you can heat metal?" she said.

"I can heat up anything," Ethan said. "You name it. I can melt it."

"Do you know what a Curie point is?" she asked.

And from there the conversation devolved into a bunch of talk of metals and temperatures and how things could vary based on altitude and crap like that. I didn't bother trying to follow along, and instead wandered over to a rifle range. I hadn't picked up a gun in sixth months, since Syke and I had gotten in our fight. She hated guns. And it's not like I was the biggest fan of them. But I hadn't been able to bring myself to shoot one since.

I grabbed the biggest rifle off the rack and aimed it down the range. Just because guns weren't my favorite didn't mean that I didn't understand them. I knew all about them. And appreciated the hell out of them.

I set the rifle against my shoulder and lined up the sights, looking at the farthest target away, the silhouette of a human. But instead of a human, I imagined it to be one of the Furies. Tish, since she was the only one left. My finger hovered over the trigger. I was going to send this final Fury off to the hell where she came from. I took a deep breath in but stopped before firing.

No. Not the Furies. Not Tish. Despite the fact that they were trying to haul me off to Tartarus, they were not my real enemy. They were only doing their job. But the problem was that I didn't know who my real enemy was. My enemy was a silhouette, just like on the target. A killer with no face. A coward, afraid to fight me in the open.

I lined up the sights again, and without a second thought, I pulled the trigger, hitting the target dead center. That would be all I needed. One shot to stop the killing of the dryads. That would be all it would take. I just had to know where to aim.

"Nice shot," Ethan said from behind me. He patted me on the back, almost like he could read my mind.

"Nice gun," I said, handing it over to him.

He took it and put it back on the rack, cradling it like it was a baby. "It's a new design I've been working on. Special request from Professor Reese."

I laughed. "Doesn't surprise me. It's got some power. Did he mention what he wanted it for?"

"Nope," Ethan said. "And I didn't ask."

We walked over to a chamber set into the side of the warehouse with a metal door and glass window. Nicole was already there fiddling with a control panel next to the door.

"Do you know what you're doing?" I asked, looking to Ethan to see what he thought about her messing with his stuff.

Nicole pressed more buttons, changing some numbers on an LED screen. "If you know the Curie point of the metal you're working with, you input it here."

"Fine," I said. "I bite. What's a Curie point?"

"It's the temperature that you need to heat the metal above in order to demagnetize it," Nicole said. She was totally geeking out about this shit. I had a feeling she and Ethan could sit around and talk about dorky engineering things for hours. No doubt Jordan would love that.

"And your spearhead is over eighty percent iron," Ethan said, taking it from me. "So we program the temperature and place this in the chamber."

"It won't melt?" I said. That would be the last thing I needed. I already thought I lost it once.

"Not so long as the temperature is controlled," Ethan said. He unlatched the door to the chamber, spinning the door handle until it clicked open. Then he walked in and placed the spearhead in the center of the small room.

"You sure this is safe?" Nicole said.

"It's safe," Ethan said. "It won't start if it detects someone in the chamber."

That said, he didn't stick around in there to test the theory, instead coming out and resealing the door.

"Then we start it and wait." Ethan flipped a switch on the bottom right of the control panel.

The room immediately lit up, as if a fire burned inside it. I pressed my hand on the outer wall, but it wasn't even warm. I glanced inside, making sure the spearhead was okay. Not that I was going to do anything about it if it wasn't. I couldn't just tear the door from the wall and run in to grab it. I didn't think my immortality could withstand that. It glowed yellow then orange and I looked to Ethan. He smiled and the light extinguished and the control panel temperature gauge dipped back to normal.

"That's it?" I said.

"Now we supercool it," Ethan said.

"And then re-magnetize it," Nicole said. "You have a neodymium magnet around here?"

Of course he did. He sent the spearhead through super cooling, then into a separate chamber for the magnetization.

"Ready to see if it works?" Ethan said, popping open the door.

"More than ready," I said, thinking of the silhouette target. I had been ready since before this whole thing had started.

Ethan used a glove to pull the spearhead from the magnetic

chamber and dropped it into my upturned palm. It was warm, like a boiled egg.

"Do you feel a pull on it?" Nicole asked, trying to grab it from my hand.

Hell, yeah, I felt a pull. But I wasn't about to tell her that. I held it out of her reach.

I closed my eyes and let it balance there. Just the smallest amount it pulled to one side. I held my hand firm so Nicole wouldn't be able to tell, and I wrapped my fingers tightly around it.

"Not yet," I said. "Maybe it needs some more time to cool off or something."

"Are you sure?" Nicole said, trying to take it again.

"I'm sure," I said, keeping it out of her reach.

Disbelief crossed her face. "I don't understand. It should have worked perfectly."

I shrugged and tried to act disappointed, even though inside I was ready to follow the magnetism and attack now. "It will. Maybe I just need to be closer to the other one."

Nicole bit her lip. "Maybe." But she didn't look entirely convinced.

I walked slowly, trying to keep up the disappointed act. But damn straight if this hadn't worked perfectly, just like she'd said it would. We walked to the front of the warehouse and to the door. I held it open for Nicole so she could leave first. The MPs were still outside, standing guard around the place.

"I'll be right out," I said to Nicole, and I quickly shut the door.

"It really didn't work?" Ethan said.

"Hell yeah, it worked. It totally worked. She just can't know or she'll want to come with me. As soon as she drops me off, I'm going after it."

"No, Achilles," Ethan said.

"No what?" He couldn't expect me to bring Nicole.

"You need to wait for me."

I shook my head. "It's fine. I got this."

He crossed his arms and stared me down. "Look, I know you got this. Or at least you think you do. But could you just this once shove that arrogant, independent part of you aside and accept my help? Seriously?"

I was about to open my mouth and say no, that I didn't want to put him at risk, but I couldn't pull my eyes away from his.

"You say we're like brothers," Ethan said. "And if that's really true, then you need to wait for me. We need to do this together. Let me fight at your side."

And at his words, I could see us there, side-by-side, fighting for revenge. And justice. And the image felt so right, like it was meant to be. I wanted Ethan with me. Needed him there.

"We should go after dark," I said, since that would keep us out of the eyes of most mortals.

Ethan grinned. "Perfect. I get off at seven. Meet me at Central Park. I'll bring weapons."

CHAPTER 30

"Can you drop me back at the gym?" I said, trying to keep the disappointed look on my face. But damn. I was so close I could smell it.

"Why?" Nicole asked as she backed out of the parking space, waving to the MPs as she did so. They didn't move a muscle on their faces to acknowledge her friendly gesture. I was tempted to give them a gesture of my own, but I didn't think they'd find it very friendly.

"I want to work out. I need to work out." I had to do something until Ethan got off work or I'd go crazy. I clenched my hands into fists to keep them from grabbing the spearhead and following along its trail even right now. It had worked. It had really worked. Nicole and all her Curie point nonsense had been right on. This was the break I needed.

"Maybe you need a drink instead?" she said, winding around

the streets of Camp Mabry.

I'd celebrate with a drink once I found out who was framing me. Vodka would never taste so good.

"Maybe tomorrow?" Tomorrow all this would be resolved.

"That's fine," Nicole said. "I'll call Jordan. He said he had something he needed to talk to me about."

There was this weird moment when I wanted to tell her not to call Jordan, but how pathetic was that? I wasn't some possessive creep. Nicole and I weren't a thing either. At all, no matter what Aphrodite or Mom said.

I gritted my teeth and said, "Tell him I said hi," which was the best I could do.

We drove in silence the rest of the way. I couldn't keep my mind off the spearhead, and Nicole didn't fill the void with snippets of conversation. Before I knew it, she'd pulled up to the curb in front of Heroes Gym.

"So see you tomorrow?" Nicole said.

"Yeah, see you tomorrow," I said. "And thanks for . . . you know . . . everything."

When the words left my mouth, I realized for the first time how much Nicole had done. She'd helped me track down Paris. She'd gone with me to visit Hephaestus and unlocked his door. She'd re-magnetized the spearhead. She'd almost been killed by the Furies. If not for her, there was no reason to believe, besides my stubborn pride, that I would have gotten this far. And with as much as she'd done, lying to her felt so wrong. Except if I'd told her the truth, she would want to come along for sure, and that presented a danger I would not risk.

"Do something for me, okay?" I said.

She cocked her head. "What's that?"

"Lock your door and stay home tonight," I said. "You know,

just to be safe."

Her beautiful eyes softened. "Aw, that's sweet, Achilles. It's almost like you care."

I held her gaze, not daring to admit my true feelings. "Just do this one thing for me. Please."

She seemed to consider my words. "Yeah, fine, I will. You don't have to worry."

"Thanks." I slammed the car door and watched her pull away, then turned to the gym.

And there were the stupid Flower Scouts.

"Hi, Mister. Would you like to support the Flower Scouts of America by buying some delicious cookies?" the little girl named Neela said, smiling like she'd never seen me before.

I patted the pockets of my jacket without thinking about it, and the spearhead jumped, as if its energy had been renewed. As if it was eager. As eager as I was to find its mate. This was really going to happen.

"Well, do you?" the little girl named Cassie said.

"Do I what?" I said.

"Want to buy cookies?"

I shook my head. "I don't want to buy any cookies. I've already bought cookies from you girls."

The dark-haired woman standing in the background stepped forward. "You'll have to excuse them. They're just really trying to—"

"I know," I said. "Earn the trip to Hawaii. You've told me."

She narrowed her eyes at me. It was the first time the smile hadn't been plastered on her face. "Well, there's no need to be rude. Just because you and your little girlfriend had an argument is no reason to take it out on my girls."

I did not have time for this or for some sour attitude from a

Flower Scout troop leader. "She's not my girlfriend," I said. "And I wasn't being rude. I've bought cookies from you three times so far. And I don't even like the cookies. They taste like cardboard. The peanut butter is gross. And how can you have a vegan Skinny Mint? That's just wrong. Milk chocolate shouldn't be vegan."

Her eyes only narrowed more. She gently pulled back on the girls. "Come on, Flower Scouts. Let's go find people who have manners." And without another word, they walked away.

Like I cared. I had manners most of the time, but now was not the time. I patted my pocket again, and again the spearhead moved. As soon as Ethan got off work, I would have justice. This would all be over.

I headed into the gym without saying a word to Keith. Just went to the back and stripped down to my tank top and sweats, taped my hands, and went at the bag. Over and over again, falling into the rhythm that I needed to focus my mind. I was Achilles. I was going to find out who was setting me up. And they would pay. Pay for the dryads. Pay for the lies. It was going to happen. I vaguely remembered Keith asking if he should lock the door when he left. I didn't respond. Only went at it harder. And faster. Instead of wearing me out, it fueled me.

I only stopped when I heard the bell above the door ring. I must've been at it for well over an hour. Sweat dripped from every pore on my body, falling to the mat. I grabbed a towel and wiped it across my face, still feeling the anger inside. This had gone on far too long.

"You're still here," someone said from the front of the gym. The voice was feminine but not Nicole.

I wiped my face again because the sweat was still coming, and I looked over. There was Elle, paused at the counter, like she wasn't sure whether she should come any closer.

I nodded and grabbed a bottle of water from the fridge, uncapping it and downing it in one swallow.

"Just working out," I said.

"I see that," she said. "I didn't mean to interrupt."

"No, it's good. I was done."

"Is Nicole here?" Elle asked.

I grabbed another water, first wiping it across my forehead, letting the condensation cool me. "No. Just me."

But the moment the words left my mouth, I realized how awkward they were. Like I had made it official that it was just me and Elle alone in the gym.

"Oh," Elle said, and bit her lip. "She was supposed to meet me here. For a private yoga lesson."

Weird. Nicole hadn't said anything to me about it. But of course she'd had a pretty unusual day, too. And I'd told her to go home. To stay home.

"You could try calling her." I grabbed my jacket off the hook where I'd draped it. I was still covered in sweat, but I didn't want the jacket out of my possession, not with the spearhead still in the pocket. Not when I was this close.

Elle took a step closer, passing the counter and in toward the weights.

"You seem a little preoccupied, Achilles," she said. She ran a hand through her dark hair, like she was trying to loosen an invisible tangle.

I shook my head and pulled the jacket on, placing my hand over the spearhead to make sure it was still there. It was solid, but unmoving.

"I'm fine," I said.

"Do you want to talk about it?" Elle asked. Another step, slowly, almost like she was hoping I wouldn't notice.

Talking to Elle about all my problems was the last thing I wanted or needed to do.

"No, and maybe you should go?" I said. "I can give you Nicole's number if you want."

For a second, her face hardened, like she couldn't believe what I'd just said. But just as quickly as it came on, it passed, until the softness was back.

"I have her number," Elle said. "But maybe . . ."

"Maybe what?" I walked up to the counter, skirting around her, hoping it would further give her the hint that I wasn't in the mood for her flirty games right now. Or ever.

"Maybe we could go get coffee," she said. "And talk. I'm not trying to impose, but you really look like you need to talk to someone, Achilles."

What I needed was to find the spear, and I started to open my mouth and tell her no. But then a wave of emotion washed over me, and I wanted nothing more than to tell Elle everything. To sit and let her listen to all the problems I'd been dealing with. She was completely unbiased. She wouldn't judge. She wouldn't tell me what to do. Or what not to do. She could listen. Maybe that was exactly what I needed. What Mom kept hoping would happen when I went to the horrible counseling appointments she set up for me.

"I . . ."

She linked her arm through mine. "Come on. I'll help you lock up."

I glanced around, like there was something I was forgetting. "I think . . ."

"It will make you feel better," Elle said. "I promise."

She tugged gently on my arm, guiding me toward the door. And I wanted to go. But my feet would not move. No matter how much I tried, I could not get myself to take another step.

"Come on, Achilles," Elle said.

But whatever spell had come over me evaporated. I unlinked my arm from hers.

"No."

"No what?"

"No, I don't want to go have coffee and talk about it," I said. That was seriously the last thing I needed to do right now.

"But . . ."

"And the other thing is that I don't know what games you're playing, with me and Ethan, but I'm not into you that way. At all." Sure, Elle was hot as hell, but Ethan liked her. A lot.

She put her hands on her hips, and the moment of anger returned to her face. "Is there someone else? Is it Nicole? Is that what's going on here? You guys are a couple?"

Who I was a couple with was none of Elle's business.

"It doesn't matter," I said.

"So it is Nicole," Elle said. She put her finger to her lips. "Or wait, maybe there's someone else. Someone from your past."

Immediately Syke came to mind, even though that was long over.

"You need to leave," I said. No question about it. I wasn't asking her. I needed her out of here. She was the most ridiculous distraction I could have had right now.

Elle inhaled a long breath and blew it out between her pouty lips. "Fine, Achilles. I'm sorry. I was out of line. It's just that—"

I put up a hand to stop her. I didn't need excuses right now. "I'm just really busy." I pulled the door open and held it for her, not even trying to smile as I stepped to the side.

She tossed back her head, shaking her dark curly hair. "It's fine. Everything is perfect."

I let the door fall closed behind her and put her out of my mind. Then I turned off all the lights and the thermostat. Only when I walked out and locked the door did I finally smile. The time had come. I was finally going to end all of this.

CHAPTER 31

I texted Ethan after I got out of the gym. "You ready?"

"Leaving work now."

I pocketed my phone and hurried along Guadalupe until I came to 38th Street where the cutoff was to get to Central Park. The sidewalk traffic thinned out, and my sensors went up. I didn't expect the Furies to show up—not this soon—but I also needed to be prepared. Odds were against it, but the odds had been against me the last couple weeks. But I made it to the park without seeing them and found a tree to lean against while I waited for Ethan.

Only then did I pull the spearhead out of my pocket and let it rest there, in my palm. The second I set it down, it spun around until it faced southwest, the complete opposite direction of where it had been facing earlier. Which meant that whoever had it was moving. But they couldn't know that I had a way of tracking them. It was my advantage.

I let it sit there, seeing if it would move, even the smallest amount, but it was stable. So I slipped it back into my pocket. That's when the tree behind me came to life.

Branches wrapped around me and tightened, pulling me snug even as I struggled to break free. Then they started crushing me, digging into my shirt and skin, pushing under my ribcage.

I struggled against them, but that only seemed to make it worse. I was sure that if they pulled any more, they would cut right through me. It was more than my body would be able to handle. But they stopped tightening, holding me so close that I couldn't move.

From another tree in front of me, a massive oak, a shape dissolved from the bark, reforming into the imposing presence of the matron of trees, Mother Dryad. Real, live, and in all her terrifying magnificence. She stood nearly seven feet tall and had thick brown limbs that could rip concrete walls in half. Her hair was bright green, like the leaves of her tree. She wore no clothes, and yet, looking at her didn't evoke the slightest of sexual thoughts. Mother Dryad transcended that. She was connected to Mother Earth in a way equal to how Nemesis was connected to the universe. She went beyond the gods. And her eyes, bright green ovals that cut into the bark of her skin, flowed like liquid.

"Why did you do it, Achilles?" Mother Dryad said. Her voice echoed around the park, but if there was anyone else around to see, I wasn't able to swivel my head around to tell.

"I didn't do it," I said, but the second the words were out, another branch snapped out and wrapped around my mouth, gagging me.

"We saw you," Mother Dryad said.

I tried to shake my head since I couldn't talk, but it wouldn't budge.

"We thought we could trust you," she said. "And you betrayed us, again and again."

She paused, as if somehow she thought I would magically be able to answer her, to defend myself.

"I held out hope that it wasn't you," Mother Dryad said. "But then Morea saw you. She said there was no mistaking it. And for that, your punishment will be death."

That was impossible. Nobody could have seen me do anything.

There was another pause, and I was sure I heard someone coming. Not that the dryads would really care. They'd lived among humans forever, knew how to make them forget.

I tried to answer. I struggled. It was no use. The dryad held me tight. Mother Dryad fixed her green eyes on me and the swirling liquid nearly hypnotized me.

"Before I kill you—and I will be the one to kill you—you need to tell us where she is," Mother Dryad said, in a soothing voice like she was going to make me do whatever she said.

I elbowed the dryad holding me from behind, but all she did was tighten her branches around my arms. How could they do this? How could they think I would do any of this?

Mother Dryad slipped closer to me until her bark skin brushed against my arms and chest. She placed her mouth directly in front of my face, breathing out the heady scent of the forest that lived inside her, that she was a part of.

"Tell me where Syke is," she said.

The hypnotic spell was broken. My eye widened, and panic ran through me, filling me so quickly, I thought I would throw up from the rage of it. Syke. No.

No.

Please, not Syke. Not any of the dryads, but especially not

Syke. Mother Dryad could not be serious.

She edged back, just the smallest amount, her steps echoing in the surrounding woods.

"Surprise, Achilles?"

I pleaded with my eyes for her to let me speak. Her words could not be true.

She reached a brown bark-covered hand out and placed it flat against my chest, directly over my heart, and she held her eyes on mine. I was sure she was going to puncture my chest with her branches and rip my heart out on the spot, as if the fact that Syke was gone wasn't already doing that. I kept my eyes wide, not backing down from her. The liquid swirled. She breathed in and out. Her grip was unyielding.

Finally, the branch uncurled from my mouth.

I sucked in a huge breath. "Syke is missing?" I hated the words. I did not want them to be true. But I knew that I wouldn't be here, now, in this situation if they weren't. I also knew Mother Dryad wouldn't lie.

"She still lives," Mother Dryad said. "I feel her life force. But it's weak. So weak."

"Gods, no," I said.

"Tell me where she is, Achilles," Mother Dryad said.

"It was not me." I spit the words out as clearly as I could, trying to convey their truth with my voice.

"Morea saw you."

"Then Morea is wrong! It wasn't me. I swear it on the life of my own mother."

Mother Dryad took another step back, pieces of her bark cracking with her steps. "Interesting. Your own mother's life."

There could be no greater vow than what I'd given. My mother's life was not something I would ever bandy about.

I pulled against the branches that still held me. "I know how to find her. I can find who did this. You have to let me go."

"You could be lying," Mother Dryad said. But the swirling green liquid in her eyes had slowed down. I don't think she believed that I was lying. Not anymore. Not after she'd seen what was in my heart.

"I could be," I said. "But I'm not. And right now, I'm your only chance to make this stop. If you kill me now, then I promise you it will stop nothing. Dryads will keep getting killed."

Dryads like Syke.

No sooner than the words were out of my mouth, my voice caught in my throat on the huge lump that had formed there. There was no reason that Syke should have been involved in this. No reason except her history with me. A history that I would take away right now if it meant that she would be okay.

Gods, please don't let her be dead. I would not be able to live with myself.

"Please," I said. "Please let me find her."

One second passed. Then two. Then, ten seconds later that felt like an eternity, the branches around me finally loosened.

"I believe you, Achilles," Mother Dryad said.

I nodded, unable to talk as air refilled my crushed lungs.

"Go find her and bring her back to us," Mother Dryad said. "And when we know who is responsible—who truly is responsible—they will pay."

She slid backward until she was once again up against the oak tree, then she melted into it, her skin and the bark merging until it was impossible to distinguish if there had ever been a dryad there in the first place.

Syke.

I had to find her. And when I found out who was responsible, they would curse the day they ever went up against me.

CHAPTER 32

I balled my hand up and punched it into my palm as rage filled me. I wanted to punch everything around me, the trees, the world, but that wouldn't help anything. I turned, looking for something to let out my rage. Ethan was just running up.

He stopped about ten feet away as anger came off me in waves.

"What the hell happened, Achilles?" he said.

"Syke," I said, gritting my teeth to keep the fury inside. How dare this happen? When I found out who was responsible, I would tear off their testicle sac and choke them with it.

"What about Syke?" Ethan said. He edged closer, staying about five feet away, and if the force of my anger formed a barrier around me.

"She's gone." I wanted to tear down the world around me. Make someone pay.

Ethan stepped forward, pushing past my force field of anger, and placed a hand on either of my shoulders. He looked me right in the eyes. "Achilles, tell me what's going on. Where is Syke?"

I focused on his eyes and tried all the things my counselor had told me. The anger was a ball inside me. It was not me. I could use it but not be controlled by it. I tried to picture the stupid ball, but all I saw was a mass of flames right in the middle of my chest, wanting to destroy the world.

"Whoever is doing this has taken Syke. The other dryads can't find her. They . . ." I wasn't sure what else there was to say.

"Okay, Achilles," Ethan said. "We got this."

The ball of flame inside me flared, renewing my anger. My enemy would pay. They would wish that they'd never been born.

"Achilles!" Ethan said.

My mind refocused on him.

"We got this, okay? We will find this bastard and we will destroy him."

I nodded, letting his words sink in. Then I reached inside my pocket and pulled out the spearhead, clenching it so hard that it nearly cut into my skin. I let the pain of it wash through me, hitting up against the anger.

"We got this," I said.

Ethan released his hands and stepped back, reaching down to unzip the duffel bag he'd dropped earlier. Inside was an arsenal of hand combat weapons. I grabbed a sword and pulled it from its scabbard, holding it aloft, looking sideways at the blade. It was so thin it almost turned invisible at that angle. Thin enough that they would never see it coming. I grabbed the black knife Ethan had made me, clipping on my side. Then I grabbed another knife for good measure.

"Enough power to destroy a god," Ethan said.

"Let's hope so." God or mortal . . . it didn't matter. Vengeance would be mine.

Ethan clipped on his weapons and threw the empty bag into the woods. I swung the sword over my shoulder and placed the spearhead in my palm, letting it realign to the southwest. "That way," I said, and without another word, we took off.

Time was critical. But without knowing exactly where we were going, there was no way to gauge distance. If Syke was somehow still alive—and I prayed that she was; Mother Dryad had felt her life force—then I needed to get to her before that changed. I knew that if I didn't, I would never get past it. Whether Syke never wanted to speak to me again or not, I could not let her die. We ran in the direction the spearhead pointed, adjusting every time it shifted even the slightest amount. I couldn't tell if it was moving, or if it was just getting more precise the closer we got.

We passed UT and the Capitol and veered south, so we could head across the Congress Avenue Bridge. Over the water, the spearhead spun in my palm, zipping back and forth, like the water was somehow throwing off the magnetism. But as soon as our feet were above the ground once more, it settled, this time pointing west.

We cut onto the hike and bike trail, running faster than any of the other pedestrians. It wasn't crowded since night had started to fall. We crossed a foot bridge, and once again the spearhead lost its bearing, but then, again, it settled, pointing slightly south, more west. Toward Zilker Park.

We cut off the path and hopped the miniature train tracks. Near a scattering of trees it looked like there was still a family hanging out, but when I got closer, I realized that it wasn't a family at all.

It was Syke.

I couldn't tell if she was still alive. She was bound to the picnic table, too far from a tree to be able to reach one. Without a tree, if she was injured, she would die. If she could have reached a tree, she could have escaped. But from the way she was slumped over, it didn't look like she was going to escape from anything. Sitting on the picnic table were three little girls, decked out in green vests. A woman stood next to the table. A woman I recognized as well as I recognized the little girls.

"Mister, would you like to buy some cookies now?" the little brat with the red curls said. She motioned to the table where boxes of Flower Scout cookies had been stacked into a pyramid.

"I don't want your fucking cookies," I said, and damn it felt good. I'd been wanting to say that from the second they started pounding on my door. Whoever these Flower Scouts were, they were not normal girls. And their leader? I didn't know who she was, but I did know she was the one I was looking for.

"No need to be rude, Achilles," the woman said, smoothing her green sweat suit. "They're just trying to earn the trip to Hawaii."

"They're not trying to earn a trip to Hawaii," I said. "And you need to let Syke go right now."

"Right now?" the woman said. "But if I let her go right now, we won't be able to have any fun."

"I don't want to have any fun," I said. "The killing needs to stop."

The woman seemed to consider this. "But killing can be so much fun. Well, it's not really the kill that's so much fun. It's more the hunt. Hunting . . . it's kind of my thing. You know. Just like fighting is yours. But you know that about me, don't you, Achilles?"

Hunting. What the hell was she trying to say?

She shook her head. "My brother isn't much of a hunter, not like me. He's more involved with parties and being the center of attention. You know, kind of how the sun is at the center of the solar system. But you know that, too. Oh, and by the way, he sends his greetings. And he says—and I'll try to quote this word for word—'If Achilles dares to touch Paris again, I will personally burn his eyelids off and make him stare into my brilliance until he can't see another thing besides me for the rest of his pathetic immortal existence.' Yeah, I think that's exactly what he said."

Oh shit. You have got to be kidding me. She was talking about Apollo. Which meant that she was none other than the goddess of the hunt.

"Artemis," I said, letting the realization sink in. This was not what I expected. It was also the worst thing that could have happened. It was one thing to know her brother, Apollo, despised me. Always had. And sure, maybe trashing his temple back in Troy wasn't the best choice on my part. But Artemis? She'd always kept her distance. There was no reason why she would fix her sights on destroying my life.

Artemis shifted before my eyes. Her poofy hair straightened into a long brown ponytail. Her green sweat suit transformed into a short green sleeveless dress with brown sandals twined around her feet. And to finish the look, a giant bow materialized, draped across her chest. A quiver of arrows sat on her back. The girls sitting on the picnic table didn't seem to notice.

"Aw, you figured it out," Artemis said. "And I'll have you know, for the record, that my girls most definitely are trying to earn a trip to Hawaii. Hard work is a very essential part of being a Flower Scout."

"Oh, yeah, and you know a lot about Flower Scouts?" Ethan said. He still held his position beside me.

"Know about Flower Scouts?" Artemis said. "Who do you think founded Flower Scouts?"

"Someone who likes crappy cookies?" Ethan said.

"No. It was me. And I don't like cookies. They give me indigestion."

"You're telling me you founded Flower Scouts?" Ethan said.

I glanced over to Syke, wondering if there was a chance that I could cut the ropes while Ethan distracted Artemis. I edged sideways the smallest amount, flexing my fingers around the hilt of the sword.

"Best organization in the world," Artemis said. "Why the Flower Scout pledge is not only a pledge for making it through scouts. It's a pledge for life. A way we choose to live."

"Yeah, well your cookies taste like ass," Ethan said. "Did you change bakers or something, because Skinny Mints used to be really good, and now they just taste like dried up cow shit?"

Artemis cleared her throat and glanced at the little girls who by this point had cracked open a box of Skinny Mints and sat there on the table devouring it. "The new baker promised us a much better share of the profits."

"Bad business decision," Ethan said. "You should never sacrifice quality for cost. Well, except those peanut butter wheel ones—what are those called?"

"Wagon Wheels," Artemis offered.

"Right, Wagon Wheels," Ethan said. "They're actually better this year. The peanut butter has a little bit more sugar."

I took another step toward Syke, knowing I had to make my move quickly.

"I wouldn't try anything, Achilles," Artemis said, stopping my next step. Almost in response, Syke let out a soft moan of pain.

"You need to let her go or she's going to die," I said.

"Who cares?" Artemis said. "Another dryad dying. That's the least of my concerns."

The few trees around us seemed to shake in response. But if they were powerful enough to do anything about it, they didn't.

"Just let Syke go," I said. "If you have a problem with me, then deal with me."

"Hmmm . . . ," Artemis said, as if she were really considering this. "It's not really me who has the problem with you."

"What? Then why are you doing this?" I motioned at Syke, still lying on the ground. She was starting to stir, as if she was regaining consciousness.

"I'm not the one doing it," Artemis said. She turned to the three little girls sitting on the picnic table. They'd already finished up the box of Skinny Mints and had started on the PB Choco-Patties. "Girls, your mothers will be waiting for you over by the parking lot. Please remember the buddy system as you walk over. And don't talk to strangers. Girls can't be too careful these days. We'll plan to meet up tomorrow near the Domain."

"We're gonna sell so many cookies tomorrow," the chubby little girl with the blond hair said.

"Not if you eat then all, Sarah," Neela said. "No more cookies for you."

"Don't be mean, Neela," Cassie said. "You know Sarah needs her cookies or her blood sugar gets low."

"That's just an excuse," Neela said. "We better not run out of cookies tomorrow, Sarah."

Artemis shooed them along with her hands. "Girls, we've talking about the bickering. That doesn't follow the Flower Scout Way."

They all dropped their heads and nodded, like they'd heard this scolding a hundred times before and like they knew exactly how they were supposed to respond.

"Sorry," one muttered after the other, and they left, trailing through the grassy area toward the parking lot.

"Young girls these days," Artemis said. "If it's not eating cookies, it's too much time on their cell phones. Or on YouTube. Or it's about boys wanting to join the troop. Some days I seriously worry about the future of Flower Scouts."

With Artemis at the helm, it was definitely a concern.

"You're not going to walk them over there?" Ethan said. Kudos for his forethought. Not that I thought it would work.

"Girls need to be independent," Artemis said. "Also, I have a protective aura placed around them. Nothing will happen to any of my girls."

I wondered if those girls knew how lucky—or unlucky—they really were.

"If you're not the one doing this, then who is?" I asked. Rage and concern battled inside me. Syke couldn't die. But Artemis could. I had the spearhead. One good throw, and it should kill her, or at least render her incapacitated. But if I killed her and she truly wasn't the one behind this, then it wouldn't stop.

"Oh, yes, that," Artemis said. "Well, you don't think Ares is the only one who's woken one of their favorites from immortal sleep, do you?"

"I talked to Paris," I said. "But you already know that."

"Right. Apollo and Paris. Such an interesting choice for a demigod. Sure, the boy's cute enough—he does have that charm— but other than that, I'm not sure why my brother picked him."

Wow. So I wasn't the only one who thought that Paris was a dickhead. But if we weren't talking about Paris, then that meant Artemis had woken a demigod of her own. Someone who held a grudge against me. A very big grudge.

"I see your mind spinning," Artemis said. "It's so typically male of you, not to have figured it out."

"Who is it?" I asked, going over the list of possibilities, not wanting any of them to be true.

"Achilles?" Syke said, propping up on her elbows. Her brown hair was a mass of tangles, and cuts and scraped covered her brown skin. Sap dripped from her wounds. "What are you doing here?"

"He's here to save you," Artemis said.

"Artemis?" Syke said, turning her head toward the goddess.

Artemis cocked her head. "Yes, yes, it's me. Bet you're sorry you wouldn't let me hunt in your sacred forests."

"Who is it?" I demanded. I'd had enough of this. "And where is the spear? Tell me now."

Artemis placed her palms together and rubbed them up and down, smiling. "I guess it is that time. Helen?"

Almost like she'd been hidden there in plain sight, Nicole appeared.

Nicole.

I could not believe it. She was the one behind it all?

Except then I noticed her hands were tied, and cuts and scrapes covered her arms and face. Her eyes were wide, not with fear, but with a burning anger that matched my own. And from behind her, pushing her forward, materialized another person.

Elle.

Elle. Of course it was Elle. How every time she'd been around me, my head had gone kind of fuzzy, like it was hard to focus on anything else. How her laughter filled the room and how every eye in the gym turned her way when she walked in.

Elle was Helen. Helen of Troy. The woman who'd launched a thousand ships. The woman responsible for the Trojan War.

Flashes from my memory filled me. Flashes specifically of the time Elle—Helen—had approached me in the past, during the war, when Paris didn't know. She'd snuck into the enemy camp and tried to seduce me. Tried to convince me to run off with her. To leave the entire war behind to sort itself out. The war she had started. She'd said she was bored of Paris. That she wanted something else. Someone more.

She'd wanted me.

She'd slipped under the covers with me in a mask of darkness. She'd told me how she dreamed of the things we would do together. She'd run her hands over my bare skin. She'd made me feel like a god.

And I'd told her to go to hell. It had taken all my will power, even back then, but I'd pushed her aside. Told her that she wasn't worth the dirt I walked upon. I'd pushed her away from me and shoved her out of my tent. I still remember the final look she'd given me as she'd walked away. Fury had burned inside her eyes. Fury that she'd buried inside herself until the time came when she'd be able to get back at me.

And now she had. Here. With the stealing of the spear and the death of the dryads.

"Are we having fun yet?" Elle said. "Oh, or would this be more fun?" She flickered in front of me, changing shape as I watched, becoming me. She flexed her muscles and tossed back blond hair. "Or how about this?" She shifted again, this time turning into Paris, with dark ringlets and a velvet tunic. Then she turned back into herself and tilted her head upward and laughed.

Fuck. That was the reason why the dryads had thought I was guilty. Helen could change shape. Could make people think they were seeing anything. That's why even Nemesis didn't know who was responsible.

"Elle?" Ethan stood beside me, still holding his sword. But it was lowered at his side. His balance was all off. He wasn't ready for an attack. Which made it all the worse when that attack came.

Artemis lashed out with her hands, and wind flew from her fingertips. Ethan flew backward, dropping the sword well before he hit against a tree and landed on his butt. He slumped against the tree.

"He was cute," Elle said. "But not as cute as you, Achilles. Nothing but a fun distraction to play around with while I hunted you." She shoved Nicole to the ground on the opposite side of the picnic table from Syke. Then she held forth her hand.

The spear materialized instantly, as if it had only been cloaked in the darkness. Its head was deep black and clean despite all the killing that it had done. The wood was smooth and brown and her fingers gripped it with a certainly that told me she was absolutely responsible for the deaths of the dryads.

"I did it for you, Achilles," Elle said. "Well, not for you. More because I was still so pissed off at you. Do you realize that no other guy has ever spurned me the way you did? I still can't believe you said no. I mean, I was using everything I had, really turning it on. And you . . . you think you're too good for me. Even today. You said no again. I don't like when people say no. It's upsetting."

I shook my head, trying to see if Nicole was okay. But when I looked back to Syke, Artemis now stood over her, each of them guarding someone I cared about a lot more than I wanted to admit.

"I'm not too good for you," I said. "That was never it. It's just . . ."

"It's just what, Achilles?" Elle said. "You don't think I'm pretty? Is that it?"

"You're very pretty," I said. "On the outside." Maybe the last part was unnecessary, but I didn't think it through.

Elle seemed unfazed as she tossed her dark hair over her shoulder.

"Do you not think I'm smart enough?" she said. "Do you wish I was an engineer like your little girlfriend here? She's really smart." She flickered again until she became Nicole, with dark brown skin and straight hair. I hated to even see her like that.

"I think you're very smart, Helen," I said. "You were always smart. You know that."

"Then what?" Elle said, changing back into herself. "If you can give me one good reason, then maybe I'll spare someone's life. How does that sound?"

It sounded like a pile of shit to me. A pile of shit that I was shoulder deep in and sinking.

Helen. Elle. Why had I never responded when she'd approached me? She was every guy's dream. A perfect female. Gorgeous. Smart. Funny. The way she made my mind blank. I'd never figured out if that was just a trick or if it was something more. Something special about her. I didn't want to be tricked, but no one did. That wasn't it. It was more. Something about the war. The way it had started. Because of her. And how she'd left everything, without shedding a tear, to follow Paris. She didn't think it out. She never had. She'd never given any concern to the wake she'd left around her. She destroyed countries, an entire civilization, with a thoughtless decision.

"You never cared about anyone besides yourself," I said. It might not be the answer she wanted to hear, but it was a truthful one.

"You're being rude to Helen," Artemis said. She grabbed Syke by the head and held her slightly off the ground so part of her body weight was supported by her own hair. Syke let out a gasp of pain that burrowed into my ears.

Elle put up her hand. "No, it's okay. He said what he believed to be the answer. And I don't want anyone to accuse me of being unfair. So, because of that, Achilles, I'll do what I said. I'll spare one life for you. You name it. Do you want me to spare your precious yoga girlfriend here, Nicole, who tried to hit me over the head with her purse when I captured her? She was following behind you. Trying to trail you. My gods, I thought she was going to pull my hair out. Or do you want me to spare the love of your life, your precious dryad, Syke? She begged me to clear your name. She told me she'd come with me willingly, that she'd give up her own life in order for you to stay out of Tartarus. It was so sweet. I almost shed a tear. But not sweet enough. So, Achilles, tell me, which one do you want to sentence to death and which one shall I spare?"

I glanced from Nicole to Syke, wishing Elle would evaporate on the spot. Artemis had woken Helen from her sleep and brought her here, to this time. Brought her to fight in whatever battle the gods had brewing ahead. But if it were up to me, I would never let that happen. I was going to kill Helen, here, tonight. And if Artemis got in my way, I would do whatever I could to destroy her also.

I glanced backward, over my shoulder. Ethan still lay slumped against the tree. His sword was only a few steps behind. But it was too far to reach. They'd never give me the time. I swung my own sword around, cutting the air with a whooshing sound. I was not going to choose between Nicole and Syke. I would save them both.

"I'm not playing your game, Helen," I said. "And Artemis, if this is your idea of empowering girls for our future, then it's seriously fucked up."

"Helen was upset, Achilles," Artemis said. "So I gave her

access to the Hall of Artifacts and helped her steal the spear. Your friend Jordan isn't the only one who knows computers. I have my own mortals doing my bidding. A couple video edits, and the security footage was as good as ever. Helen even came up with the idea of framing Paris, though we decided not to tell my brother about that. Apollo gets a bit upset if his demigods are mistreated. It was my idea to go after the dryads, just because they've always annoyed me. They're so particular about hunting in their forests. The fact that you had a history with this poor little dryad only made it that much more special."

"Here's what I want to happen," I said. "I want you both to back away from Nicole and Syke. And Helen, I want you to drop the spear. Then go back to whatever hell-hole you want to—I don't really care. Just stop this now."

I didn't expect them to listen, but I wanted to give them fair warning. The same way I'd given Hector fair warning so long ago in Troy. There was nothing unsportsmanlike about our battle. He was a worthy opponent, and I defeated him. Just like I would defeat Helen and Artemis.

Helen did not drop the spear. Instead she held it parallel to the ground and aimed right at me. I could evade it, if it was the only thing I had to worry about. But Artemis dropped Syke to the ground and placed one foot on her chest. Then she pulled the giant bow from over her shoulder and placed an arrow on the string. She aimed it at me and pulled the string back.

"Make your choice, Achilles," Helen said.

"Achilles made his choice," Artemis said. "He dies, and they both die, too."

But then the air to my right sucked in on itself, making an enormous snapping sound so loud the trees and table rattled around us, tumbling the pyramid of cookies. Tish, the final Fury, materialized from the darkness.

She pulled her red hat from her head and tossed it aside. The red snakes attached to her scalp twisted and writhed, snapping out in all directions as if they were hungry for anything and anyone.

"Nobody kills Achilles except us," Tish spat into the air. "He's ours." Then she reached up and grabbed a handful of snakes and threw them.

CHAPTER 33

I jumped forward and started swinging. I'd fought the Furies before and was prepared. Helen was not. She dropped Nicole to the ground and leapt backward, letting out a piercing shriek that brought back vivid memories of the final battle in Troy. Of her, screaming and tearing through the castle for the escape tunnels while thousands around her burned. Died because of a war she was responsible for starting with her selfish desires. But even though she moved away from Nicole, she still held the spear, and with my sudden movement, she started swinging it wildly, back and forth. Its deadly tip came within inches of me. I had to be cautious, except the tunnel of red fury in my mind made it hard to focus on anything.

The snakes slithered forward, coming from all directions, for every single one of us. Nicole was within my reach now, and I leaned forward, trying to grab her hand without getting skewered by the spear.

"Can you reach for me?" I extended my hand out as far as I could, hoping she heard me over the chaos that had erupted.

She leaned out, and her fingertips barely brushed mine. Just a little bit more. I held my head back and tried to push my shoulders out. This time, her fingers connected. I grabbed her hand with mine and flung her backward, up onto the picnic table, away from the snakes.

"You're cut, Achilles!" she said, swiping at my shoulder.

Shit. She was right. Pain exploded down my left arm, radiating toward my fingers. I switched the sword to my right hand, and clutched as hard as I could on it, even though my fingers were starting to tingle.

"It's nothing. Just stay away from the snakes."

I jumped onto the picnic bench and glanced backward. Artemis still held Syke, but she'd grabbed her around the waist and was pulling her backward, away from the snakes and away from Tish who advanced on her. Artemis still kept Syke far away from the trees, not giving her a chance of healing. Behind me, the snakes were nearly to Ethan's feet and he still hadn't gotten up. I jumped from the bench, flipping through the air toward him, landing to his side. I grabbed him under the shoulders and pulled him to his feet.

"Are you okay to fight?" I asked.

He grabbed his sword and nodded. And without a word, he began swiping at the snakes on the ground, slicing them in half, one after another. The serpent pieces writhed even as they died, flopping around with their fangs still extended. I balled my left hand into a fist, to try to keep the tingling from taking over, hoping the blood flow would eliminate whatever damage the spear had delivered to me.

"Go save them," Ethan said. "I'll take care of the snakes."

I gave one short nod and started cutting a path through the snakes, back to the picnic table. Nicole stood on top, kicking at any snake that dared peek its head over the table.

"You need to make a run for it." I motioned to the path behind me.

"Are you out of your fucking mind?" she said, and before I knew what she was doing, she grabbed the black knife from my belt and plunged it directly into the head of the snake nearest her. But she didn't stop. She stepped on the snake and pulled the blade free then stabbed another. And another. It was a thing of beauty. And Mom's words came back to me. 'She's a survivor.' I wasn't sure what Nicole's past was, but it obviously involved more than just yoga.

"Damn, you are amazing," I said. I jumped from the bench, back to the ground, and toward Helen. She was still there, in the same spot, but the fear in her eyes had been replaced with fury. Snakes lay dead around her feet, victims of the spear no doubt.

"Are you sorry you spurned me yet, Achilles?" she screamed. "Do you wish you could change things?"

The only thing I'd change was that I should have killed her back in Troy, when she'd come to visit me in the tent. I should have recognized that she was nothing but a poison that needed to be stopped.

"I'm not sorry for anything," I said. "And don't you ever mess with me or the people I care about again."

I swiped my sword forward, catching the spear on the side and almost knocking it from her hands. But she held onto it with a death grip. I kicked out, hitting her full on in the stomach. She doubled over, but still she hung on, like the spear was her life.

"You can't stop us, Achilles!" Artemis yelled from behind me.

A loud explosion caused me to turn, and I watched as an arrow flew from Artemis' giant bow and hit Tish full in the chest. Tish flew backward, slamming into a tree. Syke lay on the ground, next to Artemis, barely holding her head up.

I turned and jumped forward, dropping my sword and grabbing the spear with both hands, wrestling with Helen for it. "You need to let this go. You need to get over it. This is not right. This should not be who you are."

Helen looked at me like I'd lost my mind, even as we fought for control of the spear. "But this is who I am, Achilles. Who I'll always be."

I jerked the spear with all my strength and tore it from Helen's hands. She was no match for me. She was no warrior.

"I don't like who you are at all." I swung the spear around and jumped backward. Then, in one solid movement, I stabbed it through her stomach, pinning her against the tree.

Immediately blood oozed from the wound, and sank into the bark. The tree groaned and came to life, branches turning into arms that wrapped around Helen and sucked her inward, pulling her off the spear. She screamed with what life she had left and reached her arms out like she thought I would help her. I stepped backward, bringing the spear with me even as the bark enveloped her. Her screams became muffled then vanished completely as the bark closed over her mouth, erasing any sign of her.

"That was not a good choice at all," Artemis said.

I whipped around, just in time to see Artemis reach her hand outward, toward Nicole. Nicole flew backward, the black knife dropping from her hands, until she landed on the ground, on the opposite side of Artemis as Syke. She struggled to get away, but invisible bonds seemed to hold her there.

"Now, Achilles, I will kill them both," Artemis said.

"No, you won't," I said. "Stop this now. Helen is dead. This whole ridiculous thing with her grudge is over. This ends here. Now."

Artemis threw back her head and laughed. "You think this is about Helen and her little grudge? You think that's all this is about?"

I did. Except then I thought of Ares' words. And what Hades said. Of how factions were being formed within the gods. How sides were being taken. And war was coming. And I realized that I, just like Helen, was nothing but a pawn in their game. But pawn or not, I was not going to die, and neither were Nicole or Syke.

One shot was all I needed. One shot with the spear and Artemis would be dead. I never missed. No matter how far away the target was. This was my only chance to save them.

Without another thought, I raised the spear and threw it straight for Artemis. It spun as it flew through the air, gaining speed as it got closer. And closer. It was so close to Artemis that I could smell her death. Then it stopped and jerked sideways until the spear landed solidly in Tish's hand.

She stood there, in her red cowboy boots with a broken arrow sticking out her chest. She held the spear, eyeing it, studying me and Artemis. The snakes writhed and she cocked her head, in deep consideration. And when I thought that I couldn't stand one more second of the silence, she closed her eyes and nodded.

"That does clear things up," Tish hissed in her Texas twang. "Y'all are a real pain in my ass." Then she dropped the spear and leapt forward, grabbing Artemis with both hands, sinking her claws in deep.

Artemis howled with pain, and smoke poured from the places where Tish held on.

"Setting others up for your own crimes," Tish said. "Twisting the truth. Attacking a Fury. Murdering dryads. For these crimes, Artemis, you will be brought before the council who will determine your sentence. And your sentence, when determined, will be served out in Tartarus."

A giant flash bit into the air along with a cracking sound like the world itself was splitting. Then, when the flash was gone, both Tish and Artemis had vanished.

CHAPTER 34

I grabbed the spear and circled around, scanning the area for threats. Helen was gone, taken by the dryads. And Artemis was gone, taken by the Furies to pay the price for the crimes she had committed. Or so I hoped. I had no intention of following through and getting mixed up in the gods' business.

"It's clear, Achilles," Ethan said, hurrying over to join me. He held a knife in his hand.

I nodded slowly and scanned the area one more time, more to lower my heart rate than to expect an attack. That had been close. Way too close.

Still holding the spear, I dropped onto the ground next to Syke and Nicole. Nicole had her arms wrapped around Syke's shoulders. But Syke's normal brown skin was pale and clammy when I reached out to touch it.

"She's hurt really bad, Achilles," Nicole said.

I passed the spear to Ethan and grabbed Syke under the arms, lifting her off the ground. Her body was slick with sweat and the cuts and scrapes that I thought had just been on her face covered her entire body. Her blood, amber-colored like sap, leaked from the wounds.

"We need to get her to the trees," I said, and I took off running for the tree line. One tree wasn't going to be enough. Syke needed the healing power of her entire dryad family. I was vaguely aware of Ethan and Nicole calling out behind me, but I didn't stop. I ran fast, covering what had to be over one hundred yards, in seconds. Syke cried out from the pain but I couldn't stop. The trees were her only chance.

When I finally reached them, I took her off my shoulder and pressed her against a tree. She didn't move. Her head hung limp. I'd taken too long. The battle had taken too long. And Syke was dead.

"Please don't die," I said. "Please just don't die on me. I promise I'll do better in the future. I'll stay away from you forever if that's what you want. I'll follow through on my promises. I won't lie to you ever again. I'll spend less time in the mortal world. More time with you. I'll . . ." I didn't know what else there was to say. I'd failed Syke again.

But then the bark of the tree spread and opened to expose the hard wood underneath. Almost like it was stitching itself back together, the bark started growing around Syke, pulling her inside. She hung there, motionless, as the tree consumed her. I stared, unable to take my eyes off her. Willing her to survive.

"Please save her," I said, knowing the dryads would hear.

Then the bark closed and Syke was gone.

"Will she be okay?" Nicole said as she came up beside me.

Ethan stood a few yards back, guarding the area with the

spear.

"Gods, I hope so," I said. The thought of the world without Syke was too much.

"I'm sorry I was following you," Nicole said. "I—"

I didn't wait for her to say anything else. I grabbed her and held her against me, holding her close enough that I could feel her heart beating, needing to know that she was alive. Time stood still as we stood there in the darkness.

Then Ethan finally called out, "Okay, not to break this up, but we need to get the hell out of here."

Nicole wriggled out of my grasp. "I'm okay. I'm okay."

I looked her directly in the eyes. "Don't ever do that again. Do you realize you almost got yourself killed? Never do that again. Ever."

"Why? You act like you care or something," Nicole said.

I did care. A lot. But I wasn't about to say that.

"I just don't want Jordan coming after me with a chainsaw," I said, and we joined Ethan and got the hell out of Zilker Park, leaving the destroyed picnic area far behind.

CHAPTER 35

A week later, Ares stopped into the gym.

"Council says you can keep it here," Ares said, tossing me the spear. It might have been a little unusual for him to walk around the streets with a full-sized spear, except this was Austin. Anything went in Austin.

"Thanks," I said, catching it. "What made them change their mind?"

"They put a spell on it or some bullshit like that. You can't remove it from here, except under grave necessity. I convinced them that it was safer here than it had been in the HOA."

"Thanks for that." I balanced the spear in my hand, letting the weight of it connect with my body once again. I'd kept to myself the fact that I also still had the matching spearhead. It was back at the condo locked up.

Ares had come in full workout gear and immediately grabbed

the tape to wrap his knuckles.

"You got enemies now, Achilles," Ares said, passing me the tape when he was done, which was the sign that he intended to spar with me, not just punch a bag.

"Enemies as in plural?" I said, using my teeth to cut the tape.

"Artemis has allies," he said. "Hell if I know who they are. Lots of the gods are being pretty quiet about their alliances."

That was just perfect. I had enemies and I didn't even know who they were.

Ares and I went at it, holding back nothing as we sparred. For every blow he landed, I countered. Every kick. Every fake out and punch. Sweat dripped from both of us, but we didn't stop until finally we both threw a punch, and neither of us connected. Then we fell backward and started laughing, releasing the energy inside. It was exactly what I needed to get out the final bit of anger I'd still been holding onto from the mess with Helen and Artemis. It was enough to let go.

"Athena said something about drinks this Friday," Ares said as he toweled off.

"Athena, as in the goddess?" Nicole said, walking up.

Ares raised an eyebrow. There had been no keeping away from him the fact that Nicole knew everything. Of course he'd found out. But we still hadn't talked about it.

"Hell, yeah, gorgeous mortal," Ares said. "Though I'm thinking you need to come along also."

That right there sounded like a disaster in the making. I already had the impending visit from Aphrodite to worry about.

Nicole scowled at him in a way that made me want to give her a high five. "You really think a lot of yourself, don't you?" she said.

"Don't you?" Ares said.

Nicole only rolled her eyes.

"Fine, I'll behave myself," Ares said.

"Right," Nicole said. "That seems likely."

"Smart girl. I think you and Athena will get along really well." Then he grinned at me and ripped the tape from his hands. "So Friday night it is. Oh, and bring Ethan, I got some shit I need to talk to him about."

"It's like a party," I said.

"It's always like a party." Ares grabbed a water from the fridge and walked out, leaving me there next to Nicole.

"You live a pretty exciting life, Achilles," Nicole said. "Oh, and I really like your new decoration." She motioned toward the spear.

"Yeah, me, too. It makes me feel more . . ."

"Complete?" Nicole suggested.

"Yeah. Complete."

"So . . . Athena?" Nicole said.

My face heated up. If it was red, I could blame it on the sparring session. "What about her?"

"You and she . . . ?"

Oh gods. Why did even the simplest things have to be so complicated?

"We're friends," I said. "You know, as much as one can be friends with a goddess."

"Yeah, friends," Nicole said. "I gotcha. And what about Syke? Any word on her?"

I shook my head. That was the one loose end to this entire thing.

"I keep asking, but nothing. I don't know." I'd tried to put it out of my mind. Tried, but been utterly unsuccessful.

Nicole rubbed my shoulder. "It'll be okay."

"I hope so," I said.

I stayed a good two hours after closing, catching up on all the boring financial crap that nonetheless paid the bills. You would think that even after an epic battle that nearly ended my life, I'd have gotten some kind of financial benefit. But nope. I was nearly as broke as when this whole thing had started.

I locked up and pocketed my keys, starting the walk home. I tipped my head back and smelled the fresh air, relishing the fact that I neither had to worry about Furies attacking me or Flower Scouts approaching me to sell cookies. I hadn't seen a single Flower Scout since all the shit had gone down. Truly, I'd be happy if I never saw another one. Well, except for the peanut butter Wagon Wheels. They were still pretty awesome.

I cut along a side street then past the elementary school. Except when I got to the small park next to the school, the air went still and silent. Then a figure slipped from the tree to my right, coalescing from the bark and leaves and branches until there in front of me stood Syke.

Her skin glowed with life. Her hair was wild and full of leaves and twigs. She wore a green tank top the same color and texture of the leaves and a brown pair of shorts that showed off her amazing legs.

"Syke," I said, stepping toward her. "Oh, thank the gods. I was so worried about you." I couldn't keep the shaking from my voice. But seeing her here, now . . . relief flooded through me, releasing the tension that had become a part of me this past week.

"Achilles," Syke said, and she covered the final distance between us and pulled me into her arms. I don't know if she leaned forward first or if it was me, but then we were kissing. I sunk into the kiss, wrapped my arms around her, holding her close and letting my mouth explore hers. I lost track of time at that point.

Time didn't matter. The fight from our past didn't matter. The brewing war between the gods didn't matter. The only thing that mattered was this moment. Gently I pushed her backward, up against her tree, until the tree swallowed us whole.

ABOUT THE AUTHOR

P. J. (Tricia) Hoover wanted to be a Jedi, but when that didn't work out, she became an electrical engineer instead. After a fifteen year bout designing computer chips for a living, P. J. started creating worlds of her own. She's the award-winning author of *Tut: The Story of My Immortal Life*, featuring a fourteen-year-old King Tut who's stuck in middle school, and *Solstice*, a super-hot twist on the Hades/Persephone myth. When not writing, P. J. spends time with her husband and two kids and enjoys practicing kung fu, solving Rubik's cubes, and watching Star Trek.

For more information about P. J. (Tricia) Hoover, please visit her website www.pjhoover.com.